It lying naked up disencumbered of sitting at her side and allowing his eyes to play delightedly over her body. As I could have foretold, he was not disappointed; and soon, his eyes having drunk their fill, he permitted himself the pleasure of paying tribute with his lips to her smoothly rounded shoulders, the firm flesh of her pouting breasts, the generous but not fleshy round of her belly, and soon enough to the source of her chief pleasure, framed by the softest and finest down.

Also available from Headline:

Eros in the Country
Eros in Town

Eros on the Grand Tour

More Adventures of a Lady and Gentleman of Leisure

Anonymous

HEADLINE

First published in 1989
by HEADLINE BOOK PUBLISHING PLC

ISBN 0 7472 3309 8

Typeset in 10/10½ pt English Times
by Colset Private Limited, Singapore

Printed and bound in Great Britain by
Collins, Glasgow

HEADLINE BOOK PUBLISHING PLC
Headline House
79 Great Titchfield Street
London W1P 7FN

For the convenience of the reader
we here record a note of
IMPORTANT PERSONS APPEARING IN THE NARRATIVE
in the order of their appearance

Andrew Archer Esq, our hero.
Sir Franklin Franklyn Esq, of Alcovary, Herts.
Mrs Sophia Nelham, our heroine.
William Blatchford, their servant.
The Revd Jaundise, a singular clergyman.
A familiar *gen d'arme*.
Two old crones.
Miss Evelyn Scott, a young traveller.
Miss Dorothea Scott, her sister.
Mr Graham Scott (of York), their father.
A female travelling companion.
Two *demi-mondaines*.
Sr Nunez, a sea captain.
Carlos, a Portuguese cabin-boy.
A French *masseuse*.
The Lady Elizabeth Rawby, an aristocrat.
The Lady Margaret Rawby, another.
Wilson Nichol Esq, British Consul in Lisbon.
Sra Casado, a widow.
The Marquise de Aljubarotta, a noblewoman.
The Marquis de Aljubarotta, her son.
Miss Emily Fawcett, a young Englishwoman.
The Revd William Brarley, her fiancé.
The Sras Cazenove, two Madames.
Two *filles charmantes*.
Capt Fenton Braithwate, R.N.
Mrs Fenton Braithwate.
A Roman.
A Roman Matron.
Vittoria, her daughter.
A Pompeian youth.
His sister.
Capt Andrew Pawlin, of HMS *Scout*.

Sir Henry Beadle, HM's Governor in Malta.
Lady Beadle.
The Revd Michael Willoughby-Pauncefoot, their Chaplain.
Mr George Wilbraham, otherwise Ramkishore, an Anglo-Indian.
A number of postulants.
Lieut Thos Swinton, of the *Scout*.
Lieut Eric Blore, of the same.
Mr Twinton, British Consul at Cairo.
A belly dancer.
Mr Williams, British Consul at Prevesa.
A shepherd lad.
George, a gradoman.
Mr Percy, British Resident at Joannina.
Veli Pasha, a Vizier.
His harem, and in particular Basili and Toortie.
Hanif, an Egyptian guide.
His sister.
A Sheikh.
Mustapha, an Arab tribesman.
Mr Spiridion Logotheti, British Vice-Consul in Athens.
Andreas, his son.
Mr Eustathios Georgiou, a Greek gentleman.
Mrs Mariana Macri, a Greek lady.
Giuseppe Vitali, a householder of Constantinople.
Ali, his servant.
Mustafa, a rich Turk.
A Nubian slave, henceforth Sally.
A Bride and her friends.
Petro Panayoti, a Nyklian.
Nikitas, another.
Yanni Panayoti, brother to Petro.
Madame Panayoti, their mother.
A number of eunuchs.
Young ladies of a harem.
Capt Chas Mellor, of the *Actaeon*.
Two uncouth Nyklians.
Lieut David Knee, of the *Actaeon*.
The Revd Thos Webber, a clergyman.

Chapter One

The Adventure Begins

At half-past eight on a morning in late autumn in 1817, I, my friend Sir Franklin Franklyn (of Alcovary in the county of Hertfordshire) and his half-sister Mrs Nelham breakfasted at a coffee house in the Strand, in London, while Blatchford, our servant, went about placing our luggage on the Brighthelmstone coach, upon which we were to set out half an hour later.

All three of us were, I readily confess, in a state of some excitement, for though we had all had our share of adventures during our young lives - and I counted my age with the century's, while Sophie was of my own years and Frank two years my senior - the months ahead promised to be of particular interest, since it was our plan to follow the example of our peers and embark upon the Grand Tour of Europe.

Sophie and I, in particular, had contracted very early in our lives the disease of requiring a rapid and regular change of scene, my having spent many months making a haphazard living while travelling through the country - as I have related in previous accounts of my life; while she, through the misfortune of an early unhappy marriage and the desertion of her husband, had been thrown upon her own wits, with the result that though of relatively tender years her experience of life was that of a woman much older than herself.

I had grown up so much in the company of my two friends as to be regarded as a brother - though in Sophie's case, admitted to more familiarities than most brothers are afforded; and Frank, having inherited the estate and title of his father, had invited me to share his life in London - where to our mutual surprise we had found ourselves, willy-nilly, engaged in the running of a highly successful brothel.

Inspired by our example, Sophie had opened out a similar establishment which catered for those ladies whose husbands and lovers were unable to offer them that corporeal satisfaction to which their sex, as ours, is surely entitled. This, alas, had recently been burned to the ground; but Frank's establishment continued in a good way of business, now managed by a trusted aide.

A little over a year of such activity had, however, satiated us; and the same time in one place had filled Sophie and me with the desire once more to roam – so that it was with no little delight that we greeted Frank's suggestion that we should set sail over the Channel and see what the continent of Europe could offer us.

This was now a popular as well as an adventurous journey, for above forty thousand Englishmen and women travelled to the continent each year, and it was not difficult to come by information which enabled us to plan our journey. We had made plans to stay first in Paris, to travel on to Rome, and thence to Athens before returning to Naples and Venice, and thence home to England. We had no constraints however upon our time, and few financial constraints either, our profits during the previous year, added to my friends' fortunes, being sufficient to enable us to travel in whatever comfort was available, and to otherwise maintain ourselves in reasonable style. Thus, we determined to take what adventures should offer, and to depart at any time from our plans, should the time suggest it.

It had rained during the night, and so the roads being less dusty than usual, we placed Blatchford inside the coach, and ourselves sat outside, taking a last view of the city as we rattled through it and out on to the Brighthelmstone road.

'Well, my dears,' said Frank, 'and so we set out! To what adventures can we look forward before we once more cross the Thames, or set foot in our property here?'

'And to what profits can we look forward, from the efficient management of your house?' said Sophie, never behindhand in considering practicalities.

'All the better,' said her half-brother. 'for the knowledge of the income will encourage us to spend as freely as we might wish. To which end,' he added, 'I invite you to take a glass with me' – and calling down to Blatchford, was handed up a bottle of fine champagne, from which we drank in turn as we made our way to the coast, which we reached at four-thirty, stopping at the Gun public house on the west cliff at Brighthelmstone, where we hoped to enjoy dinner before we sailed.

The landlady having offered us the opportunity to refresh ourselves – for though relatively free of dust, we were all of a sweat from the heat of the sun – we took ourselves up to a common bed-room, where a large tin bath of water had been set. Having been from childhood familiar friends, we stripped off our clothing without mock modesty, Frank and I reclining upon the bed while Sophie was first to make her ablutions. The heat of the day, and the lethargy communicated by it, had set me in an amorous mood, and it was impossible for me not to be delighted once more, despite its familiarity from youth, by the sight of Sophie's nakedness as she wiped the perspiration from her breasts and flanks, and similarly impossible for my emotion not to be communicated to that part of a man's body where such feelings commonly manifest themselves.

I was not specially uneasy at this, for we three were without the demureness attendant on the inexperienced; and indeed it was soon obvious that Frank shared my emotion – and when, Sophie, turning, saw our state, it was with a ready laugh that she stepped from the bath and, wrapping herself in a large towel, came to sit at our sides, planting a kiss first upon my unruly limb, and then upon Frank's

'I see,' she said, 'that you wish to pay your last tribute to English beauty before the lovely creatures of the continent fall to your blandishments.' Whereupon dropping the towel to the floor she enquired which of us wished first to serve her?

The inference that she was as inclined to the game as I persuaded me to ignore the possibility that Frank would wish to claim the rights of the elder, and pressed my lips to her breasts, where still there sparkled drops of the water which had laved them; and in a moment the whole cool length of her body, stretched beneath me upon the bed, was pressed against my still glowing and hot one, soon growing still hotter by my bucking – impossible to restrain – which pleased her as much as myself.

Frank, who may have been less entirely devoted to the game than I, but was by no means without wit, in a moment drew my legs apart, and inserting his hand squeezed the flesh beneath my cods with such an amorous pinch that I, with unwonted speed, gave out my soul; and were we alone, Sophie had been unsatisfied. But having brought about the result he desired, Frank tumbled me to one side, and taking my place filled the void to such effect that his half-sister shrieked in pleasure not once but twice before he too was satisfied.

'And now, I must bathe again,' she said after a while; and did so, we following her example, though having to dress ourselves in our same clothing, our trunks at that moment – as we could observe from a window – bobbing upon the waves in a cockboat towards the Dieppe packet, which could be seen in the bay below.

Downstairs we were offered and consumed with pleasure a dinner of boiled mackerel and beef-steaks, after which Blatchford appeared to announce that the cockboat was ready to take us to the packet. This was a boat which might at best hold perhaps twenty persons, and I had some misgivings when I saw that upon the shore making ready to board her were at least thirty passengers – and the boat already with luggage on board.

A wind had arisen, and the waves were considerable; the boat, grounded upon the gravel, swaying to and fro as each wave lifted her. Nevertheless, after a dousing with spray, we managed to climb on board, and were packed close together with the other passengers, some of the ladies already in a state of fear.

Finally the word was given to shove off, and a number of men came down and attempted to push us into the deeper water, which they found an impossible task, and signalled to more friends to join them. They did so; and managed to shift the boat – but she was so top-heavy that immediately the keel left the shore she tipped upon one side and filled with water.

The panic can be imagined among the women and children, while in a moment a cry went up upon shore, and throwing off their clothing several fishermen came into the sea and began to take hold of the women and children and carry them ashore, while the crew of a nearby schooner hastily lowered a small boat into the water and began to row towards us. Frank I knew to be as good a swimmer as myself, but Sophie a much weaker one – and as ill luck would have it, she was thrown into the water at some distance from me, so that though I struck out in what I took to be the right direction, in the general uproar and increasing darkness, I missed her.

In short, when half an hour later I succeeded in finding Frank upon the shore, safe, but in as wet and forlorn a case as myself, neither Sophie nor Blatchford were to be seen – and for a while we were in despair lest they should have perished; but upon enquiring found a man who swore that he had seen them both picked up by oarsmen and carried off to the schooner, which our informant told us was a Portuguese, the *Amigo*. At which we relaxed, confident that the morning would see us reunited; returned to the Gun, and bespoke a bed for the night.

It can be imagined with what speed we leapt from bed the following morning at first light, and made for the windows – to see only the packet lying where she had lain the previous night. There was no sign of the *Amigo* – and downstairs, we were informed by a mariner that she had sailed during the night for Lisbon.

Upon our expressing surprise, he informed us that the Captain, a Sr Nunez, was of an uncertain temper, and little given to changing his plans; there would have been no chance of his delaying his sailing in order that our sister, much less our servant, should be set ashore. Blatchford, we were assured, would be set to work his passage, while Sophie would no doubt be invited to contribute to the cost of her passage in whatever way she could. This would certainly not be financial, for all her means were in the luggage which, though safely rescued, was with us upon the shore.

However, we were assured that both would be safe, for the Captain was of sound reputation, however unsympathetic; and in fine we regarded the episode as a joke, for Sophie, used to caring for herself, would doubtless upon landing make straight for the British consul; and therefore Frank sat down immediately and wrote to his man of business in London to have sufficient funds transferred to the consulate, together with a letter explaining the circumstances and confirming Sophie as a lady of means.

Having done what we could, we required ourselves to depend on Sophie's wit and Blatchford's honest good sense and strength, and to be assured that by one means or another they would either return safely to England or – knowing our plans – join us at one or other of our destinations. We successfully boarded the packet at four in the afternoon, and after an hour's delay, the wind being against us, sailed for France, cramped together in the bunk of a tiny and airless cabin.

I was glad at dawn to make my way on deck, where the packet was ploughing through considerable waves towards the French shore, which as one might expect from its being home to so volatile a race, was moving itself about in a strangely dizzying fashion, so that after a while my stomach showed signs of rebelling, and I was forced to discharge much of last night's meal, or its remains, into the sea. After that, however, I was considerably recovered, and did not see the necessity of informing Frank, when he came upon deck, of my discomfiture, being content to offer him my sympathy upon his being sea-sick, something to which I was not susceptible (his being Sir Frank, my senior, and inclined occasionally to give himself airs, it is always in my view a good thing to take any opportunity that affords itself of – not unkindly – putting him down).

Crossing the bar, we set anchor in Dieppe harbour at ten in the morning, when a police officer came on board and took our passports to send them to Paris, as is customary. Ashore, we went to Durrand's Hotel by the market place, and there were informed by the proprietor – used to dealing with British travellers – of the necessity to attend at the *gendarmerie* or police station to get new passports.

This proved a strange event, for we were ushered into a small back room in which there were already three protesting Englishmen, one of them a parson, clad only in their drawers – it being necessary, we were informed, for the minutest details of appearance to be recorded, which included scars upon our bodies and even such peculiarities as the fact (much disputed at first by him, but then confirmed by the humorous comments of his travelling companions), that the Revd Jaundise only had one ball. This fact was, at the insistence of the presiding officer, solemnly recorded by the clerk upon the reverend gentleman's passport, to his intense disgust but the scarcely disguised pleasure of his companions (he being, as we guessed, a pompous and self-important individual).

Frank and I having stripped, the officer examined us and found nothing uncommon to record; but then the presiding officer singled me out and invited me to step into an inner room, which, clad only in my under-breeches, I did – to my surprise being invited to remove them for what the man stated was an *inspection particulier*; the purpose of which did not occur to me until, having divested myself, the officer concerned placed his hand between my legs and began to toy, a protruberance in his breeches at the same time revealing an interest in my person of a nature more passionate than was likely to be required by the circumstances of his employment.

Not wishing to provoke discord at the very beginning of our journey, I restrained my instinct (which was to deal him a blow upon that part of his person which most particularly offered), and instead in what little French I had at my command informed him that I was *pas sodomatique*, to which in distorted English he replied that 'there was first times for all'; however, by insisting, I persuaded him of my disinclination, and he reluctantly permitted me to resume my clothing, presumably lest I should call out and alert the neighbouring room.

Leaving Dieppe at eight o'clock at night in a hired cabriolet, by eleven we reached the small town of Totes, about halfway to Paris, and there stopped at the only inn, which was dark and silent with not a soul stirring. After much hammering upon the door, and much shouting, a light was seen approaching a window, and an old crone peered suspiciously out at us before opening the door and ushering us into a kitchen of such astonishing meanness and dirt that it was not rivalled in that circumstance by any place I had seen in England. One small rush-light alone illuminated it, for which I was thankful, lest more enormities of filth should be discovered than could be seen within the dim circle of light it shed.

However, things soon improved, for the old woman roused another, and in very little time a fire was revived in the grate to heat eggs and *soupe-au-lait* for our supper. As we ate, the two old women hovered about us, clad only in what appeared to be men's night-shirts, rent here and there, where scaly, grey skin could be seen. It being necessary to give the horses some rest, we enquired whether we could lie for an hour or so; and after cackling together in a corner, the old women threw open a door and pointed through it. Feeling our way into a small room, offensive by reason of a fetid warmth, we soon felt our feet fall upon straw. I became conscious as I moved forward of other movements throughout the room: were our sleeping quarters shared by pigs or some other livestock? But as my eyes grew accustomed to the darkness, two human shapes could be seen lying upon the floor – presumably those either of other travellers or of people of the house. Well, however it might be, there was nothing for it but to share the space available to us, and throwing off all but our shirts, we lay down beside the other sleepers, and such were the effects of our day's travelling and of the heat that we immediately fell asleep, and did not wake until the morning sun fell through the bars of the hole in the wall which passed for a window.

It was not, however, the light which roused us – or at any rate myself – but a sound of some kind; which, as I came to myself, I recognised as female laughter, and opening my eyes saw that this emanated from two girls with whom, unknowingly, we had shared our straw bed. Had I been conscious of their sex in the night, they had nevertheless been safe, for the conditions I had seen in the kitchen would have prepared me only for equally degenerate and dirty females. I would, however, have been wrong, for it was clear no less from the relative cleanliness of the shifts they wore, than that of their naked shoulders and arms, that they were no scullions but travellers like ourselves.

As I turned, the cause of their laughter became obvious, for the two girls – they could surely be little older than girls – were observing the body of my friend, who, lying upon his back, was in sleep displaying a piss-proud instrument which, his shirt having ridden up above his waist, had attracted their attentive and amused gaze. My own eyes fixed not so much upon my friend's display as upon the fine swelling of two pairs of breasts, hanging almost in full view as their owners bent over Frank's recumbent form.

Fearing to startle the nymphs, I stayed still, amused by their amusement, and increasingly conscious of my own swelling manhood as the two girls approached their faces nearer and nearer to my friend's lower parts, in their eagerness to examine his swiving tool; upon which one made a signal to the other that she should touch it, raising more laughter – and glancing at Frank's face I saw, unmistakably, his eyelid tremble, and beneath the long lashes an indication of movement. As I did so, he contracted his muscles, and his cock moved sharply, striking the cheek of one of the girls, which caused them both to collapse in a laughter so loud that it was impossible longer to pretend sleep.

'*Bonjour, mademoiselles*,' said Frank, determined to impress; but one of the girls through her laughter immediately reponded with a cheerful 'good morning, sir,' in English; and it was impossible for us not to join in their good humoured amusement.

I had by this time sat up, and smilingly introduced myself by revealing not my name but the readiness of my similarly eager cock.

'Laughter is well and good,' Frank said, 'but does not repay me for unwittingly accommodating your gaze. Perhaps you would permit me to demonstrate the accomplishments of the apparatus you have been so admiring?'

For answer, both girls simply raised their arms above their heads and drew away their shifts, revealing in handsome nakedness two bodies as like as peas in a pod – the same proud, round breasts breaking into rosy nipples, the same handsome shoulders from which depended the slimmest arms, the same narrow waists broadening to generous hips, and sturdy thighs which in a moment parted to welcome both myself and my friend to our first embrace on foreign soil.

The two girls matched eagerness in play with beauty of body, and though they must surely have suffered from the discomfort of an earth floor covered by even so generous a mattress of straw, were quick to meet thrust with thrust, racing us to a speedy consummation, when they answered our enquiry as to their comfort with satisfied acquiescence. Taking a handful of straw, which at least was clean and fresh, we wiped first their bodies and then our own; and as we lay naked and exhausted in the reflected golden light of early morning, introduced ourselves – and they themselves, as the Misses Evelyn and Dorothea Scott, of York, travelling to Paris with their father, Mr Graham Scott, a dealer in fine fabrics.

At the mention of their father, both Frank and I must have revealed some apprehension, but the girls were quick to reassure us that having eaten and drunk well upon the previous night, he would still be safely asleep in another corner of the inn.

After a while, we all four roused ourselves, and passing through the kitchen (where one crone was already stirring a pot over the fire) found in the yard a stone trough of fresh water where we splashed and refreshed ourselves, then once more dressing in our travelling clothes. By eight o'clock both our carriage and that of the Scotts were ready; and having breakfasted briefly and made the acquaintance of Mr Scott, whose head appeared not of the strongest (due no doubt to over-indulgence in French wine, the previous night) we bade what we hoped was a temporary farewell, climbed into our respective conveyances and rattled out of the inn-yard, then covering no less than thirty-eight miles in eight hours, and by late afternoon entering Rouen, where we took rooms at the Hôtel de France and ate a splendid dinner off a shoulder of lamb, accompanied by a bottle each of Burgundy wine called Mâcon, and a pitcher of water instead of beer.

Next morning we rose at five, and after some coffee paid thirty-two francs for two places in the cabriolet for Paris; the third being occupied by a handsome young French lady, who consented to sit between us. Five horses – two in the shafts and three abreast in front – whipped us along at a great rate, which the young lady pretended to frighten her, though in truth she was excited by the velocity and made an excuse of it to throw herself now upon me and now upon my companion, her flushed face and dark, flashing eyes producing in us a fine admiration of feminine France;

increased in me when, under cover of the rug which the postillion had placed over our knees before taking his seat upon the near shaft horse, she took the liberty of placing her hand upon my thigh – I naively thought to steady herself – but soon realised it was in order that she should satisfy herself that Englishmen were built in the same manner as Frenchmen, for her hand slipped ever higher and eventually came to rest upon my swelling manhood, which she caressed through the material of my small-clothes, to my increasing agitation – but agitation I had no means of satisfying other than spending in my breeches, which, they being my best – which I had put on for my entry into Paris – I was not eager to do. Had I but known it, Frank was facing the same puzzle, the lady clearly taking the view that she should be even-handed in the distribution of her favours (and, I now think, taking some amusement at our discomfiture).

I was forced finally to take her hand in mine and place it in her own lap, after which I took the liberty of returning the compliment by some little exploration of her person – which ceased when, encountering a hand which seemed larger and hairier than might have been expected, I discovered it to be my friend's; at which we all laughed with great freedom, and rode on in mutual good-will.

We entered Paris at about five in the afternoon, having ridden almost ninety English miles, dismounting only twice to walk up steep hills, so bidden by the postillion, a rough fellow forever cracking his whip and making ferocious and incoherent cries at his beasts, but otherwise allowing them to wander as they wished from one side of the road to another.

Arrived at Paris, we took a *fiacre* or hackney coach to the Hotel Cité de Londres in the Rue d'Echiquier, and were quick to bathe and refresh ourselves and go out into the streets, walking until dark along the boulevards, which – at least as far as we went on that first evening – were wide and lined with trees, and with crowds strolling to and fro and making use of the theatres, tea-gardens, billiard-houses, coffee-houses and other places of amusement of all kinds. Though it was Sunday evening, there was no sign of Sabbath-keeping, for the streets were crowded as though they were one big fair-ground.

We sat for a while and took some coffee, and were astonished by the magnificence and elegance of the unaccompanied females who walked along the boulevards, occasionally bowing to someone they knew, but for the most part clearly engaged in plying for trade – for from time to time a gentleman would approach one, and lifting his hat address a few words to her, after which he would generally take her arm and they would walk off towards one of the many side-streets branching from the main thoroughfares.

We were exhausted from our long day's travelling, and had determined to postpone amusement of any strenuous kind until the following day; but we had reckoned without the generous temptations the city had to offer, for upon our rising and paying our bill, we had walked no more than a step when two most delectable females walking towards us smiled with all the charm imaginable: one tall and buxom, the other somewhat shorter and slimmer. Their deportment was irresistible to any full-blooded man, and we both raised our hats and bowed.

'*Bonsoir*,' said Frank; to which in a strong accent, but perfectly understandable, the taller lady replied, 'Good evening. You are searching for entertainment?'

Glancing at me, Frank bowed again – and cautiously (for while always extremely generous, he was not given to throwing his money away) enquired the dimensions of the present we would be required to give for the pleasure of their company.

'Ah, *m'sieur*,' replied the tall beauty. 'that we leave to our friends; but in general a *cadeau* of three francs would be most generous.'

At this, Frank offered his arm, into which the tall lady immediately put her own, while her friend – who had remained silent, but whose bewitching smile had continued to delight me – took mine.

We had only to walk perhaps two hundred yards, when we were guided into the hallway of a large house in the Rue de Berri, and having mounted a most handsome marble staircase, were ushered into a hallway where a maid took our hats and sticks, and then showed Frank into one room and myself into another.

'*M'sieur* will make himself ready, when *Mademoiselle* Anny will join him,' the maid remarked in good English.

The evening being warm, and the room yet warmer – despite an open window through which the sounds of horses' hooves and passing footsteps rose – I was pleased to disencumber myself of my clothing, which I hung upon the stands provided. The room was finely furnished with plain but good furniture, consisting of a capacious four-posted bed and two large arm-chairs, together with two big mirrors placed at each side of the bed, and capable of being arranged at the inclination of the occupants.

Seating myself in one of the chairs, though I waited only for a moment or two, I was through natural exhaustion almost asleep when there was a soft knock at the door, which immediately opened to reveal Mlle Anny, clad now simply in a white *peignoir*. She smilingly walked towards me, and immediately falling to her knees before the chair began to kiss and caress me, offering her lips first to my own, then with an increasing fervour tickling my ears with her agile tongue while the long nails of her fingers scratched at my nipples, then gently at my lower chest, descending until her palm fell upon my tool, which despite my exhaustion was instantly happily at stand.

Such is the inspiriting power of love that I no longer felt at all tired, and springing to my feet clasped my new friend in my arms and in a moment slipped my hands under the hem of her gown and lifted it from her, revealing a body both soft and muscular, small but finely proportioned, the breasts perfectly shaped, the lower half of the twin globes falling naturally into the palms of my hands, while my thumbs discovered the small buds which sprung from them to be hard almost as horn – yet clearly sensitive, for as I set my lips to them and tongued them, I felt a shudder run through the girl's frame.

Eager to please, she set herself now to show me all the arts she had at her command, twisting her body this way and that as her lips plied themselves upon every part of my body; I felt them now suck at my breast, now nip with small, sharp teeth at my hips, then as she knelt and took my buttocks in her hands so that the tips of her fingers pried between them, I felt an imperceptible warmth that announced her reception between those red and pliant rims of my almost bursting tool, along whose length she grazed so softly that the pleasure became like a drug in its effect, pleasing without urgency.

Though I was no longer utterly exhausted, my natural debility had the unusual effect upon me that I had no desire to inspect her own body other than by watching with pleasure as it strove to please me. I did at one point, guilty at receiving without giving, attempt to rouse myself – but she, placing her hands upon my shoulders, laid me back upon the bed (to which we had now progressed), indicating by signs that I was merely to lie and allow her to please me. This required no special determination on my part and, she matching her rhythms to my own, it was with the slowest and most charming gradation that I mounted to a peak, the culmination occurring in a lethargic but most pleasurable, lengthy swelling towards the final spasm, which, occurring, left me aglow with goodwill – after which I instantly fell asleep, to waken only with the morning light, finding myself alone in that comfortable,large bed, but covered with a quilt carefully placed about my naked form.

A dual embarrassment and amusement was mine; equalled only by that of Frank, to whose room I was shown by the maid whom I shortly summoned. He too was asleep in his naked bed; and when wakened by me confessed that his experience had been much like my own. It was astonishing to us that our two companions had – as we discovered – left the house to go to their own homes, without so much as demanding the payment they properly expected from us; but which we left with the maid, with an additional present, together with the most kindly wishes. Then descending to the quiet streets, we walked back to the Hotel Cité de Londres, where the *concierge* or person in charge of the desk regarded us with suspicion mingled with amusement, but handed us our keys without comment, whereupon we went upstairs and fell into our own beds to sleep for a few more hours, thus thoroughly restoring ourselves to our normal vigour, and ready to explore the city which lay before us.

Chapter Two

Sophie's Story

Being grasped about the waist by a naked sailor would never distress me, but that that event should be accompanied by a dousing in cold, salt water was another matter.

Our being thrown into the sea by the diligent stupidity of those in charge of the boat which was to have conveyed us to the Dieppe packet could have resulted in my death, for though a good swimmer in calm water I had not previously had the experience of sea-bathing; – and it might well have been the death of our servant Blatchford, who could not swim at all. Fortunately, however, though we found ourselves separated from the main crowd of other shipwrecked passengers, we were in the path of a small boat launched from the Portuguese schooner *Amigo*, from which a number of mariners, having thrown off their clothes for the better ease in swimming, jumped to our rescue, one seizing me about the waist and the other gripping Blatchford by his hair, and after a short time getting us to their boat, which took us up wringing wet and coughing from the water we had swallowed.

By the time the boat had been rowed to the *Amigo*, we were sufficiently recovered to clamber up the nets thrown from her side, and found ourselves upon her deck, where all was business, apparently in preparation for sailing. A tall, sturdy, dark-bearded man, evidently the captain, stood upon the poop, and we immediately approached him, when I made my curtsey and offered to thank him for the assistance of his men.

Though I fancied his eyes roamed pretty freely over my body, which was clearly discernible through the wet muslin of my dress, he paid me little attention, but merely ordered us to stand to one side – and when I asked whether we could not immediately be put ashore (for I was anxious for the safety of Frank and Andy, apart from my goods and chattels) he made no reply other than '*Não percebo!*', with a motion that he did not understand me; and as we spoke the sails fell from the masts and filled before a brisk down-channel breeze, and the schooner began to move rapidly through the water.

When I stepped forward once more and attempted to speak, Captain Nunez – as I gathered was his name – threw out his hand and pushed me aside with the words '*Basta! Estou com pressa!*'

Blatchford, angered by the gesture, himself now came forward; but with one blow of his hand Nunez struck him to the deck, and when he rose gestured to a man to take him below.

There was nothing I could do except stand, growing increasingly cold in the night air, watching the dim shape of the coast, now beginning to prickle with lights, slide past us as we made for the open sea.

At last, the sailing being completed and the course set, Nunez deigned to notice me, and taking me roughly by the upper arm uttered the words '*Venha comigo!*', and positively towed me to a stairway which led down into the body of the ship itself, and eventually to a small cabin which I took to be his own, furnished only with a table and a single chair, and a small bunk. Closing the door behind him, the Captain strode forward, picked up a blanket from the bed (of what cleanliness I had no means of telling) and clearly indicated by his gesture that I should divest myself of my clothing, which though it had now somewhat dried in the wind was still so uncomfortable that though conscious he was treating the incident as a free show – for he sat down plump on his chair and showed every sign of pleasurable anticipation – I turned my back and took off my dress and my shift, wrapping myself in the blanket.

The Captain stooped to where my clothing had dropped to the floor and, picking it up, held it to his cheek as though impressed at its quality (which indeed was fine); then opening the cabin door shouted a word or two and thrust the damp things into the horny hands of a sailor who appeared, and whose lustful grin indicated some envy of his captain's lot.

Having nowhere to sit, I half lay upon the bunk bed while

Nunez lounged in his chair, still regarding me with the closest attention. I must confess that at this moment it occurred to me that I had best ingratiate myself with him if I was to expect to be treated with any kindness – or if I was to be able to intervene on behalf of Blatchford, who I feared was in an even less comfortable situation; so I carefully arranged that the blanket should slip until one breast was almost fully in the Captain's view, at the same time extending a foot so that part of my thigh also slipped from the blanket's woolly embrace.

The effect was immediate, for Nunez, as though at a signal (which I must confess was the case) got to his feet, and began to disrobe – an event which was of no long duration, since in the heat of summer a pair of breeches and a torn shirt were his only covering.

I was prepared for the swarthiness of his body, which must surely be common in that part of Europe from which he hailed; but having moved for some time among the quality I had forgotten how little attention men of his class pay to common cleanliness, so that the dirt with which his chest, shoulders, arms and legs were ingrained was a surprise to me; his rump was however almost white by contrast, giving the effect of his wearing short trousers – except of course that nothing was disguised from my view, in particular an instrument of impressive dimensions that projected in an upward motion from a positive basket of hair beneath and around its base.

Thinking it well to show some enthusiasm, I stood and allowed the blanket to slip from me, at which a string of expletives, presumably in the Portuguese language, fell from his lips, and he strode forward and took me in his arms with a vigour and strength that could not but be inspiriting, despite the strong smell of sweat – and worse – which accompanied it. I had not, however, to put up with this perfume for long, for he was in no state (presumably suffering from a long confinement alone with his men) to delay, and lifting me so that I was seated upon the table, thrust my thighs apart and planted his tree within my thicket. I had not for some time been embraced by a true son of toil, and had forgotten the great contrast between the soft skin and silky texture of a gentleman's body and the horny hardness of those used to manual toil; the Captain, despite his rank, had clearly for many years been of the latter class, for his entire person seemed covered with leather, the skin of his arse being only slightly less rough and hard than that of his back; moreover beneath that leathern covering were great muscles corded like those of a horse, and the strength of his thighs was such that, what with the shaking of the table and the shuddering of his body against my own, I began to fear that serious damage would be done either to my person or to the furniture, if not to both, before he rode to a swift culmination; but this having been achieved with a final bounding of his hips and a cry of '*Venha comigo . . .! Depressa . . .!*' he lifted me, placed me upon the floor and threw himself upon the bunk, occupying it so completely that I had no recourse but, wrapping myself again in the blanket, to seat myself in the single chair, place my feet upon the table, and make myself as comfortable as possible; which, though 'twas not much, at least enabled me – exhausted – to fall into a sleep, rocked by the gentle motion of the schooner.

In the morning, Captain Nunez woke me by the simple expedient of thrusting a great hand between my thighs and squeezing my lower parts with more enthusiasm than amorousness; which he meant, evidently, merely as a friendly greeting – as near to a cordiality as I was ever to receive from him. He might have progressed to other endearments, had there not been a knock upon the door and the appearance of a man with a great tin mug of coffee and a bowl of some kind of sickly gruel, which he left to me while he went, I suppose, upon the business of the ship. I managed to cram some of the mess into my empty stomach, and – the man also having thrust back into the cabin my dress which was dry, though fumbled and creased – clothed myself and went up upon deck.

There, a helmsman stood at the wheel, Nunez at his side; but upon the deck in the morning sunshine five naked sailors hauled sea-water up upon a line in a bucket, and poured it over each other while they frisked upon the boards in the still chill air. It was a pleasing sight, though not one to which I was much inclined, the events of the past twelve hours having been such as to offer me more concern than pleasure.

I was somewhat comforted by a sight of Blatchford who, though there was a bruise upon his cheek where Nunez's fist had caught him, looked cheerful enough, and tipped me a wink as he worked at scrubbing a portion of the deck – work I suppose allotted to him in exchange for his passage. Being no less than a woman, I could not but be both amused and flattered by the glances I received from the frolicking sailors, who ceased their slapping of each other's buttocks and friendly attempts to grasp each other's lower parts and, with a bemused modesty, turned their backs upon me (not, I am sure, realising that to we ladies the sight of a handsome posterior is at least as pleasing as the prospect of that part of which man is usually prouder).

A not altogether unpleasant day followed; the weather was fine and sunny, and the sea being calm, the motion of the boat was not unpleasant. Though I was naturally worried about my brother Frank and our friend Andy, last seen just before the upturning of the small boat off Brighthelmstone beach, Blatchford, who managed to have words with me, told me that he was sure that as he had been hauled into the *Amigo*'s cock he had glimpsed the others carried to safety by rescuers from the shore; and also let me know that the sailors (one or two of whom spoke a kind of English) had told him that Captain Nunez, while less than a gentleman and as rough in nature as in appearance, was honest, and would set us ashore safely in Lisbon in four days, where we could contact the British Consul and hope to return to England by the first available passage. He himself was not, meanwhile, being ill-treated, and hoped that I too was being made comfortable.

I did not inform him of my entertainment of the previous night, for he was fiercely defensive of me, and I feared seriously for Captain Nunez's safety had my servant known of his treatment of me, for Blatchford, while quiet mannered and not naturally of a violent disposition – nor matching the Captain in physical strength – was of strongly independent mind, and would make a dangerous enemy.

At lunchtime, that ill-tasting slop which had been served at breakfast once more made its appearance, and not only I but Blatchford (who had a good regard for his stomach) could scarcely force it down our throats, despite the hunger which the sea air engendered. Enquiring, Blatchford found that the so-called cook was merely an ordinary seaman detailed to prepare food; and at this, volunteered his services – not being himself so trained, but having grown up in a family where food was respected, and finding that the hold contained, among a great selection of material carried by the vessel in the way of trade, potatoes, onions, and dried meat, produced by evening a substantial and delicious stew which the men delighted in, and which even brought something approaching appreciation from Captain Nunez, who in mime released my servant from deck duties on condition that he prepared our food for the rest of the voyage.

As evening drew on, I began to prepare myself for another bout with the Captain, to which I looked forward with less than eager pleasure. This, however, was not to be the case; after his stew, and no less than three bottles of wine, he retired to a part of the deck near the rear of the boat, laid himself down, and was soon snoring. He was clearly one of those men for whom women were a mere commodity like food or wine, of use when he was hungry or thirsty. After a while, I made my excuses to the crew – who sat at a respectful distance while we were eating, and later had softly sung some Spanish sea-songs, in rude but sentimental tones – and went down to the captain's cabin, where I lay myself down upon his bunk and slept well for eight or nine hours.

This undisturbed night, and a second day of lazing upon the deck, completely recovered me. The journey began to seem at least as pleasant as any I could have expected in the company of my lost companions; indeed, more so – for how could the bumping along in the close confinement of a stuffy coach be compared with this gliding over a calm, dark blue sea under a sunny sky? And, moreover, I was thoroughly spoiled by the crew. Though Nunez remained morose and distant, he did not interfere with his crew more than was necessary to ensure the passage of the ship which, the weather being fine and the wind brisk but not strong, did not require more than some of their time; and they began to spend their leisure moments at my side, learning from me a few English phrases in return for some of their

Portuguese, which is a confoundedly difficult lingo.

They were rough seamen, but apart from one oldster (the so-called cook to whose duties Blatchford had succeeded) were young and not unattractive, ranging from perhaps thirty-five years in age to a young cabin boy of maybe sixteen or seventeen, who reminded me of Andy, the friend who had grown up with our family and who was regarded by us as a brother.

That evening, after the Captain had drunk by my counting four bottles of wine while most of his men were still upon a single tankard, and retired to his place at the other end of the deck to fall into a sleep, we had songs and shanties and dances to a pipe played by one of the men. These I joined in with enthusiasm, and the men were pleased to applaud my dexterity upon the deck. Their informality with me was now greater than it had been, for inclined at first to view me as the great lady, they now realised what was true - that I am at home with all manner of men, so be they are pleasant and agreeable; and they were soon treating me as they might a sister - or, more probably, someone else's sister, for more than once I felt a hand brush against my flank or breast, in a manner sufficiently discreet to be a compliment rather than an assault.

The one person who still kept his distance was the young apprentice or cabin boy, who had clearly had little to do with women. I had noticed that during the morning ablutions, while the men now displayed themselves without modesty in my presence, he would do his best to hide on the other side of the deck from that where I stationed myself, or if forced to pass before me, while unclothed, held his hands carefully before him, or sidled past with his back to me (revealing, did he but know it, hindquarters of so delicate and well-proportioned a shape as to make any lady's heart beat more strongly).

His mates of course had noticed his shyness, and made a joke of it, saying loudly to me in broken English that he 'had still the woman unknown', which I took to mean was a virgin. At this, he reddened and became angry; and on my smiling at him blushed an even darker hue; but a new tune being struck up on the pipe, I rose and going to him invited him to dance, which somewhat reluctantly he did - however displaying a nimbleness and gaiety which were enchanting. The dance ending, we collapsed on the deck amid applause, and I saw that he was not unconscious of the rise and fall of my breast as a result of the vigour of the dance, while I could not but see the knocking at the fair flesh of his bosom (his shirt having been discarded) of his own heart, just below a left pap innocent of any more hair than the flesh of a young peach.

It was not long after this that, the air upon deck chilling as evening drew on, we all – except for Nunez, whose invariable habit it was to sleep on deck except in the roughest weather – made our way below. In the Captain's cabin, I threw off my dress and prepared, clad in my shift against the grubbiness of the blankets, to sleep – when I became conscious of a movement at the door, and turning, saw the light of the lamp glint at a crack, which seemed to suggest that an eye was placed to it. Pretending to notice nothing, I idly took a step in that direction, and suddenly threw open the door, whereat into the cabin fell the young cabin boy, Carlos.

I could not but smile at the terror upon his face; at which that terror vanished, and a delightful urchin smile, showing equal proportions of shyness and eagerness, crossed his face, and he made a short bow, then stood as though not knowing what to do. What he *wished* to do was not in question, for his eyes were fixed upon my bosom, barely concealed by a shift which was of the finest muslin, and therefore even in the dim light of the lamp revealed almost as much as it concealed of a body which in all modesty I cannot claim to be unattractive.

We both stood silent for a moment, and then – since it was clear that he would not make the first move – I leaned forward and closed the door behind him; the action bringing my upper body in contact with his own, still shirtless and bare. The contact released a spring in him, and in a moment his arms closed around me and his lips fixed on mine – but firmly closed – while his lower body pressed itself also to me, but with legs together, so that he might have been embracing the mast of a ship for all the pleasure either of us were like to obtain from the exercise.

Realising soon enough that nothing would come of the

matter unless I took things in hand, I gently disengaged myself – at which he looked disappointed, and as though I was about to send him from the cabin. When I lifted the chair and placed it upon the bunk, and moved the table to the side of the cabin, he merely looked puzzled; as when I took the blanket and placed it upon the floor. But when, bending, I took the skirt of my shift and raised it over my head, presenting to him what I must suppose was his first view of a naked female, once more that delightful grin appeared, as he realised that I was intent upon his education.

Like all young stallions, he was over-eager for the battle without having any idea of tactics; and like many, he found that his eagerness was not matched by his valour, for when I reached for the waistband of his breeches and loosened it, he first made an attempt to prevent me, and then, brushing my hand aside, turned himself modestly as he removed his clothing, hesitating to face me without the comfort of covering.

Stepping forward, I pressed my body against his back, those charming buttocks against my belly, and placing my hands upon his breast moved them in circles about it as I touched with my lips the lobes first of one ear and then the other. Soon, I felt his hands upon my hips as he reached back to embrace them, and it was in the natural course of things only a few moments before his desire to embrace me encouraged him to turn so that we were breast to breast, and I felt against my belly the eager knocking of that limb he had so far successfully concealed from me.

It has always been a delight to me to entertain a young man with no previous experience – or at least one such prepared to accept a lesson. When he is not, the whole event resembles more a rape than a pleasure; but the young person who instinctively recognises that there is more to making love than the expulsion of vital fluid can generally in a short time be brought to the realisation that a pleasure prolonged is a pleasure redoubled.

The shuddering which was now running through Carlos's body was such that I recognised that until his first frenzy was satisfied there would be no reasoning with him, and so sinking to the floor and carrying him with me, I with no difficulty, embracing him with my thighs, drew him into me, whereupon with only two plunges he evacuated, a comic expression composed of a mixture of pleasure and disappointment crossing his face. Instinctively recognising that more was to be expected of him than he had delivered, but lacking any English in which to voice his feelings, he could only exclaim in his own tongue: '*Nāõ conhecia as regras . . . Que pena! Desculpe!*' He then pressed a soft kiss upon my brow – so unexpected a gesture from so young a person that it brought for the moment a tear to my eye.

Seeing this, he made to raise himself, but by folding my legs and arms about him I made this impossible, and smoothing his back and flanks gently with my hands I felt his body begin to relax, until the tension which had made it nervous and febrile sank, and his eyes, which had been darting and eager, grew large and tender, and after a while, raising himself upon his arms, he began to examine my body with a keen and amorous interest, at first with his eyes, then with his lips. As is natural, his first attentions were given to my breasts, so attractive always to the sex. With an index finger exploring the texture of the aureate rings, he was delighted and astonished at the manner in which the complimented nipples rose and tightened to his caress, and fixed them, one after the other, with soft, warm lips; then, raising his head again and looking to see whether I was approving or displeased, tested the globes with the palms of his hand, lifting and swaying them.

By this time I could feel that his member had once more risen and was knocking at my lower belly, and sure enough in a moment he once more attempted an entry; but it was now my turn to take command, which I did by suddenly raising my body so that he fell upon his side and then upon his back, whereupon I threw a leg over him and imprisoned his thighs with my own, his instrument raising itself between them, not so large perhaps as to be remarkable, but in vigour and readiness beyond question.

Carlos was clearly surprised at my action, and looked on astonished as I ran my hands over his shoulders; but his surprise turned to pleasure as I nipped with my nails at the flesh of his breast, and with a kneading motion felt the delightful young muscles of his sides, no doubt hardened by the work of the ship, and stronger and cleaner than those of the young men of whose persons I most recently had experience – they being of a different class, and bred to work (if any) of the mind rather than the body. His hands meanwhile had fallen upon my thighs, and themselves were moving in an interesting fashion, until reaching my centre the fingers fixed upon my nether lips, and raising his head as he drew them apart, he looked with interest at a sight with which he was unfamiliar. It was no doubt equally a surprise to him that I showed some pleasure in his handling of me, which indeed was gentler than I might have expected – due no doubt to his unfamiliarity and fear he that he might harm me. Raising myself upon my knees, I crept forward until I sat astride his chest, and as he continued his exploration greeted the ministrations of his hands with yet more pleasure, until upon his seeing and testing with a thumb that tiny organ in which such pleasure is centred, I could not but gasp in delight, at the same time reaching around behind me to seize his own attentive limb with my hands and to tickle it with the same gentle attention as he continued to bestow upon me, while at the same time gently fumbling his cods.

This, however, was too much for him, for the excitement of viewing my person together with the touch of my hands brought him off, and I felt upon my lower back a spurting of liquid remarkably generous for a second exertion so soon following the first.

His disappointment upon this was evident, for he clearly felt the exertion wasted when it could have been more conventionally employed – something I have often remarked upon with gentlemen who feel that the only form of evacuation should be within a female, while it is clear that the pleasure of spending is not diminished by other means – which for the female are indeed safer.

However, I could not expect young Carlos to understand such a matter, nor could I in any way communicate it to him, other than to smile and stroke his cheek, then dismounting, by lying upon my side and placing my arms about him (in which he happily acquiesced); and despite the hardness of the boards, covered only by a single blanket, we soon fell into a sleep – from which I awoke at some time later in the night, in darkness (the lamp having extinguished itself) to feel the nibbling between my thighs of a pair of lips, and recognised that in the darkness Carlos was performing that act which in the light he would have been too modest to perform – that of planting kisses at the very entrance of a place so new and interesting to him.

It was not long before my own lips embraced his now once more engorged prick, which I found to be sweet as a nut – he perhaps coming more recently from home, being plainly more careful about cleanliness than his mates; and my embraces clearly gave him as much pleasure as he was affording myself – indeed, more, for he was not about to permit me to bring him to culmination in any other way than what he most desired, and hastily withdrawing himself from my lips, he turned and in a moment had once more pierced me in that old way common to us all, and was moving now with a careless and charming rhythm characteristic more of a practised lover than that of an *ingénue*. His twice having spent made the process slower, and I reached a happy peak of pleasure only a moment before himself; after which I heard the cabin door open and close, and was alone, but by no means unhappy; whereon not even troubling to climb into the bunk, I fell once more asleep.

The voyage to Lisbon took us only four days, so that I had no further opportunity to renew my acquaintance with young Carlos; but meaningful glances were frequently directed towards me as he went about his business upon deck, or climbing like an agile monkey in the rigging. Being a young man, I could not expect him not to boast of his conquest, and I saw the other sailors from time to time glance knowingly at me, though none of them made any gesture which could be constructed as rude or insulting – a tribute to their character. Blatchford, on the other hand, was unnaturally quiet, and I could not but suspect that he disapproved of the episode; however, it was not his place to approve or disapprove, and by simply ignoring his coolness I restored it to normalcy by the time, late in the afternoon, we sailed into the harbour of Lisbon.

Chapter Three

The Adventures of Andy

During the week after our arrival in Paris, we looked about us in order to find lodgings, the life of an hotel being inimical to perfect freedom; and in a day or so took an apartment in the Rue St Guillaume, adjoining the Hotel de Berlin, which – consisting of two spacious rooms – cost us only fifty francs a month, which was the time we proposed to stay in the city, and was most agreeable.

The city of Paris made a happy effect upon us from the first, being by comparison with London almost excessively handsome as to its buildings, and provided with a perfect variety of female beauty, which not so much caught the eye as impressed itself upon one by its presence at every view, particularly in the fashionable boulevards, where every day there was a perfect perpetual promenade of ladies and gentlemen, all seeming to share a standard of youth and beauty.

We found ourselves, one hot afternoon, upon the Quai Voltaire, which has a wonderful prospect of the river Seine upon one side and fine public buildings upon the other. The river is not to be compared either for size or use with our Thames, but there are remarkable buildings floating upon it, including a public bathing school which may be seen from the quay. Here we were delighted to see many young people at practice, clad only in the lightest of clothing, the breasts of the ladies (of every age from the budding girl to the full-blown and handsome woman) seeming almost naked under the wet vesture which clung to them, while the young men's bodies were similarly displayed by the close-fitting drawers they wore, which as for concealment had nothing to be said for them. Indeed, we remarked that such clothing marked rather than obscured the character of the bodies of those who wore them, so that there was a perpetual air of *coquetterie* (as they call a kind of flirtation), the young men admiring the ladies – sometimes with the most obvious approbation, as was obvious from the swellings barely disguised by their costumes – while the latter were not backward in responding by showing their figures off in postures which, had they been accompanied by more obvious invitation, would not have been out of place in a bordello.

Leaning upon the balustrade of the Pont des Arts and admiring this scene put us much in the mood for female company; but it seemed only in the evening that those women, whom we could with ease have approached, walked out and we had as yet no introduction we could take up.

However as we turned reluctantly from the view, a man who had been observing us asked, in French, whether we wished to take advantage of the baths which lay upon the other side of the bridge? There, he said, we would find excellent recreation – this with a tone which was unmistakable, and a gesture which was even less capable of misinterpretation.

He directed us to a gate in the parapet of the Quai, just by the bridge, which gave onto a set of steps leading down to a floating platform from which it was possible to enter a large wooden shed. This proved to be divided into a large number of cubicles, guarded by a *madame* of formidable size, who handed us each a towel and directed us to our places. The cubicles were bare except for a low wooden table and a large tub which was evidently connected by a system of pipes to the river itself.

Left to myself, I removed my clothing and was grateful (the heat now being considerable) to lower myself into the tub, the water of which was cool without being frigid. I had been enjoying it for no more than a few minutes when the door opened, and a young woman entered, who with merely a nod immediately threw off the loose blouse which covered her upper body, and clad only in a skirt approached, seized a cloth to which she applied a strongly smelling soap, and set about scrubbing my shoulders and chest.

Though clearly of a lower class, she was extremely handsome, in an almost animal fashion. The necessity for her to spend her entire life (as I guessed) in performing manual labour had clad her arms in admirable muscles which rippled delightfully below the surface of the skin, while her breasts were large but in excellent proportion to her body, and held proudly and without an excess of heaviness. At present I was able to admire her quite without emotion, the coolness of the water having for the time reduced my ardour, so that even when, inviting me to stand, she turned her attention to my lower body there was at first only an appreciation of the thoroughness with which she applied the soap and with a firm and brisk movement cleansed my thighs and buttocks, then my cods and prick – the latter, however, beginning to show some hint of approbation of the attention she paid it when she drew back the skin of its head with what seemed to be some interest (most Frenchmen, it seems, are subject to the unkind rite of circumcicion, so that she can rarely have observed a tool properly clad).

Finally, she gestured to me to leave the tub, and to lie face down upon the table, which I did. I then received a rude shock, for it seemed as though she had decided to flay me alive. Seizing a rough, dry sponge, she began to rub with the greatest vigour at my back, from shoulders to ankles, until from the slight chill to which the water had reduced me, I had recovered to a warm glow of heat. Gradually, as the blood began to circulate freely, the briskness of her rubbing slowed, and the sponge was replaced by her hands, which at first almost as rough, gradually became less so, until it was merely a pressure and a kneading movement which I felt, this, as it began to concentrate particularly on my fundament, beginning once more to rouse those emotions which had drawn me and my friend to the establishment.

With a new lethargy, I began almost to sleep, the slow palpitation of her hands conferring a peculiarly soothing pleasure as they ran now from my ankles along the outsides of my legs, then coming together at the bottom of my back and descending between the cheeks of my bottom, merely brushing my cods before returning down the inside of my thighs and calves. I lost altogether a sense of time, and only came to myself when my attendant took my hand and placed it upon her hip while kneading the length of my arm with her fingers – for I realised that that hip, which I would have expected to be clothed, was now naked – and opening my eyes discovered that indeed, whether from the warmth of her exercise or some other motive, she had divested herself of her skirt, and was now naked as I – and her flanks as fine, firm and proud as the upper part of her body. Indeed, while her figure was brown from the sun and possessed only a natural animal grace rather than the refinement of motion of a lady, it was of a sensual attractiveness almost unparalleled, and I could only congratulate myself upon the good fortune of being in the way of possessing it – which surely was to be the case?

Having worked at both my arms, my attendant now encouraged me to turn over – but showing no sign of noticing that I was now clearly ready to pay tribute to her beauty with more than an admiring glance; indeed, retiring from my reach, she began to work at my feet, pressing the soles with her fingers, and turning my ankle this way and that – then raising my knees so that they were bent, pinching and rubbing the calves of my legs. But then, climbing upon the table between my knees – which was barely wide enough to support her – she began to massage my thighs, her fingers running down them to the very valley whence my now over-eager machine sprung – but declining to caress it, instead rubbing my belly and breast.

It was impossible not to pay tribute to her by allowing my own hands to stray upon her body whenever it was within reach; yet she took no notice of this, continuing her work regardless of whether my palm was feeling the weight of a splendid breast, sliding over a fine rounded haunch, or even running between her thighs to feel the fur which clad her parts.

Finally, I could restrain my passion no more, but sitting up, attempted to seize her by the shoulders and draw her to me; but with a strength which was surprising despite her build, she threw me once more to the table; clearly I had overstepped my mark as a guest of the establishment. Yet surely I was not to be left so clearly frustrated of satisfaction?

Indeed that was not to be the case, for now she retired for a moment and dipped her hand into a small container of some kind of pleasant-smelling ointment,and standing so that her body was within reach of my hands, I felt her anointing my eager self with an unguent which was almost as slippery as soap, but yet was sufficiently resistant to allow of some slight friction; this material at first stung like fire, so that I cried out at it – but then began the most remarkable pleasure as a kindly and caressing warmth spread through my flesh, and she began to smooth my iron-firm tool from root to tip with fingers now as gentle as could be conceived. First one hand then the other ran up its length, beginning – as I involuntarily raised myself from the table – at the very base, where my cods were drawn tightly into my groin, then with a tender grip barely moving the skin upon its horny base, and finally running with a circular motion around the unclad knob, where her interest in my to her somewhat unfamiliar shape led her again and again first to draw the skin over the tip, then back again.

All this was performed with an uncommon instinct, for time and again I was upon the very edge of the precipice the descent of which grew increasingly certain – yet recognising the fact, she withdrew for a moment her hands, resting them upon my thighs or breast, before returning again to her ministrations; so that I was longer in reaching my apogee than would have been likely had she allowed me to possess her fully.

Eventually, when my whole body seemed drawn into a single knot of pleasure, she with a final gesture untied it, and in a torrent I was at once delighted and relieved; whereat she smiled and, reaching for the cloth, wiped me, and withdrew; and even when I had dressed and left the cubicle, there was no sign of her – nor would the *madame* accept anything other than the two francs which was the fee for the establishment, though I wished to leave a present for my attendant.

Frank joined me just as I left, and from his expression there was no need for me to ask whether he had been similarly pleased. We walked in silence back to our apartment, and slept an undisturbed sleep for several hours before returning to the pleasures of food, wine and society.

The rest of our time in Paris passed uneventfully. I say this with remembrance of the excitements which passed during the rest of my journey through Europe; in fact, at the time, it seemed that I was experiencing as much pleasure as any single man could hope to take in at one time. But eventually the time came when, if the full extent of my plans were to be carried through, I must leave the city.

The reader will not have failed to note that I refer now to 'my' journey, not to 'our', embracing also my friend and companion. I must now explain how it came to be that I left Paris alone.

After a fortnight of various pleasures, we were told that our stay in the city must certainly comprehend a visit to the Opera, and in order that I should cut a fine figure there, I went in the morning to the tailor's, where I suited myself with a pair of white military trousers (now much in vogue) and a white waistcoat. Frank also equipped himself with some new clothes, and dressed in new French finery, and with hair *à la Russe* we set off to attend a performance of Rossini's new opera 'The Barber of Seville', a highly comedic piece the first act of which inordinately amused me.

During the interval, we walked about in the fine *foyer*, commenting between ourselves on the beauties present, when I was conscious that one young lady in particular was staring at me in an interested fashion - and indeed, now I came to look at her, it seemed to me that I knew her.

After a moment, she approached me, and asked if she was not addressing Mr Andrew Archer? I replied that that was the case, whereupon she exclaimed - somewhat too loud for my comfort - that she had not at first recognised me out of footman's dress; whereupon I knew her for none other than the Lady Elizabeth Rawby, daughter of the Earl of Rawby, at whose house I was (as I have recounted elsewhere) for a time, in my former incarnation, a servant.

My lady's attitude to me was at first somewhat condescending, until I introduced my companion to her as Sir Franklin Franklyn of Alcovary in the county of Hertfordshire, at which, recognising that I was upon equal terms with him - and perhaps admiring him (I will not say myself) as a promising blade, she invited us to accompany her to her box, where her sister, the Lady Margaret, would be found.

The latter greeted me with equal surprise; but being as pleased to meet my companion, we were invited to spend the next act in their box, where during what remained of the interval I heard news of the household – of the Earl, the ancient Beau Rust, and my friend Signor Giovanni Cesareo, a musician who had taught me to play the guitar, and whose amorous entertainment of the ladies I had observed by accident, and then been drawn into – which prompted me to whisper to Frank, while the ladies were talking, that perhaps there might be some entertainment here which would prove more interesting even than Signor Rossini's ingenious plot.

And indeed, when the music started and the light was dimmed somewhat, it was not long before I felt the Lady Elizabeth's knee press against my own, and glancing at her met her eye and was reminded forcibly of the pleasure which we had taken together at Rawby Hall. I lost no time in placing my hand upon her thigh, whereat her own fell naturally upon the bifurcation of my breeches, and it was soon clear that she was eager to examine the method by which they might be opened. On my other side, I saw Frank pressing a kiss upon the inside of Lady Margaret's wrist, and felt sure that he would soon be invited to press his attentions further. Which was the case, for soon Lady Elizabeth rose to her feet and drew the curtain at the front of the box (something which had occurred, I saw, elsewhere in the theatre), and with that forwardness which I recalled from our previous meeting, undid and stepped out of her dress with an alacrity matched only by her sister – to the amazement of my friend, whose saucer eyes could scarcely believe what they were seeing – which comprised not simply two naked ladies, but two inordinately handsome and forward ladies.

It need not be supposed that our pride in our new clothes prevented us from discarding them, and with as little delay as the ladies; nor that when they clasped us in their arms we were slow to show our appreciation of their favours, so that soon Lady Elizabeth and I were stretched upon the single sofa the box had to offer, while my friend and Lady Margaret had fallen to the fortunately thickly and softly carpeted floor at our side.

I had a clear recollection of the warmth with which my lady had ever approached the act of love, always for her a welcome pleasure; but could scarce forbear to smile when from time to time I caught Frank's eye as her sister pressed an unusually interesting caress upon him – such as one might properly expect from a professional lady, or even from a mistress of some months' passage, but not from the daughter of an Earl upon first meeting in a public place. Her eagerness for instance not merely to accept his shaft between her upper lips, but to caress it with a dextrous tongue whose effect I well remembered, set him in a positive paroxysm of pleasure, while when she raised herself above him and, opening her nether lips with her fingers, sank slowly upon him, he was in a rapture which I feared would soon preclude further enchantment. Recalling how displeased either lady was on being denied the full accomplishment of her bliss, I reached down, gripped his right ear between my fingers, and twisted it fiercely, so that he uttered a cry of pain which must clearly have been heard even over one of Signor Rossini's *tuttis*, but which at least had the effect of enabling him to control, for a further few moments, his ecstasy.

Meanwhile, my own case was almost as serious, for the Lady Elizabeth, while lying upon me, was wriggling her body so that not only her splendidly affecting breasts were massaging my chest while her fingers played with my hair, ears, nose, and inserted themselves into my mouth in an extraordinary and tantalising motion, but between her belly and my own as they moved together like two grinding stones, was trapped my manhood, which was as near to reaching a premature discharge as Frank's – until suddenly there was a knock upon the box door which immediately sprung open, and there entered a footman in full uniform bearing a tray with a bottle of champagne and glasses.

I was prepared for an outcry and our expulsion from the theatre, as would certainly happen at Covent Garden Theatre; but the man merely stepped carefully over the panting bodies upon the floor, and placing the tray upon a side table, exclaimed, '*Pardonnez-moi, m'sieur-'dames*', bowed with averted eyes, and left.

We all four at this exploded with laughter, which, as is generally known, is antipathetic to passion; so for a while we recovered ourselves, and sitting all four together upon the sofa, drank a glass of champagne each and listened for a while to the music, the trio *Ah! qual colpo!* particularly delighting us, before the ladies, by simply falling to their knees before us and placing kisses upon that limb they could most easily reach, persuaded us to return to our previous pleasure – which we did with the greatest delight, the limber movements and charming, inventive passions of our partners' persons bringing us as much joy as we had ever experienced in the way of love; so that finally we all lay in a positive bath of perspiration, limbs shining and running, bosoms panting, in a tangle of exhausted and fulfilled delight.

We repaired, when the opera had ended – which it did almost as soon as we had dressed ourselves and resumed our seats – to an eating place near the theatre, and there enjoyed a meal and some more wine; after which we offered to escort the ladies back to their hotel. They were amused at this, claiming that it would be quite below them to be seen to reside at a place of public entertainment. They had taken an entire house only a short distance away, where they were staying together, and apparently unescorted, for when I asked after their father, the news was that he had died only a few months earlier. After we had walked with them to their door and bade them goodnight, I was able to inform Frank that, there being no brother, the sisters – for they were twins – had presumably inherited the entire estate, which was a handsome one indeed. He became extremely thoughtful at this, and addressed many questions to me about the two – which was most amiable, which most interested in pleasure, and pleasure of what sort?

I answered as best I might, and repaired to bed wondering whether his interest was more provoked by the undoubted enthusiasm with which the Lady Margaret had welcomed his amorous attentions, or by my news of the sisters' considerable wealth. Interested he was, for at breakfast the following day he asked me whether he thought it was too early to pay a visit to the ladies (it was a new thing to me to be asked my opinion upon a matter of etiquette by someone so much more in command of it than I; and I interpreted the question as showing a certain nervousness on his part as to how he should conduct himself with these particular ladies, whose predilections I knew rather better than he).

I suggested that we might properly call upon them after luncheon. He looked a little uncertain at my including myself in the invitation, but accepted my advice, and after spending the morning most enjoyably in a visit to the Palais de Justice, where we obtained tickets to view the great guard-room of the Conciergerie, and taking a glass of wine and an omelette in the open air on the nearby Quai Voltaire, we walked across the river and after a while came to the house in which the ladies dwelt.

Upon our sending up our names, there was a delay of some minutes before we were admitted to find only the Lady Elizabeth at home, her sister having gone to Versailles – so we were told – to visit an elderly relative. Lady Elizabeth invited us to sit, placing me upon a high-backed chair at some distance from the settee upon which she sat herself with Frank, whom she regarded with considerable interest, and who returned that interest. After a while, it was clear to me that I was very much *de trop* (as they say in the French language) and rising to my feet asked if I might be excused, for as my friend knew, I was waited for by a gentleman.

The trembling of Frank's mouth showed that he was aware of my subterfuge and grateful for it.

'And are you also expected by this – gentleman?' asked Lady Elizabeth.

'No, I am not,' Frank returned.

'Then perhaps you would be so kind as to remain? My sister being away I have no other company, and I fear I am easily bored.'

My friend bowed, and I turned to the door.

'Excuse me for one moment while I see Mr Archer to the door,' she said, quickly rising; and before I could protest, had accompanied me to the top of the staircase. Once we were out of the door, she asked whether I really had another appointment, which I had to own was an excuse.

'Then,' she said, 'if you pass along this gallery, turn to the left, and knock at the door which first presents itself, you will find someone who will be glad of your company.'

At which she gave what in someone of a lower station

might have been described as a wink, and returned to the room where Frank awaited her.

I did as she asked; and in response to my knock came a soft instruction to enter, whereupon to my surprise I found myself in a dressing-room occupied by none other than the Lady Margaret, dressed in a becoming *negligée* and seated at her dressing table.

'You are surprised that I have so speedily returned from Versailles?' she asked.

I admitted it; upon which she said that on being informed that we had called, she and her sister had agreed that she should absent herself, for Lady Elizabeth had been eager for a private conversation with Frank.

'It is not that we were not equally glad to see you,' she said, 'but as you are aware, we are both familiar with your considerable charms' (I must admit to being flattered by the reference), 'and since it was I who enjoyed them last night, my sister wished to try your friend . . .'

My surprise was equalled by my amusement. Lady Margaret was of course right: during my time in her father's house I had swiftly become a favourite, sharing the favours of both sisters with Signor Cesareo, the musician, so that turn and turn about I had become familiar with them both. Indeed, I had had no favourite between them, their appetites being similarly keen and their ingenuity in satisfying them equally pleasing.

Stepping forward and making my bow, I took her hand, and kissing it, undertook to fulfil any duties which she was minded to present me – then offering to kiss her lips, which she permitted, before drawing away with a shake of the head.

'Alas, Mr Archer, since last night amorous activity is denied me for some days. However, we might perhaps see how far my sister is progressing in entertaining Sir Frank?' On which she rose, and led me to a door which gave into a fine bedroom at the corner of the house, then to another which opened into a dressing-room. Against one wall of this was a low platform upon which she stepped, pointing out a little sliding panel which revealed two eye-holes, matched by those under the panel beneath her hand. We both applied our eyes to these, and saw, as by now I had expected, a clear view of a bedroom like the one through which we had passed, the bed being just beneath us. Standing locked in a close embrace near the bed as in a tableau from some amorous play were my friend and the Lady Elizabeth.

Her sister now whispered that the apertures for observation which we now used had been constructed by the Marquis St Devoire, from whom the house was rented, he being a notable rake, and having demonstrated them (with two servants as the objects) as an advantage recommending the house to any tenant.

'But look,' she said, 'they grow warmer' – and indeed, on applying my eyes once more to the viewing-place, I saw that my friend's hands had succeeded in loosing her sister's dress, which had slipped from her shoulders and fallen to her waist, revealing once more to me those beautiful red-tipped orbs which I had caressed on the previous night. I could scarcely restrain a feeling of envy and jealousy, as she began to unloose the ties of his shirt, and then, helping him to remove it, turned her attention to his breeches, which were soon – with his enthusiastic assent – also removed. In short, it was but a moment before the lady was lying naked upon the bed, with my friend similarly disencumbered of covering, sitting at her side and allowing his eyes to play delightedly over her body, bathed as it was by a golden light shed by the afternoon sun passing through the lawn curtains of the tall windows of the bedroom. The dimness of the light in the theatre box had not permitted him fully to admire the beauties which were offered him, and having only with difficulty descried the general contours of Lady Elizabeth as she administered to my own appetites, he was now eager to confirm that her shape was as attractive as he had believed.

As I could have foretold, he was not disappointed; and soon, his eyes having drunk their fill, he permitted himself the pleasure of paying tribute with his lips to her smoothly rounded shoulders, the firm flesh of her pouting breasts, the generous but not fleshy round of her belly, and soon enough to the source of her chief pleasure, offered him by the upward thrust of her loins, which became more eager as his tongue played more adventurously between the lips, framed by the softest and finest down.

Meanwhile, she was not slow to discover the extent of his manly charms. Both sisters had always had a keen appreciation of what chiefly made a man a man – I recall one afternoon spent entirely in the contemplation of a book of etchings of Greek and Roman statuary, during which Lady Elizabeth and Lady Margaret had commented with some degree of expertise upon the proportions of the male parts, conjecturing which would, upon its swelling, be most impressive in size – though asserting (to my considerable relief) that size was not necessarily concomitant with satisfaction. However true that might be – and many ladies have confirmed it to me – I have nevertheless noticed that a large peg is invariably something which at first sight draws the attention of a lady, even should it later, for one reason or another, disappoint her; and here was a case in point, for Frank had an instrument which was certainly in proportion to his noble rank and extensive property – that is to say, of at least nine inches in length, and of the thickness almost of his wrist, its knob proud and well-proportioned – upon which she now pressed a kiss, then smiling as she felt the start of appreciation with which, involuntarily, it responded to her caress.

My friend now hurried to place himself between her thighs – and was surprised when she threw up her legs so that her ankles rested upon his shoulders, and taking his tool in her hand directed it to her most tender spot, into which he thrust with energy, her thighs slapping against his sides and chest with a sound clearly heard by us. So violent a motion might indeed have been injurious, were it not that Lady Elizabeth's enthusiasm had ensured that those parts now receptive of my friend's passion were well lubricated with the unguents of desire.

It can be imagined that I did not regard the scene without feeling acutely aware of my own deprivation; and had I been alone might well have quickly made my way to their room – for Frank and I had from time to time shared a bed, if not a bawd, and previous experience had taught me that the Lady Elizabeth was by no means averse to being pleased by two at once – nor incapable of satisfying both lovers.

However, my disappointment was not to last long, for her sister was clearly aware of it, and I felt her hands loosening the band of my breeches, and soon a coolness about my loins told me – while still my eyes enjoyed the spectacle of my friend's pleasure – that my clothing had fallen about my feet; and a tickling delight confirmed that her fingers were discovering the extent of my painful and so far unfulfilled appreciation of their pleasure. The gentle friction which she then applied arousing me still further, I could not but gasp with delight, which evidently pleased her, for I now felt her kisses upon my haunches, and the light nibbling of her teeth first upon the skin there, then at my hip; then her tongue exploring my fundament, and, as I threw my legs apart, her lips enjoying the tight sack which lay between (she had ever, I remembered, tasted a pair of cods as a less venal lady would treat a sweetmeat); and finally her lips closed upon my very staff itself, caressing it with great gentleness but with an intent lasciviousness, so that what with the sight of my friend grimacing with pleasure as he made one final lunge a few feet below me, and with the delight given by the hands and lips of my mistress, it was but a moment before I laid down my life, and sank exhausted beside her.

With a courteous acknowledgement of her kindness, I made my farewells to the Lady Margaret soon after – while my friend, as a quick glance told me – was working towards a second compliment to his new acquaintance. So it was that I was sitting over a glass of wine on the pavement before a nearby café when Frank left the house.

Coming straight to the point, he declared himself mad in love with the Lady Elizabeth; or perhaps, he added, with the Lady Margaret; but certainly with one or the other – and asked whether it would be too great a disappointment to me if he left me to travel on alone while he paid court to them here?

I forbore to ask whether it was really the ladies he so much admired, or their estates? I suspected it to be both; for neither was ugly, each was passionate, and while they were equally rich they would at the same time have been similarly desirable had they been among the poorest ladies in Paris.

So, of course, I said that I was sorry to lose the prospect of his company, but entirely understood his desire to remain. And indeed was not altogether regretful at the prospect of travelling alone, for delighted though I always was by the company of my friend, it was equally true that I liked being alone, and being able to make my own decisions in my own time.

So it was that, at the end of August, I bade farewell both to my friend and to the two sisters – who appeared to be much entertained by his attention, and equally interested (without jealousy) to discover upon which of them he would settle – and leaving Paris set out for the equally great city of Rome.

Chapter Four

Sophie's Story

It was with some excitement that I had seen from the deck of the *Amigo* the coast of Iberia rise to the Mount of Cintra, and then give way to the bay of the Tagus, and the beautiful harbour of Lisbon with its city spread out around it.

The city of Lisbon is a handsome one. Only a little over sixty years ago the coast had been stricken by a great earthquake, which threw the sea up over the city, engulfing the whole lower part of it by great tidal waves, so that many hundreds of fine buildings, including churches packed full of praying people, were levelled to the ground and utterly destroyed. However, the Marquis of Pombal, their great statesman, issued orders to feed the living and bury the dead, which work of charity was quickly accomplished, and new building work set as speedily on foot, so that the Baixa, or lower city, where we first set foot, was soon as fine an example of reconstruction as could be seen anywhere in Europe (I am assured); and the city is now a mixture of this new planning and of the old buildings which, on higher ground, outlived the disaster.

We came first to the Praça do Comercio, a magnificent three-sided square, the fourth side of which faces the river. It was busy with a thousand people buying and selling, promenading and talking and observing; many of them well clad and handsomely accoutred – but together with a large number of beggars in the utmost degradation, sitting on the steps by the arcades picking lice and fleas, chiefly lice, from their bosoms and breeches, and cracking them by the tens on the steps. Not being entirely sure of the way, I approached one of the more respectable passers-by, and in a phrase taught me by young Carlos, enquired '*Pode ajudar-me – onde é o consulado Britannico*?' – at which he kindly indicated the direction in which we were to walk.

Through the Praça Rossio we passed to another square – the main one of the city – and along a fine and spacious avenue until, at the side of a well tended park, we came upon the street at which we aimed, and rang the bell of a large building – when a servant appeared who turned up his nose at the sight of us (as well he might, for we were dressed in the clothes in which we had been rescued, which by their first immersion, then rough treatment on board – in one way and another – were little more than rags).

However, when he heard my tone of speech – for he proved to be English, though with an excellent command of the Portuguese language, he took my name to the Consul, a Mr Wilson Nichol, who received us in a chamber on the first floor which matched his position as a trader in wine (his office as Consul being a complimentary one). Upon hearing our story, he was sympathetic, and agreed to make us a small allowance until we should be able to receive funds from England. Knowing a ship to be leaving harbour for Portsmouth that day, he sat me down immediately at his desk and encouraged me to write to Alcovary to instruct my mother to send me funds to his address, and guaranteed to see the note conveyed to the captain with instructions that on his arrival in my native country it should be dispatched by the first mail to Hertfordshire.

This being done, he then sent for his wife, and gave me into her care, who – we being something of a size – loaned me a gown (not of the first fashion, but decent enough), while his servant, somewhat grudgingly, performed the same service for Blatchford, his dress however merely consisting of an old pair of breeches and a shirt (no top-coat being necessary for the weather, though gentlemen of course still wore them in polite society).

Mr Nichol then handed me a purse of Portuguese money, and advised me to go with his servant to an address he knew of, which would provide a decent lodging until we heard from England – only the most expensive hotels, he said, being clean enough to receive us, and the inexpensive ones being indescribably dirty, and also inhospitable to foreigners.

With the servant we walked again through the streets, and up to the Alfama district beneath the Castle of

St George – where at last we came to a small white house in a cobbled street, with baskets of hanging geraniums and lines of drying washing splashing its walls with colour. There, Signora Casado, a young widow, received us politely with '*Bom dia – como esta*?', and showed us to a small room with a single large bed – at which I looked somewhat askance, supposing that I would have to share it with Blatchford; nor did he look comfortable at the thought. However, we were now too tired with a morning's walking in the bright sun to protest, and when the woman had left, I invited Blatchford to avert his eyes while I undressed and splashed myself with cold water from a large tub which was placed in the room; after which, wrapping myself in the single sheet upon the bed, I stretched myself out to rest upon one side of the bed, while he made himself as comfortable as possible upon the floor.

We slept for some time, and it was early evening before I was awakened – as it turned out, by the noise of water as Blatchford performed for himself the office I had accomplished before sleeping; for on opening my eyes, the first thing I saw was his naked body as he bent, with his back to me, immersing his head in the tub.

I had known him all my life, he being perhaps four or five years my senior, and employed by my father; but our relationship had always been that of mistress and man, while in London he had resided at the house of my brother, whom he had been principally engaged to serve on our tour. I had never observed him in a state of nature before – even when we were children – and even had it occurred to me to regard him as a subject of admiration, I would have restrained such an inclination, for it has always been my view that any sentimental association between mistress and servant can only end in distress for one or both. However, on this occasion I could not but observe that he was a handsome figure of a man, with broad shoulders and narrow hips, muscular thighs and – I would guess – all those attributes most pleasing to amorous womanhood.

My inspection of his person was brief, for as if he felt my gaze he half turned, and though I immediately closed my eyes, was quick to slip on his breeches, so that when I stretched and once more raised my eyelids he was decently clad, and offered to fetch more water so that I could once more refresh myself – which I was glad to do, the heat while I slept having been sufficiently oppressive to bring me out in a rank sweat – and I observed several red spots upon my skin caused by the bite of some insect or another; which later I discovered was the mosquito, very common in these parts in the high summer.

Now we set forth for an exploration of the city, and as the evening was cool walked past many of the sights – the Castle itself, from which there is a splendid view, the Convent of Madre de Deus, the palace of the Counts of Azurara, and finally the district of Belem, down by the Tagus, where the Hieronymite Monastery, the Church of St Maria and the Belem Tower delighted us – the Tower itself being a charming little castle a short way into the water, which guards the harbour from attack. It was, I am told, from here that Lord Byron only five or six years ago, swam the Tagus right across – a feat of no less than two hours' duration.

By this time we had a good hunger, and finding an eating house had some good fish (or *peixe*, as they call it) and wine (which is *vinho*) and afterwards, walking back to our lodging, conversed more like friends than mistress and servant, Blatchford having a ready wit and observance of the passing people, and being especially critical of the women, many of whom were in truth rather ugly, though some beautiful enough to claim his admiring attention – but, I was amused to notice, admiration which he gave covertly, attempting to disguise his glances from me, as though I might take offence at them.

Our evening together had reminded me that there is much pleasure to be got from conversation with those we sometimes regard as being below us, and that during my hardships – described in a former volume – spent travelling through England with gypsies and other riff-raff, I nevertheless often found their entertainment more inspiriting than that of my own class. So by the time we regained our room, I was in no mind to see the man sleep once more upon the floor, and invited him to lie upon the bed; he retired while I undressed, wrapped myself in the sheet and laid myself down upon the left-hand side, then, returning, himself reclined, clad in his breeches, upon the right-hand side.

We might have remained so were it not for the heat of the night, to which we were entirely unaccustomed; for the blazing heat of the day merely subsides by a few degrees at night, and wraps one in a thick blanket of dark warmth. Sleeping for a few hours, I was awakened to find that I had thrown off the sheet, in my sleep, and even so was slippery with perspiration; while between me and the window the light of a gibbous moon showed me that Blatchford had (whether unconsciously or not) removed his breeches and was lying naked upon his back, and in sleep (I supposed) displaying himself in just such a state as a man might be who had been without the venal society of a woman for longer than human nature could happily sustain.

I have ever been intrigued by the first sight of the secret parts of a male acquaintance, the matching of those parts normally veiled from sight to the face and character being always interesting to me; so that I could not resist raising myself upon one elbow and leaning over my companion's recumbent body to examine that part of him which was now, though subject only to the caresses of the warm night air, from time to time giving just such small leaps as would in other circumstances be the result of the attentions of a mistress, but which now were evoked (I guessed) by some happy dream.

As I had suspected from my earlier sight of him, here was an instrument as sturdy as one might expect – though perfectly in proportion; neither so small as to disappoint, nor so large as to alarm. From the dint of his flat belly, a gauze of light brown hair lay upon the skin, thickening into curls at the foot of the standing column, whose pale flesh was white in the moonlight, a single, thin purple vein rising for a quarter of its length, then dividing like the branches of a tree into a handsome decoration which might have been planned by an artist. Between the closed thighs two globes, the skin textured with what seemed goose-pimples, lay like plums upon a plate, seeming to support rather than depend from the cylinder above, at whose top, a ridge, perfectly regular, lay about the crown, itself punctured by a tiny red eyelet from which, as I looked, a small bead of liquor released itself.

I would not have been human had I not, by the sight of a

piece of work which by its perfect proportions signalled more the aristocrat than the servant, been roused to some passion; and without pausing to think of the consequences, in a moment had risen to my knees and thrown one thigh over the sleeping man, so that for a moment I hung astride, then gently lowered myself until, handling it as gently as possible, I could guide his prick, smooth and impermeable as ivory, between the lips of my cunny, liquid no less from desire than from temperature.

I was prepared, as I lowered myself so that I could at last feel his cods nestling between my own thighs, for Blatchford to awake, and – such in my experience is the passionate vigour of the lower orders, less conformable in general to being dominated by the fairer sex – to throw me upon my back and proceed with mastery; however, to my surprise, he showed no signs of waking, and even as I began to rise and fall upon him, there was no sign of disturbance, so that – his cock remaining strong as an iron bar within me – I began to wonder whether I had merely become a figment of his dream. My own movements became more bustling as I grew towards my satisfaction, until the whole bed seemed to shake, and the man's body, as I watched, began to throw off prickles of perspiration which soon were running down his sides as freely as from my own breasts and back. As the mounting tide broke within me, I seemed to feel a similar wave break from his loins, and indeed it seemed to me that an expression of pleasure passed over his face – though a moment later, in the moonlight, it was as expressionless as before.

I lifted myself from him and saw that indeed he had paid me the compliment of giving forth his essence, for traces shone upon his instrument as its slow collapse confirmed the completion of his pleasure. I marvelled that he had not awakened; or that, waking, he had been able to resist playing an active part in his own enjoyment – while at the same time being grateful to him that (if it were true) his tact would preserve a relationship between us which would enable me still to retain his services on a footing we both understood.

With which thought I fell into a deep sleep, waking only as he set down, in the morning, the butt of cold water brought from the well outside, himself of course fully clothed, and carefully averting his eyes from my nakedness.

No sooner was I dressed than Mr Nichol's servant appeared with a message that we should attend him at our earliest convenience; and when we arrived at his house, we were immediately greeted with a welcome letter from my brother Frank, enclosing two hundred guineas in English money. I was no less pleased to hear of his safety than to receive the money, sent on the day following the unfortunate incident of our near drowning, when he had evidently heard of our rescue, and the destination of the relieving vessel.

We immediately made our way to an hotel in the Praça Rossio – a handsome edifice where we were made welcome upon our asking to change twenty English guineas, considered here a vast sum – and took a suite of rooms where I could be comfortable while I decided on our future movements – which should, I had already decided, be planned so that we could meet with Frank at some place which we could conveniently reach at a time when he would be there – Rome, perhaps, or Venice.

Meanwhile, having asked the hotel management to recommend a dressmaker, I sent out to summon him to my rooms, where soon he appeared – a finicky little man with four female assistants and several baskets of clothes, all in a Portuguese or Spanish style, from which I chose several dresses, or *vestidos*, which suited me. Blatchford I fitted out in a suit of black trousers and white shirt, which suited his looks to perfection; and in which he seemed neither as a servant nor gentleman, so would enable him to accompany me in either capacity, but always as a protector, for while perfectly able to take care of myself I was not entirely without that nervousness which must attend a female in a foreign place.

By afternoon, we were most comfortably settled; and after two or three days became almost citizens of Lisbon, so familiar did we become with the city – sufficiently small at its centre to be readily explored within a restricted period. On one day we travelled to the picturesque village of Cintra, about fifteen miles from the capital, and one of the most delightful places I had seen, with palaces and gardens rising in the midst of rocks and cataracts and precipices.

On our sixth evening in the city I decided that we should visit a theatre, for I wished to hear some local music and see some characteristic dances of the country. The place to which we were recommended was in the Rua dos Condes – small and ill ventilated, so that from our box we felt as though we were suspended over a positive soup of humanity. Most of the audience consisted of men, with a scattering of women who soon proved to be of low character, for many of them were clad with relative indecency, their breasts often completely disclosed; and that they were of the prostitute class – or at least loose in their morals – was signalled by their willingness to allow their neighbours to make free in exploration of what lay beneath the long black skirts which they wore, but which were often thrown back (ostensibly for the heat) to disclose limbs with no suspicion of covering.

I cannot tell what sort of troupe performed, but the dances were all of an extremely lascivious nature – and the more freely the bodies of the dancers, chiefly female, were exposed, the more they flung themselves around in postures as revealing as they were obscene, the more vociferous was the applause. I must confess however that the spectacle was of interest, and I was conscious that Blatchford, though he pretended otherwise, was intrigued by it, and when the interval came told him that if he wished to make his way to some other part of the theatre 'for refreshment', I would not object; at which with scarcely a pause, he bowed, and did so.

I sat for a while watching the audience, many members of which had brought bottles of wine and food to their seats, and were consuming them while concurrently toying with the women at their sides. I was then addressed by a handsome woman sitting in the box next to my own, and accompanied by a handsome young man; having no doubt heard Blatchford and myself conversing, she enquired in excellent English whether I was not of that nationality?

I was, I replied.

And was I alone?

Once more I acquiesced, at which she asked whether I had seen enough of the spectacle before me?

I admitted that the show had little real interest for me.

'Then,' she said, 'will you not allow me to offer you some refreshment at my home, which is nearby?'

I happily assented, for she was clearly a lady; but would have to convey a message to Blatchford. That, she said, would be no difficulty, for she could imagine where he was – and sent the young man, who also spoke excellent English, to find him and inform him that I had no further need for him. This, she said, he would easily do, for on the ground floor was the refreshment room where not only food and drink but female company could be purchased, and she would be surprised if such a well set-up young man would fail to discover such a place.

Indeed, by the time we were at the entrance, Blatchford had made his way there with the young Portuguese, for he thoughtfully wished to assure himself that I was safe before returning to his pleasure – which, I suspected, involved a charming girl waiting near the door, who had an eye firmly fixed upon him.

My new companions introduced themselves, as we walked from the theatre, as the Marquise de Aljubarrota and her son, the Marquis. Their command of my language arose, it seemed, from their being engaged in the wine trade, chiefly with the British, and the young Marquis had indeed spent some time in London, and was already a shrewd businessman.

I was curious how it came about that I should find them at what seemed to me to be so disreputable an entertainment. The Marquise explained to me that it was upon a matter of business, for her son had recently been asked by a London acquaintance whether it could be arranged that some Portuguese dancers, whose performances he had witnessed while in Lisbon, could visit England on a professional basis, and the Marquis had agreed to examine some troupes with a view to this; however, they had so far concluded that the entertainment offered would be too rude for a London audience – did I not agree? I was forced to do so, though I could think of some places where it would be welcomed.

We had by this time arrived at the Aljubarrota Palace, an extensive and magnificent building in whose central courtyard, with a great marble fountain playing to cool the evening heat, we sat and drank wine. On my admiring the place, the Marquise intrigued me by saying that it had also been admired by Lord Byron, whom she had entertained there when he was in Lisbon with his friend Hobhouse in 1809.

'Mr Hobhouse,' she said, 'I found a snob, convinced that nothing could be good which was not English, and who did nothing but complain about the mosquitoes, the food, the wine and the people. Milord, however, was charm itself – and, as you have perhaps heard, a man of peculiar personal attractions. My son was delighted to become his friend, and I was equally pleased to entertain him' – which sentence she delivered with a smug coyness which to my eyes meant only one thing: that her familiarity with our greatest poet had, at least for a time, been a close one. But to my equal interest, I thought I saw upon the face of the young Marquis a knowing look which made me wonder whether the rumours about Byron's personal tastes were not perhaps true. I would not have been surprised, should that be the case, that he had befriended the Marquis, who was an excessively handsome man, with jet-black hair and the pale face of someone who took care to keep away from the sun, and whose marble skin, slim figure and flashing black eyes were remarkably attractive, and must have been even more so when he was of tender years.

We talked for some time, until the distant striking of a clock told me it was midnight.

'I had no idea the time had passed so quickly,' said the Marquise. 'You may not wish, perhaps, to make your way through the streets of an unfamiliar city at such a late hour. May we offer you hospitality for the night?'

I was, I confess, curious to explore further the luxury of the house, and accepted the offer with thanks; whereupon the Marquise summoned a servant with a great candelabra of six candles, and the young Marquis rose to accept his mother's charge to escort me to a bedroom. We mounted a great staircase, lit at that hour by flaming torches; and, having traversed a long corridor one side of which was aired by open arches giving into the central courtyard, the lady paused at her own door, and having bade me goodnight, kissed her son, and retired leaving me in his care. We proceeded further, when opening another door, he showed me into a fine chamber lined with dark wood, and with a huge bed hung with red velvet.

The Marquis, somewhat to my surprise, closed the door behind him, when setting down the candelabra upon a table and advancing towards me he took my hand – but rather than kissing it and retiring, held it between his own and said, in the most charming of tones: 'And now perhaps you allow a fuck?'

For a moment I thought that perhaps he had used some unfamiliar Portuguese word rather than so common an English one; but it was clear from his demeanour that he meant precisely what he said; and my not immediately demurring, took me in his arms and pressed his lips to mine, his tongue immediately exploring my mouth with the utmost impertinence.

In a moment, I threw off his embrace, with the exclamation that a young cub should watch his manners.

'I do not understand "cub"?' he said, with an ingenuous manner by no means devoid of charm, so that I could not but laugh.

'Your language,' I said, 'is not precisely the polite way of addressing a lady.'

'But I learn it from milord Byron,' he said.

'It is something that a man might say to a common woman,' I began . . .

'Oh, he say it to no woman; he say it to me,' said the Marquis, with an open and artless smile.

This, as might be expected, rendered me speechless – at which he took the opportunity to begin to unbutton; whereupon, fired no less by his youth and beauty as by curiosity, I allowed him to complete the process, whereat he revealed himself as a slim wand of a youth, who six or seven years ago must have been small and pretty as a girl, and who with long ringlets hanging to his shoulders I could imagine would have attracted any man predelicted to masculine beauty. Having permitted him to undress without protest (chiefly, I confess, from the no doubt impertinent desire to view those attractions which had captivated our greatest poet), I could scarcely raise objection now, and allowed him to assist me to divest myself of my own accoutrements and lead me to the bed.

Had I thought that he was a madge cull devoted only to the society of men, that suspicion was soon removed from me; indeed, so enthusiastic was he, and so ready to engage, that scarcely two minutes had passed before the rapid plunging with which he engaged me had ceased, and with a sigh and the words '*Estava muito bom!*' he withdrew.

'My lord,' I said (supposing that to be the proper form), 'I am sure that Lord Byron addresses the ladies with more kindness than yourself, if that is to be the extent of your love-making.'

'Oh,' he said, 'I know not about him and the ladies; but he is most kind and teach me many lessons.'

That I should not wonder, was the phrase at the tip of my tongue; but I failed to utter it, and not having been myself even slightly roused by the puppyish romping in which the Marquis had engaged, merely bade him goodnight; at which, without rancour, he gathered up his clothes, placed them under his arm, and left my room naked as he was born - a sight to which I could only suppose his servants were accustomed.

I lay for a while contemplating the red bed-curtains, and wondering whether it was in this very room that our poet had enjoyed the Marquis - and, presumably, his night's rest; but sleep then overtook me.

Next morning, neither the Marquise nor her son put in an appearance. Breakfast was brought to me in my room, after which I was shown to the door by servants, and made my way back to my hotel. I could only suppose that the Marquise was some kind of pimp for her son, and could only ponder the question whether the story of Lord Byron was true or not. It was a strange adventure.

After a fortnight, I was tired of Lisbon, and announced to Blatchford that it was my intention to make for Seville, and from there perhaps to Rome. We crossed the Tagus by boat and spent a night on the shore at an inn in a little village called Aldea Gallega, where we bought quantities of netting to protect us from the mosquitoes. We then hired a guide called Sanguinetti who escorted us, behind two pack horses, through Los Prigones, Montemenor and the town of Elvas, on the border with Spain. There we spent a night, and the following morning, having breakfasted on new bread and goat's milk, passed over the frontier to Badajoz and the small town of Albuena.

After several days, and a crossing of the Sierra Morena mountains which was excessively arduous and uncomfortable, we entered Seville and took lodgings near the Cathedral with a British woman who provided us with a single room into which we were happy to move; the city was extremely crowded, and there were no public rooms available. Blatchford and I were now more like brother and sister than servant and mistress, and though the familiarity which had marked our first night in Lisbon did not recur, we were to every other extent familiar, dressing and undressing and performing our toilet without embarrassment.

The Spanish character seems much more violent than the Portuguese: no sooner had we arrived in Seville than we witnessed a violent quarrel between our guide (on his dismissal) and another man in the street, for no reason that we could discover other than that they disliked each other's faces: a challenge to fight with knives was issued, and such a fight only prevented by the intervention of soldiery.

We stayed only three days in Seville before passing on to Cadiz, where we put up at Wood's Hotel. The landlady there being firm that she would allow no servants into her house, we passed for brother and sister, to our mutual satisfaction – I having long since ceased to address Blatchford in the terms of a servant, and he – with my permission – now addressing me as Sophia.

It was at Cadiz that I permitted myself to be persuaded to attend a bull fight, the cruelty of which nauseated me: the spectacle of horses galloping around a ring with their bowels exposed, of men shattering themselves to pieces, and of the tortured bulls themselves, was sickening to me and no less to Blatchford, and marks a difference between the British and the Spanish character that could scarcely be more marked.

I had hoped to travel from Cadiz to Ostia, the port of Rome; but was informed there was no direct sailing,but that I should instead make for Gibraltar, where perhaps I could obtain passage. The three days spent at Cadiz before we sailed were delightful ones, the bullfight apart: it is a gay and charming city, with an opera at which many handsome men and women present themselves to the public view – the girls especially fine, with long black hair and graceful forms, and the most becoming dress. Blatchford too was charmed by them, and escorted by a fellow Englishman staying at the hotel, visited a *seraglio* or *bordello* at which he informed me (for we were now on terms which permitted us to discuss it) he was entertained by females as generous with their endearments and as tender in their caresses as they were passionate in their satisfaction of the masculine urges.

It was with some disappointment, then, that we sailed at three one morning upon a frigate, for Gibraltar, and at noon the following day set foot on that remarkable rock.

Chapter Five

The Adventures of Andy

Of my journey to Rome (which took me through Lyon, Geneva, Chamonix, the Simplon Pass, Milan and Bologna) I wish to say little. I left in mid-November, and was ten days on the road – a matter of considerable hardship. Wishing to reach Italy as quickly as possible, I engaged for a seat in a diligence which, being a much improved vehicle of the latest design seating no less than twenty passengers, went at the rate of a hundred miles a day, the seven horses being changed every twelve miles. This was more expensive than I had reckoned on (though not more expensive than I could cover); however, I reflected that the saving in hotel bills more or less balanced the additional expenditure. What was lost was sleep, for the rattling over roads paved for the most part with large, uneven stones was terrible, and precluded even a doze; while the occasional hour's break at an inn only permitted a few stolen moments of unconsciousness.

However, these are remarkable vehicles, the like of which are not yet to be seen in England – capacious and lofty as to the interior, lined with padded leather, and with a large net hanging from the roof which was full of hats and band-boxes. Upon the roof itself perched six or seven more people who had paid less for the journey and sat precariously beneath a pile of luggage secured by ropes and chains, which rose as high again as the coach.

Travelling through France and Switzerland the weather was extremely cold, and the company on board not very agreeable, most of it being military and with great inveteracy against the English. I often heard the words 'God-damn' applied to me, but I never took the least notice. The conversation railed against the English, sometimes ridiculously so, but I thought it best to restrain my comment.

I was sad at rushing at so breakneck a speed through such magnificent scenery; though, upon the pleas of some of the ladies, the coachman occasionally consented to stop for a few minutes while we admired some feature of the landscape – the tremendous mountains near Montigny, for instance, and the famous waterfall known as the Pissevache (though there was little water in it). Some of the most tremendous and appalling beauties of nature were to be seen around the mountain Tête Noire, and for a while we rode along by the side of a frightful chasm with a rivulet roaring through fragments of rock at the bottom; if the horses had missed their footing we must have fallen from a height of at least two thousand feet – which caused great alarm among the ladies, two of whom, seated upon either side of me, were in such paroxyms of terror that they clung passionately to me, and I could have taken every advantage had not we been surrounded by other passengers, and had they not both been middle-aged, portly, and amuck with the perspiration of fear, which scented the whole coach.

Our way through the Simplon was perhaps the most spectacular section of the journey; the road is a wonderful achievement, sweeping as it does over the stupendous mountains with a winding course, in some places interrupted by tunnels cut through the solid rock, with long icicles hanging from the roof. Near the top, we stopped in fine and unsullied snow with fine romantic views.

Descending then to the frontier at Douane, where our bags were not searched, we passed through Milan (a city, I was told, more of commerce than of beauty – though I would have liked to have seen the original picture of the Last Supper by Master Leonardo da Vinci, had not my eagerness to reach Rome driven me on). And finally we entered the Papal Dominions at Castel Franco, where I changed a twenty pound bill at a good rate of exchange – and within a day saw the lofty edifice of St Peter's raised above a mass of lesser domes and steeples, and were arrived in the Holy City.

I need not say how pleased I was to find lodgings at the Via Condotti and to wash myself and change into clean clothes – a great luxury after ten days in the same garments.

I dined at a *table d'hôte* – an excellent meal with tolerable wine for five *pauls*, or about three shillings. At table I found myself sitting next to a young English lady who had travelled from Chamonix on the same coach, but in a seat distant from me. I had much admired her form and face, and indeed during those amorous reflections which visited me in the half-sleep which was all that could be secured during the journey, she had played a vigorous part, though when I had spoken a few words to her during our brief halts, she had seemed reserved.

It now proved that she was quite alone, and knew no one, so I appointed myself her protector. Her name was Emily Fawcett, or Em, as she called herself, and it seems that she had come to Rome to meet her lover, a clergyman who had come to the city to study at the Vatican library. Her father, the Dean of a respectable provincial cathedral, had suddenly died, and having no relatives, and being mad in love with the Revd William Brarley, she had let the house in which she had grown up, sent a missive to the address he had left her, and set off to join him.

This seemed to me to be a somewhat rash circumstance. Had she not given him time to reply, I asked, to her announcement of her visit? No, she replied, but he would be delighted to see her, and it was her plan that they should be married in Rome and return to England when his studies were completed, in order that he might purchase a living there (for her father had left a small fortune which would enable the Revd Lover to set himself up in a good way of ecclesiastical business).

I had some difficulty in persuading Miss Fawcett not to set out that first evening to find her lover; but she was mightily fatigued, and as I pointed out, it would be better that she should be fresh in spirit and body before setting out to discover his lodgings – which I promised to help her do, then escorting her to her room, and leaving her with regret at her door (she being flushed with the glass of wine I had pressed upon her, as an aid to recovery from the fatigue, and her pretty, small breasts rising and falling with an eagerness I could only attribute to the desire to greet her fortunate curate).

The next morning I offered, at breakfast, to accompany her to the house near the Via Flaminia where the Revd

Brarley had rooms. We found it a tall house of apartments, where a blowsy woman explained in imperfect English that the clergyman no longer lived there, but could be found at an address in the Vatican City. This was something of a surprise to Miss Fawcett, for her friend had previously been strong upon the evils of the Papacy, and had sworn, apart from his readings at the Library, to confine himself only to the Protestant places of instruction in the city.

However, we made our way to the address we had been given – Miss Fawcett prettily protesting that I was affording her too much of my time, and myself continually reflecting how delightful a person she was, and what pity 'twas that she was so clearly honest and so clearly devoted to the Revd Brarley (who I trusted would be worthy of her).

What was our surprise to discover that we had been directed to a seminary or school for the education of Papist clergy! Miss Fawcett was instantly of the opinion that there had been a mistake – and was just about to turn away when into the courtyard containing the main entrance to the seminary came a small procession of choirboys accompanied by what appeared to be two monks; upon which she gave a great start, and recognised one of the men as her fiancé! She made a quick curtsey to me and greeted him, clearly believing that her problems were now solved. Myself, I wondered whether this was the case – for not only was it clear to me, no less by his wearing the Roman cassock than by the circumstance of his accompanying a choir clearly just come from the celebration of the Mass, that he was now an adherent of that faith. However, it was not for me to take the matter further; and being now so close, I went to examine the splendours of St Peter's, and then upon a tour of the convent of the Capuchins, where I was shown a cross made by the devil, a painting by St Luke, and the subterranean cemetary where lie many hundreds of skeletons, with grottos made entirely of knuckles, knee caps, ribs, grinning skulls and crossbones; in each compartment of many stood six skeletons in Capuchin habits, erect against the walls and with their skins dried tight upon their bones, long beards hanging clasped to their waists and rosaries in their bony fingers.

This put me in a mood to enjoy the air; yet my walk back

across the river and in the direction of my lodging failed to recover me, for it was through an almost uninterrupted succession of narrow, vulgar-looking streets where the smell of garlic prevails over the odour of antiquity, and dingy, melancholy flat fronts of modern-built houses afford no relief.

I came finally upon the Chiesa Nuova, however, where the booksellers congregate, and there ate some food in the sun, and began to recover my spirits; which recovery was aided by my discovery of a shop entirely given over to the sale of books of an erotic nature, some of which I had seen in private hands but never offered publicly for sale – as *L'Histoire de Gouberdom*, or Tale of a Master Bugger, *The Life and Adventures of Master Silas, written by himself and now first translated from the original French edition* which I purchased, and a handsomely illustrated edition of Mr Cleland's *Memoirs of a Woman of Pleasure*, which I got not for the text (which being in French I could not well read, besides which I knew it well) but for the illustrations, which were perfectly and enjoyably obscene.

Seeing my interest, the bookseller, who, like most people here who have contact with the visiting English, spoke a little of our language, asked me if I wished for relief, and made a gesture which clearly indicated that he did not mean the relief of my bladder, but of other congestion in the same area.

Upon my signalling that I would not be much averse, he wrote down an address upon a piece of paper which was of a house in the Via Giulia, only three minutes away. This, he said, was a clean house, and that while I would find the city full of complaisant girls, many of them were poxed, and I would be wise to confine myself to the professional ladies.

I was not indifferent to this advice, for having so far in my life contrived to avoid the burner, I was not eager to acquire it. So I took myself off to the Via Giulia, where I found a fine apartment where I was welcomed by two elderly sisters named Cazenove, who ushered me into a large room, handsomely furnished, where there were three pretty *filles charmantes*. I was told I could have one for the price of fifteen *pauls*, or nine shillings, though at weekends the price was increased to a *sequin*, or ten shillings. There are, it seems, seven or eight other girls employed here, but this was the hour of siesta, when many Italian husbands make their way to the house for recreation, and the others were busy. However, if I wished it, and as an introduction to the establishment, I could be entertained by two of the girls for the prize of a *sequin*. Having had no female company since leaving Paris, I considered that I could allow myself that pleasure and, closing with the sisters, took the two prettiest girls by the hands, and was led by them to a room where heavy shutters allowed only thin streamers of light to fall upon the bed which was its chief furniture.

The two ladies politely assisted me to disrobe, one unbuttoning, the other carefully folding my clothes and placing them upon a chair. They then led me, bare as a bodkin, to the bed and, placing me upon it, turned to each other, removing each article of clothing – of which, indeed, there were few – with deliberation, and with exclamations in a strange English, such as 'It is the beauty of cunt!' or 'What a fuck is here!', which I assumed they had learned from some of my compatriot customers, but only partially understood their meaning, for they were frequently inappositely applied, as when caressing her friend's breast one exclaimed: 'Oh, but of the ankle the most handsome!'

However, their speech was not to me the most interesting aspect of the situation, and in admiring their figures – which were fuller than those of the generality of Parisian or London beauties, the breasts heavier and at their centres darker, the nipples surrounded by great circles of a light brown skin – I soon achieved a display of enthusiasm which arrested their attention and drew them from mutual admiration to a display of apparent wonder at my size. I did not, of course, take this for more than professional compliment; but nevertheless could not but be pleased when, one sitting upon each side of me, they leaned to admire, pointing out to each other those features they found most attractive – as the acute angle at which I stood, the size of the crown displayed beneath the skin (with which they were as intrigued as other European ladies), or (and here they pressed with their fingers, with many an 'Oh!' and 'Ah!') the iron rigidity of my member.

It was soon my turn to admire, which was not a difficulty;

indeed, kneeling between them as they lay one upon each side, the problem was upon whom first to graze – which I have ever found a confusion when abed with more than a single companion, and which in my experience can expose a lover to the dangerous accusation of favouritism. However here, the ladies being hired, it made no matter; and I was able to compare and weigh the differences – the slightest diversity of contour here, the mole there, the abundance of hair in one case and relative sparsity in the other – without compunction. Indeed, there was a superabundance of delight, for as I pressed my lips to the breast of one girl, the other would be nibbling with her teeth at one of my toes, or passing her hand between my legs to grasp at my cods; or upon my testing with the tip of my tongue the entrance to the pleasure-hall of one, the other would herself apply her lips to my most sensitive part, thus forcing me to rein in my senses if my pleasure was not to be brought to a too speedy conclusion.

The time passed most agreeably in this matter, until finally one of the ladies placed herself in such a position that it was impossible for me longer to resist, and in a moment, and with no more than a single movement, the accumulated juices of a fortnight were released.

'*Lei è molto gentile,*' I remarked, having once more assumed – with their charming help – my clothes.

'*Il piacere è tutto mio!*' they replied; '*un'altra volta lei dovra passare qualche giorno in casa nostra,*' which I took to be a invitation to stay with them for a whole night, to which I would by no means be averse, their company being charming and their persons delightful.

I had learned enough Italian during my journey thither to say to the sister Cazenove who bade me farewell, '*Mi rincresce tanto, ma io me ne devo andare,*' or that I was sorry to go.

'*Spero che ritornera presto – venga quando vuole,*' she replied, or that I was to come again soon, which I determined should be the case.

I determined to spend that evening in my lodgings, being quite exhausted after the rigours of my long journey and my day's sightseeing, to say nothing of the afternoon's adventure. At about five o'clock, however, Miss Fawcett appeared, in some distress, and my being the only person in the house with a command of English, and having been something sympathetic to her, chose to explain the cause to me. It appeared that her lover, upon her disclosing herself to him, greeted her most coldly, without seeming in the least pleased that she should have travelled so far to greet him, and not at all enthusiastic about her plans for marriage. Indeed, he explained to her – and not with the least shame – the fact that he was in process of converting to the faith of Rome, and planned to take their orders, which meant that he would have to undertake a lifetime of chastity.

She would not, she said, have been so distressed at this – for she respected the conscience of any truly religious person – had she not, while sitting at tea in an English tea-house near the seminary, overheard an Italian pointing it out to some English visitors as notorious not for the purity of its religious faith, but as a hot-bed of lust – and (she blushed to relate) not conventional pleasure, but (as the Italian had put it) 'beastly sodomy', for there the priests indulged themselves in 'a monstrous filthiness, and yet to them a pleasant pastime, besides their religious chanting, making songs and singing sonnets of the beauty and pleasure of their *Bardassi*, or buggered boys.'

Miss Fawcett – or Em, as she now insisted that I should call her – subsided into tears as she related this to me, clearly believing (and I suspect with truth) that her lover had suffered a conversion of more than one kind. I could not but embrace her, permitting her to weep upon my shoulder, while it was a matter of some difficulty to me (despite my earlier amorous encounter) not to caress her, for her form was delightfully warm and yielding, and her clothing sufficiently light for the blushing of her body to be readily observable beneath it.

I persuaded her to take some brandy, and by lying readily to her about its strength (saying that it was by no means as alcoholic as the English equivalent) soon made her drowsy and escorting her to her room advised her to rest, whereupon she fell upon the bed and into a deep sleep even before I could close the door (which, I must insist, I did, however reluctantly).

During the next week we became extremely friendly,

though I abstained from pressing any attentions upon her other than that of an acquaintance, if one I believed increasingly dear to her. Early on, borrowing a guitar from one of the servants (which I heard him strumming upon), though out of practice, I played to her upon it, music being a healer of hearts, as I believe; then I began to take her about the town to see the sights. We walked one day at about nine o'clock to Santa Maria Maggiore, one of the principal churches, where we found it crowded with military in anticipation of the arrival of the Pope. The church was hung throughout with crimson cloth and brilliant with chandeliers, and the altar surrounded by immense wax candles, and after a while Pius VII arrived in a sedan chair, and we obtained good positions with the help of one of the Swiss guards while, in full robes, he was borne along the centre aisle in a state chair, on the shoulders of six men, with on either side a man carrying an immense fan of white peacocks' feathers, and preceded by a long train of cardinals in full robes. I have never witnessed such a gorgeous display of pomp, and Em was equally impressed by it.

I discovered that she was an interested delineater, who took always a pad and pencils with her, and would frequently pause to draw a scene. Hearing that it was possible for strangers to visit the Roman Academy, I obtained tickets and invited her to do so, for it had a great reputation as a school for artists - particularly, though I was not aware of it, those devoted to drawing the unadorned figure. So it was that when one afternoon we were shown into a large room there, we found about thirty young men gathered around a dais upon which two others, completely unclothed, were locked in embrace, counterfeiting the battle between Hercules and Antaeus.

Miss Em, I suspected, had never set eye on the living human figure before, and despite the fact that she was the only woman in the room, set herself down with more freedom than I anticipated at the front of the room and began to sketch with interest. The models were excessively handsome, and well endowed by nature with all the manly parts - which my new friend was by no means too discreet to counterfeit, and with a pencil which remained remarkably steady.

The curiosity of the students was not a little roused by the strangers among them, and particularly by the fact that one of them was a female; it appears that this is rare, and probably only the fact that I failed to mention that my friend was of that sex enabled me to obtain a ticket for her. Her lack of embarrassment impressed them; and also had its effect upon the models, for it was clear to see that the male part of one of them – who was facing her – while not raising itself to an objectionable degree, certainly swelled under her gaze, and I saw a bead of blood upon its possessor's lower lip as he bit it, no doubt to subdue his emotions.

While their master, one Sr Della Gatta, was present the students remained silent and calm; upon his leaving the room, however, they were like mice when the cat's away, ever employed in wanton play, and gathering around Em, made a point of admiring the truth of her drawing, offering to pose for her in private should she require further study; and finally, upon their asking whether she would care to pose for them herself, I felt obliged to intervene and remind them that they were gentlemen, enquiring whether they would treat one of their ladies so. The reply was, that they would treat her a great deal less formally, which I believed; however, I persuaded them back to their seats, and we were able to continue our sketching (on my part, chiefly pretence) until Em rose, made her curtsey to Mr Gatta, and we left.

Back at the lodging, when we had enjoyed a meal and a bottle of *Chianti*, which they call a rough but pleasant wine, Em grew confidential, and confided that while she had since she was a child attended art classes in England, this was the first time she had drawn the male figure from the life; and upon further questioning confirmed that the models she had seen that day were the first males she had seen unclothed – even including those pictures reproduced in books, which, she pointed out, invariably had draperies which concealed their vital parts.

And was she, I asked, pleased or disappointed at the sight?

She replied that she found it curious, for she had had no notion that the private parts of men differed so greatly from those of women; though, she offered blushingly, she could now imagine how the act of procreation took place, helped by her memory of once seeing a dog mount another in the yard of her father's house. However, it was not clear to her (she whispered) how the man could reach the woman, that essential part of him being so small.

The reader will suppose that I was not slow in offering to enlighten her further – without much hope of the offer being accepted, for her confidences were clearly the result of her having drunk freely, and I did not believe that a few glasses of wine would make her amenable to an amorous interlude when she was so clearly a young lady of decorum. However, I had reckoned without the effect upon her of her lover's betrayal and her disgust at it, and of her first view of an unclothed young man, together with her curiosity.

In short, in a little time I found myself in her chamber, and with her hands unlacing my breeches. I was by this time roused to such a pitch that she was presented immediately with the sight of a prick at its most extensive, which astonished her, and she asked if she might inspect it. I was not slow to give her permission, or to throw off the rest of my clothes the more easily to facilitate it. At first afraid to touch, under my encouragement she at length handled me with tender enquiring fingers, admitting surprise at almost everything she found, unable to understand the usage of what she saw: what, she asked, was the purpose of the hood of skin which, like a coat, could be pulled over the head or removed from it? For what purpose were the two spheroids suspended beneath? How was it that when the skin of my thighs was smooth, and that of my belly almost so, hair should so readily grow about the base of the instrument? I answered all this as best I might, and the reader may imagine that what with one thing and what with another I was by this time in a state of excitation which persuaded me almost to rape – the lady showing not the faintest interest in being herself embraced, for every time I moved to do so, she thrust me back upon the bed and began a fresh examination.

I was forced to explain, after a time, that this could not continue; or that if it did, the chief purpose of man lying with woman would be frustrated – which astonished her almost as much as the sight of my prick had done; but I explained to her that it was only for a time that man could support such caressing as she had (unconscious, I was sure, of its effect) been conferring upon me; and asked whether she would not permit me to demonstrate to her what she was most curious of – that is, the use of the male and female parts in amorous conjunction?

I cannot now but suppose that she was more aroused by the sense of sight and touch than I had imagined, for though I had anticipated more persuasion, she was immediately sympathetic to my suggestion, and permitted me to remove her clothing – with a pleasure that increased as the body which emerged proved to be as handsome as I had imagined: her breasts were small but perfectly formed, more the shape of apples than of pears, and with nipples of the most enchanting pink tightly drawn up like rose-buds and as velvety to my tongue. Between the slimmest of thighs a triangle of dark hair marked a sex which at first she endeavoured to hide with a hand, but then permitted me gently to unveil – even with my fingers to draw apart the lips, revealing a portal so diminutive that I doubted whether I could achieve an entry without causing her considerable pain.

She was now, however, eager to bring things to a head – and to my surprise climbed upon the bed and placed herself on all fours! I had then to explain that while that may have been the posture she had observed in her father's bitch, and could certainly be employed by woman, it was not necessarily the most advantageous or rewarding pose, and persuaded her upon her back, at first simply lying upon her, my breast to hers, and my now eager prick pressed to her belly. She clearly found this pleasant, for soon she began to wriggle and to press herself upwards against me, and although I am sure she had no notion of how I intended to proceed, I felt her thighs open so that I sank between them, and could feel a wetness upon my body which signalled her readiness.

Reaching down to draw her thighs fully apart, for I wished to make the introduction of my person as little painful as a virgin could find it, I placed myself at the ready, and with the greatest care introduced the head of my tool between her lips, sliding it slowly in. The entrance was tight, but she did not demur, though I expected at every moment to meet that natural obstruction which so often proves an uncomfortable obstacle upon a fair encounter, and at the breaking of which she would surely cry out.

To my amazement, there was no such barrier, and as she let out a great sigh of happiness, I found myself sunk to the hilt, so that we lay bone to bone for a moment, before, joyful at the ease of my entrance, I began those movements which were met with as pleasant a thrusting, my prick tightly sheathed as a sword within its scabbard and her cunny embracing it with such astonishing natural affection as I have but rarely encountered even in those females most adept at love; as I withdrew seeming to draw me back, and as I re-entered seeming to welcome me with the most sanguine embrace. It was no long time before my satisfaction was complete.

Though Em's enjoyment had clearly been as intense as my own, she as certainly was eager to continue – which was a little painful to me, so that tenderly kissing her upon the lips, I withdrew, explaining that a short pause must ensue before we could continue. Why? she asked – which I could not clearly answer except to say what was true, that in this case it would not be an interval of any great length.

She now noticed my shrunken state, was interested to inspect it, and asked whether it was usual that an instrument should vary so greatly as between its limpid and extended state. Yet as she examined it, it once more began to swell, and in a very short period was once more ready for combat, when she threw herself once more upon her back; however, this time I suggested that she might care to essay another posture, and remained myself lying prone, whereupon she with great quickness of mind read my thoughts and in an instant had mounted me with all the expertise of a horsewoman (which indeed I discovered her to be, thus explaining the absence of that hymeneal obstruction which is frequently destroyed in young ladies by equine endeavour) and was cantering with an enthusiasm so infectious that once more we reached the apogee of pleasure in almost the same moment – though this time, in her paroxysm of pleasure, she leaped clear out of her seat, and was astonished and amused to observe the fountain which signalled my own enjoyment.

During the next week our pleasure in exploring the sacred city was amply reflected in the pleasure we took in exploring each other, finding ourselves perfectly matched in our amorous proclivity; Em was perhaps the most enthusiastic and natural pupil in the school of love I have ever encountered, and for enjoyment and vigour equalled any other. Enjoying her first taste of physical love, she was kind enough to praise me as a thoughtful and untiring lover – which at that time was the truth. She was enchanting company out of bed as in it; and when I began to speak of moving on for the rest of my journey, it was without difficulty that she persuaded me to allow her to accompany me at least as far as Athens, plainly informing me that since she had brought with her sufficient money for her dowry, she was now determined to spend it on pleasure before returning to England.

However, before travelling on to Naples, which I was determined to see, we were advised to remain for the balls and carnivals which celebrate the height of summer, and this we agreed to do.

Chapter Six

Sophie's Story

My first impression of Gibraltar was of a dirt and disease far greater than that roused by my first acquaintance with the most beggarly inhabitants of Lisbon. Unfortunately, this was not lessened when we arrived at the Three Anchors, a British hotel upon the rock where the best chamber stank and bugs could clearly be seen moving upon the none too white sheets of the single narrow bed which Blatchford (whom I introduced as my brother) and I were supposed to share.

I was in despair at this, but at least ordered a late luncheon – which, when it arrived, proved to be almost inedible through bad meat and a superfluity of equally rancid greasy fat.

We could not imagine what to do, and were standing outside the inn door (to be free of its fetid atmosphere) discussing our situation when we were interrupted by a stentorian voice:

'Madam,' (it said) 'may I present myself? Captain Fenton Braithwate at your service. I gather from your conversation – which you will pardon me for overhearing – that you seek accommodation?'

That was so, I admitted.

'And you will not have found the Three Anchors particularly to your taste. A filthy hole, madam, to which you are unlike to find anyone resorting who has the least taste or decency. But perhaps I might offer you the hospitality of my house? Mrs Braithwate and I will be happy to entertain you and . . .'

I introduced myself and Blatchford. We were, I said, brother and sister engaged in the Grand Tour, who were planning to sail to Italy when the opportunity afforded.

He bowed.

'I shall see what can be done in that way,' he said. 'In the meantime, perhaps you would be so good as to accompany me. Your luggage?'

Blatchford pointed it out to him, and tipping a slovenly servant to watch over it, our new acquaintance promised it should follow us by his servants. He then led the way up a steep hill towards a pleasant house overlooking the mediterranean and – dimly discernible the higher we mounted – the distant coast of Africa.

Captain Braithwate was a heavy man who seemed to have got himself with some difficulty into his uniform, from which a large belly did its best to overflow. Of perhaps fifty years of age, he was bald, and perspiration flowed freely over a high red forehead, while podgy hands kept fidgeting with the handle of the dress sword which he wore. He had, it appeared, a permanent posting with the Navy, and I presumed had lived on the island for some time, no doubt with a comfortable middle-class British wife.

I could not have been more wrong on that point. As we reached the terrace which lay on the seaward side of his dwelling, an extremely handsome dark young girl, obviously of Spanish origin, came forward and greeted him with a kiss upon the cheek.

'Maria, m'dear,' said the Captain, 'may I present Mrs Nelham and her brother, Mr Blatchford? They are upon their travels, and mean to spend some time here until they can embark for Italy. I have assured them that we can provide accommodation – though, young man, it will not I fear in your case be more luxurious than a couch in our drawing-room can provide.'

Blatchford, who was constantly amused by being for the first time in his life addressed as a gentleman, bowed and smiled.

Mrs Braithwate (for it was she) provided to be only eighteen, slim and somewhat boyish in her figure, with fine large eyes and hair streaming to her waist. She spoke good English, and immediately offered us tea, which we were glad to take; after which she offered to accompany us to the summit of the rock – which we were glad to do, having been confined for a good part of the previous day below decks. So we watched the sun set over Africa, when, descending, we spent the evening in pleasant conversation, the Captain offering some stories of his career in the navy – more concerned, it appeared, with clerical than with martial activity; while his wife sat at her embroidery, her fine eyes glinting in the light of the candle. I could not but be conscious of the discreet but obvious admiration with which Blatchford observed her, and trusted that he would not attempt her, for apart from the impropriety of offering attentions to our host's wife, it would be excessively inconvenient were we to be thrown into the unwelcome embrace of the landlord of the Three Anchors.

At ten o'clock the captain rose, and while the servants made up a couch for Blatchford in the room in which we had been sitting, I was shown into a pleasant bedroom nearby, where having bade my host and hostess a good night, I was in no time abed and asleep.

My sleep however did not last long, for in what can only have been an hour or so I was awakened by a light in my room, and upon becoming fully conscious descried, carrying a candlestick, the captain, clad in a long night-gown.

Instinctively but somewhat unwisely (for I was in my naked bed) I sat up and enquired, 'Sir, is there some calamity, that you disturb me?'

'Be assured, ma'am, there is none,' he replied, 'but I could not resist paying my respects to you, and . . . ah . . . requesting the pleasure of . . . taking the liberty of wondering whether . . . In short, ma'am, I am desperate in love with you!' And putting down the candle on the bedside table, he sat upon the side of the bed and embraced me.

Here was a pretty pickle. One cry from me, and I was assured that Blatchford would come to my rescue; the result of which would no doubt be a bout of fisticuffs followed by our having to leave the house. On the other hand, it seemed unlikely that my host would be put off with anything so insubstantial as a profession of admiration. Well, I reflected, it would not be the first time that I had had to reconcile myself to an unattractive lover in order to retain my independence and comfort. I therefore permitted him to toy with my breasts, at which he began to pant and sweat, and in a while to fumble with his night-shirt, which finally – for the process otherwise seemed likely to last for several hours – I aided him in removing, revealing a body as cumbersome and over-endowed with flesh as I had imagined, his belly hanging like a great reef over an enthusiastically extended lower limb which was, nonetheless, unlikely to shiver any timbers.

Frantic now to be engaged, he clambered upon the bed (which creaked beneath our combined weights) and positively threw himself upon me; but found it difficult to come at me because of the extent of his corpulence, which overflowed my body like a quilt upon every side, and was gathered into such folds before him that, though he made to thrust with the agility of a younger, leaner man, he came nowhere near the mark.

After a while, fearing once more that the night would be over and I entirely bereft of sleep before he had relieved himself, I whispered to him that it might be best if we rearranged ourselves, and with a great effort tipped him over and climbed atop of him where, after hauling at his belly with both hands and wriggling with my bottom in an energetic manner (which appeared to give him considerable peripheral pleasure), I felt a slight disturbance which indicated that out parts were at least in some communication; after which, following an energetic bouncing, a shaking of those fleshy paps which resembled those of a woman, a panting of that generous belly and a grunt or two seemed to indicate satisfaction.

After a while, he rose, somewhat shamefacedly climbed once more into his night-gown, and making an awkward bow, left without a word! Whereupon once more I settled to sleep, to awake in full light, with strips of brilliant blue sky appearing between the slats of the protecting shutters which were drawn across the window, and this time the more attractive figure of Mrs Braithwate standing over me, with a tray containing chocolate and new bread.

She bade me good morning with a smile, and asked whether I had spent a comfortable night, or whether I had been too hot.

I found myself lying once more completely without covering, it having become my invariable habit to throw off the bedclothes during the course of a night so generally warm as was the case in those southern latitudes. We being two women, I saw no necessity to cover myself, and merely replied that I had been very comfortable.

Mrs Braithwate seemed a little unsure of herself, and setting down her tray, sat upon the side of the bed and said with some hesitation that she hoped the Captain had not incommoded me.

So she knew of his night ramblings! I supposed that last night's was not an uncommon experience when young females were in the house. I replied it would take more than the captain's attentions seriously to trouble me, and smiled; though, I said, it seemed extraordinary to me that he should seek solace elsewhere when so beautiful a wife occupied his bed.

Did she not, I asked, find such adventuring offensive in a husband? – whereupon she replied that his person was not so inimitably attractive to her that his absence from her bed was a tragic one. 'And,' she said, 'your person is so tempting that I could not but anticipate his wishing to discover your charms at closer quarters.' Whereupon she laid her hand upon my shoulder, and squeezed it in a manner which was more loving than merely friendly.

I realised in an instant that there was another reason why Maria was not particularly distressed by her husband's adventurings, for it was clear that she was one of those women who enjoyed the company of her own sex more readily than that of the gentlemen. This distressed me little; as readers of my former adventures will discover, the attentions of my own sex, while I do not seek them out, are not inimical to me where beauty and charm are combined with kindness – which was certainly the case with my new friend. In short, it was not long before she had divested herself of the single garment in which she was clad, and was lying beside me on the bed.

The most charming characteristic of an encounter between two females is the instinctive manner in which one female knows best what pleases another: there is none of the rough treatment that is all too frequently the mark of even the most considerate male, no over-eager mauling of the most intimate parts, no attempt to prove strength or demonstrate superiority . . . Maria, as I must now call her, at first was content to explore with the most delicate enquiry the surface of my body, passing fingers and palms over the unfamiliar territory with tender apprehension of its lowlands and highlands, its brakes and woods. So light, so tender was her touch that my entire skin seemed soon to be afire, lively to each gesture; and when her tongue followed her palms in paying compliment, it was at once a relief and an additional stimulus, so that it was only with the utmost effort – informed by my instinctive knowledge that she would for the time prefer it – that I was able to continue to lie motionless beneath her explorations, until, upon her parting my thighs and approaching my secret parts, still unsatisfied after their excitation by her husband (for, however unattractive, my congress with him had still necessarily roused my animal instincts), I found it necessary to slake my own curiosity by commencing to admire my partner.

She indeed merited the top of admiration, for unclothed she was even more handsome than she had appeared before. Many of the women of Portugal and Spain had appeared portly, and displayed, when in an even partially unclothed condition, great hatches of dark hair beneath their arms which to me (who was accustomed to the English habit of trimming if not plucking the same) was unattractive to a degree. Maria's armpits however, delicately arched beneath attractive and slim shoulders, showed only the lightest puff or cloud, while her body too was smooth and unencumbered by hairs, except where one would expect to find them.

Pressing her shoulders so that she lay upon her back, I gave some attention first to her breasts which, while full were without a superfluity of flesh, but even when she was prone showed a shape undeniably feminine, without – as is so often the case – being so ample that they hung towards the side of her body. On the contrary they presented to the touch as to the sight an enviable firmness and elasticity, speaking eloquently of youth, health and beauty. Her waist was gathered to a smallness which many Englishwomen would have envied – indeed, I could almost span it with my two hands; but beneath it, her hips were generous and broad, and her thighs equally so – her legs long, but at the top of a certain thickness, though again not with superfluity of flesh, for beneath the skin could be felt firm flesh shot through with muscle.

I had only to place a hand on each thigh for them to open, revealing beneath wiry black hairs (for unlike the hair of their heads, the intimate hair of the southern woman is rarely fine, but resilient to the touch) long purple lips which, when parted, framed what I had never seen before: while every woman possesses in little a counterfeit of the male part, here was one of larger dimensions than I had previously encountered – of perhaps an inch in length, and of the size of my little finger; and upon my touching it with the tip of my tongue, hard almost as horn, while beneath my caress I felt the eager response which I would have expected from its male brother.

That this remarkable appendage shared the sensitivity of its masculine counterpart could not be doubted, for as my lips caressed it – which could be easily done – the entire lower part of my new friend rose and lifted itself as we throw ourselves upwards to meet the thrusting of a lover; and upon the occasions when I have found myself abed with my own sex, I have never experienced, before or since, one whose reactions (despite the entirely feminine charms of her body, and the completely lady-like demeanour shown in public) were so nearly that of a man.

This was indeed so thoroughly the case, that after a few moments, Maria's reactions continuing so wild, I lifted and placed myself in the position which I had occupied with the Captain – whereupon she began immediately to lift her hips and thrusting towards me to rub or grind our two persons together, so that while it was never possible for her organ to enter me, in a few moments her blushing, gasping and tensing her body revealed that she had reached her goal.

Such was not the case with me – partly perhaps because I had not the inherent tendency towards enjoying love-making with my own sex which she clearly possessed, and later admitted. Seeing this, she threw me back upon the bed, and kneeling over me, applied her tongue with such soft yet eager plunging, such kind yet wild embracings, such general yet well directed attentions, that before long I too had experienced the utmost pleasure.

We lay then for some time, our arms about each other, while we recounted the history of our lives; my own being much shortened (for as my more faithful readers will know, my short life has been overcrowded with incident), while hers recalled an education – at the hands of the nuns in the small Spanish town where she grew up – which first revealed the truth of her nature to her, so that when she was given in marriage (almost as soon as she was a woman) to the Captain, she found the expected coupling with a male as unsatisfying as it was at first revolting to her. At the prompting of some friends, she tried several younger lovers, whose attentions she found less unpleasant, but who never raised her to the joys she experienced in the arms of those same friends – who themselves were for the most part similarly given to enjoying each other in order to fill the void left by the brief and rough attentions of their own husbands, the Spanish male being even less considerate between the sheets than is commonly the case in England.

Entirely sympathetic to this story, I could not but be sad that my new friend should deny herself the embraces of a handsome man, which I said to her.

'But,' she said, 'where is one to be found? It is impossible that I should give myself to one of the common sailors, charming though they often are, for my husband would not tolerate that – nor could it be kept a secret, for there are no men here of a common status that could resist boasting that they had enjoyed me.'

From the look in her eye, however, and the way in which her hand unconsciously strayed to lie in that place to which a man would naturally direct his own attentions, I was in no doubt that she was not naturally a lover solely of women.

'How,' I said, 'if I were to say that I could introduce you to a lover who would make you happy, if only for a brief while?'

I needed not to wait for a reply, so quickly did her tongue touch her lips in anticipation; and wrapping a sheet around me I went to the door which led from the room on to the terrace. There, as I had expected, sat Blatchford in white cotton trousers, in the sun, enjoying a pipe of tobacco. I had only to whisper a word to two to him, and in a moment – for he was nothing if not quick in apprehension – he accompanied me to the bedroom. Maria did not move upon his entrance, lying naked upon the bed as I had left her, one knee drawn up so that a thigh lay back to display the treasure which she was so eager to share; one hand lying upon that thigh as if to point the way, and the other caressing a breast.

Blatchford looking at me as though to ask whether it was really the case that he was invited to partake of such delightful fruit, I simply gave him a small push towards the bed, whereupon, hastening to throw off his trousers (under which, as was then the custom, he wore nothing but his skin), he knelt upon the bed and, as he lowered his head to kiss Maria upon the lips, I, standing behind him, saw her hand reach between his legs to ensure herself that what was even then preparing itself for combat was really of so handsome dimensions as she had observed.

Though we had taken great pleasure with each other, it was soon clear to me that she was as naturally a lover of mankind as I; and it was with sympathetic enjoyment that I watched as Blatchford's sturdy haunches pumped such sensations into her body as she had evidently waited for some time to enjoy, for he was forced – fearing to alarm the house – to place his hand over her mouth to stifle the joyful cries with which she welcomed each motion of his body. Such celebration of the rites of love were impossible not to join, and placing myself at her side, I grasped Blatchford's free hand and, directing it towards the seat of my own sensations, encouraged him to explore, while I stimulated his own efforts by inserting my hand between his body and that of his mistress, and adding friction to those moving parts accessible to me.

As I had observed in Lisbon, Blatchford was entirely a man, and the delight he took in the present situation persuaded me that perhaps I was mistaken to have kept him at arms' length – though he had certainly accepted the situation without protest and, realising that I wished to keep a distance between us, had made it easy for me by making no move towards me. Having with a final thrust brought Maria to a second culmination, signalled by the screwing up of her eyes and a shudder of her entire body, he to my surprise lifted himself from her and, turning to me, raised an eyebrow, a gesture I interpreted aright by permitting him to transfer his weight from Maria's body to my own, which he did almost without a pause. I found his limb as sturdy as ever, and it was clear that his control had been perfect, for he was able to continue his motions with a perfect rhythm, so that I soon felt my body mounting to the heights so recently observed in my friend – who now lay back upon her pillows, observing us with the satisfied pleasure of the replete, and contenting herself by occasionally running her hands through my servant's hair, or raising herself slightly to slide her hand down the length of his brown back, and over the still pumping globes of his backside.

In due time, reaching down to those same globes, I clutched them to me as I met my apogee – and at the same time felt his soul released, though as to his face only the slightest twitch of eyelids veiled by surprisingly long lashes signalled that his pleasure was also complete. Lifting himself, he rolled over to lie for a moment beside us, and then, scarcely waiting until his prick had begun to fall from that acute angle at which it had presented itself, reached for his breeches and climbed into them, soberly acknowledging us by a half-nod, half-bow before returning to the terrace and resuming his pipe.

Maria was well satisfied at the adventure, and I believe – though I did not enquire – several times again took advantage of Blatchford's not inconsiderable stamina during the three days we remained as guests in that house. There being no prospect for some time of a passage to Ostia, the captain took berths for us on board the *Townshend Packet*, bound for Sardinia and then for Malta, whence we could if we wished easily return to Italy. I thought that Blatchford seemed somewhat tired as we made our way for one final time to the summit of the rock, on one of the last days of our sojourn; but failed to enquire as to the reason. On arriving at the ship, I found that we had been placed together in the single small cabin available – and wondered whether this was invariably the manner in which brother and sister (which only Maria now knew was not our relation) were expected to travel – in which case the incidence of incest in southern Europe must be expected to be higher than in the northern latitudes. We bade farewell to the Captain and Maria, who looked after Blatchford with a regret I could well understand, and made our way on board in later afternoon.

I did not expect any problem with my servant, for Blatchford was the soul of discretion and good behaviour, and I was confident that he would be guided by me in his manner – though to be honest I knew not precisely what I hoped. That evening, after we had had an indifferent meal with the captain, we retired to our cabin, undressed in perfect purity, and retired to bed in two hammocks which were all the means of sleeping supplied us, and in very short time were asleep.

The voyage was a calm one. Finding there was a little space near the mizzen shrouds unfrequented by the members of the small crew, I spent some time there simply lying in the sun, while the captain and Blatchford occupied their time shooting with pistols at bottles thrown into the water; and during the calms a boat was lowered and they fished for turtles, catching one or two which we then ate – a flesh somewhat fishy but not unpleasant. At night, it being remarkably warm for the time of the year even in these climes, I spent some time on deck, standing at the railing between the pegs on which the sheets and shrouds are belayed (you see that I had accustomed myself to sailors' language) and watched as the waters slipped past, sparkling in the light of the full moon.

I must confess that I regarded Blatchford, now, with rather more interest as a person than as a servant, but still felt it would be unwise to encourage familiarity on a regular scale. One night however, when I returned from deck to our cabin, I caught, as I undressed, a flash of reflected light from his eyes which betrayed the fact that he was observing me, and could not but wonder what emotions were passing through his mind upon his having to spend his nights in the same confined space as an attractive woman (as I took myself to be). Climbing into my hammock, I prepared for sleep, but a short time afterwards, upon looking over in the direction of my servant's hammock, I saw it was swaying with a regular and somehow suggestive motion, and as the light of the room strengthened and was reflected by the waters through the porthole, could see his hand moving rhythmically at the base of his belly, and – having first learned about carnal love from observing my brother and young Andy pleasuring themselves and each other by manual means – realised that he had been driven to such desperate means by my presence. I could not be so unkind as to permit this to continue, and so softly called, 'Blatchford, you are not the only one to feel much alone in this strange situation, and to need comforting . . .'

As I have remarked, he is nothing but quick of apprehension, and in a moment had tipped himself out of his hammock and was standing at my side. But here a difficulty presented itself, for it seemed impossible that he could climb atop of me, or that if he did so, the slightest movement would not result in our tipping to the deck. However, bending over me, Blatchford caught me up in his arms, and in a moment I was out of the hammock and standing with him in the closest embrace, his arms about my upper body and his tongue seeking mine, while by parting my thighs I was able to receive between them a tool so eager for contact with my body that it felt much as though it was carved from mahogany or some equally firm wood. So firm indeed it felt, that in a moment, lowering myself so that my lips and tongue made a snail's trace down his body, I took it between my lips to test whether it was indeed so adamantine; and found it so. In my experience, which had then encompassed exploration of the parts of a number of young men – and has encompassed more since that time, and many of them highly practised in the arts of love, and no less enthusiastic to demonstrate their skill – I have come across no other instrument so strong, so intractable, so unlike a construction of flesh and blood and tissue; and though it was sensible of my attentions – for as I gripped his thighs and with the gentlest of motions sucked upon it, I could feel an answering tremor in his body – it seemed that he could at will diminish that sensitivity, for he was always capable of extending the length of time of copulation until his mistress of the hour had entirely completed her ecstasy.

Upon this occasion I found the strangeness of the situation inspiriting. Unable to lie, we were bound to complete our congress in an upright position, which was made possible by my placing my arms about Blatchford's back, and his placing his hands beneath my bottom, raising me so that embracing him with my legs my cunny was at a level with his prick; upon which he drew me towards him, impaling me, and – being extremely strong – he was able by moving his hands to and fro to produce that motion which satisfied us both. Indeed, the strangeness of the place and the posture gave an added zest which brought me off more quickly than is my wont; of which he took no notion, but continued the movements, which in a while once more raised my sentiments – and, in short, gave me the pleasure of no less than three delightful victories before he himself was satisfied. Whereupon he gently lowered me to the ground and kissed me upon the lips not with passion but with a sort of brotherly embrace, before once more lifting me in his arms, this time to place me in my hammock and to draw over me the single sheet which was all that was necessary in the warm night, and to retire to his own place.

In the morning, by the time I was awake he had already risen, gone on deck, soused himself with salt water, shaved his whiskers, and returned to the cabin with a pail of water for my ablutions, offering me no discourtesy or intimation of familiarity, but simply a smile entirely without impertinence, and retired to leave me to clothe myself. I was, I reminded myself again, extremely fortunate in so excellent a servant.

That day we put in at Cagliari, the capital city of Sardinia, a rough and uninteresting place; sailing again, we followed the coast of Italy, now just in view, now just out of view, and saw the island of Sicily in the distance before entering the harbour of Valetta, on the island of Malta.

Chapter Seven

The Adventures of Andy

The festivities of the Roman Summer really began for us with a grand ball given by the Neapolitan Ambassador. I procured for Em and myself black cloaks, and we arrived at nine and remained until about one o'clock. All the English in Rome who were of any least respectability were invited, so the evening was of some dullness, for it was considerably more of an English ball than an Italian one. Most of the English females were very elegantly dressed, but with decorum which precluded a great deal of enjoyment in my regarding them. Most of the gentlemen were in court dress with swords.

Several large rooms were laid together for dancing, which was kept up with spirit until daylight, though we did not remain until so late. It was the most brilliant, genteel mob I ever was in, and the evening was made tolerable only by our discovering some rooms appropriated for cards, where high play was going forward between the Italians. On my pretending to wish to take part Em left me, and I for the while made way with an Italian lady, widowed for the present by her husband's concentrating upon his wagers; however, upon my placing my hand in her bosom she moved speedily away, and seeing that I had been noticed by a glowering gentleman who appeared to be the friend of her husband, I made an excuse and left, contenting myself with presenting myself again to Em, and toying with her thigh beneath the table at which we sat to eat some good food; which roused her so, that we made our excuses, and, unwilling to wait until we returned home, engaged a closed carriage and were at the game during the entire time of our driving back to our lodgings; and, pausing only to draw our cloaks about us to conceal our semi-nakedness, raced to our room to continue our happy bout.

I had heard much of the licentiousness of the Italian carnivals, and was impressed at the merry appearance of the streets by three in the afternoon, when the Corso was filled with a double cavalcade of carts, carriages and landaus travelling in opposite directions close to the footpaths, leaving a large promenade in the centre of the road for the pedestrians, who were of every class, everyone jumbled together in a common herd, and everyone masked and so dressed that it is impossible to tell an aristocrat from a beggar (except perhaps by speech). Some of the masks are very grotesque, and the favourite character seems to be the Fool. Other people are dressed as hussars, *gens d'armes*, quack doctors, poets and so on, with many a huge man dressed in women's clothes and the other sex clad in male attire. The chief amusement is pelting each other with a preparation of lime, and this is done indiscriminately, especially when friends recognise each other.

Within an hour of our venturing forth, Em had been captured by a handsome figure of a man dressed in a domino and mask, who – whatever his breeding – clearly impressed her by the muscularity of his thighs in the close-clinging tights which he wore, and which were covered in lozenges of many colours. Myself, I wandered about for some time, observing the crowd, and was then made up to by a slim, attractive woman whose cloak could not disguise the elasticity of her frame, and whose slender hands were quick to caress the nape of my neck and my chin as she laughed beneath her mask. Linking arms, we strode for a while among the others, when I became conscious she was guiding me in one direction, which proved to be a small street near the Borghese Gardens, where in a while she turned into a doorway.

I did not long hesitate to follow her, and saw her beckoning from a room at the end of a dark corridor, and there found myself in a bedroom, and the young lady in my arms planting vigorous kisses upon my mouth, which I returned with interest. She showed eagerness to unclothe me, which ambition it was my pleasure to satisfy, whereupon she fell to her knees in admiration of my body, and paid me the tribute of a kiss, the nature of which aroused me still further. However, it was now my turn to release the buttons of her jerkin, and then of her shirt, which revealed small breasts, the lack of flesh in which somewhat surprised me; but all was soon answered, for on my loosing her breeches I found an appendage which proved what a first sight of her breast might have suggested – that she was indeed a young man.

He was eager to continue (in what vein I know not) what he had begun; however, while I have had experience in that sort it has never been of my seeking, and I made my excuses – kindly but firmly – with '*Mi rincresce tanto, ma io me ne devo andar.*' Upon this he attempted to hide my clothes, but despite all his protests, which in the end included tears, I recovered them, dressed myself and left.

Outside it was now late afternoon, fine and warm, and being somewhat discomfited as well as disappointed by my experience, I strolled along the Viale del Muro Torto and turned into the Borghese Gardens themselves through a gate which stood open, attracting from time to time couples who strode arm in arm into the park and lost themselves among the trees.

I was now somewhat melancholy, and wished that I had persuaded Em to remain with me (the employment she was now upon with her gentleman I could only guess at). However, as I came to a small lake or pool, another single figure approached me with '*buon giorno*', and when I replied, went on to ask '*Mi cuol fare un piacere*?' This I knew to mean she desired a favour, and bowed – whereat she led me a little way into a grove of trees, and putting down her cloak from her shoulders, turned her back to me and with a gesture indicated a mess of lime and dirt which had struck her about the shoulders and run down beneath her dress.

Somewhat nicely, for I could not tell precisely what she meant, with '*le chiedo, scusa*', I undid the top button of the dress at the back, and with my handkerchief began to wipe away the mess. This had run down the length of her back, which was indeed a beautiful one, the backbone handsomely delineated, with the slightly swelling flesh upon each side resilient to the touch. I was forced to lift the dress away in order to wipe more, whereupon she released it at the front so that it fell to her waist, and smiled over her shoulder as I continued.

I was by now confident that the invitation was to more than a convenient cleansing and, falling to my knees persuaded the dress over her hips, so that it fell to the ground, revealing a pair of haunches which would have raised the spirits of an eunuch, so oval, so richly firm, so inviting were they. The dirt having ceased at her waist, and my having removed the last of it, I made now no further pretence, but threw down my handkerchief and commenced with my hands to stroke that most beautiful rump – whereat she instantly stood astride, her legs sufficiently apart to reveal her sex, like a rich plum inviting a bite; and upon my approaching, she bent, the better to enable me to press my lips to it and to savour its delicious, musky fragrance.

The experience was too much for a man so recently cheated of a passage at love, and quicker than I (or perhaps she) would have thought possible, I was out of my breeches and, clad only in my shirt, grasped her by the hips, and plunged into her from behind. Once I was firmly seated she threw back her shoulders and positively arched her back, so that by turning her head she could fix her lips to mine in an appreciative kiss, her long black hair tickling my cheek and shoulders, while my thrusting clearly gave her the utmost pleasure, for she reached around to grasp me as best she could, to avoid my losing my purchase.

Whether she had experienced a similar disappointment as myself I cannot say, but certainly there was no doubt that she enjoyed the passage as much as I, and when with a final throw I gave up my soul, she echoed my sigh and, turning clasped me to her, affording me my only brief glimpse of her splendid breasts, before she had seized her dress, quickly drew it upon her body, and with a shy smile half ran away towards the Porto del Popolo.

For myself, the warmth of the afternoon and my energetic play had brought me out in a muck sweat and, picking up my trousers, I made for the small pool nearby, where I threw off my shirt and plunged in, spending some minutes in a delightfully refreshing swim.

Alas, upon my climbing out, I discovered that some passer-by – no doubt as a jest – had taken my clothing, so that nothing, not a shoe, remained.

Happily, hearing that thieves abounded at the Roman

carnivals, I had left all money but a few coins at my lodging; nor was the weather so cold as to incommode me much, at this time of the year. However, I did not entirely relish making my way back in a state of nature. To make the best of it, I scaled a small tree and plucked off, with some effort, a heavily leafed branch, which holding before me I put a brave face on and was soon at the top of the Corso, where in no time I had collected a small crowd who paced behind me, making gestures and chanting slogans which certainly were not a comment upon my respectability, and from time to time darting forward and slapping me upon my naked arse – which I could not resent, for no doubt I would have laughed had I been upon their side of the question.

Fortunately we met none of the Roman guard; and fortunately the spirit of carnival, now considerably alcoholic, made everyone good humoured, and even the *ragazzo* who after some time answered the bell and let me into our house, and who was in some ill-humour at being forced to remain indoors during Carnival, laughed with me rather than at me.

However, I thought it well to propose to Em, when she returned that night, exhausted and insistent on spending some time in telling me of her adventures – which were what I would have supposed (her friend having proved himself four times in as many hours, a feat I should now have at some time to emulate if I was not to lose altogether her respect) – that next day we should leave for Naples.

The road to that city was full of interest, partly from the views – including when, which most interested me, we passed upon the famous Via Appia, or road built by Pius VI across the Pontine marshes, which we traversed in heavy showers of rain and hail. We were warned to hide any valuables we had about us, for there was some danger from robbers – though the Neapolitan troops escorted us for part of the way; and there were deterrents in the form of the heads of robbers displayed in iron cages at the road-side.

At Velletri, we were enlivened by the presence of a mother and daughter, both Italian, who crowded into our small coach. The mother, an enormous woman almost bursting out of her clothes, sat herself next me, almost overwhelming me by her size, her great arms heavy with flesh, her bosom heaving under its black dress in the close quarters of the coach, and her panting seeming to make air as scarce as gold. Her daughter, however, was another matter, being a delightful slim little thing with a pretty oval face, full lips, eyebrows narrow as though they had been drawn in India ink, hair which shone like the coat of a well-groomed pony, and bewitching black eyes which seemed to flash invitation, even in the view of her mother. She – the daughter – was sat opposite to me, and with the best will in the world I could not prevent our feet sometimes from touching, at which I seemed to feel a gentle pressure returned, and thus learned during the course of the long day's journey to Terracina, to hope for something which I dare not so far name to myself. Em, who was sat next the girl, clearly saw my interest, and with a wink of her eye engaged the girl in conversation – for she had, being quick, picked up a considerable knowledge of Italian in addition to what she had learned when planning the journey to her clergyman betrayer. What she said, I know not; except that it was about me, and I hoped a recommendation – for I had been entirely frank with Em about my delight in women, and she had not a jealous bone in her body, enjoying our love-making when it occurred, but never accounting it anything in the way of a pledge of fidelity, or even of romantic love.

Stopped at Terracina, we came to an inn a little better than is common in the country, being clean and affording us a room each (unlike some others on this journey, where we sometimes had to share a filthy chamber with other travellers, lying fully clothed on hard bunks with dirty blankets). We were offered, too, a fine supper of boiled fowl, which we all ate with equal enjoyment; the young lady, whose name I learned was Vittoria, picking up the bones and sucking them with a charming unconsciousness of the effect her gesture had upon me, who could not but regard the pretty play of her lips as redolent of promise – though I had no idea of how to come at her, even were she willing (which her inviting eye seemed to suggest). Her mother pressed food and wine upon me, indicating that she thought I needed fleshing out; she seemed continually to be behind me, helping me to wine, or placing tidbits upon my plate, and I was gracious to her, hoping further to ingratiate myself with her girl, and smiled and joked (though not understanding half of what was said).

By ten o'clock we were all yawning, and at last the mother rose, and kissing her hand to me, made her way from the room; at which I made bold upon rising to take her daughter's hand and to plant a kiss upon it, whereat she smiled, and taking a piece of paper wrote the letter seven upon it, and passed it to me in the palm of her hand. On my showing it to Em, when Vittoria had left the room, she congratulated me.

I took as special a care of my toilet as could be done with the help of a cold pail of water and some rough soap, then taking a clean shirt from my luggage and putting it on; the single small looking-glass in my room showed to my satisfaction that it was sufficient to cover my modesty were I discovered out of my room; and at midnight, after an impatient wait of half of an hour, I took my candle and left my room, making my way along the corridor past Em's room, which was numbered Four; there was only one more room upon the first floor, which was Five – and so I took my way up the stairs, and upon the next floor passed room Six, and at last found myself before that upon which the number Seven was painted.

As I softly opened it, a draught blew out the flame of my candle, so that all I could see was the dim shape of the room as shown by the light from the window, for it was a dark and cloudy night. I seemed to hear the noise of quickened breathing (my own breath now coming short with excitement) and made my way more by instinct than by sight to the bed, whereupon no sooner did I set a knee upon it than I felt Vittoria's hands reach out and, feeling the shirt about my waist, lift it to discover my person (through the coolness of the air and the apprehension of possible discovery) not yet risen from its shrunken state. Not for long, however, did it remain thus, for a sensation crept upon me which could only be the result of the application of those delightful, full, rosy lips which I had watched as they drew the soft flesh of the chicken from its bones, and which now were drawing my soul from me!

I placed my hands upon her head, feeling that fine and flowing hair beneath them, and then as she continued to minister to me, her hands upon my arse, I placed my own hands upon her shoulders, and . . .

But what was this? Rather than the slim shoulders I expected, I felt beneath my palms immense and plump flesh; and placing them below, rather than the firm and small breasts which I meant to embrace, within my palms fell great fleshy dugs! 'Twas not Vittoria, but her mother, with whom I was engaged.

I was caught like a fly in a web: for what could I do but remain? To have left the room were an insult which would not have been forgiven, and I was in no doubt that had I attempted it she would have roused the house, which would have been fatal to my reputation and – for all I knew – my life! I must also confess that, despite my early disgust at my discovery, the lady was certainly no tyro in the art of love, her tongue as educated as that of the most subtle whore in my experience, and her hands (as increasingly she proved) equally adept at rousing the spirits. Her experience was proved in a moment, when, the unhinderable motion of my hips indicating my nearness to death, she removed her lips, and falling upon her back drew me upon her. Adrift like a small cockle-boat upon a vasty ocean, I bobbed and bucked as she wriggled and rose, until seizing my prick with her hand she thrust it into that place which most longed for it – but which itself was sufficiently capacious to have swallowed half a dozen such; indeed, I could scarce feel any sensation, for though complimented often by my female friends upon my size (being perhaps not long, but certainly in breadth sufficiently satisfying) my sensations were few, my position being similar to that of a baby who has thrust his finger into a milk-pail.

This, she also quickly realised, for seizing me again, she began rubbing my instrument against that part of her person where sensation most vividly resided; at which in a moment her passion was so roused that her whole great body quivered and tossed so that it seemed that from time to time I was thrown completely into the air, only tethered to her person by her firm grasp upon the anchor which fixed me to that cove to which I had been steered.

In a while (it seemed a lifetime) one final shudder, which seemed likely to demolish the bed, and a great sigh, suggested that she had reached her goal; and feeling about me with her other hand, she signified by an incoherent cry her realisation that I had not come. Being so buffetted and exhausted, I whispered that it mattered not; but she would not have it, and laying me upon my back, she bent over and with a combination of a remarkable delicacy of touch from her fingers and the motion of her lips, soon provoked in me an ecstasy that I was in some sense reluctant to give up, but which despite myself was drawn from me.

When I made to go she showed great resistance; and I had to wait until, in twenty minutes or so, she fell asleep with my member still grasped between her fingers; however, there was no difficulty in my releasing myself, for now that I was spent my realisation of what I had been cozened into – as opposed to what I had expected – made me so angry that I shrank to the size of a hazelnut, and was quite able to leave her and return to my own room, where, there being no lock upon the door, I carried a piece of furniture and placed it there to wake me should she attempt a rape.

Next morning, the lady treated me with the utmost kindness and respect, and I must say without any indication of what had taken place. Her daughter made a great point of winking behind her hand, which I ignored; as to Em, she clearly believed that it was the young girl who had made me happy, and I did not disillusion her, for she had – as was shown by her reaction to my misfortune on the carnival night – an extremely poor sense of humour, and would only have laughed. The couple left the coach at Capua, whereupon Em made many enquiries about my delight, which I answered with what skill I could, drawing upon my experiences with other young ladies; and I believe convinced her that Vittoria had pleased me to the utmost (though she wondered at the coldness of my parting from her, for, she said, had a lover given her the pleasure Vittoria had permitted me to take, she would at least have found opportunity to kiss her farewell, despite the efforts of her dragon mother).

Naples is a most magnificent city, the Toledo as handsome a street as any I ever saw, excepting perhaps the High

Street at Oxford. We walked upon the promenade, by the sea, and had a good view of Vesuvius and the Island of Capri, and on our second evening visited the Theatre of San Carlos, which was built only two years ago on the ruins of the previous theatre, destroyed by fire. In point of splendour Drury Lane in London is far inferior; though there is much gilding, the *tout ensemble* is chaste and highly imposing, and the scenery well worthy of the house.

Upon the first opportunity we hired a small phaeton with a single horse and set off at seven in the morning to see the ruins of Pompeii and Herculaneum, those remarkable relics of past civilisation. We chose a day when the sun was bright and warm, and within half an hour were able to throw off our cloaks and enjoy the fine air of the countryside. We reached Pompeii about midday and enjoyed a meal at a hostelry there before looking over the ruins, which are indeed remarkable. The excavations are fifteen feet below the ground, the lower six to eight feet being a mixture of cinders and small pebbles, and the upper part a solid mass of earth and lava.

Halfway through the visit, the fellow who was guiding us took me apart while Em was examining the remains of a wine shop, and enquired whether I wished to see the ruins of a *bordello*, to which I replied that we would both be pleased to do so. He made a great fuss on the grounds that ladies had never been permitted to enter that place before, there being paintings of a highly indecent nature there; upon which, Em overhearing, was very determined to accompany me, and after tipping the rascal some extra coins, he ill temperedly acquiesced.

It seems, from what we were told, that at the time of the disaster which overcame the city (which was about the beginning of the Christian era) inns (or *cauponae*) and taverns (*popinae* and *thermopolia*) frequently became places of gambling and assignation, with prostitutes installed as barmaids, to convert the gambling dens into bawdy-houses – and we were shown a tablet upon which a traveller's account included the payment of eight *asses* for favours accorded him by a maid-servant during his single night at an inn. A sign had recently been unearthed in the Via dell' Abbondanze, which we also saw, and which was much like a poster of our own time; it bears the sketch of a woman with legs apart, and the information that an establishment boasts three young female employees (*asellae*) able to satisfy the traveller's every whim. These were sometimes known as *pornai*, who were the lowest class of prostitutes; *hetairai* were companions, versed in conversation and polite behaviour, while *auletriades* were entertainers chiefly equipped to sing and dance, but sometimes available for more intimate pleasures.

However, the establishment whose remains we now saw had been built, or at least wholly converted, for one purpose - for it had a cock carved above its door - and it amused us to compare it with the house in Brook Street, in London, which (as I have related elsewhere) Sir Frank and I had equipped and run as the finest brothel in the city. Here was a group of rooms about a central, open hall, where we supposed the girls would stroll in the cool of the evening, and receive their customers (the emperor having decreed that such houses should not open until the ninth hour). Upon a table here was a collection of amulets and good-luck charms, some in the shape of cocks with wings and hind legs, and with bells attached to them - worn about the neck of gentlemen, but sometimes also of ladies - which much amused us. Here too a small stone carving showed an erect prick placed as the central column of a temple, thus illustrating the devotion of many people to the god Priapus - which extended not only to love-making between humans, but also to thc love of animals, for we were shown a sculpture of Pan in congress with a goat, which looked uncomfortable for both god and creature.

The reverence with which these ancients regarded the male instrument is to be seen everywhere in the city of Pompeii: paintings upon the wells show again and again the worship of models of a part of the body in our time normally hidden from view: we saw an illustration, for instance, of satyrs drinking wine and watching a woman with limbs scarcely covered annointing with oil a large prick in front of which a naked girl is about to strike with a whip another, who bends to receive the blow, while nude dancers circle them in an orgy of lascivious movement; the whole scene being remarkably inspiriting even to modern men and women.

Upon the walls of the smaller rooms were paintings of men and women enjoying congress in every conceivable position, illustrating the services offered by the girls. As we enjoyed them, so both Em and I began to feel keenly the desire to celebrate our visit to the house by reminding the ghosts of the *hetairai* that we modern men and women still enjoyed the same delights as they. My hand indeed stole out to fondle Em's pleasing bottom while, believing our guide to be otherwise engaged, she laid her hand upon my thigh – but a cough revealed that the fellow was indeed watching us, and in a moment beckoned to me, and in the good English which he commanded (through the common visits of travellers to the spot) informed me that it was possible upon payment of a small sum to command the attentions of a young girl – for it was usual for visitors to the house to find themselves inclined to celebrate the priapic rite.

I informed the man that my companion and I merely wished for a place where we could be alone, to which he replied (no doubt believing us to be utterly degenerate), 'Why the same meat when different comes?' and informed me that he had a young brother who would be pleased to act with Em some of the scene depicted before us. She, being as usual disinclined to allow me a secret conversation, had made it her business to overhear, and expressed her willingness to meet the young man – who like magic appeared, within a couple of minutes, accompanied by the girl whom I was invited to love: evidently our guide kept them in readiness for just such an eventuality as had now occurred – though I was surprised that there should be a young man kept in readiness for the convenience of ladies, which seems to suggest that in Italy a woman's requirements are more openly acknowledged than in England, where my friend Sophie's scheme for the satisfaction of just such female desires met with astonishment (however successful her house eventually became).

The two young people were, to our pleasure, extremely handsome, and might have stepped from one of the frescoes we had been admiring – young, slim, dark-skinned and agreeable; and leading us to a room where a rough awning of sack-cloth had been thrown over the open roof, and a platform of earth covered with a layer of clean straw, they without a moment's delay removed their clothing – which action we in a moment matched. Making love *al fresco*, as the Italians term it, is always a pleasure where discovery is not likely; my first experiences of pleasure in the exercise of my masculinity had been – as I think is the case with many – in company with my friend Frank, when in the woods at Alcovary we experimented with each other's bodies, and were soon (though not to our present knowledge) spied upon by Sophie, who used her knowledge to seduce her half-brother, and later myself, into enjoying the female company for which we were made. Those memories are pleasant enough; but to throw off one's clothes in the balmier climate of the south, where even in deep shade the airs played about our bodies like warm water, and the breezes which flowed between and around our limbs were like the caresses of some invisible and delicious companion, was yet more pleasurable.

However, we had more corporeal companions, also; they were lithe and handsome, and quite apart from the physical delights offered by their bodies, it was a pleasure to observe two such handsome creatures – almost like twins, with black curly hair not only upon their heads, but elsewhere – and for once my disinclination to admire hair upon the female body was overruled, for the shining tight curls of hair beneath the arms of the girl somehow increased the air of natural wildness which made her resemble a young animal rather than a human, while between her thighs a similar generous display increased the suspicion that she was dryad rather than woman. The boy, too, wore tight curls not only upon his head and below his belly, but upon his chest, while even his small, round buttocks were a mass of shining black hairs, so that he looked like nothing so much as one of the satyrs cavorting upon the frescoes. Both were sleek as young colts, indeed, and being so young (as I guessed, not a year older than myself) and unpractised in the sophisticated arts of love, their gestures were as unmannered and free as could be, the girl offering her breasts to my lips with the most open pride, while the boy's delight when Em, admiringly, took his prick between her lips in proper tribute to its firmness and elasticity, was unfeigned.

Taking advantage of our recent discoveries, we tried some of the postures we had recently seen depicted upon the walls of the *bordello*; but despite the athletic build of our companions found some of them difficult to impossibility – as when, for instance, Em was invited to sink upon her young friend's instrument, but facing his feet rather than his head, which she found uncomfortable; or when my companion wished me to penetrate her while standing upon my right leg, my left embracing her, while she balanced upon her left leg, passing her right about my waist.

Nevertheless, the enthusiasm of our young friends and the pleasure they afforded us passed the time most agreeably, the cool air making our couplings (which, it being at the top of the afternoon, the heat of the sun would otherwise have made productive of a rank sweat) delightfully inspiriting – until our guide, appearing around the corner of the room, informed us that a party of English tourists was approaching, whereat my girl drew me upon her and, embracing my waist with both thighs, milked me in a moment dry of pleasure, while a foot away the young satyr, lying beneath Em, thrust upwards with his hips until she collapsed with a cry upon the straw.

It was with surprise that I noticed (I believe Em did not) that he had not, himself, ejaculated those male juices which normally flow at such times; and as we were drawing on our clothes, I asked him in private whether this was usual with him; whereat he said that he 'kept himself' for Rosanna, the girl who had so happily accommodated me; for she and he were to be married next spring, and their recent activities were to enable them to gather together sufficient money to buy a farmstead in the neighbourhood.

Touched at this – for surely it was remarkable in him that, even with a partner so willing as Em, he could restrain the utmost joy in order that it could be dedicated to the one he loved – I gave him three *pauls*, at which his joy was so great that he immediately caught up his girl in his arms, and with a merry '*addio*!' left us. As we left, the English party was, in the hands of our former guide, being split into two so that the ladies might take a rest in the shade while the gentlemen were escorted to the villa we had just left. Bowing to them, we made our way back to the phaeton, and drove off for Naples under the suspicion that ours had been a more enjoyable visit than that of our compatriots would be.

We spent some two months in enjoyment of Naples, but there is little to recount of them; it is a city much given to theft, and the adults pass on their expert experiences in that field to their children, for the streets swarm with partially-clad *lazzaroni* who are expert pick-pockets, so that it is best to keep your handkerchief in your hat, and your watch well secured with a strong guard. It is also a dirty city, with the porticoes and colonnades used by the inhabitants to relieve themselves, and the courtyards of palaces and hotels, the porches of private houses, the staircases and landings similarly employed, people getting down from their coaches wherever and whenever the need arises. It can be imagined how unpleasant the heat renders such places.

But there were attractions, however, not least in the freedom the place offers to those seeking relaxation: the Neapolitans are a good-looking race, at least when young; the city seems full of little brown children jumping about stark-naked, the bigger ones dancing with castanets; and the sea is used as a common bath-place, for walking by it one sees people of all ages throwing off what few clothes they wear and bathing themselves without the smallest ceremony, then walking and sporting on the shore perfectly naked – a custom we were happy to enjoy, and which resulted in several happy encounters with pretty young Italian girls, while Em, the whiteness of her skin carefully preserved by her with the help of an umbrella, was sufficiently unusual to attract many salutations from the men, some of which she invited to a conclusion satisfactory to them both.

However, in time, we decided that our explorations should continue; it was still in my mind to make for Athens, and to that end, after making a few purchases for the journey, we set off in a *voiture*, passing through picturesque country to Avellino, where we stopped briefly, since Em wished to make a sketch of the Douane, a very ancient building; but we were such an uncommon sight that about a hundred people soon gathered about her, pointing and pushing; at which she had to give up her venture, and we made on through the mountains to Asiano.

During the next few days we passed through the valley of Bovino, a very wild, mountainous country much infested with thieves – indeed we saw a gathering of about twenty men who our driver nervously informed us were about to attack; but seeing another *voiture* nearby, they decided against the venture and let us pass. A little way onward, we saw at each side of the road the heads and hands of some robbers, taken two months ago, the skulls in iron cages with a hand and arm under each, supported on a pyramid of stonework.

Eventually, we reached Bari, and after some enquiries found that no ship was to sail for Greece for some time, but that one – an English man-o'-war, the *Scout* – left the very next day for Alexandria. Would it not be interesting to change our plans, and cast our eyes on that miraculous beast, the Sphinx? The idea no sooner occurred to us than we accepted it, and, passing for convenience as Mr and Mrs Archer, took passage under Captain Pawlin, an intelligent young man who appeared to know the Mediterranean well, and welcomed us warmly, entertaining us to a good dinner and introducing us to his officers. That evening, under a clear sky and upon level seas, we set sail for Egypt.

Chapter Eight

Sophie's Story

The town of Valetta, the chief place in the island of Malta, looked particularly interesting as it hung over the grand harbour in which we lowered our anchor. It was without hesitation that, having bade farewell to our friends – the captain of our vessel being eager to press on to his next port of call, which was on the northern coast of Africa – we saw our belongings packed and accompanied them in a small boat to the shore.

Upon the advice of the captain, we made immediately for the mansion of the Governor, Sir Henry Beadle, who we were told was an hospitable kind of a person. The streets of the town were vertiginous to a degree – and so much so indeed that in many places they consisted merely of steps, with a single narrow strip of ground at their centre upon which sleighs could be drawn, carrying heavy goods – as, for instance, our luggage, which was willingly so conveyed by two Maltese youths whom we had found lounging about the quays and waiting for whatever work presented itself.

Upon our giving our names in, the Governor immediately sent for us to come to him, and not merely received us politely, engaging us for dinner that evening, but also offered to allow us house room – an offer which we were glad to accept, having no plans of that sort. Sir Henry was a tall, lean man, somewhat like a stork, and dressed in a rusty suit of court clothes, with tarnished gold epaulets falling from his thin shoulders. He sent for his wife, a plump, red-faced beauty of indeterminate age, who might have come that instant from the washing-tub of a farmhouse in a remote corner of Staffordshire. But she too, good woman, received us most pleasantly – I guessed that not many people of quality called at the island (and indeed there was still talk of the time, only a few years ago, when Lord Byron himself was there, and cut a swathe through the young ladies of the town).

Lady Beadle having escorted us to our rooms, which were perfectly decent, though furnished in the style of the 1750s; and having commanded hot water and bathed ourselves (feeling distinctly soiled with sweat and dirt after some days' confinement in a ship, where the only water available was salt, which is not efficacious for cleanliness); we sallied forth to see the town – which did not take a quantity of time, it being pretty small, though in places elegant, with for instance a pretty little theatre where performances sometimes take place.

We strolled for some time upon the fortifications, which culminated in a platform constructed to hang above the fine harbour, and from which there was an excellent and impressive view of the multifarious shipping which gathered there from ports all over the Middle East. Finding ourselves then hungered, we made acquaintance at an eating place in the main square with a somewhat peculiar local food known singularly as 'breads', and consisting simply of that comforting substance, still warm from the oven in which it was baked, and spread with a conglomerate of olive oil, tomato paste, raw onion and crumbled cooked fish. This sounds sufficiently horrid – but as I have often had cause to remark, food which we would spurn in our own country tastes often good enough under clear skies and a hot sun, as was the case in this circumstance.

We spent the afternoon again strolling about the town, until it was time to prepare ourselves for the evening's dinner party. Blatchford dressed once more in his anonymous black, and looked fine enough; I was concerned lest the dresses which I had bought in Spain might not be sufficiently elegant for the drawing-room of the Governmental Residence; but I need not have worried, for when Lady Beadle received us she proved to be clad in a gown which, if indeed it had originated in London had done so during the last century, and not its latest decades. She greeted us with great kindness, however, and introduced us straightway to her chaplain, the Reverend Michael Willoughby-Pouncefoot, who appeared to recognise Blatchford (doubtless from his sombre garments) as a kindred spirit, and immediately attempted to engage him in discussion of the most recent opinion in British ecclesiastical circles of transubstantiation; which Blatchford received by informing him that he believed the Prince Regent to be in favour of it – at which the chaplain was reduced to a somewhat confused silence.

The only other persons present were a merchant and his wife, of a provincialism even more considerable than that of Sir Henry and his lady, and whose conversation was all of the trade in British smallclothes which he hoped to establish with the Chinese.

After a while, we retired to the dining-table, set for eight people – though, as I had noted, we were only seven. Just as a watery soup was served (and the absence of wineglasses explained by a short but vigorous lecture from Lady Beadle upon the evils of alcohol) the door opened and a tall figure came in, the gentleman making his apologies to Lady Beadle and then taking his place in the vacant chair opposite my own.

Here was a most welcome addition to the table: a man in his middle twenties – as I surmised – with a somewhat olive complexion, and enormous black eyes below clearly marked eyebrows, lips of a generous fullness, and an expression of intense interest in everything about him – including, I could scarcely forbear to notice, myself. I could not but note his fine, delicate hands and long, apprehensive fingers, which handled his knife and fork with a delicate poise that suggested a natural sophistication which only I, in that company, could match.

I was not able, alas, to communicate with him during the meal, other than in the way of passing the condiments or returning an occasional glance; for my attention was occupied by the chaplain, who alas had been placed next me, and who attempted immediately to explain the arguments of a thesis he had been writing on antidisestablishmentarianism, and to seek my advice upon its publication in London. However, while attempting to answer sensibly even the most stupid of his questions, I was conscious of an interest in the newcomer, and somewhat sensible of an attention I felt he would pay me should it be possible. Upon the ladies withdrawing (after the consumption of a few wizened apples and some crumbs of cheese), I immediately enquired of Lady Beadle what could be his origin? – for I was certain he could not have been born upon that island.

'He is,' I was told, 'a most interesting young man of some twenty and three years, who was the irregular product of an association between an officer of the British India Company and the daughter of a *rajah* or prince of that country. Upon his birth he was immediately recognised by his father who unfortunately died shortly afterwards, and the boy was taken (with the heart-broken permission of his mother) to England by his uncle, and there educated at Harrow school, which I believe to be much admired as a place of learning by the aristocracy. Not long before the time came for him to leave and return to India, news was received that his mother too had died of the cholera; and he now found himself in possession, though yet a minor, of a large fortune left him by his parents.

'He was determined to return to the country of his birth, and on doing so became interested in the religion of his mother's forefathers, and studied it with many teachers. Wishing to bring the knowledge of it to the western world, he has established here, at Hal Tarxien, near Valetta, a monastery in which he has been teaching a number of young men and women its observation.

'As a Christian I cannot, of course, approve this;' the good woman remarked, 'but Mr George Wilbraham is a young man of such parts that it is impossible not to recognise him, and he commonly dines with us once or twice a month.'

This was indeed interesting, and though by no means of a naturally religious disposition I could not but feel an interest in the young man's history, and to wish to make his acquaintance; so I invited Lady Beadle to introduce us, which she did on our rejoining the gentlemen. He pressed my hand engagingly, his eyes assaulting my own with a most direct approbation. He had evidently been speaking to Blatchford, for he immediately expressed his regret at my widowhood, and hoped that my travels were helping to remove the lethargy and despair which followed the loss of a beloved consort (at which I gathered that their conversation had not included an explanation of the total abhorrence in which I had held the late Mr Nelham, nor my pleasure at his decease).

Almost at once, he followed those few words with an enquiry about my present plans. He understood, he said, that my interests were wide, and wondered whether I would care to visit, with my brother, the establishment at Hal Tarxien, for I might find the establishment interesting.

'In what do your studies consist?' I asked.

He looked about to ensure that we were not overheard, before replying – for, he said, some people might not comprehend his words in the sense in which, he was confident, I should.

He then revealed that the chief interest of himself and his community was in the study of the theory of *Tantra*, and asked whether I was familiar with it. I said I was not, whereupon he explained that it was based upon certain ancient Hindu texts which had foreseen an age when man would be 'without restraint, maddened with pride, ever given over to sinful acts, lustful, gluttonous, cruel, heartless, harsh of speech and deceitful.'

'Can it be doubted,' he asked, 'that they referred to our own time? But fortunately, the ancients also proposed a cure, and our philosophy holds that the universe and everything in it participates in a secret energy which is at the heart of all being, and that that energy can best be tapped during the mutual joining of man and woman.'

My interest grew.

'Even before I knew anything of Tantric yoga,' Mr Wilbraham proceeded, 'it seemed strange to me that Christianity and indeed all other religions of which I had experience, recognise the power of love as the vital energy of our being – but at the same time seek to repress it, speaking of it as though it were always and everywhere sinful.

'The Hindus, I discovered on opening my studies with an ancient scholar in Benares, see the progress of a love match as a formal pattern, almost a dance, which is as inevitable as it is rewarding. It begins – if I do not bore you . . .?'

I shook my head vigorously.

'It begins,' he went on, 'with *smarnana*, or thought – when one first sets eyes on a person with whom one wished to be united' – and I could not but be conscious of a meaning look in his dark eyes as he spoke the words. 'Next is *kirtanam*, or discussion; third *keli*, or keeping company; fourth *prekshenam* or what we call flirtation; fifth *guhyabhashanam*, or intimate conversation; sixth *samkalpa* or the desire for a consummation of love; seventh *adhyavasayam* or the determination to love; and eighth and lastly, *kriyanishpatti*, or the act itself.'

And what, I asked, made this process any different from the normal method of courtship employed in any civilised society; what, indeed, elevated the act of love itself from a simple enjoyment to a religious rite?

Ah, he replied, this was the mystic nature of the ceremonies devised by the ancients, and which he taught to the young men and women he had gathered together. These were secret, and had been established in order to fulfil the theory that if man could discover how to prolong for more than a few seconds that momentary paroxysm with which the act of love was concluded, he would discover a greater vision of himself and of the order of the universe.

'Through the study of Tantric yoga,' he claimed, 'man can achieve the potency which enables him to extend ecstasy for half an hour or more.'

'And you have accomplished this?' I enquired.

'Certainly,' he gravely responded, 'and can teach it.'

'To men as to women?'

'I have received no complaints from the fairer sex,' he replied with a smile. 'And as to your intimation that the act is nothing different from a normal copulation, why during *maithuna* or sacramental union, the woman is no longer simply a woman, but the goddess Parahakti herself, while her lover ceases to be a man, and becomes the incarnation of the god Shiva.'

This keenly inspiriting conversation was now interrupted by the irritating advent of the Reverend Willoughby-Pauncefoot, who brought a clearly bored and dispirited Blatchford towards us.

'Mr Wilbraham,' he said with a supercilious smirk, 'Mr Blatchford and I have been discussing St Colman of Kilmacduagh, and whether the fly which was said to have made it its business to mark his place in the book he was reading, or the cock which carefully woke him five minutes before morning office, were independent agents or under the direct instruction of the Almighty. Might I enquire your opinion on the matter?'

My new friend declined, on the grounds that he had little knowledge of the fauna of the Celtic nations. The chaplain bowed sharply and took his leave – there was, I observed, little love lost between them.

Mr Wilbraham addressed himself again to me and to Blatchford.

'I believe,' he said, 'that Sir Henry has offered you the hospitality of the palace; but if you have an interest in looking over our community, and perhaps of receiving some instruction, we would be pleased to offer you a room. I am sure, Mr Blatchford, that your sister will tell you of our establishment and the work we do there . . .'

I felt it proper at this stage to inform him that Blatchford and I were not in fact brother and sister, but that we travelled together for convenience's sake.

'And I am sure,' I said, 'that my friend will be as interested as I in your proceedings, and as happy to visit you.'

'Excellent,' he exclaimed. 'Then can I look forward to seeing you in the morning?'

We assented, and he shortly afterwards took his leave.

Sir Henry and (especially) Lady Beadle were surprised and somewhat concerned at our expressed intention of visiting the monastery (as she called it); and indeed the lady warned me of the dangers of mixing too closely with the common men and women we should meet there, who were not, she explained, of the best households in the island, but had apparently been picked specifically for their lack of education in western ways. 'Almost,' she said, 'as though Mr Wilbraham had chosen them for their lack of good Christian morality.'

I thanked her warmly for her warning, and retired for the night – Blatchford however coming to my room and sitting upon my bed to hear of Mr Wilbraham's establishment, which he agreed sounded interesting – 'though I have had enough religion tonight from that d****d priest, to last a lifetime,' he said. However, he was all for our visit, when I had explained the nature of the Tantric religion, for he averred the one objection he had always had to courting a young lady with a view to connection with her, was that the resultant ecstasy was too soon over (though he used a commoner expression than ecstasy).

It was noon that day before we were able to wrench ourselves away from the palace, for Lady Beadle took me off to her boudoir (a little, ill-furnished room in the corner of the house) in order to discover from me the latest news of the English court, which I was obliged to invent, ornamenting my tales with what details I could remember from my conversations with my friend Viscount Chichley and his wife; but was able to interest her, and out of my kindness complimented her on being able in so distant a place to keep so closely in touch with current fashions – something she was most pleased at.

After a light luncheon we made off in a hired equipage for Hal Tarxien, which proved to be a mystical place where ancient peoples had constructed temples for their use in worshipping an unknown god or gods in temples half or entirely beneath the ground. Near these a small range of buildings had been constructed, and we were greeted at the gate of the enclosure by a young woman dressed in a flowing saffron-coloured gown or robe, who clearly was expecting us, and escorted us to two plain rooms, next each other, with only a simple bed and a single cupboard to furnish them.

There she indicated upon the bed a robe similar to her own, and suggested that I should put it on, which I did – its being of good cotton, cool and graceful; though Blatchford, I was amused to observe, was less at home than I was in this – to him – curious garb. We were then taken to a central courtyard, where we saw Mr Wilbraham and a group of young men and women, all similarly clothed, and seated under a canopy. He greeted us warmly, but when we addressed him by name, informed us that here he was known by his Indian name of Ramkishore.

We sat and sipped a cooling drink, served in large bowls, sweet and refreshing; then he announced that that very evening we were invited to attend the secret ceremonies of the place – which indeed we did, but omitting to report my impressions of it I prefer to remark that on the following evening I was myself schooled to participation, and will describe the ceremony as I experienced it when fully informed and practised.

The rite of *maithuna* invariably took place in the afternoon, when the heat of midday had given way to a cooler but still warm air, and when the sun slanted down through deeply set windows to shed a faint light within the darkest temple, which was dimly lit also by a single lamp. A container of bright scarlet flowers (I know not their name) also stood there, with a silver platter bearing small portions of freshly cooked meat and rice, two glasses and a pitcher of water, and one of wine (the latter representing the element, fire).

Ramkishore (as I was henceforth to call Mr Wilbraham) and I first repaired to a neighbouring smaller room in whose floor was set a bath, and there bathed ourselves from head to foot in cool water. He then donned a robe similar to his everyday one, but in fine silk, and left while two of the maidens anointed my body with a sweet-smelling ointment and then clad me in my own silken robe, leading me to the larger chamber, where Ramkishore was sitting with legs crossed and hands placed upon his knees, taking in deep and regular breaths. Around the room, in the centre of which was a low altar or ceremonial bed of stone upon which a thick quilt was spread, sat the dozen young men and women of the place, all of an age of around twenty, and all somewhat similar in appearance – with the slightly squat bodies of the Maltese people, well built and without corpulence, but somewhat more substantial than most westerners – including myself and Blatchford, as well as the leader of the group himself.

I seated myself beside Ramkishore, when after a moment or two he performed the ceremony known as *panchikarana*, offering me some cooked meat and taking some himself, while chanting a *mantra* or prayer: '*Devata chava siddhaye* . . .'

Standing so that two of the young men could unloose my gown at the shoulders, allowing it to fall to my feet, I was then led to the central altar, and there – known now as the *shakti* – sat upright while Ramkishore, the *sadhakta*, stood before me gazing with admiration at my naked body, 'the awakener and embodiment of bliss, the unsullied treasure house of beauty,' as he termed it, quoting from the ancient writings, which describe the *shakti* as 'she whose slender waist, bending beneath the burden of her breasts' ripe fruit, swells into jewelled hips . . .' The adoration of the body of the *shakti*, I was told, was a vital part of the ceremony, and indeed without it what followed would be null and void.

Ramkishore then performed the rite of *nyasa*, placing the tips of his fingers first upon my heart, then upon my forehead and eyes, then the hollow of my throat, the left and right ear lobes, each breast, the upper arms, the navel, thighs, feet, and finally my secret parts or *yoni*, as they are named. All this time he continued to chant the prayer '*Hling . . . kling . . . kandarpa . . . svaha . . .*'

Two maidens then stepped forward and released his robe, which revealed a body of quite striking beauty, perfectly balanced, slim yet fully-formed, and with a *lingam* (as they call the male instrument) of impressive dimensions, yet once more perfectly proportioned, which presented itself to me in a properly complimentary erection – its length balanced by a proper thickness, and its head round and full. As was always the case when Ramkishore displayed himself in nakedness, a gasp of admiration was heard from the girls present – if not from the young men, who no doubt felt that their own *lingams* were of equally admirable proportions, and only naturally regretted that the admiration of their friends was so cordially directed at the body of their leader!

I should say that upon other evenings, when a young man and young maiden were being instructed, there was not an atmosphere charged with such tension, perhaps because the participation of Ramkishore, with his knowledge of the rites, was necessary to their full apprehension. However, to return to my description of the ceremony, I was not permitted to touch the body of Ramkishore, though my interest was of course keen; instead, I was prompted to lie back upon the couch, while he took his place upon his left side, at my right hand.

Now, the two girl attendants raised my legs by bending them, at the knees, and folded them towards my chest. Ramkishore then swung the upper part of his body away from mine, so that his *lingam* was in proximity with my *yoni*. My legs were then lowered, and his right thigh placed between them, so that we lay pressed together as closely as was possible without actual congress – though now reaching down one of the girls took his *lingam* in her hands and placed it so that its splendid head lay just between the lips of my *yoni*.

The girls then retired, and sitting each beside a young man, joined in the chanting of the *mantra* as we lay completely still for over half of an hour.

This will appear to the uninformed to be a curious and perhaps unsatisfactory manner of making love; and yet the result was most remarkable, for at about the twentieth minute a rising tide of pleasure very slowly mounted, seeming to flow between us at the point at which our bodies were joined. This was most gradual, at first indeed indiscernible, so that I believed the experiment was to be a failure; but then gradually was conscious of a faint warmth, growing to an emotion perfectly irresistible; and at about the thirty-second minute of our congress came a sudden access of sensation which was so intense that I feared for my sanity. Still we did not move – except that our bodies were shaken by a quite involuntary movement, a paroxysm of bliss which was marked by the community, whose chanting rose to a peak, then dying away as an intense feeling of peace engulfed me.

After this we lay for some time, feeling our energies now withdrawing one from the other, until it was possible for us to part. The intense sensation of oneness is known, I was informed, as *samarasa*, and it is unusual of achievement so early as I achieved it, Ramkishore congratulating me, and the girls being envious of my attaining it.

In private, after the first such experience, what was my astonishment to discover on examining my *yoni* to find that there was no sign of that liquidity which I expected to mark the occasion. I was later informed that the ancients insisted that it was improper for the male to give forth his essence during the rite – a thing which makes it difficult of achievement by any but those with the utmost control over their emotions, and impossible to the libertine or the voluptuary. Ramkishore later informed me that upon the first occasion of his union with me, his pleasure was such that he had the greatest difficulty in containing himself, and only did so by the ancient practice of holding his breath and at the same time turning his tongue backward as far as he could against the roof of his mouth – a remedy which I have since with some success recommended to those men whose pleasure is spoiled by a too speedy consummation of the act.

When the participants of the rite were two of the postulants, rather than Ramkishore himself, I noticed more keenly the difficulty they had in containing themselves, the young men frequently being unable to resist the occasional small movement which betrayed a natural instinct; upon occasion they were unable to prevent the spilling of their seed, which Ramkishore assured me was a venial sin, but lowered the occasion from that high standard which it should attain. When he himself was a participant, however, though sometimes I believe the girl concerned did not experience the height of passion I had felt, the expression upon his own face was transcendental, and it was not difficult for me to believe that indeed something of the spirit of the god Shiva had entered into him.

If the whole matter was strange to me, it was even more a mystery to poor Blatchford, who despite all Ramkishore could do never succeeded in grasping the spiritual implications of the rite, and moreover, though he was entirely enthusiastic at the prospect of maintaining congress for half an hour, did not entirely approve of the way in which this was to be done.

There was some difficulty right from the moment of his entering the ceremonial bath, for he was entirely unable to prevent himself from assisting the ravishing girl of seventeen who was his first partner to bathe herself, her splendid dark beauty and generous person attracting his hands like a magnet, though the attendant maidens explained that such attentions were out of place at such a time (if, clearly, they were not entirely unwelcome to the girl in question!).

Then, when as instructed he took up his position standing in front of his naked *shakti* in order to admire her beauty, that admiration went further than the simple tapping of her breasts and thighs with the index and middle fingers of the right hand, as advised; instead, he applied his palm, to the underside of those breasts, and bent to fix his lips upon their delightful pink nipples - again not to the girl's displeasure, but to the distress of the matron whom Ramkishore had placed in charge of the occasion.

The maiden herself was clearly not unimpressed by the dimensions of Blatchford's *lingam*, when it was revealed to her; but contrary to his clear desire merely observed it rather than immediately attending to its obvious need. He clearly welcomed the moment when he was instructed to lie at her side, and when, upon her thighs being lifted by the attendants, a *yoni* of delightfully welcoming proportions was revealed, a dark fig in which a scarlet aperture seemed to cry out for stopping, he did not hesitate to thrust himself into her, immediately beginning those motions of his familiar (to me) muscular buttocks which usually delineated congress.

A cry was heard from the young men and women who looked on, and who appeared not to have seen such a sight before; so that the exclamation was perhaps of pleasurable admiration rather than of scandal - though I do not know, I cannot say. Blatchford's action was also a great surprise to the *shakti*, who was equally unconscious of the actions of normal congress, but whose lower body began unconsciously to react to her partner's movements, so that they were soon giving an unconscionably good imitation of what my friend would have described as 'a good fuck'. So, what with one thing and what with another, the temple was soon full of enquiry, though voiceless, as to why none of them had been shown this energetic motion, which seemed capable of giving such enjoyment, and without the long period of inactivity demanded by the rite they usually practised? Several of the watchers got to their feet, indeed, and made their way to the altar, kneeling there to inspect at close range the manner in which, rather than merely nestling at the entrance of the *yoni*, this man's *lingam* was busily bustling, entering and withdrawing with alacrity and enthusiasm.

The matron was by this time in a muddle of emotions; though older than any of us present, she could not have been of more than thirty years, and was not unmoved by the spectacle - for she had no doubt herself experienced similar congress, and was only by her admiration for Ramkishore devoted to the rite which he had first shown her; she was certainly by no means uncertain of the difference between the *kriyanishpatti* and what was now proceeding, and on stepping forward to attend to part the lovers, found 'twas impossible – indeed, the only result was that Blatchford, finding an even more splendid pair of breasts within his reach, pulled her down towards them so that she unbalanced and for a moment made a third in the amorous struggle.

However, she released herself and hastily left the hall – which was the signal for the young people around us to depart entirely from their roles as mere spectators, for though her presence had restrained them, they were all impatience to try this new sport, and on her disappearance threw off their coverings and in a moment were, in all corners of the temple, attempting to emulate the couple upon the altar, some imitating their posture, some very speedily concluding that there was more than one way of killing a cat, and finding with natural quickness their own way to heaven – though upon one girl attempting to welcome her lover with closed thighs, I had to point out to her the necessity of embracing him with more than her arms, which she was quick to learn and to thank me for.

Ramkishore, whom the matron had gone to fetch, no doubt wisely declined to intervene, probably realising that it would by now have been impossible to separate young people engaged on their first unsupervised amorous intercourse; however, next morning he read a lecture about the lowness of appetites which could only be satisfied by such unaesthetic and carnal activities.

The following evening he supervised Blatchford's second attempt to submit himself to the Tantric discipline, somewhat with more success at first, though to one who knew the latter it was clear from the rolling of his eyes that he was having the utmost difficulty in remaining still during the first seven or eight minutes of connection with yet another charming girl; and although he managed to restrain himself so far, in the end it became impossible, and with a cry of 'Bugger this for a lark!' and one buck of his hips, he gave up an ample supply of that essence which the Tantric ancients would have had him conserve.

Several times during the next two weeks he was asked

whether he would not rather abandon the attempt, for Ramkishore was naive enough to suppose that he was serious in his intentions; an unfettered supply of charming young persons of the opposite sex, who by now (alas!) were all eager to experience lying with him, would have been too much for a stronger man than he. In the end, Ramkishore could not but notice that there was some eagerness to partner 'Mr English', as he was known; and though it was the custom that the leader himself should chose the partners for each *maithuna*, it was also usual that a different girl (and normally youth) should be chosen each evening. There was some irritation among the youths that while on alternate evenings I was again and again chosen for the rite, I was invariably partnered by Ramkishore himself, at which muttering was to be heard – so that I was by no means sure that the impact which we had had upon the ordinary run of events at Hal Tarxien was entirely beneficial.

Moreover, it must be confessed that after about three weeks I was beginning to be somewhat bored at the continual repetition of the *maithuna*, and despite the extraordinary sensual experience which it offered, to be more than ready for normal congress; the sight of Blatchford once and again enjoying it, despite the best efforts of his instructor, was no help, and in time I came to the conclusion that it was time my friend once more attended to my needs. So one afternoon, made amorous by the heat and the wine I had drunk at lunch time (for wine flowed freely there, as the ancients recommended), I concluded that if my body was not positively to suffer, I must find the release of a less rarefied congress.

Happily, the tool was at hand: making my way to the next room, I saw my friend clad only in that decently furry pelt with which nature had endowed him, half-asleep upon his bed. Before he was properly awake, I was kneeling at his side, and had applied my lips to that limb which had not experienced such a caress for too long – such an exercise being apparently unknown at Hal Tarxien.

Blatchford was by all means inclined to comfort me in the way in which I most wished, feeling the lack of an experienced consort – the attentions of unschooled young girls has a certain charm, but can in time pall (difficult though it may be for some of my male readers to believe it). In no time he was applying his tongue in that inimitably knowing way to my belly, thighs, and *yoni*, while my lips were renewing acquaintance with his *lingam*, which if anything seemed to have grown in stature with the practice it had received during the past few weeks, and whose smooth sturdiness I was happy to prepare for the place in which I trusted soon to receive it.

However, a shadow now fell across our bodies, and on hearing a soft oath from my lover, I looked up to see the figure of Ramkishore standing above us, and looking so melancholy and disconsolate at the sight before him that I fancied he must burst into tears.

I could not but sit up, my eyes somewhat cast down, for I did admire the young man and was sorry to be the cause of distress. I glanced at Blatchford, and with the smallest motion of my head dismissed him, who with his usual amiability, though somewhat glumly, stood up, and, that so substantial tool already drooping, made his way from the room. Lifting my hand and taking his, I drew Ramkishore down to my side, and bade him not be sad – for though I had been interested in the experiments in which he had so kindly allowed me to participate, I must confess (I said) that normal congress was still more attractive to me, for the manner in which they conducted it at Hal Tarxien was to me somewhat monotonous; did he not find this to be so?

He then admitted that such a form was the only congress he had known, for his teachers presented it as the only form in which true *kriyanishpatti* could be conducted; and confessed that his curiosity at – for instance – the posture that he had seen Blatchford and I adopting was considerable, for how could the *yoni* receive the *lingam* when man and woman lay head to toe?

The only way in which this could be explained was what I now adopted, persuading him from his robe, and placing myself in position showing him that the compliments which a woman could pay a man with lips and tongue were not to be disdained. The trembling of his body, like that of a plucked string, conveyed the fact that he was not unmoved by this; but why, he asked – when for a moment I paused, the tension of his *lingam* making it clear that otherwise the episode would come to an untimely end – why should we lie head to toe, for surely I could minister to him in this way simply by kneeling before him?

I then must explain that it was not unknown, in the West, for a man to offer to a woman the same tribute as I had been paying him; which in a moment he seized the idea of, and with the most tender sensitivity began to explore my *yoni* with his lips – and soon I discovered one advantage which had perhaps not been realised by those ancients who taught the cultivation of the muscles of the tongue for the purposes of helping to restrain too quick a conclusion in the act – never had I felt so insinuating, so intense, so dextrous a petting in that way!

Indeed, as I continued to reveal to him the multifarious ways in which man and woman could pleasure each other, his body reacted like that of an untamed colt, first over-quick, then gradually recognising the discipline which alone brings pleasure to full fruition; could I but have had him for a month, I could have made of him a lover quite irresistible; and indeed as it was, though perhaps I never received the transmission of that peculiar eruption of emotional intensity offered in the final moments of the *maithuna*, my own pleasure equalled his if not in originality at least in completeness.

We occupied ourselves for the whole afternoon, Blatchford being so good as to stand guard, informing those who came in search of Ramkishore that he was privately instructing me – a mirror image of what actually took place. No less than six times, such was his stamina, did he return to the fray; upon the first occasion of his dying, he gave forth an astonishing torrent of essence – not having completed the act, he told me later, for over six years; by the end of the afternoon and after the final battle, a single pearly drop was all that remained as evidence of his pleasure.

He was not seen that evening, when I took my seat with the others while two of our friends performed the ceremony. Blatchford was nowhere to be seen (the absence of one of the younger girls being explained by the fact that she was suffering her monthlies – something which Blatchford later informed me was an untruth). Next morning, Ramkishore came to me full of apologies – which of course I assured him were not required; but he said that he believed he had betrayed the commission he had accepted from his teachers – and though I did my best to console him, was disconsolate. I was forced to agree however when he suggested that perhaps it was time that Blatchford and I removed ourselves from the community – though he was kind enough to say that should I wish to remain he was sure that I could become a sublimely inspiriting *shakti*.

It was with some regret and some relief that we parted from the community and from Ramkishore – regrets shared, I believe, by the young girls, and relief shared by the young men. In Valetta we bade farewell to the Governor and Lady Beadle – who was extremely curious about our experiences; whereat, somewhat naughtily, I informed her that she would find the rites there extremely interesting, and that she should pay the community a visit and insist upon being present at the ceremonies. This, I trust, will bring some light relief to the no doubt monotonous life led by the lady in this distant colony. In the meantime, we joined a ship which was part of a British merchant convoy for Patras and Prevesa, and sailed for new fields of pleasure.

Chapter Nine

The Adventures of Andy

Now embarked on my first lengthy ocean voyage, I was a little apprehensive lest I should suffer from sea-sickness – as indeed was Em; but within twelve hours of our leaving harbour at Bari upon HMS *Scout* we had both our sea legs (as they put it) and felt as secure as on dry land, though aided it is true by the calmness of the voyage.

The heat was extraordinary, even for summer, Captain Pawlin assured us, and for our convenience rigged up an awning of canvas for'ard of the main-mast, upon an area of deck forbidden to the crew, where we were able to sit in the shade, and where after some time I stripped myself merely to a cloth wrapped about my loins, while poor Em had to suffer to remain in a dress, which though of thin stuff was nevertheless stifling to her body in the heat.

I asked Lieutenant Swinton, an amiable young man of my own age whom the Captain had kindly deputed to care for our wants, whether it would be proper for her to uncover, or whether it might cause some difficulty with the crew; to which, blushing furiously, he said that he could ensure that nobody would disturb us, and that if the young lady wished to – er – divest herself of – er – her upper and outer clothing, there would be no inconvenience to the discipline or running of the ship. Em, relieved to hear this, thereupon removed her dress, and we were more at ease, with the lack of clothing and the soft sea breezes cooling us. Lieutenant Swinton had however, while presumably warning the crew to keep clear, failed to report to the Captain, who suddenly coming upon us at luncheon-time – to offer us a glass of wine – found us asleep in a state of nature more apposite to those landspeople Adam and Eve than to life upon the water. No doubt he attempted tactfully to leave us, but stumbled over a piece of ship's equipment and woke us. On seeing his discomfiture we could not but laugh, whereupon he too, seeing that we were not embarrassed, laughed also, and in short sat down in his uniform and took wine with us.

I could not but notice that his glances at Em, while suitably disguised, were nevertheless of admiration; and later that afternoon, lying half asleep, noticed that, despite the young lieutenant's warning, the faces of members of the crew occasionally appeared in the rigging which overhung our resting-place, and twice was sure that the young man himself peeped around the corner of the canvas shield to glimpse Em's person (which indeed was worth a glimpse, having filled out somewhat with the many meals of pasta – a kind of paste the Italians eat much of, accompanied by sauces of meat or tomato – and was now more to the taste of the average Englishman than perhaps it had been when she first arrived in Rome, when she was somewhat lean and hungry).

When, after supper, she had gone to our cabin and I sat drinking with the captain, I thought it proper to bring up the question of our privacy, not in order to insist upon it, but to wonder whether the lieutenant had been right in suggesting that our freedom might not endanger discipline.

'Sir,' Captain Pawlin said, 'you are on an English man-o'-war, where a century of the lash has instilled into our men instant obedience to orders; why, if Mrs Archer were to walk the deck from one end to another entirely naked, the men drawn up upon either side, not one muscle would be moved!'

I took leave to doubt it, for surely – particularly when men were as deprived of the company of womankind as upon ship – it would be beyond nature?

The Captain insisted, and both of us having enjoyed our bottle, after some argument concluded a bet on the above circumstances; which I then was obliged to explain to Em – who fortunately took it as it was meant, in good humour.

In the morning, Captain Pawlin attempted to retract, but I was firm that the wager, having been made, should stand: and in Lieutenant Swinton's presence and that of Lieutenant Blore, the first officer, with Em standing by, the conditions were drawn up – that the ship's company should be mustered in two lines from stem to stern, and that Mrs Archer – as I had named her – should walk unclothed between their ranks, the wager being that not a single muscle would stir. The question of what should be wagered then arose. It was clear to me and to Em that by their covert glances the officers would have liked to have included some familiarity with her as the prize, but were shy of suggesting it in her presence. She then put forward that if the Captain lost, the cost of our passage from Italy to Alexandria should be borne by himself; whereas if we lost, we should provide an entertainment for the ship's crew – which, she said, she would not be particular on, but it should be something they would be pleased to remember in their old age!

They agreed; and so it was that late that afternoon, just as the blazing heat of the sun began to fade to a pleasant warmth, the entire ship's crew of some fifty men was mustered upon deck and addressed by the Captain. They were, he told them, upon duty, and a ceremony was about to be performed which would be new to them; it was vital, however, that they should remain at their posts, and any man moving would be subject to severe punishment.

The men were clearly surprised at this, and knew not what to suspect; and when the doors of the rear cabin were thrown open, and on to the deck stepped Em, as bare as the day upon which she was born, I hoped for success, for the men could not control their expressions, which were of mixed astonishment and pleasure.

In the broad sunlight Em then walked the length of the ship, slowly and with perfect grace – such grace that even I, who had been familiar with her now for some time, could not forbear to admire the lascivious swaying of her rear, the proud projection of her breasts, the careless swing of her arms, and the charming smile with which she showed how little affected she was by that curse of so-called civilisation, modesty.

Standing at the Captain's side, I could scarcely conceal my triumph when I saw, perfectly clearly, those movements which in the great majority of the men before us, proved that however motionless their bodies remained, there was one limb whose apprehension of my friend's beauty could not be controlled; I was able to point out to Captain Pawlin that several muscles in fact moved during Em's stroll; something which he could not deny, particularly since (when he began to protest) I was able to point out that a certain bulge in his uniform trousers indicated that he too had joined in the tribute.

When the men had been dismissed, and we met in the officers' cabin, however, the Captain and lieutenants protested that I had taken an unfair advantage, for it was, they said, impossible that any man worthy of the name should restrain his admiration of so beautiful a lady to the extent I demanded: 'a man whose cock did not stand – pardon the expression, ma'am' – with a bow to Em – 'before such beauty I would not welcome on my ship!' he said.

I asserted however that the conditions of the wager had been particular – that no muscle should move; and they were forced to agree that by the letter of the law, they had lost the bet, and in the end the Captain smilingly agreed to waive the fee for our voyage; at which Em came in to claim that she was of his own opinion, that the wager – while won in its particulars – had been unfair, and suggested that we should nevertheless entertain the company in some way which would reward them, and promised that we would show them something if the crew was mustered upon deck the following evening.

When I asked, upon our being alone, what sort of entertainment she would offer, she replied that while in Naples she had met a person who recalled the *tableaux* shown there by Mrs Emma Hamilton, later the mistress of the hero, Lord Nelson, and suggested that we should counterfeit some of them. Upon my objecting that to present patriotic and sentimental *tableaux* to the crew of a man-o'-war would provoke mutiny, she said that she meant those tableaux privately presented by Lady Hamilton to her closer friends, and on her describing them to me, I wondered whether a riot of another kind might not be provoked; however, the discipline observed by the crew heartened me, and I agreed. Whereupon, Em sent a messenger for Lieutenant Swinton, who she thought could help us; and with his nervous agreement, we spent the next day planning our entertainment.

The crew of the ship, when again mustered, found a

space of the deck now furnished as a bedroom – or at least with a deck-cover made comfortable by a pile of blankets; and as dusk fell and the deck was illuminated by the light of lanterns which shed a romantic glow, Em and I made our bow, and fully clothed began to embrace, slowly becoming more passionate until, in a silence which was almost tangible, we began to disrobe each other and to demonstrate all those familiarities with which lovers prelude a passage at arms.

No sooner however were we naked and in each other's arms, than I drew away and lifted a finger as though to listen: and, leaping to my feet, strode to one of the small boats laid up upon deck nearby, and from it, protesting, dragged Lieutenant Swinton, the young man protesting vehemently, but betrayed by the large ship's telescope in his hand, with which it was to be assumed that he had been watching us.

There was a great laugh at this, and several shouts of a more or less obscene nature, questioning the lieutenant's ability to tell a man from a woman (which indeed might possibly have been near the truth, for in our rehearsals we had discovered that apart from the solitary entertainments of boyhood, he was indeed a virgin).

Now, we spent some time discussing in dumb play the penalty for his spying, and finally, pointing first to myself and then to him, Em indicated that he had the advantage of me in being clothed; whereat there were cries of 'Get 'em off!', the lieutenant continuing to protest – and I believe honestly, for although we had with difficulty persuaded him to take part in our show, upon promises of pleasant reward, now that he was faced with the reality and the faces of fifty rude lookers-on, he would have liked to retract; so his struggles, as I held him and Em divested him of his clothing, were real; and when he was quite naked, there was more laughter as his manly parts were seen to be so shrunken as to be almost indecipherable to the eye. I could not but pity the boy, thinking what I would have felt in his place; and indeed, thought I saw a tear start to his eye, and began to believe that we were too cruel. Em, however, now, clasped his naked bosom to her own, and sank with him to the floor, where he was content to be kissed but, when she began to reach downward, showed unwillingness to allow the familiarity and pushed her away (as we had planned, but I fancy indeed with some reluctance, for I began to see a stirring where all had previously been minuscule and unassertive).

However, in accordance with our scrip, I now came behind the boy and holding him by the arms raised him to his feet, while Em, kneeling before him, approached and began to toy as a squirrel might with a nut, with curiosity and tenderness mixed, first lifting the swelling tool upon the palm of her hand and gently stroking it with her fingers, then feeling beneath, to weigh the cods and examine their roundness, and rising to her feet – her breasts brushing the whole of the lieutenant's body from knees to chest (who had now ceased his struggles and was looking more than content with his situation) – planted a kiss upon his paps, his shoulders, his neck, and finally his lips.

I was by this time myself in a state of some excitement, and I fancy that the lieutenant's confusion, though no doubt pleasurable, was compounded by the apprehension of a large and clearly excited prick at stand against his buttocks (which I could not help, being still keenly appreciative of Em's beauty). I whispered an apology to the boy and, engaging his attention reminded him of the part he was supposed to play, whereat he made a counterfeit of aversion, wriggling his body to escape my clutches, but at the same time making sure that such wriggling brought him into even closer propinquity with Em's body – who now however stood back and pointed to the hatch-cover nearby, which we had prepared for the occasion by fixing ropes to its handles. In a moment, we had dragged Swinton thither and tied him by his arms and ankles so that he lay flat upon the cover – flat, that is, except for his sturdy young cock, which once at stand showed no indication of failing to remain erect whatever indignity he might suffer.

A cheer arose from the ship's company when Em, standing astride the lieutenant's recumbent body and beginning to lower herself towards it, made the nature of that indignity clear; and indeed by the time the tip of the subject man's instrument brushed the strands of gauzy hair which decorated the entrance to her bower, it was sufficiently lubricated by an unusual spending of that liquor which more freely enables entrance, and she was without the least obstacle able to sit astride him, the audience having in clear view the length of his cock as it vanished slowly within her body, allowing him a pleasure now mirrored upon his face (for he had long since ceased to act any reluctance).

There now began a rhythmical clapping with which the men, no doubt in a state of some envy, marked the slow rise and fall of Em's body, to the captive lieutenant's increasing excitement and joy. I, meanwhile, stood somewhat abashed, for I had now no part to play, and entirely naked as I was, and still under the passion of the moment, I saw no way of satisfying myself – until Em, catching sight of me and marking my predicament, beckoned me forward until I stood astride the lieutenant's chest, and she was able to take my tool between her lips (another cheer!). The lieutenant was now in such a state of frenzy that I believe he knew not what was happening to him, for his hands were caressing Em's breasts and sides, my own thighs and cods, quite regardless of sex or inclination; and indeed our hands met and grasped at that very moment when, my energy finally spent, I threw myself backwards just in time for my vital liquor to spirt forth over Em's shoulder (for unlike some women, she was averse to my spending in her mouth), and he, with the shriek of a young boy brought to the finishing line for the first time by a beautiful woman, gave forth his soul and brought Em to her own fulfilment.

This was astonishing to me, and I believe to Em; for it is unusual enough for two lovers to come off at the same time, while for three to accomplish that accident must be most rare.

We had been, I do believe, so occupied that we had forgotten for a moment that we had an audience – until, as all three collapsed (the lieutenant easily throwing off the ropes that had only pretended to bind him), a veritable roar of applause broke over us, in a mixture of clapping and cheering and whistling that the most generous audience at the London theatres would have found it difficult to equal. Captain Pawlin and Lieutenant Blore came forward with a blanket to cover Em, while Lieutenant Swinton (or Tom, as we now called him) and I merely clutched our clothes to our bodies and with an uneasy bow made our way to the Captain's cabin. There, Captain Pawlin was already pouring a glass of grog for Em, and congratulated us on our performance, which, he said, be believed was unusual in His Majesty's Navy, for although sometimes on occasions some members of the crew dressed as women to provide entertainment (which, he said, begging Em's pardon, sometimes ended in more familiarity than was usual between men), he dared swear ours was an entirely individual concert!

Later, he took me aside. 'You are, sir, a man of unusual liberality,' he said, 'in allowing your wife to dispose her favours elsewhere, even in your company.'

'Em is her own mistress,' I replied, 'and I would not dream of circumscribing her.'

'Then, sir,' he said with some hesitation, 'I wonder if you would object should I . . . aroused, I confess, by the nature of your performance, I would wish . . .'

'My dear Captain Pawlin,' I said, 'if you wish to pay your attentions to Em, you may do so, for me; I cannot of course promise an accommodation, for that is a decision she must make. However, my feeling is that you may be successful' – for I had seen Em, on occasion, admire the captain's fine bearing.

He bowed, and shortly afterwards was seen to whisper in Em's ear; upon which she nodded, and left the cabin, when shortly afterwards he got to his feet and, with what may have been a blush or perhaps merely the effect of the sea winds upon a naturally ruddy complexion, made his excuses.

Left alone, Tom, Lieutenant Blore and I drank another bottle, after which the latter rose and took his departure. I expressed to Tom the regret that the first lieutenant was the only one of us not to be satisfied; whereat he said no, that his predilection was for a young mariner whose arse was (as he somewhat crudely put it) a natural funnel to his desire. 'For,' he said, 'I have also tried it, under the circumstances of a long voyage; but I fear Miss Em – I mean, Mrs Archer – has now shown me such an example of female loveliness that I shall never again be satisfied with rump!'

Curious about the practice, I enquired as to its pervasion,

whereon Tom assured me that it was common as between officers and men, sometimes despite the men's objections, who had to agree or be subject to the lash on some excuse or another. But after all, he said, they suffered as much from the lack of female company as the officers, and most found some relief in the embraces of their own sex, while happily reverting to a more normal course when on shore. True bonds of affection, which he would not hesitate to call love, very rarely were formed, though one celebrated case upon the first ship on which he sailed, had resulted in a midshipman and one of the officers breaking ship at the island of Samoa, and eluding all chase, so that he supposed they were still living like husband and wife, and, he hoped, happily so. This was revelation to me, but I saw no difficulty in believing it – nor could I condemn it, for where men are confined together for long periods of time without female company, these exchanges of passion are surely bound to occur while human nature remains a vital force in conduct.

During the remainder of the voyage we were accepted as members of the crew and, while there was much exchange of candid rough humour, every man aboard treated Em with complete respect. There was some slight embarrassment with Lieutenant Blore, for having made the captain happy, and so publicly accommodated young Tom Swinton, she felt it only proper to offer him companionship, not realising that his emotions were centred upon his friend; he rejected her with the utmost politeness and composure, however, and when I had explained the situation to her she was quick to offer him her apologies, and to insist upon meeting his lover – which embarrassed him still further, since it was the custom with the men to ignore such partnerships; however, the young sailor was produced (a pretty fellow, somewhat girlish in looks but masculine in conduct and as excellent at seaman's work as any of his companions), and Em was interested to meet for the first time – she said – one of his sort, the madge culls of our cathedral cities being more prone to concealment than upon ship.

We were permitted to live quietly during the rest of the voyage, though as we approached the end of our journey young Tom's face grew so long that Em persuaded me (without difficulty, for I liked the boy) to sleep on deck so that she could entertain him for a whole night in our cabin, and in a proper – though narrow – bed; his expression, as of a cat who has been given the freedom of the cream bowl, being thanks enough to both of us.

The day before we were due to reach Alexandria the weather turned sour, and in the evening while we beat about and about and made little progress, there were signs of an approaching storm, the horizon being covered with big, black clouds, and lightning breaking from all quarters. About nine o'clock we were obliged by the heavy rain to retire before the wind, the lightning and thunder became terrific, and we feared some accident, as we were now near the shore. I went on deck, wrapped in my cloak, to witness this war of the elements, and found we were now driving along before the wind with all our sails furled except one jib. The rain poured down and the lightning was the most tremendous I ever saw, with only short intervals of total darkness. Our captain and crew were all firm to their posts and displayed much intrepidity.

After the storm had passed, the moon appeared and most of our sails were set again, and with a wind in our favour, by morning we were at Alexandria and received a pilot on board, who did not take the wheel but gave his directions to the helmsman. We dropped anchor about ten, and found about two hundred vessels around us in the harbour, nearly all loaded with corn; only two of them English. We bade *adieu*, with some sadness, to our captain and crew, whom we now regarded as friends (and who from the three cheers they gave as we departed, had similarly warm feelings for us).

The houses of the town, which is a small place and now utterly unworthy its name, are mostly whitewashed and have flat roofs, and a wretched boy conducted us to the only two taverns in the place, both small and dirty, and each unwilling to accommodate us. We went then to the British Consul, who received us cordially and made a room available to us. He said there was no plague in the town at present, and had not been for five years, so he could offer a clean bill of health. There was now no danger in travelling in Egypt, and we could proceed up the Nile without molestation. The Pasha is extremely well disposed towards the English, and his army had been ordered to offer protection to our nation.

The narrow streets are full of people, most of them poorly dressed, and the women veiled so that nothing is seen but their eyes. Some of them are said to be beautiful, which I hoped at some time to be able to prove.

The following morning at ten we left Alexandria on donkeys, with large comfortable saddles but no stirrups or bridle. We travelled all day by the Bay of Aboukir and crossed the Lake of Edker in a ferry, at which the donkeys caused a great deal of trouble and four men had to carry them aboard. We were on the road for almost eight hours, and met with bad fare at a mosque where we were obliged to sleep in common with several Greek and Turkish travellers of a low description, and were awakened several times by noise, and saw in the lamplight that several of the men were in congress with each other, apparently a common consequence of the religion of the place, which denies to men the use of women except in marriage.

At day-break the next day we started once more, reaching Rosetta in two hours, where the British Consul assisted us in hiring a boat to carry us up the Nile to Cairo, a journey which took us three days of steady progress; the wind was sometimes, by the bends of the river, rendered unfavourable to us, whereupon our eight or nine Arab crew stripped to their skins, jumped overboard, swam with a rope to the shore, and towed us till the boat got into the wind again. They then plunged into the water and swam to the boat, where they reclothed themselves with their only garment, a coarse blue shirt. This they did before Em, and without the slightest modesty.

The Arab men seem to regard European women with some contempt, perhaps because they are not veiled as their women are. Certainly they afford them no privacy, and Em had the utmost difficulty even in answering the calls of nature without a grinning seaman overlooking all. Upon seeing her pale face, the fishermen standing up to their waists in water, would haste to higher ground and lifting their tools in their hands, wave them as though in greeting, which she found immeasurably comic (an attitude which further scandalised the crew).

However, we fetched up in Cairo without difficulty, and there took lodgings in a relatively clean inn and were able to explore the city, the bazaars of which are interesting in their busy, even frantic, money-making and trading. The streets are narrow and the houses miserable, and no doubt fine harbourers of the plague. The streets are crowded with all nations and ranks huddled together, from the stately Turk on his charger to the half-naked and miserable Arab. We generally rode on asses, and it required care to avoid being run down by a camel or squeezed against the wall. Upon our first excursion, I saw a procession for the Pasha's three sons, who were to undergo circumcision (or the cutting of the foreskin of their tools) that evening. They were about ten years old, and each mounted on a superb horse. They all looked very sad and held a handkerchief to their mouths. They were followed by an execrable Turkish band.

Expressing to the consul, Mr Twinton, my disappointment at not catching so much as a glimpse of the vaunted beauty of the Arab women, I was invited by him to watch an exhibition of dancing one evening during our week in the place; and was unable to persuade him that Em could be present, for that was never known, he said, and might cause a riot against us.

The place to which he took me was a plain, large room with cushions on the floor on which he and I sat, while the band of two musicians – an old man and a young boy – sat with strange stringed instruments on more cushions at the side. Upon a nod from Mr Twinton, they struck up, and there came in three girls, their faces veiled, but their bodies quite naked except for a small scarf twisted about their loins, and necklaces and bangles on their necks and hands.

Their dancing consisted chiefly of their upper bodies remaining still, but their lower bodies revolving and turning as though scarcely connected with the rest; it was indeed almost impossible to believe that any woman could so twist her hips and rump without the rest of her torso turning to accomodate them. The other singular movement was of the belly, which itself jumped and revolved like some live thing, or as though there were an animal within it, for it sank and rose, circled and panted with an extraordinary vivacity.

I was not especially pleased at the display, nor excited by

the girls, who though shapely were not unusually beautiful; and when Mr Twinton enquired which I would like, replied none of them, at which he urgently whispered that I must make the acquaintance of one, or all would be whipped for not pleasing me; he recommended one in particular – whereat I accepted the offer, and when he gestured to the girl in question she came forward and taking me by the hand led me to a neighbouring room, where she first bowed low before me, then with great deference and care removed my clothing, raising her hands with foreign exclamations obviously mean to express amazement at my beauty, which I took with salt, as being merely compliments she paid to all.

Naked, I stood scarcely knowing what to do, for she showed no signs of lying down with me; but pressing her hands on my shoulders, she persuaded me to the cushions, where beginning at my feet she stroked my whole body with her hands, gradually raising herself so that her own body gradually slid the length of mine, her breasts, which were full and comely, caressing my skin, the nipples almost scratching (for they were, as my fingers told me, almost calloused, and with skin as hard as that of my thumbs).

Having with her hands sufficiently aroused my passion, she reached into a nearby jar and taking some white and greasy substance, spread it upon me, and then kneeling removed her scarf, revealing herself more naked than I had expected, for all hair had been removed from her lower parts, the lips of which, perfectly bare, she set welcomingly ajar with her fingers, then introducing my prick, which by some alchemy she seemed to draw within her as though into a vacuum.

Then began that movement of her hips and belly which had been expressed in the dance, and which now gave me the most amazing and unequalled sensation; for as she moved, so her thighs remained locked about my hips, and my prick, firmly gripped as it seemed by a ring of elastic flesh, could only move with her while my torso remained still – an experience which I can scarcely describe, for though at first painful, it soon became excruciatingly delightful – a fact my face must have revealed, for though still veiled, she seemed to smile, and regarded me with keen attention. I was later told by Mr Twinton that these ladies are educated to examine the eyes of their lovers, the contraction in which signals the approach of the utmost pleasure; and indeed, time and again as I was about to give forth my semen, she reached down with her hand and gripped my instrument at its base, squeezing it almost painfully so that my emotion sank – then beginning again those gyrations which in a moment roused me again to the utmost pitch of pleasure.

At length I could stand it no further, and upon her once more reaching down to prevent the bursting of the dam, caught at her hand, and with a loud cry accomplished my evacuation; upon which I could not – however improperly – but take her in my arms and raise her veil to plant a kiss upon her lips. To my astonishment, the face revealed was not that of a young girl but of a woman well past middle age, and the lines of whose face by no means matched her still firm, slim and attractive body. She smiled, I think perhaps a little wanly, at my expression; whereat I could not but complete my gesture of kissing her, which she received gracefully, then rising to her feet, bowing and retiring. I was joined by Mr Twinton, who had retired with another of the girls; and he handed money to the old man, who he explained was their uncle, and ran the establishment on behalf of his grandson, the young boy musician with him. Upon my remarking on the circumstance of the woman I had been with being so much older than I expected, he explained that the exercise of their dancing – which he called 'belly dancing' – was remarkably efficacious in maintaining their figures, and claimed to have seen a grandmother of almost eighty with, still, the body of a twenty-year-old – a circumstance I described to Em, who was exceedingly interested by it, and made me describe the dancing and to attempt to aid her in counterfeiting it; which when I found it difficult, she wished to see performed; however, this was an impossibility.

But now we prepared once more to travel up the Nile, this time on a large *felucca*, or ship with one huge sail and a crew only of three men, towards Upper Egypt.

Chapter Ten

Sophie's Story

Our voyage from Malta was quiet and peaceful, compared with the others we had undertaken. The captain of the *Colt*, Lieutenant Newman, was a silent and morose individual who kept himself to himself, not even taking his meals with us; while the crew was equally disinclined for our society. This was of no great pain to us, who were happy after the events of the past month to take our ease, abstaining even from love, and merely lying at leisure (when the weather permitted it) upon the decks, conversing little, and enjoying the peace of the wide ocean while gentle breezes wafted us into the Ionian Sea, and eventually into the channel which separates Cephalonia from Zante, with the high hills of Peloponnesus rising above the town of Patras.

We went ashore here to stretch our legs, during the three hours or so while the *Colt* took on provisions, and having purchased some fresh fruit, returned on board and sailed on the evening tide, north past Missolonghi and through the channel between Ithaca and Santa Maura to Prevesa, where we saw a huge full moon rise over the hills which skirt the Bay of Actium.

We were now in the domain of the Ali Pasha where, on landing, the British Consul, Mr Williams, kindly showed us the Pasha's palace (only one of many owned by that ruler). This did not promise well for the comfort of his court, for it was only a kind of barracks, where bare walls and scurvy living quarters were provided for the servants, though we were told that when he visited the palace – which had been only twice in the past fifty years – the Pasha brought with him enormous quantities of rugs, cushions and other furniture, which made the place luxurious; and one room we were shown perhaps had been magnificent, for its marble floor and walls were fine, though now dirty and uncared-for

This was the harem, but for boys rather than women, the Pasha it seems being much inclined to sodomy, something which in this country is counted a merit through the example set by himself and his courtiers, though little practised by the ordinary people – fortunately, for otherwise the land would swiftly be unpeopled!

The Pasha himself is now over seventy years of age, and, having dominion over the whole of Albania, Epirus and part of Macedonia, one of the most powerful men in the Ottoman Empire. We were told he is also one of the most cruel, having raised himself from a petty leader of bandits to the position of so great a ruler, and jealous to protect that position against all comers.

Before travelling to his court, we decided to make a brief expedition to the site of the ancient city of Nicopolis, which Mr Williams assured us was of great fame, and which we should see. We travelled there on donkeys, in solemn procession – Mr Williams, Blatchford and I, and two servants with a basket of food and cooling drinks – sherbet, as they call a mixture of pressed fruit from which the juices are extracted.

There was little enough to see of Nicopolis, that once great place being now buried under the ground, and the few walls to be seen being used for sheep pens and the land everywhere neglected. Nevertheless, it was a most beautiful spot, and walking through some groves of olive to the shore we sat within view of the sea and ate a simple meal, after which, the men and servants being inclined to sleep, I strolled for a while along the coast to where the sound of tinkling bells betrayed the presence of a shepherd and his wards. He was a handsome youth, picturesquely clad in a white tunic (thus displaying what I could not help noticing was a handsome pair of legs) and his black, curly hair hung above a forehead and face which reminded me strongly of those classical statues I had seen at the museum in London, recently brought there by Lord Elgin.

The lad did not hesitate to come forward and stare quite frankly at me, giving the impression that perhaps the paleness of my skin was unusual to him. We shared no known language except that of our bodies, and that struck immediately a common note. When he waved his hand towards a grassy knoll, I did not hesitate to recline upon it, whereupon he lay at my side and within moments was lifting the skirt of my clothing in an attempt to discover whether the whiteness of my skin extended to those areas not offered to his view. This having been ascertained, in course, by the removal of my clothing, it was my turn to be surprised that his body, above the lower thigh and excluding the neck, face and arms, was almost as white as mine (the people of the place considering the light of the sun to be unhealthy). The whiteness of his body was not, however, unhealthy, for his skin was of a fine olive sheen, and seemed to the sight as to the touch slightly oily, so that the muscles of his chest and thighs were highlighted by the sun striking them.

That a passage of love took place between us will scarcely be doubted by the attentive reader, who is by now conscious that while by no means insatiable, I am enthusiastic for the pastime; which was upon this occasion enhanced by the beauty of the spot, the vigour and comeliness of the youth, the warmth of the sun and several days' abstinence on my part. In short, the only source of any discomfort was a large thistle which punctured my skin - but sufficiently near the moment of my ultimate satisfaction to be zestful rather than a distraction.

Scarcely had the youth, having smiled his acknowledgement and kissed my hand in token of appreciation, risen and strode off to collect his straying sheep (all but one of which had strayed, that one seeming a kind of pet, with a white combed fleece decorated with ribbons, which had stood throughout watching us with a keen attention that in a human might have delineated jealousy), when Blatchford and Mr Williams appeared, having waked, and noting my absence come to find me. They could scarcely have been unaware of what had passed, since they came upon me as I was replacing my clothing; while the shepherd, still in sight, had not yet troubled - in his anxiety to round up his charges - to resume his tunic, which was slung about his shoulders. Mr Williams however showed no embarrassment, and indeed asked me jocularly whether I approved of the young men of the country, and having received my assurance that I had been given every satisfaction, remarked that he was not surprised, since it had probably been the first opportunity the youth had had to come at a woman for some months, for he would have been distanced from civilisation while guarding his sheep upon the hills.

We passed the boy again upon our return journey – still unclad, but with the modesty to seize his pet sheep and hold it before him. I remarked to Mr Williams upon the unusual event of a shepherd making a friend of one of his flock; but he explained, with some blushes and equivocation, that during their long separation from humanity it was common for the young men especially, whose blood was hot, to keep a favourite sheep, well groomed and combed, as a mistress – which upon the one hand interested me and upon the other somewhat discomfited me, having so recently lain with a youth who was also the lover of an ewe! However, I reflected that the diseases which a woman could catch of a man were probably a great deal more ruinous than those which could be caught from such another animal, and went comforted on my way.

On the following day we set off for Joannina, in the heart of Epirus, where the Ali Pasha holds his court – for I was determined to pay my respects to the ruler. Mr Williams recommended that we hire a gradoman or interpreter, one George, who was about twenty years of age, and of handsome appearance, though somewhat lean and of a physique which resembled my own rather than that of a full-grown man.

From Prevesa we went by boat to Salora, the port of Arta, where we found the only lodging to be in a barracks next to ten Albanian soldiers of the Pasha, indescribably filthy and rude, who spent their time drinking, belching with the loudest and most signal reports, singing (in a strange and horrible style) and smoking long pipes. They accepted us immediately upon friendly terms and, though I feared they might attack me – there being no other female close by – their eyes seemed to be rather for young George, who evidently took the same view of them that I did, and appealed to me for protection; whereupon by the occasional caress I indicated that he was for my own personal use – which I was somewhat sorry to find he took no advantage of, though it certainly discouraged the attentions of the licentious and brutal soldiery.

Our journey now became somewhat arduous: eight or nine hours' travel each day upon the back of a mule prepares one for nothing but exhausted sleep. George was particularly watchful, and finding that during the first two or three days Blatchford and I were particularly sore from riding, picked some herbs and made a poultice which he applied to our rear parts, and which were of a great comfort. Again, he took no liberties, cleansing and comforting the sore place with the solicitousness of a maidservant.

Upon the fifth day we came in sight of Joannina, its minarets glittering across a lake through the orange and lemon trees and groves of cypresses through which we passed – the lake spreading its expanse at the foot of the city, the mountains rising abruptly from its banks.

As we approached the main gate our pleasure was somewhat mitigated by the sight of a man's arm, evidently recently torn from his body and hanging by a string from the gateway, evidently to discourage thieves. This was a reminder that we were now in the realm of a despot!

Mr Williams had given us a note of hand commending us to the British Resident, a Mr Percy, who received us kindly and ordered that a part of his residence should be made ready for us. Upon my demurring and asking whether we could not take rooms, I was informed that visitors were so rare that it was the custom that they should not be permitted to pay anything for accommodation; so we agreed.

Mr Percy had no wife, and was an unusual figure in the city, for he was taller than most men of the place, with a fine head of very fair hair made whiter by the action of the sun; even after some years of residence he still made a stir when he went forth, and small crowds would often collect to see him pass.

I was sorry to hear that the Pasha was absent on a journey; and when I expressed a desire to see his court, Mr Percy remarked that 'twas impossible, women not being admitted to the palace (other than the close relatives of the Pasha, themselves kept in strict incarceration).

I considered this while I washed myself, and upon a sudden inclination took some of George's clothes and dressed myself in them, and upon entering the room where Mr

Percy was, was amused that far from recognising me he immediately asked who I was, whether I was a member of Mrs Nelham's party, and which room I was to occupy? On my revealing my identity he was at first somewhat displeased, but then at length laughed, and admitted that he had been entirely fooled, for I made a most striking young man. After a while he was forced to agree that properly disguised, and with the utmost care, I could possibly enter the palace undiscovered – though leaving me in no doubt that discovery would be extremely uncomfortable for us all. However, he had a strong sense of fun, and the idea of playing a prank upon the Pasha's unpopular Vizier, Veli Pasha – his second son – was irresistible.

Blatchford was less sanguine, and strongly expressed the wish that I should reconsider; while George was terrified at the idea. However, I had not come all that way to miss such an experience, and next day an Albanian tailor was summoned to provide me with a proper costume for a young man visiting the court – for which he measured George, delicacy and custom preventing my approaching him on such a matter. When the costume appeared, that same afternoon, it was a handsome one – long white kilt, gold worked cloak and crimson velvet-laced jacket and waistcoat; and a handsome figure I made in it.

While waiting for the summons to court (the Vizier having been informed that a young English milord, Nelham, wished to attend upon him, we saw something of the life of the city, including a fine wedding procession and the ceremonies attendant upon the beginning of the Ramadan or Mohammedan Lent, when pistols and guns were fired in every part of Joannina at the rising of the Moon, and the minarets of the mosques were illuminated. All day long the Turks fasted, while the night was a time for amorous visits, puppet shows, jugglers, dancers and story-tellers. Heavy drums were beaten at midnight to call the faithful to the mosque, but the feasting and carousing lasted until day-break.

Blatchford, at Mr Percy's instigation, attended at a Turkish Bath, where he was, he told me, first sluiced in freezing water, then in boiling, then extensively beaten by an old fellow whom they called a rubber, and attacked by another man upon whose hands were bound rags soaked in brine; at which he declined to indulge himself further, made an excuse, and left the establishment before reaching the inner room where the washing took place (by, Mr Percy told me, *uno bello giovane*).

Word having reached me that the Vizier would receive me upon a particular day, Blatchford helped me with my necessary disguise, binding my breasts with a length of cloth so that they lay as flat as possible – which was the only counterfeit necessary, the kilt ensuring that the difference between the male and female form was possible of discovery only upon its being removed, which was not my intention. My hair having been cut short during our stay in Salora, as a prophylactic against the lice, I resembled a young man so closely that (Mr Percy assured me) discovery was surely impossible, short of a familiarity not to be expected.

I was warned once more, however, to be greatly careful, for Veli Pasha was if anything crueller and more obdurate than his father. Blatchford and George attended me to the door of the palace, where they ceremoniously took leave, carefully addressing me as 'milord'. I was then brought by attendants to a large room whose floor was of the finest white marble, with walls of tiles of splendidly rich colour, gold and blue predominating. Here, large scarlet ottomans stood, upon which men sat who were presumably members of the court, they being mostly of a great age.

All nevertheless threw themselves to the ground prostrate upon the appearance of Veli Pasha, a man of middle age, handsome but of a hawk-like visage and with beard and moustaches thoroughly waxed. He received me standing (which was a great honour) kissed me upon both cheeks and then full upon the mouth, and holding my hands made many professions of his admiration of England and the English, of whom he was convinced (he said) I was a high-born example, for I had small ears, which was invariably a sign of excellence of breeding.

After we had drunk sherbet, he invited me to view his harem – something I was most curious to see, for I had heard much of these gatherings of young women kept specifically for the satisfaction of their lord and master, and was interested to see how they appeared and how contented or otherwise they seemed to be.

The Vizier, preceded by two splendidly accoutred servants who accompanied him everywhere, led me along several corridors to a ceremonial gateway guarded by two more tall servants, and through a beautifully wrought iron gate which led to another large room, this time with a fine pool at its centre, with a fountain. Eight or nine figures sat or reclined on the scarlet ottomans about the walls, but this time did not rise to greet the Vizier; nor did the three or four others who were playing in the water emerge at his coming, but continued their sport.

The scene was no more and no less what I had expected – except that all the figures were of boys or young men between the ages of perhaps sixteen and twenty. I might of course have expected this, for I had heard of Veli Pasha's predilection; but somehow the idea had not occurred to me. Nor had it occurred to me that the Vizier clearly shared the view of a number of men of this part of the world – that every Englishman was more interested in boys than in girls, and had indeed probably travelled thence for the purpose of solicitation. At all events, he drew me by the hand around the room presenting me to all the boys, who held their hands together as though praying, and made small bows to me. These, Mr Percy later informed me, were the sons of some of the best families of the city, who were rewarded for the commandeering of their children either by great favour or, should they show the slightest sign of disapproval, by exile – the boys in whichever case being forfeit, for the Pasha and his son were absolute rulers.

Through his interpreter, Veli Pasha then informed me that he had to go to a meeting of his court, and trusted that in his absence I would be pleased to enjoy the amenities of the harem; he hoped later to be able to entertain me in his private rooms. He then addressed a few words to the boys, who made obeisance; and left me alone with them.

Upon his leaving, two of the boys came forward and led me to a pile of cushions upon the floor, on which they invited me to recline. They were dressed in trousers of white silk, the upper part of their bodies bare except for the most splendid pieces of jewellery – necklets and bracelets of gold and precious stones. The rest of the boys gathered around, and we were joined by those others from the pool, still wet and neglecting to dry themselves (the room being warm); all of them curious to see the stranger and eager no doubt to favour him, since that (I guessed) would raise them in the estimation of their master.

Scented water was brought, and my hands and face gently bathed; then the boys began to loosen my clothing, no doubt anticipating amorous play.

I must confess that so much young masculine beauty displayed about me and, clearly eager to please, roused my spirits to an engaging degree, and though I realised the danger I might be in, I did nothing to prevent their fingers untying the tapes with held my tunic, and removing it – then turning their attention to the fastening of my shirt.

Their discovering that my chest was carefully bound somewhat unsettled them; they perhaps wondered whether I had an injury? But on my not resisting it, they began to unwind the bandages. Their surprise when my breasts were revealed, and resumed their normal shape, was considerable – and yet not to the extent I had supposed; it occurred to me that they perhaps believed me to be an eunuch, for the chests of those persons, I believe, sometimes assume female proportions.

However, it gradually dawned upon them that I might not be what I seemed, for they soon curiously and closely examined me, and at length raised my skirt or kilt with curious fingers, revealing of course that I was neither male nor eunuch, but a creature still stranger to most of them – a woman!

Some of them seemed frightened at what they found, even perhaps believing me to be deformed; but one of them in particular chattered excitedly to the others in their natural language, with gestures which I interpreted as explaining what they saw, he presumably having had some knowledge of women before entering that place. Indeed, in a moment he threw off his own trousers (not having been one of the bathers) and revealed himself in such a state as proved he was, though young, a man – and with movements of his hands explained the course of events which followed upon a male and female meeting in amorous concourse.

This had the result that the boys could scarcely believe it and, placing me upon my back like an upturned turtle, spread my thighs in order that they could closely examine how I was made; as they did so I was amused to see that, unaroused before by the presence of a guest they believed to be a man, they now all showed unmistakable signs of carnal interest.

There was no doubt that they all wished to try me; but clearly this was impossible in sheer terms of numbers – or, rather, in terms of time, for there was none who was not in some way a beauty whom I would have been happy to entertain, the Vizier's taste being not for the namby-pamby, and all the boys unmistakably masculine – I believed in natural inclination as well as in appearance. Here, then, was a peculiarly slim and inflective waist, there a breast like a shield of polished teak; here fine hands which commended themselves by their gentle insistence, there an engine of magnificent proportions, which would have been welcomed by any spirited female.

I expected almost to be raped; and was touched by the fact that they stood back and allowed me to make the choice of whom I would receive. This was no easy one, but eventually my eye fell upon the small youth whose reaction to my person had been least surprised: to demonstrate the way of the natural world I would need a partner who had at least some idea of what was to occur! He was also an attractive youth, his mischievous glance promising a familiarity with lascivious tricks, and the limber flexibility of his body suggesting a natural inclination for amorous play.

It soon became clear that the fact that he had been educated to please a man was no bar to his pleasing a woman; not only did he woo me with eyes, mouth and fingers, but when – without too much delay – the moment came for him to present his perfectly formed and firm organ to my *yoni* (as I still called it), there was no question but that it would make a triumphant entrance – as it did, to the mingled wonder, amusement and applause of his fellows, who had all approached as closely to the seat of pleasure as was possible for so many onlookers.

My partner's enjoyment was not so uncontrolled that he did not remain for several minutes in charge of events, the natural and vigorous movements of his hips demonstrating quite clearly the action which his fellows no doubt hoped to emulate – their ambition growing indeed so eager that they soon became jealous of his possession, and attempted to draw him from me; and this failing, began to excite him further by tickling and stroking, until finally, upon one of them thrusting a forefinger into his fundament, he uttered a cry halfway between protest and enjoyment, and gave up the ghost.

Out of a sense of duty I felt it proper to accommodate as many of the boys as possible, and had offered myself to seven or eight of them within the hour (the offer in each case being enthusiastically accepted) when the sound of the gate being thrown open signalled the return of the Vizier. I threw off, to his chagrin, the boy who at that moment was in the saddle, and the rest had scarcely time to dispose themselves about the room – several throwing themselves into the pond so that the water could cool their ardour – and I to thrust myself into my kilt and shirt, before he reappeared.

Upon my rising to receive him, he strode towards me and immediately with enthusiasm greeted me with the customary three kisses – at the last of which I felt not only his tongue searching my mouth, but to my considerable apprehension, his hands raising my kilt and seizing my bare arse, clutching me towards him so that I could feel his masculine organ stirring excitedly. I feared immediate disclosure, for the shape of a woman's rear is entirely different to that of a boy's; but either he had never known the curves of the female backside or in his excitement failed to notice the difference, for all he showed was pleasure in the naked flesh.

Through his interpreter he expressed the hope that I had been well entertained. I had indeed been well satisfied, I replied (which was nothing less than the truth); whereupon he suggested that I be shown to the quarters set aside for me for that night.

I expressed surprise that he wished to do me the honour of entertaining me for so long a period; but – perhaps fortunately – he took this as mere politeness, and strode out along the corridor so that perforce I could do nothing but follow him – to a fine set of rooms where he left me, informing me that he would return in an hour, when he trusted I would be rested and ready to enjoy some food and drink and 'other entertainment' – the upward movement of his bushy black eyebrows leaving little room for doubt what that would be. Indeed, his last glance, which passed discursively over my body in intense admiration, would have been complimentary had I not known that he was mistaken as to my gender.

As soon as he had gone, I explored the rooms: in the first, in which he had left me, there were merely cushions and low tables; next to it, a room with a sunken bath of fine marble (there seemed no other stone permitted within the palace); and beyond that a room whose purpose, with its low couch scattered with many cushions, was clear. The windows all gave upon a central courtyard, and were heavily barred. I opened the outer door – but there stood a guard with the look of a man not to be trifled with. I closed the door again.

Sitting now upon the floor, I almost gave way to tears, though it is not my way: I was dismayed not so much by the prospect of having to entertain the Vizier, but the certain knowledge that his disappointment upon finding me female would be equalled by his fury at being disappointed, for there could be no question that he was capable of seduction by the female sex, his disposition being (I had been assured) indissolubly fixed. I feared, indeed, for my life, for we had heard tales of women who had betrayed their husbands being sewn into sacks and disposed of in the lake; and if that were so, with what at least equal cruelty would the Vizier revenge himself on me?

After perhaps twenty minutes, I had still thought of no way of escape. But then to my astonishment I saw a small black head appear around the corner of the door of the bathroom, finger to lips. It was the boy whom I had first entertained, accompanied by another of the harem-boys, who to my surprise addressed me in a kind of English.

It seemed that before being admired and consequently kidnapped by Veli Pasha, the latter had been a servant to Mr Percy – and perhaps more than a servant, for he addressed me as 'ducky' and 'dear', which is not in my experience the language in which a footman addresses his master. However, I did not care what he had been to Percy; for he explained that he and Basili, my limber lover, had come to remove me from the palace before Veli Pasha could discover the secret of my sex – and incidentally to escape themselves, for (he explained) though enjoying the luxury of life in the harem they were already sated with love of their own sex, and had long suspected what they now knew to be true – that equal if not greater pleasure was to be had from womankind.

Taking me into the bath room, they indicated a gap in the wall where a water pipe lay, through which water was pumped, they said, from a cistern above the harem – which was the way they had come. I pointed out that while I was not fat, my hips were broader than theirs, and it was impossible that I should make my way through the passage. But that, they said, was not the idea – after all, it would only lead us back to whence they had come. No, we should be leaving by the main gateway!

On my incredulity appearing upon my face, Toortie (for such was the somewhat strange name of the second boy) explained that this plan was perfectly capable of success: once we had emerged into the street an accomplice would be ready, prompted by a note they had smuggled out by a complaisant servant, to conceal us and remove us to the British Residency.

But how to avoid the clutches of the guard? Why, they said, by a ruse used by the best thieves, who at night could visit any house and escape even if they disturbed the householder. Young Basili pointed to a large jar in the corner of the bath room, which on my examining it proved to contain scented olive oil, which was used, it seems, to remove grime and to oil the body after bathing. Slipping out of his loincloth, he dipped his hands in the oil and generously applied it to his body. Then, 'catch me!' he exclaimed, and upon my attempting it I discovered that my hands were entirely unable to take purchase on his slippery torso.

I will not disguise the fact that the sensation was agreeable as the two boys employed themselves in ensuring that every plane and surface of my body was covered with the oil, until I was slippery as a salmon. They then turned their attention to each other, and with my help rendered themselves in a similar case – making particularly sure that their masculine parts were generously oiled – which I believed was for the pleasure of having me handle them, but they explained that this was one of the areas of the body by which, were such attention neglected, a man could be caught and held; something Basili demonstrated upon Toortie, which gave the latter more pain than pleasure. However, I will not say that it was with any reluctance that they permitted me to oil those interesting parts, together with their small, round buttocks and slim thighs; nor that it was with much hesitation that I gave them my aid. However, when Toortie – who was one of those boys with whom I had not had connection in the harem – sought to persist in greater familiarity, I kindly but firmly dissuaded him, for the business in hand (I said, persuading him to relinquish what he at that moment had in hand) was too serious. There would be time for play after our successful escape.

The difficulty and danger of the attempt was clear to me, though perhaps because of their youth and the excitement of the occasion it did not seem to concern the boys. However, I took courage, and we three gathered in a huddle behind the door, myself pressed against Basili's back, and Toortie's body, trembling slightly – from what cause I could not say – against mine. Then at a signal all three let out a tremendous howl – at which almost immediately the door was thrown open by the guard, concealing us behind it. After a moment he strode forward into the centre of the room, then began to make his way towards the bath room – when, on silent naked feet we crept from our hiding-place and without his cognisance left the room, running along the corridor to the top of a staircase, then down it, the stone cold to our feet.

At the bottom of the staircase we came face to face with a second guard, who came at us immediately – though without crying out, perhaps because of his astonishment at the sight of a naked woman in the palace of a man to whom the sex was inimical.

Toortie and I easily eluded his grasp, though I felt his hands slide over my shoulder; Basili was not so lucky, for hearing a scream I turned and saw him held by the hair of his head. Toortie was by now out of the door, and the guard bellowing; upon an instinct, from what source I cannot say,

I merely stood my ground and commanded him in a loud and firm voice, 'Stay, infidel, in His Majesty's name, and release that person!'

He cannot of course have understood the words; but something in my tone of voice affected him, for indeed he came to attention and released Basili. Before he could think again, the boy and I were in the street, where we were in a moment hustled into a bullock-cart and hidden beneath evil-smelling straw as it rattled off down the road. We heard behind us the brouhaha; but our pursuers were hindered rather than helped by the crowds, most of whom were entirely aware of Veli Pasha's cruelty and concupiscence, and therefore disinclined to assist his servants.

No one betraying us, we came safely in time to Mr Percy's house, where Blatchford greeted me with special pleasure, though surprised to see me crawl stark-naked from a bullock-cart, accompanied by two equally unclothed young men. Percy, on the other hand, immediately threw his arms about Toortie, who seemed almost equally pleased to greet his former master. No news ever came out of the Pasha's harem, and since the boy's disappearance there had been no sign whether he was living or dead.

It was now necessary, Percy agreed after hearing our narrative, that we should leave the city as quickly as possible. There would certainly be an immediate search, the indignity the Vizier had suffered in being deprived of the boys (no less than his fury at hearing that I had not only escaped, but was female rather than male) being intolerable. Indeed, a noise from the street now indicated that a house-to-house search was already under way.

Hurriedly, I threw on a loose gown and established myself in bed in my room. Blatchford and Percy met the men, who forced their way into the house and announced their intention of searching it from roof to cellar. They began, indeed, on the roof, with a large cistern which we had considered but fortunately rejected as a possible hiding place for Basili and Toortie.

Coming to the closed door of my room, they demanded who was within, and Percy explained that it was a sick guest. They still enforced entry, the door flying open. I lay attempting to look as ill as possible – not difficult, for I was indeed pale with fear. They approached the bed, which almost shook with the trembling of the limbs of Toortie and Basili, one upon either side of me under the loose sheets.

Happily, being told my illness was believed to be the cholera, the men were afraid and removed themselves; and I heard Blatchford explaining to them through an interpreter that there had been indeed another woman staying in the house who had expressed the intention of entering the Vizier's palace disguised as a young man; but she had not been seen since, and he was shocked to hear of her escapade.

Perhaps because of the natural authority of which Blatchford was in command, and perhaps because the people of that country have some respect for the Englishman, they accepted the story and eventually departed, carrying the profoundest apologies from Mr Percy to Veli Pasha for any disturbance which might have been caused by so unregenerate a countrywoman as that unfortunate wretch whom they trusted to see no more.

The men having left, Percy appeared with wine, and he and Blatchford sat upon the side of the bed while we enjoyed it. After a time Percy seemed by his glances to be inviting Toortie to accompany him to some other room, for what purpose I could only guess; but the trembling approach of the boy's hand upon my thigh, beneath the sheets, indicated that his wishes were otherwise – and, believing honesty to be the best policy, I openly avowed to the Resident my wish to reward the boy for his help to me; whereupon Basili, guessing my intention, leaped from the bed and taking Mr Percy by the hand led him from the room, Blatchford with a wink following them.

My intention that Toortie should explore the *terra incognita* of a woman's body employed no remarkable powers of persuasion, and his eagerness grew with familiarity. He had at his disposal considerable and arousing skills – the chief weapon of the catamite, as I guess, being lips and tongue, which he employed with a skill astonishing in one so young. I have found few experienced lovers capable of conveying such pleasure, and am almost tempted to suggest that every man should undergo a course of instruction from a catamite – a suggestion however which I fear would be doomed to rejection by most men.

Despite his own excitement and enjoyment, he thus raised me twice to the pitch of pleasure before, after kissing me finally upon the lower lips, placing himself between my thighs and allowing himself the pleasure of residing there until he had reached his apogee; when with a delighted smile, he saluted me upon both cheeks. In a moment, Basili, returning, found us in a pleasant languor, and affirming (through the lips of his friend) that he had for the time satisfied whatever demands Mr Percy had made of him, curled up with us, and we all fell asleep – to be awakened by the ever watchful Blatchford before dawn next morning, who during the night had arranged for our leaving the city – this time with myself upon a fine horse, accompanied by the boys disguised as female servants and mounted on donkeys.

I believe them to have been recognised at the gate; but that the guards turned their eyes the other way. Veli Pasha, though ruling the city firmly, was cordially disliked, and the temptation to let some victims slip away was great.

So we travelled on towards Saliora, on the Gulf of Arta, and reached it after two full days; halfway there, the boys descended from their mounts, and embracing me for the last time, with delight threw off their female clothes and made their way – with many a turn and a wave in our direction – to a village where some of Toortie's relatives lived, and where, I trust, they still happily reside, living a happier, less effeminate existence.

Chapter Eleven

The Adventures of Andy

Our journey up the Nile was a delightfully slow and relaxing one. On several days there was little, if any wind, when our three native boatmen would either take a line ashore and gently tow us upriver, or would even plunge into the water itself and swim – this having a greater effect upon them, cooling them from the heat, than on the progress of the vessel. This latter exercise, however, they soon ceased after the first day upon which we saw three or four very large crocodiles sunning themselves upon a mud-bank, who at our approach slid into the water. We were informed that they were peaceful creatures, who only attacked when hungry; since however there was not sufficient communication between us enable them to facilitate a reliable decision as to the state of beasts' digestions, they took the safe line, and remained on board.

For our own part, I produced my sketchbook and pencils, and, poor artist though I am, attempted to record something of the scenes we passed, which included pyramids and other ruins, small villages – the houses of which themselves seemed in a permanent state of ruin – and the natives, who for the most part were friendly and amiable, waving to us as we slowly glided past.

For food we depended on what we could find; for meat, chiefly upon sheep, which were sometimes presented to us, we, as Europeans, being the objects of respect and even veneration – or were sometimes bought; they were always live, and had to be slaughtered by a member of the crew, who generally received the fleece as recompense.

We paused at Meidum, Beni Suef, Tell el-Armana and Asyut, and there examined some ruins; more elaborate and interesting monuments were to be seen at Baliana and Abydos. But it was at Dendera that we prepared to be impressed, for we had heard that the great Temple of Hathor, the Golden One, was on no account to be missed, and were indeed eager to examine it. Upon going on shore we asked who was the best and most knowledgeable guide, and after some minutes a tall youth presented himself as Hanif – one who knew not only the temple but the history of it. Engaging him, and our impatience mounting, we set off without waiting for the donkeys we had hired, and were halfway to the temple (which lies about a mile from the river bank) before we were overtaken by our mounts. Em mounted hers and rode comfortably; mine had however no saddle, and its spine was so sharp that I was soon in distress, and walked the rest of the way.

The temple was as impressive as we had been told, with its splendid wall, its fine *mammisi* with carvings of the goddess suckling her son, and the main building supported by six gigantic columns – the great hall having more massive pillars, some fifty feet high and thirty-five feet in circumference, with astrological signs painted upon the ceiling (for the ancients thought much of this art; I wished that my friend Sophie could have been with me, she being a practitioner of it).

Hanif was an excellent guide indeed, with elegant if unusual command of our language. He showed us the Hall of Offerings, faintly lit and mysterious; the Sanctuary, lit only by a single torch, and the surrounding Corridor of Mysteries which, as we entered it, was alive with a myriad bats, making the air thick above us with the fluttering of their wings.

We were then led up one of two great ceremonial staircases – along the walls of which were depicted in exquisite carving representations of the processions of Pharaoh and priests, who – especially at New Year – would carry the gods to the roof of the temple to be blessed by the light of the sun: for as goddess of love, our guide explained, Hathor had as consort Horus, who would visit her annually from his temple at Edfu, to lie with her in a chapel upon the roof of this place – as a result of which their sons Ihi and Horsematawi were born.

Upon the roof we were shown two pairs of chapels, one of which was sacred to the goddess's love, and upon the ceiling of which another zodiac appeared. In the centre of its floor stood two altars or couches of stone, smooth as silk, which – Hanif remarked – were the connubial couches of Hathor and Horus. I asked whether anything was known of the rites which took place there, and he said that yes, these secrets had descended from ancient times through the family of the priests of the time; and that he had heard them from his father, who had got them from his father, and so back to the times of the Pharaohs.

On my asking him to describe what took place, he said in a soft voice that he hesitated to do so in the presence of Em, for they were concerned with the union of man and woman, which western ladies were in his experience too modest to hear. Em, who as usual was determined to know all, remarked that he could not shock her, and that indeed she would be most interested in seeing these rites. Were they ever performed?

Hanif then admitted that sometimes couples who were childless would come here to imitate the rites, in the hope that they might conceive; and that he was accustomed to play the part of the priest at such events. Indeed, there was a couple coming here tomorrow, and if . . . .

But Em suggested that while we could not stay for that, she and I would be delighted to play the parts of the god and goddess should he be content to instruct us – and whispered me to show him some gold, which I did, and which had the immediate result that he signalled to another man who had been hovering nearby, and who now appeared with a large jar of palm wine – for, Hanif said, the gods were worshipped through the consumption of alcohol, besides which (he whispered to me) it, together with the heat of the sun, invariably removed any objection on the part of the female to performing in the light of the sun an act more usually performed at night. I forebore to tell him that in my experience no such encouragement was necessary in this case.

While we had been drinking – in the manner instructed, which involved the balancing of the jar upon the forearm and its tipping backwards towards the mouth – a matter which needs considerable practice to perform it to perfection – Hanif had vanished, and now reappeared dressed in a pure white gown apparently of silk, or some silken material, and accompanied by a beautiful, tall maiden similarly clad, whom he introduced as his sister, and who would accompany him in presiding at the rite.

Hanif then approached me and, with great diffidence, and watching every moment to see if I demurred, helped me to unclothe myself, while his sister performed the same office for Em. Bare as two bodkins, we were then led to the two altars or beds, and encouraged to recline upon them, their surface worn smooth by the bodies of who knows how many supplicants?

Hanif and his sister then stood between us, she next to me and her brother next to Em, and began an incantation certainly directed at Re, the Sun-god, for every moment they raised their hands and faces towards the sky, then bowing towards the east. After a while their continual chanting began to make me drowsy, as a repeated sound will do, so that it was in something like a trance that I saw the priest and priestess turn to one another and, with many reverences, divest each other of the silk gowns, baring their olive-brown bodies to the light - a pleasant sight, for each was handsomely made.

Now, turning once more to the east, the couple laid their hands upon us - Hanif turning to Em and his sister to me and, first touching our brows, then our eyes, mouths, breasts, thighs, knees and feet and finally our middle parts, the incantations continuing. Finally, Hanif lifted Em's left hand and placed it upon his member, which I saw was admirably firm and upright, while his sister took mine and carried it between her thighs; they then returned the compliment, the girl's fingers placed below my cods and supporting in the palm of her hand an object which indeed needed no support.

After this they made no movement - yet a sort of electricity seemed to flow between us, for a tingling spread from the girl's hand through the part it touched and on through all my limbs, while I could feel my own hand positively vibrating with power, and was dimly conscious through the extraordinary emotion aroused that her body was arching as if in the throes of considerable pleasure. Our emotion grew more and more intense (Em later confessing a similar experience), until I could no longer contain myself, and with an involuntary lifting of my loins I bedewed the palm of the beautiful Egyptian with a limpid tribute. Glancing to my right I saw that Hanif had similarly anointed Em's hand; that the two women had experienced a pang quite as intense and pleasurable as ourselves could scarcely be doubted, from their expressions.

I had assumed that the ceremony was now ended; but no. Turning to his sister, Hanif took her in his arms and embraced her, then they both turned to me, and taking me by the arms raised me and led me to where Em lay, apparently in a miasma of gratification. I was at a loss what was expected, for it was barely two minutes since I had given up the ghost, and while never slow to recover my vigour, would need some time to collect myself before I could engage in a new passage of love.

Yet as Hanif's sister passed behind me and stood with her body pressed to mine, and her hands upon my hips, to my amazement my phallus, almost with a life of its own, began to lift itself once more into an upright position. Hanif had now approached Em and, taking her feet in his hands slid her body on the polished stone until her knees were at its edge, and parting them, he laid her person open upon the very side of the altar, so that the girl, guiding me forward, could bring me to the point at which she and her brother could guide my prick within those familiar portals. They then laid their hands upon my buttocks and seemed without force to encourage me to a regular movement which, again, I was not conscious of performing; it was as though some outside force held me, and was using me as a tool in its power, a golden elixir springing in my veins and forging me with my friend in a consummation keener than any we had hitherto experienced.

That Em felt the same force was evident from the expression of her visage, which was of someone experiencing a pleasure keener than was bearable; and indeed as I reached my own climax, a cry almost of pain came from her lips, causing the birds around the temple to rise into the air with a fluttering of their wings, giving out their own raucous cries.

I think that I must for a time have lost consciousness, for

the next thing I was aware of was lying upon the warm stone in the shadow of a wall, my nakedness covered by one of the while silken robes; nearby was Em, in similar case. Hanif sat, clad in his ordinary clothes, some feet away, while his sister had vanished.

Needless to say we wished to reward him for such an experience; but he rejected our offers, saying that the tribute had been paid to Re and Hathor, for the essence of our bodies had gone to strengthen the power of those gods in their land. We could not doubt but that what we had felt was some remnant of ancient magic, nor that Hanif and his sister were indeed descended from those ancient priests whose power had supported the Pharaohs upon their thrones. We returned to our *felucca* in a thoughtful mood.

No incident for the remainder of our journey upon the Nile had such a remarkable effect – though this is not to detract from the wonder of the sights we continued to see. From Dendera we continued upriver with a strong northerly breeze, reaching Assuan and exploring the island of Elephantine and the remarkable buildings at Philae before proceeding to Abu Simbel, where we had to cross an immense heap of sand fallen from the 150-feet high cliffs and covering the gigantic statues of Rameses which stand before the temple there.

We were sorry to find that the door which had been opened with such perseverance by the explorer Belzoni had been again closed by falls of sand; but upon our offering them sixty *piastres* our men cleared away sufficient sand for up to insinuate ourselves into the temple, excavated from the limestone rock. I never witnessed a finer effect than upon first entering this temple, each of us with a candle, the united light serving only to create a dreary gloom throughout, everything having more the appearance of shadow than of substance.

Returning to Cairo we visited the great pyramids at Gizeh and the enormous Sphinx, only the head and shoulders of which appear above the sand. But then with a caravan of two dromedaries (for Em and myself) and camels for the servants, we struck into the interior, for we were interested to explore at least a little of the great desert, taking with us a good supply of green food for the animals, and oranges, dates and vegetables for ourselves. About ten miles from Gaza, we came upon a tented village – the home of a tribe of wandering nomads led by their Sheikh, who was affability itself, especially upon my introducing Em – for these people are unused to the open and spirited appearance of western women, and much beguiled by their white skin.

We were entertained to a supper of meat the like of which I had not previously tasted, and whose origin I did not enquire into, preferring not to know it. The quantities of palm wine which accompanied it made us all more easy, and some dances which were performed by three of the tribeswomen – before an audience of ourselves, the Sheikh, and eight or nine elders (though some were comparatively younger men) was most interesting, allowing Em to see what is called 'belly dancing' and which I had witnessed in Cairo some weeks before.

The Sheikh now asked me about the attitude of western women to the art of love, and whether they were as accomplished as the women of Egypt – to which I could only reply that my knowledge of the latter was insufficient for a judgement. Em, who had as usual been listening to our conversation, claimed herself the equal of any native woman in the matter, and having done so openly to the Sheikh was challenged to prove it, and accepted the challenge – though not realising, I believe, that the contest was to be a public one. However, at a sign from our host a place was cleared at the centre of the tent, where the food had been laid, and a thick rug was spread, with some cushions; the Sheikh then rising, and standing with legs apart and hands on hips, clearly inviting her to approach.

It was not possible to refuse, for fear of offending; though our reception had been kind, we had been warned of the volatility of the tribesmen, and that it would be best to humour them. Moreover, the Sheikh was a fine figure of a man, and I am not sure that Em would in any case have wished to decline the honour proposed. Rising in her turn, then, she approached the Sheikh, and without taking her eyes from his, unloosed her clothing and revealed her body to him – at which a gasp of pleasure went up from the assembled elders, and particularly from the youngest of them – a young man perhaps of only seventeen years of age, though with the full jet-black beard of an adult.

The Sheikh too was clearly pleased at what he saw, and in his turn threw off his clothing, and taking Em in his arms embraced her, the contrast between his weathered and brown limbs and her own – though these now somewhat more bronzed with the sun than would have been the case in Hertfordshire – being an instructive one; as indeed was that between his body and that of almost any European, for though thick-set and strong limbed, his person was almost hairless, lacking that virile growth upon chest and thighs which we expect as a sign of stalwart masculinity.

Now, bending to cup Em's buttocks in his hands, he lifted her, and, she spreading her thighs to throw her legs about his hips, without any other aid proved his interest by pulling her upon his engorged prick, which could clearly be seen to enter her – to the admiration and applause of the company, which now began a slow and regular clapping to which the Sheikh timed his thrusts. This went on for some considerable time – until Em, perhaps considering that some variety was called for, placed her hands upon the Sheikh's chest (not at all panting from the effort), and thrusting herself away, fell backwards so that the upper part of her body, with those enchanting breasts which I still found entirely captivating, showed themselves to the audience, which received too a clearer view (they now to a man standing and swaying as they continued their rhythmical clapping) of the connection between them.

Slowly, the Sheikh now knelt, until Em's shoulders touched the ground – the youngest of the men coming forward and placing a small cushion beneath her head – and seizing her ankles, raised them until they fell upon his shoulders, all the time continuing that jogging motion which clearly gave his mistress as much pleasure as himself. This posture, too, continued for some minutes; after which he raised himself upon his heels, lifting Em at the same time, and fell backwards so that he rested upon his feet and hands, resembling rather a table with four legs upon which Em was now seated – and it was her turn to control the couple's movements, which she did by rising and falling upon her lover's body.

The Sheikh was now, as it seemed to me, beginning to

show signs not of fatigue but of that excitement which is the prelude to evacuation; and Em, I believe noticing the same thing, quickened her motion until her partner lowered himself to the ground, and lay utterly reposed while she continued her motions, the clapping of the company increasing in pace – until with a shudder that betrayed the tension which had mounted in him, the Sheikh gave a wild cry and, lifting her by the hips, gave proof to the onlookers that his pleasure had culminated.

A general congratulatory applause then followed, and the Sheikh, covering himself, kissed his hand many times to my friend, while the three dancing girls (who I had noticed standing somewhat sour faced in the background during the display) came forward with towels to mop her perspiring flesh.

We stayed for only about half of an hour more, in order to take more palm wine and to receive the renewed congratulations of the Sheikh – to Em for her vitality and stamina, and to myself for having the fortune to be her regular companion; then we retired to the small tent which we had been allotted for the single night during which we planned to stay with the tribe.

We both fell swiftly asleep; but I woke, some while later, to hear a rustling nose. Fearful of snakes, scorpions or some other creature, I held up the little lamp which burned upon the floor between the two rugs on which we slept – and saw first a hand then the head and shoulders of a man wriggling beneath the side of the tent. It was the young man who had been among elders of the tribe, and whose open-eyed admiration of Em had been particularly marked.

He saw me watching him, but continued his entrance, finally dragging his legs and feet after him into the tent and, with a glance at the sleeping Em, whispering to me in broken English that he was amorous of her, and wished to ask her to allow him a taste of her body.

I was amused and not angry, for his action was just such as I might have taken in his place; but could not speak for Em. However, I did not dissuade him from trying her, and when he bent languorously over her and placed a kiss upon her breast, which lay open to view, she woke and, as I had guessed, seeing above her a pleasant, open visage, reached up and drew him down to her.

I will not intrude upon their coupling to describe it, except to report that the limited space restricted it to the simplest passage of love; however, it displeased neither of them, and the young man touched his forehead in recognition of my hospitality as, once more kissing Em, he left (whereat she smiled drowsily and lapsed once more into slumber).

We slept late next morning, and were awakened by a murmuring noise as of an assembly. Throwing on our clothing and leaving the tent, we found that the forty or fifty members of the tribe, men and women, were assembled in a circle not far from our tent; and on pushing our way to its centre, we found the Sheikh, clearly displeased, clasping a raw-hide whip and standing over the naked body of a man, tethered by hands and feet, face downward, to four posts driven into the ground. His face was turned towards us; it was our visitor of last night.

Em stepped forward immediately – to be told by the Sheikh that the young man, Mustapha, had been discovered leaving her tent, and must suffer the punishment for consuming the fruit sacred to his leader. She was not pleased at this, not considering her body sacred to anybody – much less to the leader of a tribe of rustic savages. However, nothing she could say had an effect, and when murmuring began at her intervention, I was forced to take her by the arm and draw her back, attempting to persuade her to leave the spot; but she would not.

Now, the Sheikh raised the whip, and without a moment's pause brought it down upon the body of the prostrate youth, raising a weal of red upon his body; again, and again, the whip rose and fell, in each case at a distance of perhaps half an inch from its previous path, so that soon six or seven tracks criss-crossed his thighs and buttocks. His teeth had closed on his lower lip, to prevent his crying out – but with the eighth savage stroke, a moan escaped him – at which Em tore herself from my grasp, ran forward, and threw herself upon the boy's body, receiving upon her own back the lash intended for his.

At this, the Sheikh, furious, threw down the whip, strode forward and seemed about to tear her from the victim; but at the last moment relented, impressed, as I believe, by bravery which would not – could not – have been displayed by women of his tribe.

In short, Em was forgiven; but not Mustapha, who was banished from the tribe for the rest of his natural life. Naturally, we offered to take him with us to Gaza, where engaging a small mud house of a single room, inferior but at least relatively clean and private, we invited him to remain with us until he had considered his future.

On that first night, when we arrived, we discovered the wounds of his beating to be sore and painful, and one or two open and bleeding; at which Em, on his advice, took some herbs which were recommended for their curative purposes, steeped them in water, and bathed his back; which I could not help observing, by the shifting of his posture and the frequent need on his part to thrust his hands beneath him and rearrange his person, was pleasant in more than a medicinal way.

Next evening, he asked whether she would be so kind as to repeat the bathing; but it was quite clear that, the wounds being much recovered, this was more for his pleasure than for any curative purpose, and indeed after a few minutes Em, realising this, began to massage rather than bathe his naked back, and this led to other adventures in familiarity which resulted in a repetition of the congress he had originally sought, and which I had perforce to witness, there being no other room in the house, and Gaza not being a safe place for foreigners at night.

To my surprise after some opening familiarities, Mustapha gently turned Em so that she was kneeling with her back to him, and encouraged her to place her forearms on the ground, so that with her arse raised in the air her cunny stood out as though positively inviting an entrance – which was soon affected, his placing his hands upon her shoulders as he moved. This placement, she commented, gave her much pleasure; it was called, he said, 'the sheep's posture' – at which we were both amused. But it appears that in this country much study is given to the relative possibilities of making love; each is given its name, and carefully taught to young men as soon as they are ripe for congress, usually by one of his mother's relatives. During the next week, to his own pleasure and Em's equal enjoyment, and to my interest he demonstrated some of them, occasionally being generous enough to teach me to perform them.

There was, for instance, 'putting on the sock', which consists of the woman lying upon her back, whereupon the lover sits between her legs, placing his member between the lips of her person (which is opened with the thumb and first finger), then moving so that the very head of his cock rubs against her until it brings forth that liquid which reveals her readiness for congress; at which he completes the act.

Several of the attitudes have the names of animals – such as 'the frog's congress', during which the woman lies upon her back and raises her thighs so that her heels are tucked above the cheeks of her arse; the man seats himself close to her, his thighs beneath her buttocks, and putting his knees under her armpits and grasping her by the shoulder, lifts her upon him. 'The goat's posture' is however less strenuous, for the woman now lies on the ground on her right side, the right leg extended, while the man crouches over her, lifting her other leg so that it lies over his thigh, and enters her from that position.

Being slim and supple, Em found little difficulty in mastering these contortions, though 'the somersault' at first defeated her, for it entailed her lying upon her back and pulling her legs up, keeping the knees straight, until her feet touched her forehead. This, she found completely impossible, until Mustapha showed her a trick which, he said, taught it first to those women who were new to it. Inviting her to don a pair of those loose trousers which the Arab women wear, he then pulled them down until they were about her ankles, and encouraged her to bend down until he could pull the waistband about her neck; trussed thus, he tipped her upon her back, and penetrated her. She found this uncomfortable but, she said, supremely titillating; and he assured her that with practice it was a posture she could complete without the aid of clothing.

Upon my complaining that I was somewhat neglected, he offered with Em's consent to demonstrate something which was a favourite means of congress with many Arab men, though uncomfortable to the women. Fastening cords to Em's ankles and hands, and throwing them over the beam of the house, he raised her until she was a little way off the floor; when, my lying beneath her, she was lowered until her essential womanhood embraced my willing manhood, then raised and lowered by the cords until my pleasure was complete. This was not one of those postures Em was most comfortable in, as I could appreciate; nor was it one which particularly commended itself to me, though I must confess to some excitement at experiencing it, and it was evidently meant as a compliment to me (to whom I believe Mustapha was grateful for my forbearance, though to be honest it would not have made any different to Em had I objected to their pleasure).

If 'the hanging posture' did not particularly please her, she was extremely pleased by 'the congress of love', during which the woman lies upon her right side and the man upon his left, with his bottom leg stretched out; the other leg is throw across the woman's waist, while her left leg is raised to embrace his body. In this posture she found it possible to caress those parts of Mustapha's body which gave him most pleasure, while he could similarly enjoy her person with more freedom than was allowed when the posture was more strained.

I must confess that my own reaction to the remarkable display offered by Mustapha was that it tended to turn a loving passage into a circus display; and while I certainly would not deny that some postures, while initially uncomfortable, gave much pleasure, the trouble taken to assume them and – frequently – the precaution necessary if one's member was not altogether to slip from its proper home during congress, made it impossible for me to enjoy myself as was my wont. However, it was clear from the first that Em found every new position a challenge and for the most part a pleasure, and many is the night during which I was kept awake by the sounds of their experiments – the imprecations when one in error fell off the body of the other, or the exclamations of pleasure when they succeeded.

I was beginning in fact to find the time tedious, and was about to suggest to Em that we should think of travelling on, when one morning a messenger arrived on camel back, and was engrossed for some time in urgent conversation with Mustapha. When this ceased, he took Em apart and was for some time closeted with her; whereafter she came to me, and with some display of shyness – uncommon in her – told me that the messenger had come from the tribe we had so recently left; that the Sheikh had been slain in a quarrel with a neighbour; and that the next in succession to leadership was none other than our acquaintance, who had done her the honour of inviting her to return with him as his consort.

Naturally, I did my best to dissuade her, pointing out that she would no doubt be but one of a number of wives, and that she had no experience of a prolonged stay with so uncivilised a people – but she was clearly besotted with her new lover, and was determined to accept his invitation; and upon her apprising him of her consent, I must confess that his joy was most persuasive, and that after we had bidden an affectionate farewell – for we had become close during the weeks of our travelling together – they were a picture of affection and happiness as they rode away together upon a magnificent white stallion which she had purchased for him. The extent and duration of her happiness I cannot guess at; I never saw her more.

I had by now had enough of Egypt, and returned with the greatest possible speed to Cairo, whence I set sail for Turkey, and after a restful voyage had the pleasure of setting eyes upon the Seven Towers just as the sun cast its morning tints over the gilded cupolas and tall, graceful minarets of the Queen of Cities.

Chapter Twelve

Sophie's Story

Once more we were at sea – and once more I discovered that in degree of noise and bustle a sea journey is not much quieter than one by land: at night, for instance, the piping up of the various watches must not be omitted: a long, shrill whistle first rouses you, followed by the hoarse cry of 'All the starboard watch!' Another similar prelude is the forerunner of 'Hands to shorten sail!' or 'Watch make sail!'; and as if this was not in itself sufficient to wake one, the purser of our present vessel had a bantam cock which invariably responded with a long, loud crow. I was in favour of the death of that creature, but he was a great favourite among the crew, and I could tempt nobody to be his executioner.

In due course we sailed into Porto Leone – the ancient Piraeus – which is so narrow at the entrance that there is only just sufficient space for a vessel to pass. We immediately went on shore, and, for the pleasure of it after some time on board, sent our baggage ahead by donkey and walked towards Athens along the old road, very little of which now remains, it having been destroyed by both Greeks and Turks.

At length the Acropolis burst upon our view and, as we toiled up the hill of the Areopagus, the Temple of Theseus presented itself. Passing along the miserable collection of mud and stones here dignified with the name of a wall, we entered the renowned city, once the seat of civilisation and the arts, but which at present consists of little more than an assemblage of wretched hovels, the principal buildings having been nearly all destroyed. The town has a population of perhaps ten thousand people, pressed within a wall the whole circumference of which one can walk in under an hour. There are under thirteen hundred houses, four hundred or so occupied by Turks, the rest by Greeks and Albanians. There are no inns or hotels, and visitors have either to lodge with private citizens, or find a house for rent. Near the gate, I immediately saw one good house that had been rebuilt, and a little further on, a still larger mansion on speculation – which I immediately entered into negotiation for, and took for a month at a low rent.

This mansion, of splendid appearance, turned out to be smaller than it seemed; however, it allowed Blatchford and myself a decent bedroom apiece, there was a good room for sitting, barely but properly furnished, a dining-room and servants' hall with a mud floor; but the servants, consisting of two pretty sisters and a boy who was a relative of some sort, a man who cooked, and another man of all work, seemed content, and as they came with the house, I was pleased to engage them.

Next day I made a ceremonial visit to the English Vice-Consul, Mr Spiridion Logotheti – a Greek gentleman who received me with many compliments, and immediately invited me to lunch. I accepted, and found that in the absence of a wife (for whatever reason) Mr Logotheti produced his son, Andreas, a gawky youth of perhaps fifteen, who sat opposite me at table. The apple of his father's eye, his tastes were deferred to in all things, and he was clearly spoiled. He paid me the most marked attention, complimenting me upon my beauty and asking whether all English ladies were as well shaped (English women being as scarce in Athens as social graces were with that young man).

We were served *soupa avgolemeno*, or egg and lemon soup, followed by *chtapodi stifado me kremidia*, or octopus stewed with onion, which may be an acquired taste, but I have yet to acquire it. As I attempted to deal politely with the mess, I felt Andreas's foot gently insinuate itself between my own, and with a meaningful sinuosity make its way up the calf of my leg, and even further. For this exploratory purpose, he had removed his shoe, and I could feel his toes wriggle as they reached the flesh above my knee.

I would not deny that there are occasions when such attentions would not be entirely repugnant; but one look at Andreas's face – now a little flushed, so that the yellow pustules of youth stood out even more clearly against the skin – convinced me that I was under no obligation to contribute to his education. Whereupon, still apparently concentrating on the pieces of gelatinous octopus upon my plate, I slipped my own shoe from my right foot, and reciprocated the motion he had started, lifting my foot until it could be placed between his thighs and I could feel beneath my instep a bulge which represented his chief present emotional interest. Lifting then the pepper pot to spice my food, I contrived a gigantic sneeze – the muscular spasm of which expressed itself in a kick which brought a shrill cry of pain from the impertinent boy. His father, bewildered by the simultaneous sneeze and yell, knew not what to think; my own view of the situation however had been sufficiently well expressed to Andreas, who now neglected any further tribute, and after lunch left the room even before I took my leave.

Mr Logotheti kindly procured for me and Blatchford a pass to visit the Acropolis, still under the control of the Turks; and arranged for the Waiwode or governor of the city, and the Disdar, his servant in command of the site, to be sent a present of tea and sugar which would better procure our entry.

After a good night's rest, we set out to see this masterpiece of the world on the following day. Passing the ruins of the Temple of Victory, we soon arrived at the gates of the Acropolis, where we found several English visitors endeavouring to gain entry, which was resolutely refused them. My pass however admitted Blatchford and myself, and we explored the ruins – for the place is a wreck, the *Propylaea* or vestibule nearly destroyed, though the columns are exceedingly beautiful; the *Erechtheon*, whose southern portico is still supported by five caryatides, is in a better state, but the neighbourhood temple, which was until a year or so ago reserved by the Turks as a harem for the women, suddenly fell in, and crushed the whole of its unfortunate occupants to death. The Temple of Theseus, one of the most perfect examples of ancient architecture, remains wonderfully complete, neither time, war nor the hand of man having yet invaded its sanctity.

We refused the offers of several apparently disreputable persons to act as guides, for we wished to explore the place alone. However, towards the end of our walk, we fell into conversation with a Greek of elegant appearance, evidently a gentleman. Mr Eustathios Georgiou, as was his name, was able to tell us much of the sad modern history of Athens, and proved an extremely pleasant companion – a man of middle years, tall and handsome, resembling much those ancient heroes of Athens portrayed in art – as, perhaps, Hector or Achilles.

I invited him to be our guest at dinner that evening; and upon his enquiring whether he might bring a friend – a lady – I was pleased to include her in the small party.

This was the first time for many months I had entertained anyone to a meal, and I was sorry that it must be with a cook whose ways I did not know, and to food of whose attractiveness I was much in doubt (to judge by the dish I had tasted yesterday). However, I talked to the man in the kitchen, who in his bad English assured me that, provided the necessary money was forthcoming, he would do me honour.

Mr Georgiou was accompanied, upon his arrival, by a handsome lady of his own years, introduced to us as Mariana Macri, over whose hand Blatchford bowed low and lingeringly, so that I could distinguish his admiration of her generous figure, much of which was indeed displayed under the loose robe which she wore. Mr Georgiou was himself dressed, also, in the classical Greek manner.

My cook did better than I would have imagined possible: first came *caccavia*, or fish soup; then *rouli me makaronia*, or rolled beef and macaroni, with a sauce of tomato and that strong-smelling vegetable garlic, of which the Europeans are so fond, and of which (despite its lingering qualities) I too have formed an appreciation. This was accompanied by *melindzanopita*, or a pie of some vegetable which I did not know, but which was sweet and pleasant; and finally *mila sto fourno me kastana*, or baked apples stuffed with chestnuts, and a selection of *ghlyka tou koutaliou*, or jams and jellies, which were taken with glasses of Greek brandy. This on top of some good wine, though with a somewhat curious taste as of resinated wood, put us all in a pleasant mood for conversation, to which we settled with cups of very hot, very black, very sweet coffee, drunk here almost like a soup, so full are the cups of the fine grains.

I was most interested in the Greek myths, having read something of them in the library of a house I had bought in London which had been full of books on the subject (to which I was admittedly first led by the somewhat intimate illustrations, for the library was that of a gentleman who had something of a taste for such things). Mr Georgiou, after reminding me of some of those legends with which I was familiar, remarked that while I clearly had a considerable knowledge of the traditional fables, I must also be aware that there were a number of the tables of the ancient gods which were not translated, but remained known by word of mouth, and in a few old manuscripts, their being somewhat licentious in tone.

Both Blatchford and I were interested in this, and invited Mr Georgiou to repeat some of these ancient myths, which he did:

'You will know' (he said) that one of the first inventions of Zeus was the delightful emotion which accompanies the drawing together of man and woman. Had he not done so, who would have found it convenient to spend so much time in the courtship and conquest of the opposite sex? And were they not accompanied by such delicious feelings, who would contemplate the comic fumblings, bounds and itches which accompany that act which results in the propagation of the human race?

'Zeus' error was to make the act of love *too* delightful: so much so that not only humanity, but the gods themselves found lovemaking irresistibly attractive. Zeus himself, as you know, had at least five wives and many mistresses in Olympus and, descending to earth, made conquest – sometimes in ways so devious that they would be condemned in humans, let alone gods – of innumerable women, among them Niobe, Danae, Semele, Europa, Leda, and so many others that it would be tedious if not perhaps impossible to list them all.

'Before I go further, let me disabuse you of the notion – too often entertained by those who do not know the true myths of our country – that it was simply the delight of the capture that first set Zeus off upon his extra-marital adventures. He was, as no doubt you know, married first to Metis, a delightful creature as beautiful as she was wise. He was devoted to her and, having a respect for law and order, was faithful to her for some thousands of years. The problem was, however, that he revered her *too much*. Time and again, when she wished to spend time with one or other of the Muses, or to gossip with Hera or Hestia, he, eager to prove his connubial devotion, would take her off to bed; where, the world and he being young, his inexperienced essays in the art of love bored her to distraction.

'In the end, being wise among the gods, Metis confessed to him that for much of the time he was in her bed she was forced to spend her time contemplating the social order, or calculating how many stars shone in this constellation or that – these being more interesting to her than the coarse plunging between her thighs which was all he knew of love.

'Shocked at this, but reasonable enough to accept the rebuke, Zeus did a little research among the other inhabitants of Olympus, and discovered that things were the same with other married couples – that Amphitrite was bored with Poseidon, while Melia found Apollo a bore. Something had to be done. So, after a long discussion with Aphrodite (who even when time was young, was an expert on the subject) Zeus invented – adultery. From that time until now, wives have complained little of boredom, and the gods have wasted little time in their boring marriage beds, but at the least temptation have taken off for other shores.

'Of course, problems arose as a result of this new pastime. Zeus, for instance, as chief of the gods, declined at first to taste the new pleasure of betrayal. This was partly because he felt his position of authority, and partly because he married as a second wife Themis, daughter of Uranus and Gaea, and the author of the law which regulates the moral order. My own opinion is that he married her because he thought he should ally herself to such wisdom, rather than for any other purpose. But inevitably, at last, it was his turn to be bored; and for the first time he decided to discover the delights of the new occupation he had invented. He took to it like a fish to water, and in time became as eagerly preoccupied as any of his fellows with the chase and what followed it, so that ill became him to rebuke his fellow gods for lying between others' sheets. But there came an occasion when things went too far.

'Electryon, High King of Mycenae, had given his daughter Alcmene, a girl of the most outrageous beauty, as wife to King Amphitryon of Troezen; but alas for them, Zeus, with his insatiable desire for love, set eyes on her, and coveted her. Her beauty, he saw, was as cool and chaste as that of the moon – the flesh of her breasts and thighs white as silver, her hair black as jet, her lips red as cherries; and her calm and reserved attitude was just such as to inflame the hot passions of the king of the gods.

'Eager to possess her, he contrived that before consummating the marriage, Amphitryon should go to war against the Teleboans and Taphians, and with that skill at impersonation which was his peculiar talent, turned himself into a complete replica of the absent husband: his own enormous, hirsute haunches slimmed and refined, the broad shoulders narrowed, the great beard more elegant and tractable – in short, he became the very model of a warrior hero, and in this guise entered the bedroom of Alcmene.

'The latter, brought up to honour rather than to love men, was surprised and – truth to tell – somewhat dismayed to see her husband return so soon; without knowledge of what should be expected from a husband she had been relieved when he had been called away so soon; her virginity was by no means a burden she was eager to lay down.

'Now, lying upon her bed in the lightest of night-gowns, she was disturbed by the vision which burst upon her. Zeus, under the guise of Amphitryon, was clad as for battle: that is, with no superfluous clothing, for in those days and in the heat of fighting men did not wish to be encumbered – thus he wore simply the cross-garters of leather, a brief tunic of the same material, and cuirass and greaves of silver; as he put down the huge silver shield which he bore, he revealed fine muscular thighs which rose into a brief skirt of white cloth; and his anticipation of pleasure was such that this was held up, in front, by a massive tool of godlike proportions (for Zeus did not go so far as to exchange for a mortal prick an instrument which had been tested and tried, strengthened by the practice it had had over the millennia in engaging goddesses and human women in turn).

'Alcmene, innocent that she was, had no notion what this strange sight might be: while she had seen naked men before – as a spectator at the games, where the participants were not hindered by dress – that part which, especially as her imitation husband laid by his clothes, showed itself in an engorged state, had hitherto been nothing to concern a maiden. She was inclined to believe that her husband was deformed, or that some terrible wound had resulted in the thing she saw before her; upon the god-man inviting her to place her hand upon it, she did so with such tenderness and apprehension that the emotion engendered by the feathery gesture still further ignited his passion, and he fell upon her like a thunderbolt.

'She very soon discovered the good that this new limb could do her; and joyfully and prolongedly experienced it, for Zeus before coming to earth had taken the precaution of ordering Helius to quench the fires of the sun and instructing the Hours to unyoke their team and spend a day at home – so that the one night he spent with Alcmene had the length of three, every hour of which was enlivened with pleasurable games and instruction, at the end of which Amphitryon's wife, no longer a virgin, considered her husband the king of men (though not what he was, the king of gods).

'Meanwhile, the battles in which Amphitryon himself was engaged had drawn to a close with a victory over Pterellaus at Oechalia, and he was ready to return home. In order to postpone this event, Zeus had sent his messenger, Hermes, with a notice to delay (because King Creon, Amphitryon's patron, wished him to pay court); this would give the god time to reassume his proper shape and return to the slopes of Olympus, his passion for the time sufficiently slaked.

'Hermes was one of Olympus's most beautiful gods – the image of an earthly athlete, his lithe and graceful body admired even by his fellow gods. He knew how handsome he was, and normally wore only a simple *chlamys* tossed over one shoulder – decoration rather than clothing, for it concealed nothing; the winged sandals on his feet enabled him to travel more fleetly than the wind, and he had seen perhaps more of the earth than any other god.

'Because of his beauty, he was regarded by Zeus with some suspicion – for the greatest of the gods was deeply jealous of any rivalry in that department. Hermes was therefore careful to perform all Zeus's errands to perfection, and when the time came for him to take the message to Amphitryon set out in good time.

'The problem was that Hermes shared with the other gods that partiality for love which led to so many confusions; he had had notable affairs with Persephone, Hecate and Aphrodite, and despite the supernatural accomplishments of the goddesses was equally admiring of human women.

'As he flew towards Thebes and Amphitryon, he passed through a wood, and there (unhappily for him) came upon a deep and dark pool in which a nymph was bathing. Nymphs were, as they still are, remarkable for their charm and beauty, and this one – whose name was Xenaea – was among the most handsome; she had all the charms of the most lovely of human women, to which was added that special bloom reserved for the deities of the forests. She was, in short, quite irresistible – and, not pausing to remember the importance of his journey, Hermes did not resist her.

'The moment she saw him alight upon the bank of the pool – a tall, splendid figure, the dappled sunlight falling upon his limbs, his round, winged hat upon his head, winged sandals upon his feet, and bearing the *caduceus* or winged staff decorated with entwined serpents, Xenaea had no doubt of his identity, and in order to make quite sure that she had captured him, turned and floated for a while upon the surface of the still water, making sure that he appreciated her beauty. The ruse had the desired effect, for if he had not already made up his mind to have her, he would have been caught by the entrancing sight which was before him: the nymph with her dark hair spread out around her, moving gently in the water; the blackness making all the more pallid her limbs, spread wide as though to show him all her delights at once.

'Throwing his wand to the ground and not even pausing

to remove his hat, he held out his arms to her, and in a moment, all dripping, she was folded in them, pierced by that other wand, and the birds in the trees around them, the animals of the forest, even the plants which grew in the clearing around the pool, fell still and silent as they watched a positively Olympian demonstration of love.

'But now we come to the crux of the matter. When he had decided to make love attractive – for the purposc, as he explained, of continuing the race of gods and men – Zeus had seen no reason to confine the pleasure with which he endowed the act; therefore he put no term on its continuation. In due time, pleasure having mounted in the loins of the lover, that fluid spurted forth which carried the seeds of generation; but in contrast to what happens today – when man has to rest, sometimes for too long, before continuing the act – this did not coincide with a shrinkage of that part from which the fluid gushed. In short, a man or a god could continue to make love for as long as he wished. And in this case, so beautiful was Xenaea and so enthusiastic Hermes that there was no reason to halt the mutual flow of passion: on and on he ploughed, pleasure undiminished; a froth of perspiration bathed the lovers – torrents poured from his limbs, while hers blushed with hot blood.

'It was, in short, four days before they were satiated: and even then were finally halted, not so much by that, nor even by exhaustion, but by Xenaea's having to return to her duties in another part of the forest. It was only upon getting to his feet, when the fresh airs of the wood cooled his body and returned him somewhat to his senses, that Hermes realised that twenty-four hours had passed since he should have delivered his message to Amphitryon.

'The latter, not receiving it, had as a matter of course, eager to see his bride, returned to his home, where at last day had broken, and Alcmene and Zeus had ceased their coupling and were lying full of a pleasurable languor upon their bed. The god, more wakeful than his mistress, was warned by the cries of the guard, and disappeared with such speed that Alcmene was conscious only that one moment he was there – the next, gone. But wrapped as she was in a mist of pleasure, she thought in her half-waking state that her husband had merely gone to answer a call of nature.

'In a moment, Amphitryon appeared, standing over her, and to somewhat to her surprise decked out again in his fighting gear. Perhaps, she thought, it was undignified in a King to appear naked before the servants, and he had for that reason once more put on his clothing. However, he now threw it off, and in a moment leaped upon her, eager to follow his victories in war with a victory at home.

'Sadly, he was received somewhat coolly.

' "What," said Alcmene, "we haven't slept a wink all night, and now you want to plunge again between my thighs?"

'It would have been a much duller man than Amphitryon who would not have realised that something was amiss; and upon his consulting the seer Tiresias, he was informed that it was Zeus himself who had entertained his bride.

'This affair had several unfortunate results. For fear that he should be accused of incurring divine jealousy, Amphitryon never dared to sleep with Alcmene; she had to resort to a succession of servants, for the most part smelly and uncouth, and the memory of Zeus's divine rollicking gave her a divine discontent which prematurely aged her.

'As for Zeus, his anger with Hermes was legendary: and yet he realised that he himself was at fault – for if he had thought to put a term to lovemaking, Hermes would not have stayed so long with his nymph, the message would have been delivered, and he could have returned again and again to Alcmene's bed (which now was impossible, for reasons of pride: a god who runs from a husband cannot be said to have improved his standing).'

So it was that despite protests, Zeus waved his divine hand and men were smitten with the curse of premature ejaculation: but only a very few scholars (said Mr Georgiou) know the true reason.

His account had delighted us, and since the evening was scarcely half over, I asked whether he had not another legend with which to delight us?

'Only one,' he said, 'and that grew out of the other – but if you wish to hear it . . .

'The question is often asked, why it is always men who chase after women, rather than the other way about? After all, it cannot be supposed that women find any less pleasure in lovemaking than men? Yet it is rare that we find one of them intriguing, laying plots, conniving to capture a man.

'It was not always so.

'When the world was young, the sexes hunted each other with equal passion. This was true of gods as well as men: Aphrodite, for instance, was certainly pursued by the gods – she had, after all, a beauty which stirred every male creature who saw her; but she also took a wicked pleasure in stirring the desire of any god who came within sight. Few escaped her wiles; and when Zeus wishing to punish her gave her the sweet desire to lie with a mortal man, she pursued them with equal fervour – beginning with the Trojan Anchises, whose beauty rivalled that of the gods, and going on to many others.

'Not even ridicule could rein in her lust: married to the ugly and ill-graced Hephaestus and engaged in a violent affair with Ares, she was at one time caught by her husband in a golden net that he had forged, and displayed in the most lascivious posture to any who cared to look. Unfortunately for Hephaestus, this sight merely advertised her beauty and made the queue of lovers longer.

'The other goddesses, seeing the pleasure she clearly obtained, and bored with their own husbands, joined the chase, and for a time it was open season throughout the world as men fled from importunate women. Remember, at this time no term had been set to lovemaking, and caught by an insatiable goddess a man could find himself imprisoned for months; and after the first three or four days, even the immortal arts of a goddess paled – moreover, several businessmen were ruined by being kept from their ledgers, wars were lost because the captains of armies were locked in a softer combat, and students remained ignorant because their masters were receiving lessons of a different kind.

'At length, as I have told you, Zeus with one gesture reduced the unrestricted length of a single engagement to a finite time. His fellow gods and fellow men were on the whole not dismayed – they could still spend an hour or so in pleasurable dalliance, paying the tributes of kisses and caresses to their mistresses and, if upon the final engagement their pricks were not possessed of everlasting power, the pleasure was the same; and there was time left for other kinds of sport, or even for business. (The edict gave great relief, too, to those *ephebes* like Ganymede, Zeus's favourite, who were the subject of admiration from their own sex; whereas in the past consummation had frequently lasted so long that they were incapable of sitting down for some days, now things were better ordered.)

'However, the women were less happy. They had not been constrained by Zeus to a limited time of enjoyment, and were perfectly happy to lie with a lover not merely for hours, but for days – even weeks. Now, after a mere two or three hours, their lovers would leap from bed and away.

'Such was their disgust at the change of manners that they with one gesture declined to hunt and became instead the hunted; and, ever since, it has been man who has been the pursuer and woman the pursued – for, they said, why should we take the trouble to purvey our wares, to spend days or weeks in the seduction of men, when we are too often left unsatisfied?'

Mr Georgiou ceasing his tale, we were entranced with it, and thanked him.

Was it the case, I asked, that the Greek people more closely followed the examples of the ancients than was the case with us?

'I cannot say,' he replied, 'for I have never travelled beyond these shores. But certainly there is little hesitation, when temptation offers a delightful companion – as yourself, my dear Mrs Nelham . . .'

'Nor,' said his companion, 'do the ladies of this city regard it as fair that the men should always be the seducers; those of us who appreciate the art of love are not so sated with the compliments of our fellow Athenians that we do not wish to offer hospitality to handsome strangers –' with a look at Blatchford which spoke such volumes that he immediately raised her hand to his lips, then pressing them to the upper part of her bosom – whereupon placing her hand at the back of his neck and throwing back her head, she encouraged him to find with his lips the nipple of one full breast.

Mr Georgiou was, I believe, despite our applause at his somewhat indelicate narrative, a little nervous that I should reprove Mariana for her forwardness; but far from it, I looked to him for similar entertainment. For some time I had felt in need of the comfort of an elder lover – Blatchford, be it remembered, was only a year or two my senior; while my loving exchanges had recently been exclusively with boys even younger. Mr Georgiou, while by no means old, was no youth; there were even some grey hairs among those black upon his head – and as, from the corner of my eye I saw Blatchford and Mariana sink to a reclining position upon the couch where they sat, I reached out my hand and placing it upon the gentleman's arm, asked whether he would not do me the honour of embracing me.

He immediately smiled, pleased, I have no doubt, at my honesty; and looked about as though he expected to be led to another room. However, this would be cooler than the bedrooms – which were inappropriately on the top floor of the house – and so with a smile I sank to the floor, where I looked up at him as he removed the full shirt and narrow trousers which were his costume.

From where I lay, the foreshortening (as artists call it) presented me with an admirable view of the part I was most interested to greet; which, with a shock, I realised was surrounded with a decoration of entirely white hair. My surprise must have shown for, kneeling, he assured me that this denoted no lack of power – or, if his vigour was perhaps not what it had been in his youth, there were other means of satisfying my appetite – which proved the case, for having raised my gown and slid it from beneath me, he began by turning me upon my stomach (somewhat to my discomfort, fearing that he was about to address me in a strange manner) and with the utmost lightness began to stroke my entire body, starting at the nape of the neck, and drawing his hands down my back, over my buttocks, down my thighs to my ankles – then up again, and so down.

After a while, the entrancing tickling this roused became so pleasant that involuntarily I threw my legs apart, whereupon the tips of his fingers made their way between, to linger there in an equally inspiriting fashion.

It was not long before I felt bound to turn, and doing so was delighted to see that with full vigour a promising instrument now showed itself amid the cloud of white hair; yet he would not permit me to touch it, but continued to stroke my body, now encircling my breasts, catching my tight nipples from time to time between a finger and thumb, and now concentrating on those lower lips which were positively inflamed with longing - heightened rather than assuaged, in due course, by the longer and more liquid caresses of lips and tongue.

In short, by the time he drew himself up and swung his body into the position from which he could fully engage me, I was as ready for the attack as Alcmene had been with Zeus, and could not forbear, as I felt him enter me, to throw my legs about him and lock my ankles together behind his waist.

The ensuing ride was one of enviable distance; indeed, in the middle of it, I was amused to catch sight of the rueful face of Mariana peering at us, together with those of an embarrassed Blatchford; for it seemed that he had concluded his passage of love considerably earlier than she would have wished.

Soon after, however, with a second wind he engaged her again; to expire only a moment after Mr Georgiou in silence made a final thrust of his hips, bringing about (I suppose) his own satisfaction only a moment after he had raised me to the third or perhaps even the fourth ecstasy.

Blatchford informed me later that his lady had equally delighted him, whose tricks were so lascivious that they had brought about his premature decease. So we both had cause, after bidding our lovers farewell - with hope of further meetings - to view with complacency our introduction to the land of such poignant legends and such stoutly satisfactory reality.

Chapter Thirteen

The Adventures of Andy

Approaching the great city of Constantinople, our ship sailed close under the lofty wall of the seraglio garden, separated from the sea only by a narrow wharf. Shady groves, bowers of oranges, roses and jasmine, lofty cypresses and wide spreading plane trees embosom the elegant pagoda-shaped buildings which comprise the kiosks of the palace of the Sultan and his women's apartments, all painted in bright colours which sing in the sunlight.

Near one of the seraglio gates is erected a large wooden house where disobedient slaves await their punishment – either by garrotting or decapitation, the bodies then thrown into the sea; or sometimes women who have displeased, or even merely failed to please their masters are sewn into sacks and thrown, weighted, into the River Bosphorus, where divers have seen them upright, gently swaying in the tide inside their sackcloth coffins.

But all this was far from my thoughts, for the scene was much more one of beauty, especially when, sailing around the promontory of the Golden Horn, all the beauties of Stamboul, Pera and Scutari burst upon the view. Looking towards the seraglio point is the richly gilded palace of the Sultan, with a gate that glitters like polished gold, surrounded by trees. Further distant is St Sophia and the other mosques, whose golden domes and graceful, tapering minarets tower above the painted buildings, dark cypresses and fine plane trees which clothe the seven hills. Thousands of roses hang on the trellis work which adorns the gardens of the palaces and villas along the shore, while the harbour teems with ships, numberless small boats called *caiques* – narrow pointed canoes with long beaks – shuttling between them and the shore.

Upon our anchoring, I took one of these, into which the

crew piled my small amount of luggage and, landing, invited one of the men who lazed upon the waterfront (among many others who were conducting business with frenzied activity) to conduct me to a house where I could lodge. This man (dressed as they all were, in a red hat or *fez* just large enough to cover the top of his head, a thin transparent shirt with large sleeves, and cotton drawers fastened to the knees) led me immediately to a comfortable lodging-house kept by one Giuseppe Vitali, where I took a suite of three rooms upon the ground floor – an outer sitting room, a bedroom and next to it a room with a small sunken bath of marble (this a surprising luxury in an European house, but common here, where cleanliness is a prerequisite).

Mr Vitali, finding me a stranger to the town, offered his servant, Ali (a name as common in these parts as Tom, Dick or Harry) to show me the sights – an offer which I accepted immediately and with pleasure. A wily, thin man who clearly knew his way about, he took me first to the bazaars – narrow streets crowded with traders who bought and sold anything which came to hand, and which had an extraordinary smell, proceeding not from any misdemeanour but from the many scent and perfume stalls at which attar of roses, jasmine, musk, lemon essence, sandal wood and all the sweet odours that form part and parcel of a sultana's toilet were to be bought. From time to time a man would come forward and smear portions of these delicacies on my face, hands, lips, to induce me to purchase.

I made a delicious lunch from Smyrna figs, dried dates, plums and cheese, which was a pleasure; then Ali stated that he knew of the performance, that afternoon, of the ceremony of the Bride's Bath, if I would care to see it.

Upon his explaining what this was, I was not hesitant in acceding to his offer, upon which he led me to a large house where, upon his passing to the attendant a handful of coins, we were admitted to a balcony from which, through a grill which concealed our presence, I looked upon a fine, large room with marble sofas, a sunken bath at its centre.

Ali explained that two days before, a young virgin had been chosen for a rich man's bed, and this ceremony was the ancient method of preparing her for the honour. About the room sat perhaps thirty handsome girls, who I was told were themselves all virgins and who, upon the present ringing of a bell, very hastily threw off their clothes, appearing without other ornament or covering than their own long hair, braided with ribbons. Two of them now proceeded to the door which when it opened admitted the chosen girl, conducted by her mother upon one side, and a middle-aged lady upon the other.

The two older ladies were elegantly but soberly dressed. The bride, however, who seemed perhaps about seventeen, was very richly clothed, shining with jewels; but, led to the centre of the room, was soon divested of her clothing by the other girls, appearing with them in a state of nature. Two of her friends now produced silver gilt pots of perfume and began a procession which passed around the room, the others in pairs joining behind, the leaders singing a strange-sounding song (a song of compliment on her beauty, Ali explained to me in a whisper), followed by the others in chorus.

It would not be easy to convey the beauty of this sight, most of the girls being extremely beautiful and shapely, their oiled bodies perfectly smooth and polished by the frequent use of bathing (a passion in this city both for men and women).

The procession coming to an end, the bride was led to a central couch and placed upon it by her smiling companions. Now began the ceremony of preparing her body for her lover's admiration. It appears that while they are virgin, the hair upon the bodies of the girls of this place is allowed to grow in a natural way. But a girl presenting herself as a bride, whether to the Sultan or to a humbler groom, must strip the hair from every place except her head – the same rule applying to her groom, for once puberty is passed it is regarded as a sin for man or woman to have any hair upon the body. The removal of such hair was the custom which was now be to observed.

In a moment, a matron came forward bearing a quantity of *rusma*, a paste made of a certain mineral with that name, like to the dross of iron, reduced to a powder and mixed with lime and water. Several of the bride's friends approached and, each taking a small quantity of this paste, applied it lovingly beneath the armpits and between the thighs – where it was left for only ten minutes and upon the parts being washed with hot water, the hair was fetched off cleanly and apparently painlessly. There is a science, it seems, in removing this paste at just the right time, for its strength is such that were it left too long sticking on the place, after eating off the hair it would corrode the flesh. *Rusma* is an enormously valuable thing, and being in much use in Turkey, yields the Grand Signor of the place a considerable revenue.

Having disposed of the private hair, the maidens now turned their attention to the other parts of the body, for not a single hair must be left – not in the nostrils or the ears, for instance, whence they are removed by tweezers. This having been done, each of the girls approached and in turn made the most complete and intimate inspection of the bride's person, the tender appreciation of whose beauty could scarcely have been exceeded by the most interested bridegroom; and I was assured that indeed this practice, especially among the ladies of the Sultan's harem, deprived of the carnal company of men, led to many cases of lesbian attachment between them.

No man who could help it, I was informed (as we watched the delightful ceremony below) would allow his wife to attend a public bath if he could afford a private one; but otherwise, it is essential not only for sanitary reasons, but on religious grounds. The baths are owned by men, but they do not do the washing themselves, rather employing women to wash those who come without a slave or servant. But most women go in parties of perhaps twenty at a time, and wash each other in a friendly manner – one neighbour with another, and sister with sister. But it is common knowledge that as a result of this familiarity in washing and massaging, women fall very much in love with each other, so that one often sees a woman in love with another just like a man and woman – and Ali informed me that Greek and Turkish women, on seeing a lovely young girl, seek occasion to wash with her just to see her naked and handle her – many women going to baths outside their own neighbourhood to do this, although the custom is to go to the baths in one's own district. So women often stay together at the baths (if they go early in the morning) until the dinner hour, and if they go after that they stay nearly until evening.

We had to leave the house before the ceremony was quite over, for had we been discovered by leaving at the same time as the women there might have been the most unpleasant consequences. It was difficult for me to remove myself from my vantage-point, however, for it is remarkable how much more naked a woman appears when she has been depilated; and Ali, by his observation of my careful movements, clearly realised the state of arousal which I was in, for he asked whether I would not like to accompany him to a house of pleasure nearby. This was something that for the time I denied myself, however, for I wished to acquire a personal servant for the time I was in Constantinople, and asked Ali's advice upon it, for I wished to do so immediately.

It would not, perhaps, have occurred to me to buy a slave, had not Ali taken it for granted that I should do so. It seems that this was not only convenient, but would be an excellent investment, for a girl or boy who has been bought untrained can, when he or she has been taught the rudiments of service, be re-sold for a considerably higher sum.

I was taken, then, to the slave market, in a square yard three sides of which were occupied by low stone buildings with wooden sheds projecting in front. These were divided into rows of cells, each having a window and door opening into the wooden enclosure. Within these dens – and they exactly resemble the cells usually occupied by wild beasts – the slaves are kept, either penned up in the inner compartment or lying about like cattle in the open space in front.

All the slaves on offer, many of them most miserable in appearance, appeared to be Nubians. Many years ago, they were more commonly white – from Georgia and Circassia – but lately have been brought from Egypt, Abyssinia and Central Africa; according to Mohammedan law, slaves captured in war become the absolute property of the victor, and, as any title to property could be transferred, the slave-dealer having procured his slaves from an African chief or Arab kidnapper can legally commit his right to any Mohammedan customer who cares to pay the price. These slaves, Ali told me, came chiefly from the upper reaches of the White Nile, from Kordofan, Darfur and Dongola, as well as the Bagirimi district to the north-east of Lake Chad, and had arrived only within the past day or two (the rate of sale being speedy), packed into tiny boats, or made to cross the Sahara partly on foot and partly by camel, reaching the coast at Tripoli, Tunis or Morocco. Several of the boys to be seen looked particularly sick, and Ali explained that they had probably been castrated during the journey, for sale as eunuchs.

The state of the poor souls for sale was such that I wished that I could buy all of them; when I think of the very worst conditions under which I worked as a servant in England and compare them to that cattle market, I was full of pity for the slaves – which increased as I continued my inspection, for they were dirty and clothed only in ragged blankets – though I must confess that (I suppose because they were born to no other inheritance) they chattered unconcernedly among themselves, and were to all appearances not unhappy.

As I stood gazing at the scene, the ruffian keeper (and never did a vile, debasing occupation stamp its character more indelibly on the physiognomy of man) led one of the black victims forth to meet the speculating caprices of a fat old Turkish man.

She was a young woman who could scarcely have been more than seventeen or eighteen years old and, as the keeper stripped the blanket from her, leaving her standing proudly, altogether without covering yet without shame, I could see that she was extremely handsome, her body firm and upright, plump without being fat. The keeper began – though of course I could not understand his language – to praise the firmness of her muscles and the robustness of her limbs, at the same time pinching her tender flesh so that she could not but cry out in pain. He then tore down her eyelids to exhibit the healthiness of her eyeballs, and wrenched open her mouth to prove that he practised no deception in speaking of her age.

The man, her putative owner, made free too in feeling her body, passing his hands over her breasts and thighs without caring to hide his pleasure in such an action, and with a slavering look that convinced me that if he bought the girl her duties would certainly not be confined to the kitchen. Now he began to haggle like someone purchasing a cow in the cattle market. I asked Ali how much he was offering, who said that he was standing out for a price of one thousand *piastres*, or only about twenty pounds – at which almost without thinking I stepped forward and offered fifteen hundred *piastres*.

It was the worst thing I could have done, for a Turk hates to be bettered by a foreigner, and he immediately increased his offer, and though I topped him to the amount of two thousand five hundred *piastres*, I could go no further, and he clinched the deal, and seizing the girl by the forearm, scarcely giving her the time to cover herself with her tattered blanket, made off into the crowd.

Ali, who had been plucking nervously at my arm during the barter, now informed me that the buyer was Mustafa, one of the richest and most avaricious men in the city, who would have been determined that I should not, especially being a white man, get the better of him; but agreed with me that he was a villainous creature, and himself pitied the girl, who would (he said) be made to serve her master in bed, and then upon his becoming bored with her, would either be sold off cheaply or simply disposed of – by which he seemed to mean murder.

I made some effort to interest myself in choosing another slave for myself; and was shown a window from which a solitary female looked, whose head was covered with a linen veil. On seeing our approach, she looked at me through its folds, then instantly removed the veil, and a pair of brilliant dark eyes shed their lustre upon us from a pale face. Nowadays, Ali told me, there were seldom white slaves for sale in the market, and when they do appear they are disposed of at a great price; the beautiful captive into whose eyes I gazed was a Georgian, neither bashful nor timid, who saluted me with smiles, letting down her raven locks and trying to captivate me by making her beauty appear to the greatest advantage. She had been, Ali told me, exposed to sale for several days, but no one had offered to purchase her, the sum demanded being exorbitant, for her proprietor was a rich man and could afford to wait until someone consented to put down the five thousand *piastres* at which he valued her.

My thoughts, however, despite the great variety of choice,

continued to revolve about the beautiful young girl who had been dragged away by Mustafa; and on my telling Ali that I might perhaps return tomorrow to the market, he escorted me back to my quarters, where during the evening again and again I could not restrain myself from thinking of the poor girl and the fate which awaited her. Finally, I asked Ali where the fat merchant lived – information which he was able to give me, for the man was well known. Later in the evening, consulting a map of the city which I had acquired, I found myself making my way to the house of Mustafa: which lay, as I found, behind tall walls surrounded by trees, with only one door, stout and unforceable (even had I thought of breaking in).

It was now beginning to be dark, and I had made up my mind to return to my lodging and attempt to forget the whole episode, when from over the wall I heard what seemed to be a cry of pain, and in a female voice. Almost without realising what I did, I caught at a low branch of a tree and in a moment had swung myself up into its branches and was able to look over the wall, which gave into a garden beyond which the white walls of a villa could just be seen.

In another moment, and equally without rational consideration (which indeed would have been death to such a project, my being a foreigner in a strange place – even now, a Turk for mere sport may reach for a pistol and shoot at any white person he happens to observe while looking out of his window) I swung myself to the top of the wall, and had dropped quietly within the garden.

The first thing I did, to secure my retreat, was to feel my way in the increasing gloom along the wall to the door, and to unbar it – a difficult feat to perform silently, for there were no less than four massive bars, and a lock to be turned (from which I removed the key, dropping it into my pocket).

I then made my way, walking upon the grass at the side of the pathway, towards the villa and a lighted window which I could see there, and which proved unguarded by shutters, open to the cool air. Standing in the shadows, I looked within, and saw immediately the fat Turk, sitting upon a pile of cushions with his back to me. Before him, and facing the window, stood two enormous black men holding between them the unclad body of the slave-girl. Far from a willing captive, her eyeballs were revolving, their whites shining, and her teeth were gleaming as she snarled at her torturers – for so I presumed they were, since one held a whip in his hand, and there was a mark upon her belly which had undoubtedly been caused by a stroke of it.

I had assumed that the two men were eunuchs, having heard that these were much employed in private houses, especially where the men were jealous of the honour of their wives and conscious of the continual inclination to sensuality underlined by the sultriness of a hot climate. However, I was soon disencumbered of the notion, for at a signal from Mustafa, the man upon the right hand side let go of his victim, whose arms were both seized by his accomplice, twisting them behind her back, while the first undid the knot which fastened his loincloth and, dropping it at his feet, revealed not only the fact that it was his sole garment, but that – far from his being emasculated – it had covered an organ of generation whose proportions were in complete accord with his size and strength.

It was clear to me, by the way that the girl was now held – bent backwards so that her middle section was thrust outwards – what was to follow – either because Mustafa enjoyed watching the deflowering of a virgin, or because he could not himself perform the act. However, the naked man, evidently feeling no emotion of fellowship with his countrywoman, now strode towards her and, while his comrade grinned and held her arms more tightly, ran his hands from her shoulders over her breasts and belly until he could grasp her legs at the knees and with an effort (for she still fought with a silent determination) tore them apart, baring her not only to his sight but to the attack of his tadger, with which he prepared to spear her as a fisherman would spear a fine and shiny fish.

The sight provoked me to actions which were at best extremely unwise, and at worst might have been fatal. Groping at my feet, I happily found a sharp stone and, gripping it in my right hand, I leaped with one unthinking movement through the open window and in a moment had landed with my left arm about the old man's neck and the stone pressed into the small of his back. Whether the simple silk shift which he wore was his usual garb in the warmth of the evening, I do not know; but it was fortunate, for he felt immediately the sharp edge of the stone, and as I had hoped, believed it to be a knife. The two men dropped the girl, who immediately backed away from them; but when they moved towards me, a simply applied pressure to the stone resulted in a squeal from their master, who then uttered a command which stopped them in their tracks.

I was now very much under the disadvantage that I commanded no language likely to be understood by anyone else present; nor did I wish to reveal my nationality (the old man being unable to see me). By smiling at the girl and moving my head, I persuaded her to sidle past the two men and make her way to my side; I suppose that she thought that whatever might be the perils of an attempted escape, they would be no worse than the fate accorded by any misguided loyalty to her owner.

On finding her at my side, I let go my hold on the throat of the old man and, giving a final jab with the stone (at which he screamed like a stuck pig, though it could not have done more than barely puncture his skin) jumped to my feet, and gripping the girl by the hand was in a moment out of the window and running towards the garden door. The girl matched me stride for stride. At the door I thrust her through it, produced the key from my pocket, turned it in the lock behind her, threw the key as far as I could into the blackness of the night and with a run and a leap caught a branch which again enabled me to reach the top of the wall and drop to the ground beyond it.

The villa stood in a part of the city not densely populated, and we were able to run for some distance in the shelter of trees and bushes without anyone seeing us. But then, the number of houses gradually thickening, came the moment when I realised that my appearance with a naked Nubian slave at my side would provoke some comment – not at the fact of her being a slave, but because, for a people devoted in so many ways to the exercise of sensuality, the Turks are extremely modest, and it is not the custom with them to display their bodies in public.

Happily I was myself wearing one of my shirts from home, generously cut in order to help guard the lower person

MEMO

Hotel Pulitzer

prinsengracht 315-331
1016 GZ amsterdam, holland
phone 020 - 228333, telex 16508
telefax 020 - 276753

Best Western

from cold during the winter – indeed, I had been about to discard it altogether as too warm for these climates, but providence had prevented it. Now, hastily stripping it off, I thrust it over the girl's head, when it fell almost to her knees, and looked only slightly different to the long white dresses often worn by the Arab women (though more commonly by their men).

This left me naked to the waist, but I simply had to trust that this would be excused as a westerner's eccentricity; and indeed though I received one or two glances of pure antagonism, we safely reached my rooms, where the girl, immediately upon my closing the door, abased herself to the ground, and seizing my feet began to kiss them in gratitude.

I raised her at once, of course, and by gesture tried to make her understand that too great a display of gratitude was inimical to me; but in the end the barrier of language appearing too great, was forced to send for Ali, who upon entering the room and seeing the girl – now standing modestly against the wall, still dressed in my shirt – went immediately as pale as was practicable in someone of his race.

At his enquiry I had to confirm that this was the girl whom I had failed to buy at the market; and that I had obtained her – by subterfuge, I explained – from Mustafa, who I had to confess was probably not especially delighted at her decision to leave him. However, I declined to respond to Ali's expressions of fear at what might be the consequence – and he himself admitted that it was extremely unlikely that her former owner could identify the girl; and while he might remember me from the market, it would be excessively difficult for him to prove anything against me – while his two servants would have an equal difficulty, for to them it seemed that all westerners looked alike!

My mind considerably eased, I asked Ali to discover the girl's name – which proved to be entirely unpronounceable; so I gave her the name of Sally, which brought for the first time a smile to her lips, seeming to her to be irrepressibly comic. Ali also explained, at my bidding, that I would be happy if she would care to remain as my servant – inviting him to use that term rather than the word for 'slave' – and that upon my leaving the country I would give her sufficient money to enable her to set herself up in some quiet way of business, or at least to make it unnecessary that she should again have to offer herself as a slave.

She was – unsurprisingly – delighted by the offer, and Ali undertook to explain to her what would be her duties – which indeed would be light enough, consisting of looking after my wardrobe, serving my food, keeping my rooms clean.

It now occurred to me that I had made no arrangement for sleeping accommodation for Sally; but both my sitting room and bedroom were generously provided with cushions, and it would be easy to make a pile of them upon which she could sleep for the night. I began to do this, but she, concerned that I should do nothing unbefitting a master, seized them away from me and herself piled them into a corner – though to what purpose, I doubt she knew.

I then went into the bathroom and removing my clothing began to sponge myself down, for I was still hot and sweaty from the activity of our escape. Sally, following me into the room, enquired by mime whether I required hot water; and on my shaking my head, took from me the cloth and soap and, encouraging me to recline upon the marble shelf which stood at the side of the bath (no doubt for such a purpose), first soaped my body then washed it clean in delightfully refreshing cool water.

As this exercise progressed, the effort of her dipping the cloth in the cistern and transferring it to my body resulted in her becoming almost as wet as I, the shirt which she still wore becoming soaked with water and sticking to her body, which I did my best not to notice, being determined to make no amorous movement towards her – for I did not wish her to think that my motives in saving her from Mustafa were those of one who merely wished to substitute one rapist for another. Indifference became, however, increasingly difficult to counterfeit for, encumbered by the wet sleeves of the shirt – which she did not think to turn up – and by the heaviness of the linen compared to the lighter material which is commoner wear in the East, she now attempted to unbutton it in order to remove it; and having difficulty with the buttons – for dress is more often tied, there, than buttoned – appealed to me for help; whereat I had the pleasant task of revealing the slim length of her body, with entrancing round, plump breasts, a well-shaped belly in which the navel was only a darker dint than the almost purple skin around it, and a furrow which (Turkish customs not being her own, and she not yet having been introduced to them) was guarded by a thatch of curly, black hair.

Upon my finishing my task, she motioned me to turn upon my face – which I was quite relieved to do, for by this time my cannon was showing definite signs of an ambitious elevation – and, taking some oil from the jar which always stands in Turkish bathrooms (and which in this case smelled delightfully of sandal wood), began gently to massage my neck and shoulders with surprisingly powerful hands, moving down along my backbone to the small of my back, then encompassing my buttocks, thighs, calves and feet – to the individual toes – then once more persuading me to turn over.

There was no doubting my condition, as I did so; but yet she took no notice, merely continuing to massage my body with a strong tenderness which certainly did much to calm me after an almost unduly exciting evening.

I must confess that I was reminded of the last similar experience I had had, in the establishment by the Seine, with my friend Frank; and despite the distance I had decided to keep between us, would certainly have not resisted had Sally offered me solace of a more intimate kind. However, she completed her massage without – even while attending to the inner portions of my thighs – so much as touching my more intimate part, even by accident; and finally stood back, placed her hands together in an attitude of prayer, and bowed her head, remaining with her head still bowed while I stood up.

I was by now sorely tempted to lay siege to her – and who could imagine that, with a debt of gratitude and in the knowledge of what was expected of a slave, she would not have consented? Yet she looked so charming and so innocent that I merely reached out my hand and, taking her chin in it, raised her head and smiled at her – whereupon a delightful smile spread over her somewhat snub but pretty features. I then took her by the hand and leading her to the sitting-room laid her upon the cushions, and repaired to my own bed where I cursed myself for a sentimental fool, and spent a great deal of time concentrating upon matters archaeological and mathematical in order to take my mind from her body and bring myself to a state of relative calm, from which I eventually relaxed into sleep.

Next morning early, with Ali to accompany us and interpret, I walked with Sally to the market, where it was my intention to accoutre her respectably (she being dressed for the time in a shift-like covering which he had produced from some corner of the house). After an hour, and with no great expense, she was transformed, and we left the shopping quarter in some style, she now resplendent in chemise and trousers of linen, a small round cap, neat and close-fitting, embroidered with silk, which looked enchanting amid her black curls, and a cloak or *dullimano* which hung from her shoulders.

I must confess that I was proud of the transformation I had achieved at the price merely of a few *piastres*, and stood back for a while watching as she strode ahead with that noble carriage shared by all her people.

But now came a clatter of horses' hoofs, and the people in front of us scattered; a man on a fine white horse came towards us and reined in just in front of where Sally now stood, confused at the fuss and noise around her. The man regarded her for a moment, then gestured to two other horsemen behind him – whereupon one spurred forward, bent, lifted the girl from her feet, flung her across the crupper of his horse, and the three were gone!

It was too late for me to do anything but, aghast, enquire of Ali what had happened.

'They are the Sultan's men,' he said, 'searching for new girls for his harem.'

Chapter Fourteen

Sophie's Story

At the suggestion of Mr Georgiou, I set out one morning soon after his inspiriting lecture on ancient Greek myths, to visit Poros, the ancient city of Troezen, once inherited by Theseus from his mother, and whence he brought his wife Phaedra, who there fatally met her stepson Hippolytos. It was, he said, a peculiarly beautiful spot, and moreover reached by a two or three-hour voyage across the gulf of Salamis, which I would find delightful.

This was perfectly true; but I enjoyed it alone, for Blatchford, who was as a matter of course to have accompanied me, was suffering from that especially English complaint, a cold in the head, and leaving him snuffling and sniffing at home, I took a small vessel from the port of Piraeus, and in due course turned into a little channel which ran between Poros and the village of Galatas, upon the mainland of Peloponnisos, that part of Greece which is itself more or less a large island.

Apart from the pleasure of the sail over calm bright-blue seas, the prospect of the land was entirely delightful: orange and lemon groves stretched down to the water's edge, so that the beaches which surrounded the place seemed almost an extension of them, the bright yellow of the lemons echoed by the yellow of the sands.

We arrived at about ten o'clock in the morning, and by the middle of the day I had walked through most of the town of Poros, the houses of which are most pretty, being painted by custom each a different colour. I then engaged a boatman to row me across the narrow water which separates Poros from Galatas, which took but a few minutes. This was such a small place that again to explore it occupied me only briefly, when I decided to stroll a little in the grove above the village, to enjoy the coolness of the air under the trees. This occupied me with such pleasure that I was unconscious of the passing of time, or indeed of the distance I had covered.

After a while, I came upon a clearing where the most beautiful horse was tied to an olive tree and grazing upon the scant grass. I naturally approached the beast, which proved most gentle – though clearly also noble and spirited – and made much of it; so occupied that I did not hear until the last moment a footfall behind me, when, turning, I found at my elbow a young man who in though appearance swarthy was at least as handsome (but perhaps, as I thought then and later found to be true, only half as tame) as his animal – tall, finely built, and, in his white shirt with large sleeves, and black trousers cut closely to his thighs and calves, the very picture of a half-tamed savage.

He addressed me courteously in what I assumed was Greek, but later appeared to be the language peculiar to his own part of the country; upon which I smiled, but assured him that I understood not a word. Clearly, he did not understand me either – but indicating his horse, asked me with gestures whether I had not been admiring him – to which I nodded. Waving his hand, he then invited me to try him, which I was not at all disinclined to do and, placing my foot in the hands which he courteously held for me, was in a moment in the saddle – when, to my surprise, with a single leap my gypsy jumped up behind me, seized the reins, and by a swift and sharp clapping of his heels, set the animal off at a wild gallop, through the olive groves, and in a moment across open ground away from the coast and towards the hills beyond.

I should not, of course, have been surprised at this; I should not, of course, have fallen for the trick; I should not, of course, have wandered without an escort so far from the village – but, as my reader will by now have discerned, I am not a person of whom caution is an invariable governor. I now tried by seizing the reins and pulling upon them to bring our career to a halt, and indeed succeeded for a moment in interrupting the stride of the beast which was bearing us; but when, after an imprecation and a jerk had failed to dissuade me from my effort, I felt the man's teeth fix themselves in the nape of my neck, with a nip just sufficiently strong to make me feel he was master of me – and indeed I should confess that the closeness with which my back was pressed against my companion's body and the strength of his thighs emcompassing not only the horse's body but my own had already somewhat reconciled me to my fate, the bite he gave me thus being inspiriting rather than otherwise.

I had little opportunity however for rational thought, being jolted and shaken by the onward rush of an animal which seemed tireless. We must have ridden for quite three hours when, among pine-clad hills, we galloped into what seemed to be an ancient ruin – an amphitheatre near which was a raised round building surrounded by columns, which sheltered a number of men who, as they gathered around us, I saw to be as wild – but none as handsome – as my captor.

Reining in his horse, he lifted me by the hips and with the greatest of ease swung me from the beast's back, so that I almost fell to the ground, stiff from the long ride. The men were less interested in me than in my abductor, who produced from about his waist a belt from a pocket of which he extracted a small bag of gold coins, at which there were expressions of pleasure from all. Their leader, as he clearly was, then turned to me and spoke several sentences – but seeing that I failed to understand, drew himself up to his not inconsiderable height and, with a bow, clearly pronounced the word: Panayoti – which I took to be his name.

In turn, I made a small curtsey and pronounced the name Sophie, which after several tries he succeeded in repeating in a recognisable form.

Indicating myself, waving my hand about me, and raising my eyebrows, I attempted to enquire what he wanted of me; but he simply smiled and bowed and, taking me by the hand, led me away from the others – to what fate I could only conjecture, until passing through a few trees we came upon a place where a quick-running stream made its way into a natural basin in the rock, comprising a bath some eight or nine feet square of the clearest and most limpid water. Hot and tired from the ride, I welcomed the sight, and waited for him to retire, so that I could refresh myself. However, instead of doing so, he merely sat himself down upon a rock overlooking the pool, and continued to observe me.

No doubt a becoming modesty would have better announced my station as a lady, but my need was greater than that position would have served, and seeing no other way for it I stripped off my clothing and plunged into the water, which indeed was quite as refreshing as it appeared. The gaze of my companion (whose name I had surmised was Mr Panayoti) was equally as cool, but while unrelenting was clearly not entirely dispassionate, and I could not but be flattered by his attentions, while conscious that it was not unlikely that I would in due course be called upon to endure them at closer quarters. Indeed, as I stepped from the water to see him removing his shirt, I was prepared for an immediate attack (and not, to tell the truth, entirely antagonistic to the idea). However, stepping forward, he simply placed it, still warm from his body, about my shoulders, and began to rub my body with it – which he did until I was not only dry, but glowingly warm and rosy; after which he helped me into my clothing without once making a gesture which even the most modest of women would have found reprehensible.

Now, we returned to the ruins, where a fire had been kindled and there was a smell of roasting meat. What beast had been sacrificed, I know not; but the flesh was appetising, and fresh fruit and a flagon of wine, passed from lip to lip, were satisfying after my adventure.

Mr Panayoti was utterly in command of the group; the others, though friendly, keeping their distance, and none of them addressing me until he signalled to one to come forward, to whom he spoke in his language, and who then – to my surprise – addressed me in what passed for English, though with an accent so abominable that it took some time before I could understand what he was saying. Eventually, however, Nikitas (as the English-speaker was called) informed me that the tribe were of Charouda, upon the east coast of the country, some miles to the south and across the mountains. Panayoti, the head of the village, invited me to come there with him as his bride. He was, Nikitas observed, a rich man (by which I understood him to possess a flock of goats, several horses, and his own house), and to be the undisputed leader of the countryside.

I asked Nikitas to thank Mr Panayoti for the compliment, but to inform him that I must return to Athens, where my friend awaited me, and that even the opportunity to wed the owner of several goats and horses could not tempt me from my course, which was eventually to return to England.

Nikitas looked terrified at this and, clutching his groin, whispered to me that his leader would remove an important part of his body were he to convey so unwelcome a message. I had nothing more to say upon the subject, other than to contemplate the possibility of escape – which clearly could not be for some hours at least, since the darkness had now fallen (suddenly, as it does in these regions) and the shadows beyond the ring of light shed by the fire were unwelcoming. Nikitas conveyed some sort of answer to Panayoti which presumably contented him, for he smiled and took another bite at the meat he held in his fingers, the grease running down his chin and dripping on to his chest.

I asked where we were, and Nikitas said the place was called Epidavros, or in the ancient language Epidaurus, sacred in olden times to the god of medicine but now utterly deserted except for those who came to study the ruins. Was this often? I asked – to which he replied that almost every week men came, often foreigners, to examine the ruins of the building in whose shelter we sat, and which contained fine carvings. I determined to attempt to leave a message of some sort before we left that spot – for it was clear that I was to be forced to travel with the band to their destination.

But now Panayoti got to his feet, and gestured in dismissal to his followers, who without argument got to their feet and, picking up the blankets upon which they had been sitting, retired from the circle of firelight. Their leader now picked up some branches of wood which lay about, and placed them upon the fire, which spluttered anew, the flames jumping and shedding a flickering light upon the great columns which rose above us.

Panayoti, raising his hands above his head, stretched himself – and I could not deny a resemblance between him and the figures which I could dimly see carved upon the blocks of stone which surrounded us, and which represented, I supposed, the athletes of the olden days. I prepared myself once more for his approaches, again not altogether unwillingly; but he made no motion towards me other than to indicate a blanket which lay a few feet from where he stood; whereupon I advanced and reclined upon it, in a not altogether fearful state of anticipation. But he himself now lay down, some small distance from me, and turning his back appeared immediately to sink into slumber.

I also, after some time, being tired by the events of the day fell asleep – to be awakened early the following morning by the sun shining through a gap in the trees and falling upon my body. During the night the simple dress which I wore, and in which I had slept, had risen up about me so that my lower body was bare; and the first thing I saw upon regaining consciousness was the figure of Panayoti, leaning upon one elbow, and regarding me with considerable interest.

I was not unaware that the golden light of the early sun was flattering to me, and (whether through the action of some forgotten, warming dream, I could not tell) was ready to engage, and without too much hesitation drew my dress over my head, then lying back with my hands beneath my head to await his advances.

To my astonishment, no such thing occurred. That he found me attractive, I could not doubt; and indeed his first action was to unbuckle and remove his trousers, revealing a weapon as strong and ready for action as could be hoped. But instead of approaching me, he simply lay, half reclining, and in a moment began to toy with his instrument, running his fingers along its length with a slow, caressing motion. I was of course aware of this method of self-gratification, for many years ago I had observed it in my half-brother Frank and our friend Andy, as they first discovered their manhood and that means of placating its urges. Questioned, they had described the action as the employment of Mrs Palm and her five daughters. However, that such a solitary form of enjoyment should be employed before a lady whose every motion made clear her willingness to engage, was something new. Perhaps, I thought, it was the custom in this country that the woman should make the first move – and to try if it were so, I crawled towards Panayoti and, reaching him, threw a leg across his thighs, in such a position that the possibility of ready congress could no longer be denied.

I was clearly in error, however – for with one movement Panayoti thrust me backwards so that I tumbled away from him, and held up a hand to repulse any further advances, while at the same time the action of his other hand quickened, until in a moment the jetting forth of essential liquid signalled some kind of satisfaction – though certainly not for me, who through the sight of so splendid a man spending his energy on satisfying only himself (and, I was sure, in not so enjoyable a fashion as I could have devised for him) was thoroughly confused between ill-temper and a different passion.

Upon Nikitas reappearing and my discreetly questioning him, it appeared that it is the custom, for no man of the Nyklians (as the people of Panayoti's country were called) would dare to approach a female before she had been approved by his family, which would occur when we had reached Charouda, after a journey of perhaps a week.

The men being engaged in clearing up their camp and preparing for their journey, I was able to discover a piece of paper which had been used to wrap food and, with a piece of charcoal from a sharp twig burned in the fire, was able to write upon it a brief message indicating that I had been kidnapped by bandits and was being taken to Charouda (which I hoped was the proper spelling), together with Blatchford's name and present address in Athens, imploring whoever found the message to send it to him. I had not much hope of success, for who knew when the site would next be visited, and by whom? But discovering a particularly handsome piece of carving, which I assumed would be of special interest to any visitor, I carefully deposited the writing below it and hastily retreated – not a moment too soon, for Panayoti immediately came in view, and led me once more to his horse, upon which in no short space of time I was again mounted, and we set out upon our journey.

This was by no means a comfortable one, and if I had not been used by that time to travelling for extended periods upon horseback, I might well have been severely disabled by the experience; however, my friend Nikitas (for so I believed him to be) had the same knowledge of the use of herbs as George had had during my ride to Joannina, and was no less tender in the application of the poultices he made of them; though declining any familiarity, which was a comfort to me, for what with exhaustion and pain, I was by no means inclined to commerce of an erotic nature .

I was able, later, to trace upon a map of the Taygetus mountains the journey we made through them: at the time I could only take pleasure in what I saw of the countryside – and despite my discomfort, there was indeed considerable beauty to be seen, illuminated often by sunlight which fell in shafts through rifts in the mountains and upon the countryside below, where poplars, willows, aspens and plane trees grew upon each side of the many small streams, and where olive groves lay speckled green beyond them.

Charouda, when we reached it, was a tiny village; and Mr Panayoti's family lived not in it, but in a dark tower about half a mile from the place – and as I looked, I saw that indeed many towers were to be seen about the landscape, more or less hidden by the black shadows which were cast by the hills.

I had, during the journey, questioned Nikitas about the style in which our companions lived, and about the Panayoti family, and heard a strange tale in response: how some centuries ago the countryside had been thickly populated, and it began to be extremely difficult to obtain and secure sufficient land to produce the necessary food – whereupon family quarrels and feuds had arisen, and families began to build and live in these towers, which could be the better fortified against their relatives.

The Panayoti family had been of great consequence, and for a century had been the only one which had the right, in the neighbourhood of Charouda, to roof its tower with marble. During this time there had been much intermarriage – for families of consequence could permit matches only between their sons and daughters and the children of people of equal consequence; it being a great dishonour to contract with a peasant or villein. Thus stepsister and stepbrother had often married, and even (it was rumoured) brother and sister, the rule of the church and the law being but thinly observed in this remote country.

The consequence of this was that within recent years

there had been cases of imbecility within the Panayoti family, and attempts had been made to rectify the matter by marrying outside the district. However, a great rivalry had grown up between Petro Panayoti (my captor) and his younger brother Yanni, over the pursuit of a handsome girl from Pyrgos, just along the coast, and each had barricaded himself into his own tower, bombarding the other whenever he approached with ancient cannon (though I am told there were no injuries, or at least few, and those only among the peasantry). The consequence was that the girl's family had refused to entertain the approach of either brother, and the two men had retired in dudgeon, each determined however to prove to the other his superiority in the matter of acquiring a bride suitable to prolong the race. It was for this reason that Petro had made his way so far to the north – for the people of this part mistrust anyone from the western side of the mountains – and for this purpose that he had kidnapped me.

Upon our arrival at Charouda I was greeted at Petro's tower only by two elderly crones and a gaggle of indifferently handsome girls. Petro escorted me to a bare but not altogether uncomfortable chamber high in the tower, and enquired of Nikitas whether I had been informed of the honour which was to be done me. He replied (so he told me) that I was perfectly aware of it, and had acquiesced – explaining later that I had no option in the matter, for otherwise I would simply be turned out into the countryside and left to starve.

This indeed seemed good reason for making no protest, though upon my asking when this proposed marriage was to take place and being informed that it would be the following afternoon, I was not sanguine of my chances of escaping a match for which I was convinced I had not been born and brought up an English gentlewoman.

The next day dawned as little like a wedding day as could have been expected in that remote spot. Awakened from a deep sleep in a not uncomfortable bed, I was brought fresh bread and milk by Nikitas, who by now had taken a position almost as maid to me (and was, or seemed, so indifferent to the various states of undress in which he found me, that I wondered whether he was not perhaps a nelly (as we sometimes called those men who prefer their own sex). However, whatever his predilections, he was kindly and pointed out how charming was the weather, which was the least of considerations to me. I was left alone for the morning, except for one brief visit from my bridegroom to be, who still addressed me only with gestures, and was distant and polite – yet clearly a man of vigour, so that I wondered afresh that he should have been able so completely to ignore my charms during our journey together. He came now bringing one of the two crones, who – Nikitas explained – was his mother. She came forward, prodded me here and there with gnarled fingers, and appeared satisfied; whereupon they both left me once more.

At I suppose about three in the afternoon – for it was an hour or two after I had been brought an indifferently roasted leg of some animal or another upon which I made my luncheon – Madame Panayoti appeared once more, now accompanied by two of the young men of the tribe (who I supposed were to act as policemen, in case I should try to escape), and signalled to me to accompany them. Seeing no one else in what appeared an empty house, I did so, and was mounted upon Petro's fine steed, the cause of my present predicament, which was led by its bridle into the small village and to the single notable building in it, the church of Michael the Taxiarch, down by the sea – indeed almost upon the beach, amid positive orchards of prickly pear, some of them growing over forty feet high.

Had the occasion been otherwise I would have taken time to admire the place, for the little golden basilica was pretty enough, several small cupolas crouching around a central dome; and inside, the frescos were freshly painted and charming. But the focus of my attention must be the tall and, I admit, handsome figure of Petro Panayoti, standing before the altar with a somewhat fragile looking priest, the aisles crowded with his followers – some thirty or forty of them.

As I walked up the aisle towards Petro, I made up my mind that the fact that I had been forcibly brought hither, and that my consent had not been sought, neither did I understand a word of the service which was now beginning, would necessarily disqualify me from being a lawful wife to the man who was about to wed me. However, my decision need not have been taken, for no sooner had I reached the altar, and was about to stretch out my hand to take that of my groom, when, with a great cry, a mob of men rushed into the church from the still open door at the west end. They were armed not only with all kinds of sticks and stones, but with a few ancient muskets, one of which exploded with a considerable noise, blowing the nose off a carving just to the left of the altar and causing the priest to fall to the ground in a faint.

The next few moments were all confusion, Petro leaping to join his men in the fray, but not only outnumbered but apparently outwitted by his opponents – for as I stood bewildered I was seized about the waist from behind, swung over someone's shoulder and carried bodily from the church by a side door, then thrown across the saddle of a horse, which galloped away at full speed and for several miles, severely shaking me and depriving me of my breath and almost of my senses.

At length, we drew up, not before Petro Panayoti's tower, but another similar one, and I was taken from the horse's back – more gently – and carried through the door.

There was a considerable contrast here, for the walls instead of being bare were hung with fine tapestry – uncouth in design, but rich in colour; there was some furniture, again rough but at least imitating comfort. I was placed upon my feet, and sank with some relief into a chair, whereupon I found a flagon held to my lips from which I drained a draught of pleasant wine. I then was able to see my captor, in the light from a great, but barred window – and was immediately in no doubt who it was: clearly Petro's younger brother, Yanni, of whom Nikitas had told me. The two were dissimilar in build, Yanni being slender where his brother was sturdy, his face less formed, yet full of character; his features more gentle, though no less masculine.

Seeing me regarding him without fear and apparently without anger (for what would have been the purpose of such an emotion?) the boy, for he cannot have been older than perhaps nineteen or twenty, drew himself up and bowed, then addressed me (to my surprise) in a few words of English:

'You, Petro, no,' (with a firm shake of the head); 'you, me, yes.'

Well, that was clear enough, and there was nothing to be done about it, for though there was apparently no other person in the tower at present, I was as much in this boy's power as I had been in his brother's; so I merely inclined my head in a dignified manner, meaning – as I intended – neither approval nor disapproval. At this, he gestured to me to rise and, taking my hand in his, led me to a curving staircase within the wall of the tower, which led up for two storeys, eventually turning into a bedchamber where I supposed I was to be left for the time. But no; for with a smile he pointed to the bed which occupied most of the floor, then to myself, saying with infinite meaning: 'You, me, now – Petro' (shaking his head) 'too late.' And lest I should be in danger of misunderstanding his meaning, he began to disrobe.

Had I been offered the choice between him and his brother, all things being equal, I would scarcely have known what course to take; I had not had the opportunity of studying Petro as closely as I was now able to study Yanni – but he had been a brave figure of a man, and whatever I felt about being linked to him in a form of forced marriage, the prospect of my marriage night had not entirely filled me with horror. However, Yanni was probably a gentler conqueror – for while he had begun to throw off his clothing with a fine air of unconcern, now, clothed only in his breeches, he paused, clearly less ready to stand naked before a female than he had at first appeared.

To encourage him, I drew my dress over my head, then releasing the band which held my single undergarment to my waist, permitted it to fall to the floor – revealing to him, as I guess, a figure the delicacy and whiteness of which he had previously never seen the like. The effect was dramatic: his eyes widened, a grin spread across his face, and he positively tore off his breeches, giving me no time to inspect his person before he fell upon the bed, my body beneath his own.

Astride me, he held my waist tightly trapped between his thighs, what appeared an entirely satisfactory instrument lying upon my belly, its head just below my breasts, which he presently seized with his hands – the elasticity of their plump roundness further inspiring him so that he positively leaped into the air, forcing one leg between my thighs, then reaching down to part the other so that he could present his cock to its proper aperture.

However, I was having nothing of this; though quite ready to entertain him (for as my readers will by this time have discerned, I am at no time altogether reluctant to converse with a handsome man) I was not prepared for what would have been virtual rape – and my strength having no doubt been confirmed by my recent journey, I gave a fine buck with my hips which threw him off me – and indeed off the bed. Though this was merely laid upon the floor, his sudden arrival upon the stone flags together with the manner of his unseating was a surprise to him, and the look of astonishment upon his face was such that I could not but grin.

His discomfiture would no doubt soon have turned to anger, and being entirely in his power I had no wish for that; so immediately leaning towards him took him by the elbow and drew him back upon the bed, but this time making sure that he reclined with myself at his side; I could see by the tensing of his muscles that he was making ready for another attack, but placed my finger upon my lips, and then my hand upon his breast, gently forcing his head to the pillow, whereupon I kissed him as gently as woman ever kissed man, taking his lower lip between mine and sucking upon it with the utmost tenderness, then passing my tongue over it and seeking within his lips for his own tongue, which after a moment's hesitation met my own in inexperienced but clearly delighted pleasure.

My right hand had meanwhile stroked his side and, reaching his hip, now made its way gently into the fold where thigh met belly, and further, to where the first prickling of hair announced the nest from which (I was confident) a tiger was ready to leap – and indeed in a moment, the shudder which ran through his whole body no less than the confident wand I felt upon my palm, announced that I need have no fear that my actions had in any way decreased his own readiness.

Sliding like a snake upon his body, I trailed my tongue now from lips to chin, from chin to neck, from neck to breast, and pausing only to grace with a kiss each pap –

surrounded only by a downy hair or two – past the dint of his navel and to the thicket from which a tower only less impressive and less fortified than that in which we lay, now rose in all its eager splendour.

I had thought that a young man of Yanni's position must surely have had experience with local maidens – but my attentions were clearly entirely new to him – which led me to presume that his knowledge of love-making had previously been limited to the sight of horses, dogs or farmyard animals in congress. Certainly he could not repress a yelp of surprise and pleasure as, drawing back the skin which veiled it (for like the other youths of this part of the world, he had not been cut) I allowed my tongue to caress the round head of his tower, then sliding it within my mouth so that it was surrounded by a warm and silky darkness in which, by its throbbing, it was more than happy to rest – though not for long, because his youth now insisted upon more volatile action, and more gently but as firmly as before, he took my by the shoulders, drew me up upon him, and then cleverly turned me so that I was lying upon my back.

His reason was clearly that he wished for a culmination, for he knew nothing of how to please a woman; however, I was by now more than somewhat aroused by his own pleasing shape, no less than by his eagerness, and willingly opened myself to him, being by this time lubricated by those pleasant juices which facilitate intercourse. His instrument was not of enormous size, but was of a sturdy vigour which did not diminish even after – within a few thrusts – he had relieved himself of his initial eagerness; he continued without pause, more gently and in a rocking motion during which his eyes never for a moment left my own, to press home, then to withdraw – then raising himself upon his elbows so that, gazing downwards, he could watch with what I realised was for him an unprecedented performance.

Again, after a few moments, I felt his thrusting increase, and a convulsion of his buttocks announced a second joy; yet still he did not cease his motions, upon which I for the first time reached my apogee, enfolding his waist with my thighs so that I could press my heels against his arse (something which pleased as it surprised him). And for ten minutes more, we enjoyed each other, reaching a final pleasure almost at the same time, when he almost immediately slept, his body heavy upon my own, his head upon my shoulder. Despite the discomfort, the exertions of the past hour together with the events of the day had tired me, so that I too fell into a sound sleep.

This was disturbed only by a violent shock, as I awakened to find my lover's body lifted from mine and opened my eyes to see him held firmly by two men, one upon either side, while above me stood none other than his brother, Petro, looking down upon me with an expression composed of a mixture of scorn, disgust, desire and anger. With a gesture he ordered his men to hold Yanni in place, while unloosening his belt he opened his clothing just sufficiently to release that weapon with which, in a moment, he was ravishing me.

Chapter Fifteen

The Adventures of Andy

Upon the abduction of Sally I was distraught, for I had taken a liking to the girl, and having rescued her from a fate which I had imagined to be considerably worse than death, it was in the first degree dismaying to have her whisked away from under my nose to join the harem of the Sultan.

Having regained the security of my room, however, I gave the matter more rational thought. There were two courses open to me: I could entirely forget the girl, or I could set out to rescue her. I dismissed the first immediately, as unworthy. However, I was under no illusion that to penetrate the harem of the Sultan, situated as it was at the heart of the Seraglio, would be as simple a matter as to enter the house of Mustafa.

Suddenly I recalled an incident which occurred (and may be remembered by those readers who have been persistent in following my adventures) when a house of pleasure which I helped my friend Frank to keep, in London, had suddenly been visited by the watch; it was then a law in that city that only women might supervise brothels, and the discovery that I, a man, was in charge would have resulted in its closure. With the help of a female friend, I had disguised myself as the Madam of the place, and for a time had carried the deception off with respectable virtuosity. I looked now into the mirror. My cheeks were more liable to a sturdy growth of beard than they had been then, but my complexion was clear, and I wore my hair long. I stripped off my clothing. The absence of bubbies I could not help, any more than the presence of an obvious masculine appendix; the growth of hair upon my arms and elsewhere on my body, however, was another matter. But wait . . .!

Though Ali was confused at the instruction, I sent him to the bazaar, and he soon returned with some of that paste, *rusma*, which I had seen the girls use to remove the hair from their bodies at the bridal ceremony. As soon as Ali left me, I applied the paste – not, I admit, without some trepidation – to my arms, legs, buttocks and even my chin. Judging the time with care (for I had no means of knowing for what period I should let the stuff remain, and merely removed it when I began to feel a smarting of the skin), I found that indeed the light hair of my arms and legs came away with it, leaving them as smooth as any girl's, while my chin too though still perhaps a little shaded was much smoother than it was wont to be.

Then I took some of the clothes which I had bought for Sally, and without too much trouble climbed into them. The fact that the dress hung loosely about my person disguised my lack of breasts, and otherwise, as far as I could see in the small looking-glass, I made a presentable girl, my face for the most part obscured by a veil. I rang the bell for Ali.

His first action upon entering the room was to rail at me in the language of the place, then attempting to thrust me from the room; and it was not until I addressed him in my normal tone of voice that he apprehended who I was – at which he first burst into laughter and then, no doubt realising my plan, looked extremely frightened. But his fright was nothing to the terror he expressed when I confirmed that my plan was to get myself chosen as one of the Sultan's harem, and thus to penetrate to the inner sanctum of the Seraglio. I had no idea, he said, of the cruelty to which the Sultan descended; a quick death would be the least fearful fate that would await me. But he could not dissuade me from my course, and next morning at midday – when the men instructed to search the bazaars for likely women came there – I was present among the crowd, having been escorted unwillingly thither by Ali.

Two or three girls having been chosen, the man whom I recognised as having been instrumental in seizing Sally, came towards me, and reaching out took me by the chin and turned my face towards him. I was apprehensive that, however carefully I had used the paste, he would feel a roughness to the touch; but it was not so. I regarded him steadily, with a gaze that I hoped would be considered as spirited yet not impertinent. He then opened my mouth and looked at my teeth, and seemed to be considering whether they did not reveal me as older than my appearance warranted; but on his asking Ali a question, the latter's quaking reply seemed to satisfy him. He held out my arm and ran his hands up its length and, stepping back, regarded me anew for a moment, then without more ado gave a command to an underling, who immediately thrust me into a closed carriage which was waiting nearby.

There were several other girls in the carriage, all clearly terrified, and clinging together for comfort; upon two of them attaching themselves to me, I did my best to restrain those feelings which must inevitably rise when a young man finds himself enfolded in the arms of delightful charmers between whose bodies and his own there is interposed only a few thin sheets of clothing. My attempts failed, however, for upon one of the girls thrusting her hand into my bosom, she found not the equivalent of her own no doubt charming protruberances, but a flat surface; whereupon she automatically transferred her hand to that other place where evidence of sex is to be found. Happily her shriek was taken by the guards as evidence of her fear, for in a few rough words they clearly instructed her to be quiet – which she was, though her excited whispers communicated my secret to the others, while placing my finger to my lips I enjoined their silence.

Having no jot of their language, I could not explain how I came there, and in women's clothing. They might I suppose have thought me some kind of ambitious eunuch, but each in turn testing the evidence, they found that I had not been deprived of that evidence of masculinity which those sad gentlemen lack. Clearly they were puzzled; but were not inclined to give me away.

In twenty minutes we had reached the summit of the hill upon which the Seraglio stands, and the imperial gate, *Bab-i-Humayun*, which led straight into the Court of the Janissaries, guarded by fifty *kapici* or gatekeepers. This court was still public, for here stood those who wished to place petitions before the Sultan. Our vehicle did not pause, but rolled on through the central gate, or *Ortakapi*, past the *Ciliate Odasi* or Room of the Executioner, below which are the dungeons into which the unfortunate people are thrust who have displeased the Sultan. We then came to a stop and were ordered to descend, just within the Court of the Divan, and found ourselves standing under a canopy supported by ten pillars, eight in front and one on either side, all of fine marble except for one, which is of granite. Above us, the pointed roof flashed in gold on a ground of brightest blue, sparkling with many curious stones.

Now we were marched off through the gate of felicity, or *Bab-i-Sa'adet* (so called because through it pass the ladies of the harem as they enter the private apartments of the Sultan) and came to the hall of the black eunuchs.

Here I must briefly break off my narrative for some words about these extraordinary creatures, many of whom were to be seen on all sides. Deprived at an early age – and by cruel methods which I will not relate – of their manhood, they are trained thoroughly in their duties by their seniors, and from the first made conscious of their position by an excellent allowance of money and clothing. They are entrusted with taking and receiving messages between the Sultan and Sultanas, as well as transacting other business, and can rise to positions of great power – as it might be that of *Kislar Agha* or Chief Eunuch, *Hazinedar Agha* or Grand Treasurer, or *Oda-Lala*, Master of the Chamber; if they have no great title and are engaged to serve the women, they are addressed by the names of flowers, such as Hyacinth, Narcissus, Rose or Carnation – this in compliment to the women they serve.

I am frequently asked, when it is known that I have had some experience of these half-men, whether they experience any feelings of love as we know them. The answer is that if the cruel cut was made at a time when puberty has taken place (a dangerous practice, but one not unknown), the mind has already begun to comprehend the promptings of nature even if actual intercourse has not taken place. The creature, then realising what he has lost by his castration, is frequently visited by the most awful and irreconcilable feeling of loss but no amorous emotions. If the operation took place when the man concerned was a child, continual attendance upon women creates a knowledge, all too late, of what might have been, and a feeling of terrible resentment is experienced, coupled with a mingled feeling of revenge and despair. In each case, then, there is dissatisfaction – and most eunuchs are ill-tempered, morose, childish, petulant, revengeful, cruel and arrogant – all of which makes them excellent guardians of a harem, for the sight of a normal man (other than their master) seeking connection with their charges immediately provokes in them nothing but the desire to see him punished.

It is frequently asked whether ladies whose only male companions are eunuchs are tempted to irregular friendship with them, despite the limitation on their manhood. This might be so but that these are not attractive beings. The physical effects of castration are not only complete lack of bodily hair (normal, in any event, with the men here) but a feminine, cracked voice and a gradually increasing flabbiness of the body accompanied by obesity and ugly wrinkling of the skin in later life. Among other effects may be mentioned a weak bladder, loss of memory, insomnia and bad eyesight.

However, strange though it may seem, they do often evoke affection – and are often devoted to particular charges, for it is quite incorrect to imagine that the castrated male loses all desire. In the history of the harem, it must also be confessed that many marriages of eunuchs have taken place, by special permission of the Sultan (who knows that the tie can not be a complete one). Such marriages may nevertheless be successful, not only on the plane of imagination. Indeed, I have found an account of a visit made by an Englishman to Constantinople a century before my own, in which it is stated that eunuchs 'have commerce in a manner unknown to us, and amongst themselves have ways of supplying the defect, and it is not to be wondered at that these miserable Creatures who have no other knowledge of themselves than that they are made for the use of Man, should give themselves up to all manner of lusts and sensuality, in which they say that they exceed all Women.'

But to return to my narrative: we were now received by the Mistress of the Harem, a large and forbidding woman of swarthy complexion and dark looks, assisted by a pleasanter younger woman who seemed more sympathetic. They escorted us through two further courtyards, then up a set of stairs to a room which was laid out as a bedroom, with mattresses in a row around the walls – in one of which was an opening giving on to a balcony, so that the Mistress had a continual sight of the room, in order to discipline her charges. It was then announced to us that we should prepare ourselves for the Sultan's bath, and were given robes of silk to put on. Our being left by the Mistress, her assistant confidentially told us what to expect: that after we had bathed, we were to put on these robes before passing into the hot room, where the Sultan would, from the obscurity of a screened sideroom, inspect us. We must not be surprised at what then occurred, she said; for the Sultan, who had a sense of humour as well known as his cruelty (and not always unconnected with it) had had our robes constructed so that the seams were stuck together rather than sewn; upon the heat melting the glue, the robes fell to pieces, revealing the wearer naked to the sight.

The other girls looked meaningfully at me, who could not hope to survive such a revelation; and one of them, delving into the pockets of her garments (for we still wore the clothes in which we had been taken) produced a packet of pins, and in a moment two of the girls set about pinning together one of the garments, then folding it carefully and returning it to me. I could only smile my thanks, for the Mistress had now returned; privately, I could only guess at the reward the girls hoped for, in return for their assistance.

Now, we were taken along the corridor known as the *Hammam Yolu*, or Corridor of the Bath, which we were told connects the Sultan's rooms with the *Hunkar Sofasi* or Royal Saloon. We then entered the unclothing room, the floor of which was covered with heavy Persian rugs, and where low sofas upholstered with cushions lined the walls. Here we removed our clothing, the girls attempting to shield me from the view of the Mistress, who happily was preoccupied with other matters, giving orders to the four black eunuchs who served the place – and whose eyes I had more reason to fear than hers. However, I was careful to keep my back to them – modesty being not uncommon with girls new to that place; and having been careful to remove the hair from my arse as well as my legs and arms, could hope that no trace of masculinity would be noticed at a cursory glance.

Next we entered the warm bath, a most beautiful room all in marble, where water heated by some furnace fell from a fountain into a trough which, raised on a marble step, spread the whole length of the room – narrow and long, like ordinary western baths. Here was a grave danger, for we entered the bath naked; however once more my fellow captives were careful to huddle about me so that, moving with some speed, I was able to enter the bath unrecognised, when by dint of slumping low I revealed only my shoulders and face to the onlookers – who, no doubt being used to such sights, were not peculiarly attentive. Nevertheless, it was a comfort to me when two of them brought forward a pile of sheets in which we could wrap ourselves; drying our bodies, we then passed into a small room where our robes were laid. There was a short difficulty in recognising my specially prepared one, but, a girl discovering it (by pricking her finger upon one of the pins), it was handed to me. Clothed in these flowing gowns, we were then escorted into the hot room, where the sight of a large window disguised by a grill made it clear whence the Sultan could view his captives, and I took up a position as distant from it as possible.

It was not long before the heat had the effect of which we had been warned: first a seam here, then one there, of the robes my companions wore, gave way, revealing a palpitating breast, a long thigh, a delightful shoulder – until I was the only one whose body was not fully exhibited. I could not gauge the effect this might have upon the Sultan, but indeed, so susceptible was I to the delights displayed around me that I had continually to remind myself of the mortal danger in which I stood, or I would have found it impossible not to succumb to the temptation to bestow a caress or two upon one or other of my companions.

After perhaps half an hour, by which time we were almost faint with the heat, the door was opened, and we were led back along the corridor and into a reception room, where we were handed each a *dizlik* or pair of linen drawers cut very wide and drawn around the waist by a tape or string, and a *gomlek* or loose shirt or chemise. These I hastily slipped on while still protected by my robe, completing my costume with the *yasmak* or veil, of fine muslin, which though very thin – so that the features could be seen through it – nevertheless added to my confidence that I might yet evade discovery for some time. Before we left that room, the chief eunuch – notable for a splendid costume in gold and silver – entered and presented a handkerchief to one of the girls, a plump and pleasing dark-haired beauty – which it seems indicated that she was required to attend upon the Sultan that night. Half in fear, and half feeling the compliment, she was led away to be instructed in the etiquette of the occasion (which included, as I later learned, entering his bed at its furthest end, first embracing his feet then working her way upward).

It was now time for resting, and we were taken back to the sleeping quarters, which I realised extended around all four sides of a courtyard, the balcony hanging over the open yard itself. I longed to explore further, to see whether I could find any trace of Sally; but it was impossible, for no sooner were we left alone, than the girls about me left their beds and crowded around mine. These included four who had been added to our number in the baths, and who must now be appraised of my sex. Though I had no knowledge of the language, I could not be in doubt that they received the news with incredulity, for in a moment my shirt and drawers had been torn from me, and what seemed a hundred curious fingers were passing over my breasts, and examining my private parts which despite the precariousness of my position responded as might be expected, this causing no less amusement than admiration – as indeed did the hair between my legs, for even those girls who had had some knowledge of men had seen only those who were rendered completely naked either by *rusma* or by razor, and so with interest and some apprehension tested the springy hairs with their fingers and the palms of their hands.

Many were the questions that were put to me, which I recognised by tone of voice but could not answer; I believe it may have been thought that I was dumb, but that a particularly rough tug at that hair of which I speak provoked me to an exclamation in language which would not have been comprehended even by a foreigner well practised in polite English.

It was clear that the girls had never seen the body of a European before, and exclamations of surprise and (I am bound to say) admiration were many at the whiteness of my skin and, I assume from the gestures made, the rosy pink aspect of the flesh at the head of my prick; for gently pulling back the skin to reveal it, they moistened it with their saliva to make it shine, and when their ministrations caused, involuntarily, a small bead of liquid to spring from the tiny aperture there, admiration and even pleasure continued the keynote. A difficulty swiftly arose, however, from the fact that all the girls – and there were perhaps a dozen – wished to approach at the same time, and each, having gained a position of advantage for the inspection of this curiosity, was unwilling to relinquish it; so that soon there was a babble of noise and bustle which could not but attract attention, and indeed in a few moments a cry indicated the presence of an impressive black eunuch, who caught several of the girls and sent them spinning towards their beds. Those closest to me hastily covered me with a sheet – but upon their retiring, the man (if I may so describe him) was clearly suspicious, and, approaching my bed, stretched out his hand to whisk away the sheet, when a sudden shriek from one of the other girls attracted his attention, she pretending that she had seen something – a snake, or perhaps a spider? – to alarm her; and while the eunuch's attention was distracted, another girl substituted herself for me, my rolling along until I reached another bed, where I was half concealed by several bodies; the eunuch, returning, whipped away the sheet, revealing only the attractive and unquestionably female body of the substitute – at which he gazed about him in some perplexity, but then at last retired.

I made several attempts to discover whether any of the girls spoke my language, but only with disappointing results; and the intent of my questions was mistaken, in that the girls seemed to be under the impression that I was enquiring which of them should be favoured by my nocturnal attentions. This was a task I could not neglect, nor was I permitted to make a choice, for in the end they engaged in some kind of lottery, apparently drawing straws to denote the winner, the lot falling on a handsome girl, somewhat stouter than I might have chosen – plumpness being considered an asset in that country – with full breasts whose nipples were surrounded by a dark aureole of almost a violet hue, while her honeypot, devoid of sheltering foliage, pouted below a belly which in England would have been more natural to a portly gentleman of bibulous habits. A friend bringing her the inevitable jar of oil always to be found in Turkish bedrooms, she immediate began to anoint herself ready for the fray, covering her parts with a gleaming liquidity.

There was no question of privacy, for each gesturing with her finger on her lips to enjoin her friends to a careful silence, the other girls formed a circle about my bed while the honoured favourite drew back the sheet with which I had modestly covered myself. There was a murmur of disappointed surprise at the sight of my fallen wand (the threat of discovery by the eunuch having deprived it of its stand); but in a moment, while the chosen one engaged in a sort of belly dance at the bedside (not the most inspiriting of sights, though clearly meant to rouse my spirits!) two others stepped forward and began to fondle my cock and balls in the most delicate manner, which had an immediate result – whereat Fatima (as I think of her), thrusting her helpful friends aside, threw a huge thigh over my body, and parting her lower lips slid them like a cap over my limb.

I must confess that the sensation was extraordinarily pleasant; though I would have chosen a tighter quim, this one, made slippery as it was with oil, caressed me with all the sensible gentleness of the most careful of palms, its lips sliding down the length of my staff, stroking each surface as it went, until (so generously proportioned was it) it seemed positively also to engulf my cods. The lady then began slowly to rise and fall so that she seemed to draw forth my soul with each vertical movement, relaxing to comfort me with another embrace as she sank downwards, and meanwhile with her fingernails scratching a pattern of curves and darts about my chest and belly, my shoulders and arms.

It can scarcely be doubted that the other girls were stirred by the sight, leaning forward for a close view of my dibble as, itself now anointed with oil, it slid into view, occasionally reaching out to add a caress to those I was already receiving. But a mere spectator's role was not sufficient to encompass their growing warmth, and in a while they were embracing each other, some retiring to one or other of the beds, where they lay embracing, breast to breast or reversed so that the head of each could be buried in her friend's lap; others, while remaining spectators, blatantly thrust their hands between each other's thighs, lasciviously kissing, tongue meeting tongue, or with their fingers nipping each other's breasts – all in silence, so that the scene resembled more a prurient painting than anything in real life.

The reader may be surprised that I did not almost instantly give up the ghost; and I shared that amazement even at the time – yet each time I approached the zenith, some subtle change of rhythm, a slight pause, a cruel nip of fingernails at a nipple, delayed the explosion, until from sheer exhaustion and by concentrating my mind not on the scene around me, but on my memory of the body of my dear Sophie (in what part of the world, I wondered, could she now be travelling?) I so heightened my spirits that my muscles gathered themselves into a culminating knot – at which, either feeling or sensing it, my companion lifted herself from me so that the juice of my pleasure merely fell back upon my own body, a hiss of pleasure and admiration marking the girls' sight of it.

Happily, in a few minutes, they had retired – some to a single bed, some to one shared with a friend; and the one oil lamp which had lit their pleasure showed only a room of apparently sleeping, innocent girls.

I waited until the regular breathing seemed to indicate that they all slept, then rose quietly from my bed, and drew on only my *dizlik* or drawers – for should I be recognised, I had no wish to to be encumbered with a skirt – and made my way out into the corridor. Slowly I walked around it, the dark well of the courtyard on my right, pausing to peep through the doorways into the gently lit rooms in which the girls of the harem slept; though they were dimly lit, it would certainly be possible, I believed, to see Sally's dark head against the whiteness of her pillow. I kept a sharp look-out, of course, for the eunuch guards, once flattening myself into a convenient alcove as one passed (wishing that I had a skin as black as his, but fortunate to escape detection).

Finally, I came to a room in which not one but a number of dark heads could be seen – it was a place devoted to those girls who were not of local birth, but were mostly Nubian, and so much darker. The difficulty was that I feared I would not recognise my girl among so many. However, I crept in, and upon my knees crawled from bed to bed, as close as I could get, examining each face as carefully as I could. Once, I believed I recognised the girl – but then decided it could not be; then, almost last of all, I was sure. Sally lay, a trace of wet upon her cheeks showing that she had fallen asleep as she wept; she had thrown back the sheet so that the upper part of her body was bare; one arm lay with the hand palm upwards. Very gently, I reached out my own hand and placed it on her palm. A gentle pressure resulted in her eyes opening. Still half asleep, she smiled as though recognising me – but then I had to throw my hand over her mouth to stifle the cry which came to her lips as she realised that it was not a dream creature, but truly myself who was at her side.

I gestured to her to follow me. She rose naked from her bed and reached for her clothing. For the same reason that had dissuaded me from dressing as a woman, I shook my head as she picked up the *gomlek*, and she too left the room clad only in the loosely cut linen drawers.

It was now a testing time, for I had no knowledge of the Seraglio buildings, and could only rely upon my sense of direction. The sea, I knew, lay to the north and east of the place; and that offered the best means of escape (I now realised that my haste to thrust myself into the adventure of rescue should not have prevented me from laying plans for our leaving Constantinople should I be successful – but it was too late now to repine). Near the room where I had found Sally, a staircase descended to the ground floor. Here, one eunuch nodded, asleep on guard at the doorway. On bare feet we slipped past him and out of the *Haremagalaer Dairesi*, or eunuchs' quarters (I am able to describe our route through a later examination of a plan of the place). Turning left through a courtyard, we found ourselves right in front of a guardroom where more eunuchs were, this time awake, but concentrating on a game of chance, and so sitting in a pool of light which no doubt rendered it difficult for them to see our figures as we slipped past. Now, we were in the *Altonyol* or Golden Road, a splendidly decorated tiled corridor which runs along one side of Sultan Valide's courtyard and continues between the suite of the *kadins* and the harem mosque.

Here now was the *Kafes Tasligi*, or Courtyard of the Cage – part of the quarters where the Princes of past Sultans were imprisoned for the whole of their lives, lest they should be tempted to regicide. And now we found a small doorway, the gate of which providentially lay open, and which led us into a garden. The night was almost entirely dark – yet the stars shine so brightly in this part of the world that it was quite possible to see the shapes of the cypress trees, the outline of the buildings, the many ornamental pools and fountains. As we ran over the grass, I wished again that my skin was as dark as Sally's – for as I looked at her I could see merely the white of her *dizlik*, looking as though it moved of its own volition, her dark body almost invisible to the eye.

Reaching a tall wall which was clearly insurmountable, we followed it towards the north-east; then after a right-angled turn, to the south-east where we finally became aware that we were near a gateway, which however lay beyond a lower wall, still high enough to be impossible to climb without a ladder. Nearby a long deep pool of water lay still within its white marble basin – and looking at it in desperation, I noticed that the golden carp swimming in it, the faint light of the stars reflecting from their gilt bodies, appeared to vanish as they approached the wall where the pool ended.

Holding up my hand to Sally, to make her remain upon the edge of the pool, I sat upon its side and slid into it. It was just shallow enough for me to be able to stand with my head above water. Walking to the end, I put out my hand – and discovered that, as I had supposed, there was a gap or tunnel beneath the water, where the the wall ceased. The question was how long the tunnel was, and where it lay. I ducked my head beneath the water, and attempted to see – but all was inky darkness. I lifted my head from the water. A faint glimmer of light in the east showed that dawn was about to break. Discovery would then be certain; equally certain would be an awful punishment. With some difficulty, I removed the drawers that were clinging about my legs in voluminous, wet folds and so would make swimming almost impossible. I then beckoned to Sally, who as she sat upon the edge of the pool, similarly drew off her *dizlik*, then I gently pulled at her arms, and unquestioningly she slipped into the water – with some bravery, for I realised as she clung to me that she could not swim. As I held her with my hands beneath her armpits, I kissed her upon the lips, and then turning her about so that she lay with her back against my chest, I mimed a deep breath, and when she imitated me, placed one hand firmly over her mouth, ducked beneath the water, and kicking out with my legs plunged into the tunnel.

I need not say with what relief I discovered that it was of only four or five feet in length! Without difficulty we broke water in another pool which lay at the side of the *Hekimbasi Odasi* or Chamber of the Chief Physician, which lies just inside the *Ucuncu Kapi*, the Third Gate of the Seraglio. Here, for the first time, we found guards who were awake and vigilant. As I stood wondering what to do, I realised that Sally had climbed from the water, and vanished into the night. I too emerged – hiding, shivering, behind a bush – and then heard to my consternation the low laugh of a woman, not far away. The guards heard it too – for a moment stood irresolute, then began to run in the direction of the sound. Reluctantly, but realising that the girl was providing me with a means of escape, I left my hiding place and ran for the gate – passing through it without incident; and pausing, found that almost instantly Sally was at my side.

From that place the ground fell away swiftly towards the sea, and we half ran, half fell down a grassy bank, coming to rest at last not too comfortably in a thicket of somewhat prickly undergrowth. We lay still for a while; and, throwing her arms about me so that I felt her cold breasts against my chest, she gave me an affectionate embrace which spoke of her gratitude.

From the gateway there was no sound, and at last we felt able without danger to get to our feet and make our way along the water's edge. The dawn was by now golden, and the light sufficiently clear to make us visible to anyone who happened to be passing – which was no comfort, for while a European, properly dressed and accompanied by a Nubian slave-girl, might have passed with reasonable safety through the city, the sight of a naked white man and an equally unclothed girl so near the Sultan's palace would attract not only attention but action!

We broke, then, into a trot – and rounding a rocky promontory discovered a *caique* or small boat drawn up upon a patch of sand, and without hesitation climbed into it; taking up the oars I began to row out into the waters of the Bosphorus.

By what extraordinary luck – or by what intervention of those gods who look after adventurous Englishmen – I know not, in twenty minutes or less, seeing a vessel under sail moving towards us, I descried the English flag; and when she was within hailing, stood up and by shouting attracted the attention of the men on board. She hove to, and took us aboard – not without some surprise and even certain ribaldry at discovering a fellow Englishman sharing a boat with a black girl, and both as bare as on the day upon which they were born.

The ship turned out to be HMS *Actaeon*, sailing from Constantinople for England, via Athens, under the command of Captain Charles Mellor – a name somewhat unusual, which on my enquiring I found he shared with his brother, Mr Frederick Mellor, whom I had helped, some years previously, to a marriage with a young lady in whose house I briefly played the part of music-master. This made it the easier to convince him of the truth of a narrative unusual enough to tax the credulity of any man; and upon my explaining my circumstances, and that while my ready money had been left in my rooms in Constantinople – where an attempt to retrieve it would have disastrous consequences – I possessed at home the means to pay for my passage, he moved the first lieutenant out of his cabin, which was then devoted to myself and my servant – for though the captain offered that she should be bedded in the fo'castle, I was not sanguine of the British tar's ability to withstand temptation to the extent of not violating her, especially since, clad in the borrowed white trousers and shirt of a midshipman (whose pleasure in lending her his clothes was tantamount to orgasm) she appeared, even to me who knew her, immeasurably delightful.

It would be less than honest not to report that Sally showed her gratitude to me for her rescue as soon as we were alone; nor that the agility, firmness and generosity of her young body afforded me very adequate recompense for what had been, though dangerous, an adventure I would not have missed. Two days later we briefly paused at Athens, where with borrowed money I was able to buy both Sally and myself some proper clothing; then set sail for home - but first, for Naples.

Chapter Sixteen

Sophie's Story

The respect with which Petro regarded the conventions of his ancestors served me well, for the fact that we had already been in close proximity for some time without his being able to satisfy his natural physical regard for me (his mother's consent to our marriage first being necessary) had heightened his emotions to such an extent that within a few moments of his falling upon me, he was forced by a natural culmination of those emotions to cease pounding his body upon mine, and rose from his recumbent posture to adjust his dress, looking scornfully upon my own nakedness as he did so.

His brother Yanni, meanwhile, had been held by two of Petro's men so that he could not but see my degradation, and his face was flushed and angry. Now, Petro, turning to him, without more provocation struck him across the face with the back of his hand, and gave an order which resulted in the younger man being dragged still naked as he was from the room, followed by his brother. I rose immediately and clothed myself and, seeing that the door had neither lock nor bolt, tried it – expecting, however, what I found: that it was guarded, outside, by another of Petro's followers.

For about an hour, I was solitary, and left to wonder what fate awaited me; for I had seen enough of life to know that of all conflicts, those between siblings were frequently the most rancorous; and that no man feels so degraded as one who has been overcome by the wiles of a younger brother. After some time the door opened, and in, carrying a jug of water and some bread, came none other than Nikitas – who I was delighted to see, for though I had no reason to suppose that he was anything but faithful to Petro, at least we could communicate in some form of English. I questioned him as best I could about Petro's intentions towards me, and was informed that there could now be no question of our marriage, since I had been sullied by another man. This was no particular disappointment to me; neither, however, was it a comfort, for it was followed by the statement that my fate would be to be taken to a remote part of the hills and left to live or die according to the whim of the Creator.

Was there no appeal against this fate? I enquired.

None, replied Nikitas, and with a not unkindly – though helpless – gesture, laid his hand upon my shoulder; then left me once more alone.

It seemed an age before night fell; and long after that when the door opened once again. I was still awake, my apprehensions as to my fate being too keen to allow me to sleep; and when I saw by the light of the lantern he carried, that it was Nikitas who had entered, I wondered for a moment whether perhaps he had had pity and was about to rescue me somehow from my imprisonment; but no – he merely gestured to me to follow him, leading me down the turning staircase and through a doorway into the room beneath my own – which was handsomely furnished, warmed by a bright fire burning in a large hearth, its bed occupied by Petro, who glowered at me, and barked out a command to Nikitas who, without emotion (though I guessed that he would have spared me if he could) set down the lantern upon a table, and bending, seized the hem of my garment and drew it over my head, then taking me by the shoulders pushed me towards the bed.

I was not altogether unwilling, for here was the opportunity of making myself agreeable to my captor; if he was not permitted to marry me, perhaps he might keep me as mistress, which would at least enable me to make plans for an escape – though where I should go did I escape, I had no notion, for I knew nothing of the country; and knew of no likelihood of any Europeans being within reach.

It was also the case that Petro was now very considerably more attractive in appearance than he had been since we first met – when indeed he had seemed to me an heroic figure. He had presumably made a special toilette, that morning, in anticipation of his wedding day; his beard was neatly trimmed, his face and hands (and for all I knew, body) clean – which had not been the case during our journey, when none of us had had the opportunity for such care. Hearing the door close as Nikitas left, I stepped forward until I reached the edge of the bed, and leant to take the sheet and draw it back, exposing the body of my captor.

I had not previously had the opportunity to observe this at leisure, except upon the occasion when he had briefly exposed it to me at Epidavros; and I cannot but admit that it was an object which it was impossible not to admire. Sturdier than his brother, Petro was a man who had clearly spent his whole life outdoors for, apart from a whiteness about his loins, his skin was tanned a deep brown from head to foot, and beneath the skin at his every movement could be seen the rippling of muscles which denoted him a powerful animal. In another respect, too, he seemed closer to the animal kingdom than most men – for he was uncommonly hirsute, not only his chest, arms and legs but even the upper part of his back, being covered by a close, thick layer of short black hairs, which felt to the hands like the pelt of a deer. I was for a moment reassured, however, for there was no sign of his arousal to be seen; no giant pole rose from between those brawny legs to frighten me; his instrument, though large, was relaxed and quiescent, lying upon one thigh like a sleeping puppy.

I had little time to admire what was undeniably a pleasant picture. He took no time to observe my own body – which, without immodesty, I may say has been considered by many men to be worthy of a slow and careful appreciative examination – but at once reached up, took me by the arms, and pulled me down to the bed. There, his caresses were neither tender nor solicitous; in the first instance, he turned me so that I lay beneath him and, throwing himself upon me, sat so that he pinned me to the bed, his heavy thighs embracing my sides, and placing his still relaxed instrument between my breasts, closed them upon it with his hands and began thus to massage it – upon which in a few moments I began to feel its swelling growth.

It seemed to me that if I was to preserve my life my ambition now must be to prove a bedfellow so delightful that despite convention he could not bear to part with me, and to this end I turned all my experience. This, as my more loyal readers will appreciate, is not negligible; but it will be realised that just as each man is different in his inclinations, so under normal conditions it is a matter of trial and error to discover what most pleases him. Under these circumstances, a lengthy period of experiment was impossible; so I gambled upon the proposition that subtlety was not something that would most please my lover – not only because of his appearance, virility and masterfulness, but because of the gentle manners of his younger brother (siblings often going by opposites in these matters) – and finally because, as I guessed, Petro was still angry at what seemed my treachery, and so would be best pleased by a violent meeting.

This was confirmed when, as he still wriggled upon me, his cock now grown so large that only its stem lay between my breasts, the rose-tipped bulb protruding under my chin, I reached up to take both nipples between my fingers and administer a sudden and (as I hoped) painful nip to each, digging my nails into the soft flesh around them. The shout which resulted was so loud that the door of the room was thrown open and a guard appeared – to vanish, however, as speedily, upon a cry from Petro in the impossible language of the country.

That my roughness had pleased as much as it surprised him, was clear (I guessed that his previous connections had been with women whose manners could not be compared with those of, let us say, the beauties of May Fair or Kensington). Now, raising himself upon his knees, he thrust himself at my face, and taking his instrument between my lips, I sucked upon it with a will, at the same time passing my hands behind him and seeking between the mounds of his arse for his cods, and there scratching at them as a ferret will scratch for a rabbit.

Before long, he found this motion too inspiriting, and threw himself backwards, panting for a moment as he looked down at me, then reaching for my breasts and kneading them as though he kneaded dough, at the same time forcing his body between my thighs. With one gesture, I now threw my legs up so that they passed over his shoulders – when lifting himself he was with a single thrust embedded in my body as a peg is into timber, and was butting it home with a motion so generous that it seemed as though the very bed must fall.

If the previous example I had had of such an attack had led me to suppose that Petro was incapable of a sustained effort, I was now disabused of the notion. I knew enough, however, to realise that the tension of deprivation may alone reduce a man to such a sudden explosion; and on this occasion it was amply proved that such had been the case – for while from time to time he paused to take breath, Petro showed himself capable of an almost alarmingly sustained energy. While not in general attracted by the rough manners of country lovers, I must admit that his attentions were inspiriting – and more, I would defy any woman to be unmoved by a similar experience; the continuance of a rhythmical motion for perhaps forty minutes must through its friction alone result in excitement, while simple animal exuberance, if displayed (as now it was) by a handsome man, however little in love, must have its results – in this case, my being raised no less than five times to the peak of pleasure, which I did not hesitate to show in scoring Petro's back with my nails (which he seemed to enjoy rather than be deterred by), in digging them into the flesh of his arse, and manipulating his cods (though circumspectly, for even the most generously ambitious lover must find roughness in that area less than charming).

Finally, even this astonishingly rapacious man permitted himself to be defeated, and with a bull-like bellow (which did not bring the intervention of the guard, from which I guessed that it was a sound which had been heard before) after one final thrust of his loins collapsed upon me.

For a moment, we rested; after which, upon his lifting himself from me, I sought to make myself agreeable by gently caressing his cheek. But it became clear that however much he may have enjoyed our second carnal encounter, I was not to be forgiven, for he roughly put my hand away, and when I attempted, with a corner of the sheet, to wipe his sweating chest and belly, again made a gesture of dismissal – and in a moment called out so that Nikitas, who had clearly been within earshot, entered, and taking me by the arm raised me to my feet, handed me my gown, and drew me from the room even before I could put it on.

Pitying me, I guess, he took me not to the cold room which I had left, but to another – perhaps his own – where a small fire burned, and encouraged me to dress myself; which I did. He then, in his broken English, explained that Petro would sleep, and that I could remain here until first light, when I must be returned to my cell, where the master would expect to find me. I asked what had happened to Yanni, but received no reply. Nikitas then going, I fell upon the narrow bed and almost immediately into a sleep – and almost before I knew it, was shaken and waked to find a cold light at the window, and the fire in ashes.

Taken back to my former room, I huddled as best I could into the cold bedclothes (which were few, the people of this country apparently being impervious to cold – and indeed for most of the year the nights are sufficiently warm to make any covering supererogatory). In an hour's time two of Petro's men appeared, and taking me by the arms dragged me – though I did not resist, resistance being obviously vain – to the ground floor, and out through the doorway. Petro was nowhere in sight; clearly my responses to him had not been so salutary as to make me irresistible. I did not even see his face at a window as I was hustled, my hands now tied behind my back, upon a cart which stood outside the door of the tower, and with one man whipping up the horse and the other half sitting upon my legs, we made off along a painfully rough road. I thought I caught a glimpse of Nikitas' face at a window; but then we rounded a corner, and soon were moving along a track above the village of Charouda, the sea sparkling a brilliant blue beyond it – and the view such that had my circumstances been other, I could not but have admired it.

Only an occasional shouted conversation between my guards (the noise of the wheels upon the rutted track making normal conversation impossible) interrupted the monotony of the journey. We saw no other human beings, and only one horse – a handsome beast with a bright red rug or blanket thrown across its saddle, grazing unattended at the side of the road. Our cart slowed a little, as though its driver was considering whether the strange beast was worth stealing; but no doubt there are sanctions against robbery even in such a place, and we continued our rough way.

In perhaps half an hour, we stopped; the horse was uncoupled and, my hands still tied, I was lifted from the cart and thrown across its body. One of the two men then mounted it, turned from the track and galloped up the slope away from the track – on for perhaps half an hour, until we were in a solitary place, stony and with sparse grass, surrounded by high hills, with no sign of human habitation.

Dismounting, the man lifted me from the horse's back; and turning me, unloosed my hands. Then, without so much as a pause during which I might have appealed to his good nature, he leaped on the back of his beast, stuck his heels into its flanks, and galloped from sight.

I have been, in the course of my life, in very many difficult situations; but this was undoubtedly the most difficult. I was alone, dressed only in a single, thin garment, in a desert place far from human habitation – and even further from *civilised* human habitation. Already the sun was high, and the ground beginning to give off a haze of heat. Fortunately, the season was such that it would not be sufficiently hot to be a danger – yet I knew that, when night fell and darkness came, the cold would seriously incommode me, should I not be able to find shelter.

I looked around me.

I was in a sort of flat arena, almost like a circus ring, surrounded by bushes and brush, above which in every direction save the one from which we had come, rocky ground rose, ever steeper, towards the hills – nay, mountains! – around us. There was no question of taking any decision which way to walk. There was only one. Yet I knew we had galloped for half an hour, by my guess, from the time when we had left the track; this must mean that at least ten, and perhaps as much as fifteen miles lay between me and the pathway. Retracing my way it would take some days to reach the village – and even then, I would merely be returning to the area ruled by Petro.

I was ready by this time to sit upon the ground and burst into tears. But such is not my way. Hitching up my skirt, I began to trudge along the way we had come – a way which could not be dignified with the name of road, or even of pathway, being merely a relatively clear track of rough grass.

I had been walking for perhaps ten minutes when I thought I heard something other than the spasmodic bird-song which was the only sound in the still morning air. I stopped and listened. Yes – as I had thought – the trotting hooves of a horse! My first reaction was to shout and scream at the top of my voice, lest I should not be discovered. But then – was it my former captor, returning? Had he been instructed to kill me and relented, but now thinking again of his duty, or in fear of Petro's revenge, was returning to accomplish the task? I looked hurriedly about me. There was nowhere to hide but the bushes: and into them, reckless of thistles, I plunged, throwing myself down thoughtlessly, so long as I was out of sight of the rider – who now came nearer, until the hoofbeats slowed, and the beast seemed to have come to a halt almost where I was.

I held my breath. Then, as I lay with my head folded in my arms, felt something warm touch my forearm. Lifting my head, I looked straight into the eyes of a small, brown snake.

No doubt there are some who could have contained one terror in the face of another. I was not she. Unthinkingly, I let out a piercing cry, leaped to my feet, rushed from the bushes – and found myself almost beneath the neck of a horse, which with its rider was simply a black silhouette against the sky. With a gasp, but in silence, I fell to the ground in a swoon.

I awoke to find myself cradled in a tender pair of arms, my forehead bathed by a handkerchief dampened by water from a bottle which was now held to my lips – and held by none other than . . . Blatchford!

When I had ceased weeping – which from a mixture of gratitude, relief and pleasure, took some time – he lifted me to my feet and having assured himself that I was uninjured, lifted me to the back of his horse (which, I saw from its red blanket, was the very one we had passed upon the way) and set off at a comfortably leisurely pace, explaining as he went how he come to be there – that my message, left with so little confidence at Epidavros, had been found very soon after my departure; that the very finder had returned to Athens immediately and sought him out, and that by dint of riding hard, changing horses frequently, and taking almost no rest, he had arrived in the neighbourhood of Charouda early that very morning. Turning off the road near some cliffs outside the village, he had heard cries, and come upon two men about to thrust another, whose arms were bound, from the top of a high cliff – the victim's spirited resistance and cries attracting his attention.

Being on the side of justice, which is scarcely ever that of the strong, my friend intervened, and surprise being on his side had sent one of Petro's bully-boys off the edge of the cliff before he could look round; the second put up a fight, but Blatchford being no soft touch, soon found himself battered and deprived of his weapon – so made off, whereupon Blatchford released his victim, who – the reader will be unsurprised to learn – was none other than Petro's brother, Yanni.

It was only a little time before the two men realised that they had something in common – that is, concern for me. Happily, Yanni was able to describe the place where he believed Petro would order me to be stranded, and advised Blatchford on his course of action; which was to hide himself by the wayside and watch for us, then following at a discreet distance.

To make my story short, by mid-afternoon we had reached the place where Blatchford had left Yanni, who in the intervening time had gathered together a small supply of fruit, which we ate, and, refreshed, considered our next movement. Yanni encouraged us to accompany him – which we did, myself on horseback, the two men walking – to a shepherd's hut about four miles away, at the head of a cove where the shore slanted down to a small natural harbour fed by a stream of fresh water. We were all pleased enough to throw ourselves into this and refresh ourselves, and as we lay upon the bank in the shade of an olive tree, the beads of moisture slowly drying upon our bodies, Yanni suggested (though his English was almost non-existent, his meaning was clear) that he could within a day or so muster sufficient friends to make an attack upon his brother's tower, with the hope of capturing him. There was no love lost between them, and we were left in no doubt what Petro's fate would then be.

I must confess to being less than delighted at the prospect of taking part, even by association, in such internecine murder; my chief aim was to leave the place altogether, and to return as speedily as possible to civilisation. Though Blatchford said little, I could see that he felt much the same way – but, as he said to me, he knew nothing of the geography of the place, and we would need to be set upon a reliable way if we were to succeed in returning to Athens.

Despite the problems we faced, the day's exertions had been such that all three fell into a sleep there upon the bank, just above the point where the stream fell from a rock into a shallow pool at the head of the beach, to disperse its waters in the sands.

I was first to wake, perhaps three hours later – my feet bathed in sunlight, for Sol had moved about so that he stood only some degrees above the western horizon. The two men lay, still asleep, one upon each side – and both, I was amused to see (for we had naturally not reclothed ourselves after our bathing, the warmth of the day making it unnecessary), in that state of arousal which often visits the sex during slumber. Not for the first time, I wondered at the generosity of nature in providing our sex with lovers whose corporeal appearance was so varied. Yanni, slender, lightly built, his body (in contrast to that of his brother) almost hairless, his face open and youthful under the curly brow; Blatchford, more thick-set, his body hardened by a life of not inconsiderable labour, his visage more set in years but, though manly, not un-tender.

As I regarded him, the latter's eyes opened and met my own, and with an involuntary modesty he reached down a hand to conceal his state – whereat I could not resist a smile, since our familiarity was such that such concealment was purposeless. He took my meaning instantly, not only removing his hand, but reaching for mine and carrying it to the same place – at which my gratitude to him for his honest loyalty and the hardships with which he had burdened himself in my interest overflowed, and I gently pulled him towards me, so that by merely throwing a leg across my body he was able to present his prick to that target with which it had so long been familiar, and in a moment, clasped in each other's arms, we were enjoying each other with a comfortable lethargy – being still almost half asleep.

Whether through any noise we may have made or simply through circumstance, Yanni also awoke, and at this (for us) inconvenient moment. His reaction was an instant one: knowing that Blatchford was my servant, and assuming that commerce between us in the matter of love could be the result only of attempted rape, he immediately threw himself upon us, wrenched Blatchford to his feet, and with a single blow – which by luck more than judgement found its target – sent him to the ground. Blatchford was back upon his feet on the instant, and the two were at grapple, falling to the grass and rolling over and over in an attempt to better each other – but without doubt that Blatchford would be the victor, his opponent being younger and less muscular; and indeed before long the former was astride the latter and pinning him down by the shoulders – himself grinning, for he understood the intervention and even applauded it!

Between us, we were able to explain the situation, so that Yanni, though with an ill grace, eventually shook Blatchford by the hand and – neither I nor my friend being now in the same mood, and the sun going in – took ourselves to the deserted shepherd's hut, where we made a fire at one end, and at the other spread out some clean straw which we found in a byre at the side of the hut. Upon this we spread the red blanket, and upon it, after we had eaten some food from Blatchford's pack, placed ourselves for sleep.

The reader will by now have overtaken me: indeed, it is true that the blanket was small, and that three adult bodies, each attempting to remain upon it rather than upon the prickly straw or bare floor, were in such close connection that familiarity was certain to ensue. My feelings were friendly for both men – to Yanni in sympathy for his position, which was not entirely divorced from his attentions to me; and to Blatchford, as I have explained, for other efforts in my behalf. The latter emotion must be strongest, and interrupted once, the proximity of the Greek boy could not prevent me from renewing my protestations of gratitude, which resulted in my friend once more taking his rightful place, which he occupied with that mixture of eagerness and delicacy, vigour and respect, enjoyment and sentiment which were ever the mark of our occasional connections.

It was, I imagine, something new for Yanni to find his flank pressed against that of a lady in course of entertaining another gentleman, and after trying unsuccessfully to keep his eyes from our bodies, made golden in the light of the fire, he frankly lifted himself upon one elbow and made a pleasure of observing us. From observance to participation was but a short step. Alas for him, Blatchford was a skilful lover for whom speed was never concomitant with enjoyment, and it was clear that Yanni found the waiting at last unbearably tedious, and stretching out his right hand placed it upon my bosom, caressing it with a pleasing tenderness, then passing it down my body until the meeting of my belly with my lover's made it impossible of further progress – or so it seemed until Blatchford (somewhat to my surprise, but clearly enjoying the intervention) raised himself upon his arms so that we touched only at that point where his tool entered and left my body; which permitted Yanni to caress the surrounding flesh, to find with a fingertip that pleasure-button which in the ordinary course of lovemaking is frequently and sadly neglected; this immediately brought me to a gasping culmination, and by transferring his attention to the core of flesh below the prick but above the cods, and administering a lascivious pinch, Yanni was able also to bring Blatchford off; whereat the latter obligingly rolled from me, and Yanni without hesitation took his place.

I was by this time, however, so lubricated by my enjoyment that I scarcely felt his instrument within me; and so persuaded him to dismount when, turning him upon his back, I gave him once more those attentions which had so surprised and delighted him upon our first encounter. These for a time pleased him as well; but he was eager for congress, and after a while impatiently turned me upon my face and, lifting my hips, entered me from behind, toying the while with my breasts, belly and thighs and the surrounding countryside. This gave me a new pleasure, and the sight also roused Blatchford once more – whose turn it now was to feel the outsider in our endeavours.

There being no intervening, for it would have been a shame to deprive Yanni of his pleasure, in which he was so entirely engrossed, my friend took a path which I would not have expected of him – by spitting upon his palm and lubricating his tool, then, placing himself behind Yanni, discovering that path to pleasure more often occupied by those men whose enjoyment is commonly with their own sex. Certainly I felt Yanni give a start – whether of pain, pleasure or simple surprise – at the approach, but it seemed to strengthen rather than disturb his pleasure, and in short the three of us were within five minutes in a state of exhausted pleasure which resulted in our falling again into a sleep, our limbs so interwoven and tangled that it would have been difficult for an onlooker to have connected which foot with which knee, which hand with which elbow.

I awoke some hours later to silence and darkness. The fire had gone out, and the hut was still except for the regular breathing of my two friends. Yet something had awakened me. I lifted my head from where it lay (upon one or other thigh), and lifted myself upon an elbow. Whoever was upon my left side moved sleepily, and the hand which had been upon my breast dropped into my lap. I remained still for a moment – and heard the snapping of a twig outside. A goat? Blatchford's horse? But no – there was surely a footstep? And surely – a whisper?

I shook the shoulder nearest to me, and heard Blatchford mutter something, half-asleep – but before I could shake him again the hut was full of noise as the door burst in, and figures bearing torches, knives and swords stood staring down upon us. Someone laughed, roughly. Another made a gesture, and in a moment Blatchford and Yanni were yanked to their feet, their limbs bound and gags thrust into their mouths. I made a move towards them, but myself was restrained, and my own hands tied. My two friends were thrust through the door and into the darkness beyond. I was alone with two men – the two who had disposed of me, earlier.

They exchanged a word, and one laughed, thrusting his hand crudely between my legs. Was I, unprotected, to be raped and killed? And what was to happen to my friends – in particular to honest Blatchford, who had risked so much for me, who through my stupidity had put myself in this stew?

But no – the men evidently had their orders. One led the way from the hut and the other followed, pushing me before him. Outside, I saw in the distance lights going up the path to the top of the hill above the cove; but to my surprise, I was pushed the other way – down on to the beach and along the soft, wet sand – for the tide was ebbing – stumbling in my bare feet, my flesh creaming in the cold night, to where the first man's torch showed me a small boat, with a fisherman's net hanging over the bow. The first man pulled this away and threw it to the sand, then reaching inside lifted a single oar and threw that too in the direction of the beach. Then he turned, and picked up my feet, and I was placed, with a rude bump, upon the damp boards of the tiny craft, and in a moment felt it rock, and heard the grating sound as the two men pushed the boat the few feet from sand to sea. A final acceleration, and the waves took her, and the tide gripped; the dim reflection of the torch began to fade.

I did not cry out. What was the use? The men would have been sufficiently rebuked for my first escape – they would not connive at a second. I tried to move, but could only scrabble with my feet – until, after a few minutes, I got my back against the piece of wood which served as a seat, and by pushing and wriggling raised myself until I could see the dim shape of the shore. The night was half clouded, and there was not a light to be seen. As I watched, the slowly shifting silhouette showed me that the tide was drawing me further and further out to sea.

Chapter Seventeen

The Adventures of Andy

We had just cleared the southernmost tip of Cape Tenebros and turned east, when a sudden storm grew up during the night, and – though I was not aware of it at the time – forced the *Actaeon* to run before it to the north, along the west coast of Peleponnisos. By the time I awoke, at about seven in the morning and went on deck for my usual morning constitutional, the storm had fallen, and we were almost stationary upon a windless ocean, just within sight of a coastline above which rose a handsome range of hills.

A small knot of seamen was gathered at the bow, pointing into the distance, and upon joining them I saw what they had descried – that is, a small boat adrift upon the sea: the only thing in sight. There being no officer on deck, I sent for Lieutenant Knee, the first officer, who like myself felt that the matter should be investigated lest the boat should contain some person in extremity. It was impossible that the *Actaeon* should approach – for we were virtually becalmed, and the small craft was to windward of what wind there was – and a boat being launched with two men to row, at Lieutenant Knee's command I took charge of it.

Within a quarter of an hour we had come within range, but our cries met no response; upon drawing alongside, we found that the drifting craft was indeed occupied, for upon the boards at the bottom of the insubstantial vessel lay the unclothed body of a woman. Leaping into the boat, I raised her in my arms – to discover with what amazement and horror, that the body was that of none other than my friend Sophie, whom I had last set eyes on on another craft, as we were prepared to leave England what seemed a lifetime ago.

To my relief, I found her breathing, though unconscious. Taking off my shirt, I laid it over her and lifted her as gently as possible into the *Actaeon*'s smallboat, and urged the men to row as swiftly as possible back to the mother craft, where with some difficulty we lifted Sophie on board and down to my cabin. Sally, still abed, greeted with no small surprise my arrival with the naked body of a female in my arms! However, she soon took charge, fetching water and bathing my friend, then, as she stirred, administering some brandy, which in due course resulted in her stirring - and recognising me with surprise and joy.

Captain Mellor had already, apprised of the situation, decided to run back for Athens, believing that medical attention would be a prerequisite. But Sophie's recovery, once she had recognised me and realised her safety, was dramatic and speedy, and within half an hour she had described the circumstances under which she had been cast adrift by Petro's servants. Her collapse and unconsciousness had been from fear and exhaustion rather than from positive illness, and she pleaded with the Captain that rather than making for port he should arrange a party to rescue Yanni and Blatchford, should they be still alive - and we had hopes of this, since Sophie had only been cast adrift early that very morning, and there was some reason to suppose that any vengeance Petro wished to visit upon his brother and Blatchford would wait until the full light of day.

Upon hearing in what a predicament our old servant had been placed, I too was eager to assist him if that were possible, and Captain Mellor was no less determined. Upon questioning Sophie we laid in towards land (a small but sufficient breeze now springing up), and coursed along the shore until a village came into view which Sophie confirmed was that of Charouda.

A small party was now made up, of six of the crew, led by Lieutenant Knee, an exquisite youth but of considerable spirit. Sophie was determined to accompany it - as I was, but argued that she should remain in safety. However, we were forced to accept the fact that only she might guide us to Petro's tower, and only she would recognise him; so fitting her out with a shirt and trousers borrowed from the youngest member of the crew, we agreed that she should make one of the party. As we were about to put to shore, Sally also appeared, dressed in some of my clothes, and making – as Sophie did – a very presentable youth; at which the men gave a cheer, and though I was not anxious to add another female to the party, could not dissuade her, especially since she seemed particularly devoted to Sophie, arguing that two women together would be of more effect.

We put to shore in two small boats, the *Actaeon* having dropped anchor in deeper water away from the little port. We hid our firearms about our persons – those of Sophie and Sally being thrust down the front of their trousers, which conveniently gave their figures a more near approximation to the masculine than had previously been the case. When we had landed, Lieutenant Knee – who among other accomplishments spoke fluent Greek, which while his ship was in port had been of assistance to him in procuring for his amusement youths of a similar disposition to his own – assured the small group of curious villagers that gathered, that we were merely in search of fresh water and provisions. We then began to stroll about the village as though with the interest of mere tourists, when Sophie was soon able to recognise the church at which she had been so nearly married to her villainous kidnapper; and from that, could indicate the path which led up the hill towards Petro's tower. With a few words, Lieutenant Knee instructed us to scatter, making our way separately, and still with an apparent casualness, in that direction, when, he said, we should meet at a discreet distance to plan our attack.

Forgetting that they had the appearance of young men, I gave an arm to each of the ladies – which in fact attracted no undue notice from the villagers, the youths of the country frequently being seen to walk with their arms about each other, or even to publicly embrace, in the way of friendship – and we walked quite openly up the path, while the men, singly or in pairs, disappeared among the olive trees.

In about twenty minutes we came within view of the tower – and very forbidding it looked; though with no sign of habitation, which suggested that it was unguarded or that Petro was unconscious of any reason to be uneasy – as well he might, since his brother was in his custody, and it is notorious that leaderless men are of small danger. Nevertheless, we made for shelter in a grove of trees, not at this stage wishing to be seen; and as, from this shelter, we looked towards the tower, a group of men came around its corner from the other side, where the main door was; and in the midst of them two horses, upon the backs of which sat two figures whose hands were bound; I recognised at once our former servant, and presumed that the slighter figure next to him was that of Petro's younger brother, Yanni. The tightness with which Sophie gripped my elbow confirmed the supposition.

The group of men came to a stop beneath a large, gnarled olive tree halfway between us and the base of the tower – and now followed, from the tower, another figure which was certainly that of the leader Petro – and clearly intent on the crime of murdering his brother, for walking towards the others he made a gesture in response to which two men seized from the backs of the horses loops of rope which had been set there, and casting one end of them up over the branches of the olive tree revealed that the other ends were set, in nooses, about the necks of Yanni and Blatchford.

I had no idea where our companions were, but clearly there was no time to be lost. I turned to encourage the girls to produce their pistols – but found them already in their hands; and without a word to each other, we broke from cover and ran towards the group with a shout.

The result of our sudden appearance was in several ways interesting: the group of men first started, then broke. Two of them ran towards us – but upon my firing my gun into the air, stopped (for they were unarmed) and took to their heels. At the explosion, the horses equally took fright and reared, throwing Yanni and Blatchford to the ground – though happily without injury to their necks, for the ropes had not been secured. Producing a knife from her pocket (surprising female!) Sally ran forward and cut them loose, while Sophie and I confronted Petro who with great courage – for he too was unarmed – walked steadily towards us.

When he showed no signs of stopping, Sophie levelled her gun at his breast, and held up her other hand. Looking directly into her eyes, Petro could not but be conscious of her intention to shoot if she met with resistance, and came to a halt. At this moment his brother came forward, and before I could stop him, seized my own gun and, aiming it at his brother, pulled the trigger. At the same moment, however, Sophie struck at his arm, and the ball hissed no more than an inch above Petro's shoulder. Yanni turned furiously upon my friend, but she placed her hand upon his shoulder and made a calming gesture which after a moment he accepted.

She then called out a name, and from the direction of the tower came a rather dishevelled man whom she addressed as Nikitas, and who, it turned out, spoke a sort of English. She bade him explain to Yanni that in civilised countries combat to the death between brothers was considered an enormity, and that an accommodation must be reached between them. I had severe doubts as to whether this could be accomplished – but to cut my story short, we entered the tower (still keeping a careful watch upon the disgruntled Petro), where after a long discussion, Nikitas explained to us that the brothers had agreed upon a parting, and that Yanni had agreed to accept a sum of money on condition that he left his brother in possession of the land which had been their father's – Yanni by his nodding and smiling agreeing.

Petro then vanished, and there was a pause – during which I took the opportunity of properly greeting Blatchford (whose pleasure at seeing me was only equalled – nay, necessarily surpassed! – by delight at Sophie's rescue of him and her fellow captor) and hearing from him some outline of their adventures since I last saw them. Petro then returned with a large and extremely heavy coffer which I could only infer contained gold; and, with Blatchford and Yanni staggering under the weight of it, we issued forth to be confronted by a fierce band of armed men – our friends from the *Actaeon* who, under Lieutenant Knee's eager command, were about to storm the tower!

We loaded Yanni's box upon one of the horses, and still with our arms prominent – for we did not trust the surly Petro, who viewed every one of us with the same disapprobation – made our way back to the village, where upon our bidding Yanni farewell, he pointed first to himself, then to the *Actaeon*, floating in the distance, and then to the box – meaning, as I did not doubt, that he should be taken on board as an additional passenger. Our attempts to convey that we were under sail for Italy elicited from him only an enthusiastic nod and a few words in English, such as: 'Me – Italy – good!'

Lieutenant Knee was of the view that his captain would agree to transporting the man, especially in view of a considerable profit which might be expected to ensue; and so we all set off back to the *Actaeon*, where indeed Captain Mellor acquiesced in Yanni's request – first however having asked my permission, for there being only one spare cabin, not only Sophie but now Yanni must share the accommodation formerly affording but cramped room for Sally and myself. I had no hesitation in agreeing, for my delight in seeing my old friend and being instrumental in recovering her from death, was unbridled. Sally appeared to be already devoted to her, so there was no problem in that direction; Blatchford had clearly now attained a position of trust in which his presence would not incommode Sophie – indeed, I had already suspected what proved to be the case: that his position as her servant had given way to something more familiar. However, Yanni, I believed, must agree to sleeping upon deck; there would certainly be no room for five people in our small cabin; and I had no doubt that he was used to the open air.

That evening we had a considerable banquet – or, rather, a festive meal, for the food available to us was only of the simplest; yet there was plenty of grog, as the seamen called the heavy rum with which they were supplied, and by the end of it we all felt a solidarity in friendship. I must confess that I was somewhat jealous of Sophie's preference for Yanni, for I could not but notice that the latter's gestures towards her – in planting from time to time a kiss upon her neck, or (as I suspected from their closeness) a caress of a more indelicate nature beneath the table – were not unwelcome; and indeed I must admit that he was a personable young man, whom some education in civilised manners would no doubt turn into a reasonable facsimile of a gentleman. Blatchford, I noted, was much preoccupied with the person of Sally; he had not, I suppose, been in close proximity before with a person of colour, and his admiration was obvious – and not merely based upon his observation of her person, for I had already schooled her in an approximation of decent manners, and her natural grace and beauty rendered her the most agreeable companion, and not only at night. I was happy to notice that not only Blatchford but Yanni was clearly disturbed by her handsome appearance and manner, and even while caressing Sophie had an eye for the attractions of the other.

The time came, in due course, for our retirement, and I was firm in bringing forth a blanket and pointing to a sheltered corner of the deck, where with some reluctance Yanni laid himself upon a folded sail and prepared to make his bed. On Sophie, Sally, Blatchford and myself reaching our cabin, the latter lady without hesitation removed her clothing and laid herself in one of the two hammocks which hung in that confined space, immediately appearing to sleep. I immediately took Sophie in my arms and for the first time since our last evening together at the Gun public house at Brighthelmstone planted a kiss upon those tender lips which I had known since childhood.

Her own response was no less eager than I might have hoped, for in an instant she was unbuttoning my shirt and had drawn it from my shoulders, and her lips were playing upon my breast, shoulders and sides as, sinking to her knees, she drew my trousers also from me, taking my swiftly swelling prick between her palms and caressing it with a tenderness made up equally of affection and longing – for while her warm and succulent lips moved gently over its surface, her hands were already at the cheeks of my arse with a trembling grasp which bespoke a desire for a fuller congress. Blatchford, at our reunion, had turned away and, stripping to his trousers, laid himself curled in a corner, as inconspicuous as possible – showing that tact which made him ever the excellent servant.

The reader will not hesitate to believe that it was with the greatest pleasure that I unveiled those beauties which were none the less agreeable to me for their familiarity – for however we may enjoy those pleasures which come to us in the way of adventure, it can never be with anything but affection that one looks once more, after long parting, upon that mole nestling between breast and armpit, that spring of hair below the belly, that particular turn of wrist or ankle which are familiar to us through former and loving acquaintance.

While it may sound ridiculous to those who have not had the experience of returning to safe harbour after adventures in other ports, it was with peculiar and nostalgic satisfaction that I felt my member slide into the warmth of my dear Sophie's purse; and though the conditions were not ideal for a passage of love (and no one who has attempted congress in a hammock can but be aware of its shortcomings as a bed of love) our enjoyment was of a mingled eagerness and tenderness, a mixed lubriciousness and affection, that resulted in a bittersweet culmination such as was especially satisfying, I believe, to both of us; and we fell into a deep sleep, inextricably joined together not only by my still being tightly clasped within her arms, but by her thighs perforce still enclosing my waist as we lay in the confines of the hammock.

I do not know at what time I awoke; but it was late, for the candle which was our single light had burned out. I was conscious that it was a noise of some kind that had awakened me, and indeed heard again the sound apparently of someone eating a particularly luscious fruit – that delightful slobbering which is impossible to restrain as one enjoys the sweet flesh of perhaps a ripe pear. However, I was conscious that the sound was also accompanied by a groaning as of someone in pain – and, reaching to the shelf at my side, struck a steel and lit the fresh candle that always stood at the side of the other.

The clear light which ensued revealed the reason for the sounds: for the hammock which had contained the body of Sally swung empty at our side, and upon the floor directly below our hammock I saw her delightful black bottom raised into the air as she knelt above a recumbent male body, between whose thighs her head was thrust, and from whose lips escaped the groans I had heard, while it was Sally who was clearly enjoying a particular fruit.

I felt Sophie's body shaking upon mine, as she could not but giggle at the sight of Blatchford's face – for of course the man was he! His eyes goggled as he saw us looking down at him – at the same moment concerned that I should be angry at his presumption, and so enchanted by the sensation provoked by the ingenious lips and tongue of the black girl that he could form no words, nor look other than a man whose spirit is raised to a degree at which nothing can be felt but ecstasy!

Needless to say, I was not inclined to rebuke the boy – I had been too conscious myself of Sally's attractions to feel any surprise at his attentions to her; and indeed for the rest of the voyage we shared very amiably both the cabin and each other's company, clearing away the inconvenient hammocks and instead spreading upon the floor of the cabin some folded blankets which made a sufficiently comfortable bed into which we were happy to fall. The confined circumstances under which we found ourselves were turned to advantage by our pleasure in each other's bodies; and though it might be thought by the reader that, awakened at night by the motion of the ship or merely by desire, we might find it difficult to know into whose arms we were slipping, such was in fact not the case. Indeed, while it was sometimes the case that upon stretching out a hand, I found it resting upon the member of my male companion, it was the work of but a moment to transfer my attention to one of the ladies – and these were easily distinguishable, from their forms being so dissimilar: Sally's frame being slender and muscular, her legs and arms hard from past labours, and her breasts plump but small and firm as little apples – while Sophie was more generously built, her haunches broader, her breasts fuller, and her body soft as any gentlewoman's (though I was surprised at the muscular strength of her thighs, through her recent journeys on horseback).

During the day – and for the remainder of the voyage – I attempted to teach Yanni more of the rudiments of the English tongue; a ready pupil, by the time we reached Naples, he had a reasonable command of it. He also wished to educate himself elsewhere, for he – like Blatchford – evidently was entranced at his first meeting with a girl of ebony skin; and on the second night at sea showed considerable determination to accompany us to our cabin. This, however, would not do, for it was small enough even for the four of us – and moreover, I heard Blatchford firmly say, pointing to Sally, 'Her, wife to me!' which was something of a surprise, but had the effect that the Greek once more repaired to his bed in the open air, and we to our cramped quarters, where Sophie and I immediately fell asleep, disturbed however two or three times during the night by noises which indicated that Blatchford and Sally were engaged in activities which under other circumstances might have indicated connubial bliss.

On rising at my usual hour and going on deck, this time with my fair companion on my arm, I found the day fine and already sunny; and on walking to the bow, where the tangle of blankets and sails denoted Yanni's sleeping place, took hold of the sheet and threw it back – whereupon the fresh young face of Lieutenant Knee appeared, dressed not in His Majesty's uniform, but that of Adam, and warm from the arms of our Greek friend. Upon our reception of that vision, showing we were not shocked at it, the young Englishman admitted to his preference for his own sex, and Yanni, meeting our eyes with equal frankness, shrugged his shoulders and uttered the opinion that 'Man, woman, she same, except no children' – which is indeed one way of looking at the matter. His ready reception of the lieutenant's attentions did not, however, stand in the way of his admiration for Sally, which reached the point at which I discovered him and Blatchford squaring up for a fist-fight upon deck, which was intended to resolve the dispute as to whether Yanni should be allowed to enjoy Sally's favours (the latter, I believe, still being under the impression that she should offer herself to any male person who wished it – the legacy of her slavery).

I put a quick stop to this, as being inconsiderate to our hosts – and indeed, Captain Mellor would I think have seriously disapproved of such conduct. Questioning Blatchford on the matter, I found him seriously taken by the girl; and loyalty to him as a servant encouraged me to make it clear to our Greek companion that further attentions to her would be as unwelcome to me as to my servant, whereat he offered Blatchford his hand, and subsequently confined his admiration of Sally to caressing her with his eyes – which Blatchford still disliked, but about which he could do little, especially since Yanni went out of his way to be pleasant in every other particular.

On our arrival at Naples, we took rooms in an hotel, where we could make preparations for our return to England; and I talked seriously to Yanni. His box, having been transferred to the hotel, turned out to contain sufficient gold to make him a welcome citizen of any place on earth. He expressed the intention of seeing something of Italy before returning to Greece and, upon our application to the Greek consul, an interpreter was found who would accompany him, and translate for him. His first enquiry was where he would find the best virgins, which enquiry was received indifferently by the interpreter (a middle-aged gentleman of impeccable antecedents); his adventures after we left him, I can only guess at – but I imagine that they included some amorous incidents, for his high spirits were obvious, and he had had no congress with females since he left his native shores.

Meanwhile, I had arranged that Sophie's belongings should be sent for from Athens, and myself had acquired funds upon application to the local bankers; so we were able to shop for those personal articles which would enable us to travel in comfort.

My only uneasiness was for Sally, who, unfamiliar with a western city, viewed Naples with wide-open eyes – though not without pleasure, being dazzled by the clothes and jewels to be seen there. On my enquiring what she wished to do, I received no sensible answer – and was not inclined to leave her to her own devices in the city, where there were mean-minded people among the population who would be quick to take advantage of her, and would reduce her to much that condition of slavery from which I had lifted her. (Indeed, a servant brought me a message from a fellow guest at the hotel, a Comte de Vassilion, an elderly Frenchman, enquiring 'How much for the nigger?' – an enquiry which I spurned with an uncomplimentary epithet.)

I was aware that the familiarity continued which had established itself on board the *Actaeon* between Sally and Blatchford. Though I had of course taken separate rooms for them, it was clear that only one was occupied – at least at night; and more than once I had found the two embracing – not carnally, but by the way of simple affection, hand holding hand. Thus it was not altogether surprising to me when the problem of Sally's fate was solved by Blatchford's coming to me and asking whether I would have objection to his wedding the girl, and her accompanying us to England.

My reply was, in short, in the affirmative – though only after questioning him closely as to his feelings for her; for undoubtedly there would be some difficulty with those people to whom the unfamiliar is ever disturbing, and who might be inclined to view a black girl as a circus side-show, finding any excuse to denigrate her. But Blatchford was able to assure me of a genuine affection which would ensure their happiness, and I was happy to give my consent – though the actual marriage was to take place in London – this not, however, disturbing the relationship between them, which was cemented by her calling herself 'Mrs Blassh', and saving the expense of my taking two rooms for them on the long journey through Rome, on across Switzerland to Paris.

That journey passed uneventfully – the exclamations of wonder with which Sally greeted every different view from the windows of our carriage permitting us to see Europe through her eyes, and thus taking new pleasure in the sight.

In Paris Sophie and I were naturally all eagerness to find her half-brother, Frank, and to relate our adventures. On our going to the house which had been taken by the Ladies Elizabeth and Margaret Rawby, I found this occupied only by an elderly German Baron, whose major-domo informed me that the two ladies had left some two months previously, for London.

There being nothing more to interest us in the city, we hurried to leave, and as speedily as possible posted ourselves to Dieppe, whence upon the first available vessel we made to Brighthelmstone and thence to London. It was no inconsiderable pleasure to us to see the spires of the city greeting us as we passed over the bridge – even the chill air and dank drizzle failing to curb the enthusiastic admiration of Sally, whose face, gazing from the window, was greeted with considerable interest by passers-by.

Drawing up at the door of Frank's house at Brook Street, Sophie and I leaped down, and were soon greeted enthusiastically by our friends there – who also embraced Blatchford and received with kindness, if some confusion, his dusky companion. For Frank, however, we were directed to the house of the Lady Elizabeth Rawby, in Park Lane, where, pushing aside the footman who attempted to detain us, we ran up the main staircase and burst into the salon – where indeed we found our friend, lying entirely unclothed (and this at four in the afternoon) drinking chocolate with an equally under-dressed Lady Margaret.

It may be supposed with what energy we greeted each other, the lack of clothing of our brother failing entirely to inhibit our embraces – and when he explained that, on the very day following, he and the lady would be united by marriage, she also was included in our delighted greetings.

The rest of the day was spent in retailing our adventures – and though I had heard of Sophie's doings, and she of mine, they were re-told for Frank's benefit, new details ever emerging – which included Sophie's blushing admission of her amorous connection with Blatchford, which she had failed to offer me, as being possibly embarrassing to that good man while we were so closely in company.

On hearing of our servant's devotion, and of his wife to be, Frank insisted that they be sent for; which was done, and upon their arrival they too joined in the exchange of memories – Sally in a speech now very creditable to one who had only begun to learn the language a few weeks previously.

Our pleasure in each other, and in retailing all which had occurred since we were last together – which included Frank's courtship of Lady Margaret rather than her sister (the latter now being on honeymoon in Edinburgh with the MacInch of MacInch, a parsimonious but extremely rich Scot) – lasted through the excellent meal of which we partook, and into the late evening, when we sat around a large fire in the great salon; and, as the wine flowed, our affection for each other became such that we could not but join caresses to verbal compliments – and, in short, before long were in a state of nature, ready to exchange those compliments which level master and man, mistress and maid.

It must be admitted that much attention was given to Sally's ebony limbs. Black persons were at that time scarce, and young women particularly so; and Frank and his lady – though assiduous in asking Blatchford's permission – were eager to examine the phenomenon, which they agreed was fine, the bloom of firelight on the jet skin making an unusual effect; and when Blatchford, eager to enjoy his lady, joined her, the proximity of white and dark flesh, each asserting its desire for the other, was inspiriting to a degree that Frank and his lady were soon also embraced.

Sophie and I for a time sat, one at each side of the fire, with the figures of our friends, entwined in each other's arms, between us; affection was so much the foremost emotion in my mind that I was unprepared for combat - and Sophie, I believe understanding this, merely came to my side and took my hand. However, after a while, she knelt and placed her other hand upon my person, and in a while, as she offered her lips to mine, its gentle movements had the effect which no man can deny a loving female, and when she raised herself and sat astride my knees, it was without difficulty that we were joined together in the same manner - though perhaps more placidly - as our friends.

Whether or no it was the effect of her experiences in Malta, I cannot say, but my eagerness seemed somehow to be controlled by Sophie's quiet motion, so that it seemed a century before the slowly rising torrent of my emotion was released. In the meantime, I was able once more to enjoy the familiar weight of those much-loved breasts in my palm, to feel once more the line of her spine, leading to that delightful jointure of buttocks; to taste once again the limber tongue, to feel the sharply-pointed, small teeth with my own; and, looking down, to see with pleasure my tool, glistening as the light of the fire caught the smear of juice upon it, as, rather than thrusting, it was drawn, then expelled, then drawn again, into that heaven to which all male parts aspire.

Before we knew it, Frank's wedding day had dawned - announced by a servant who cannot but have been surprised, upon entering the salon to draw the curtains, to see six unclothed figures happily sprawled before the dying embers of the fire - and one of those bodies, moreover, as black as coal.

Frank, expressed the wish and was joined in it by his lady, that I should post as speedily as possible to the vicar of St George's Church in Hanover Square to arrange that Blatchford and Sally should be joined in matrimony at the same time as my friend and Lady Margaret. The Revd

Webber, enquiring as to the religion of the second bride, and having the situation explained to him, expressed severe doubts upon the subject; for all he knew, he said, she was a pagan. This was highly likely, I said, but no doubt a solution could be found; and upon my promising a considerable donation to the church funds, and explaining that the Lady Margaret Rawby particularly wished the marriage to take place in tandem with her own, his objections were waived.

So it was that the fashionable crowd, gathered to watch the marriage of the daughter of the Earl of Rawby, were surprised to see her followed by a bride whose (hastily purchased) white gown was vividly contrasted by a body black as pitch – while a few recognised in the sturdy figure of the groom, Andy's servant – who, it may be said, had welcomed many a man in the congregation to that admirable brothel whose excellence I have chronicled elsewhere.

After the wedding breakfast, both couples set off – Blatchford and Sally to Alcovary, Sir Frank and Lady Franklyn to Bath – upon their honeymoon. Sophie and I returned to Lady Elizabeth Rawby's house, where at Lady Margaret's invitation (who had charge of it) we were to stay for the time. That night, as we retired – and we saw no reason to occupy separate beds – I could not help reflecting, as I considered the sleeping face of my friend upon the pillow, upon the pleasures of matrimony. Yet we were both young, and Sophie, I believed, was no more ready than I to settle into a dull routine.

Perhaps – who knew? – there were other adventures yet ahead of us.